OPERATION JOKTAN

Center Point
Large Print

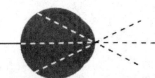

**This Large Print Book carries the
Seal of Approval of N.A.V.H.**

OPERATION JOKTAN

—A NIR TAVOR MOSSAD THRILLER—

AMIR TSARFATI
AND STEVE YOHN

CENTER POINT LARGE PRINT
THORNDIKE, MAINE

This Center Point Large Print edition
is published in the year 2022 by arrangement with
Harvest House Publishers.

The text of this Large Print edition is unabridged.
In other aspects, this book may vary
from the original edition.
Printed in the United States of America
on permanent paper sourced using
environmentally responsible foresting methods.
Set in 16-point Times New Roman type.

ISBN: 978-1-63808-310-8

The Library of Congress has cataloged this record
under Library of Congress Control Number: 2022930338

AMIR DEDICATES THIS BOOK TO . . .

God, the Creator and Sustainer of all things. May Your will be carried out in my life, my ministry, and the world.

My wife and children. It is your love and support that carry me through the days of separation and sacrifice.

The hundreds of thousands of followers and supporters of Behold Israel. Some of you are like angels sent from the Lord to encourage us, come alongside us, and pray for us. Thank you for letting God use you to be His blessing.

STEVE DEDICATES THIS BOOK TO . . .

My God, the Sustainer of my life. I lay Your gift back down at Your feet for You to do with it what You will.

Rick, your face was the first I remember seeing when I woke up, and that's when I knew it would be all right.

Wes, it is an honor to once again be your huckleberry.

ACKNOWLEDGMENTS

First and foremost, we want to thank the Lord for His faithfulness. Through good and bad, He has always been there. In Him alone are perfect peace, unfailing hope, and everlasting love.

Amir thanks his wife, Miriam, his four children, and his new daughter-in-law. Steve thanks his wife, Nancy, and his daughter. Although God is our foundation, family is the framework that holds us up and keeps us strong. Thank you so much for all your sacrifices over the years.

A big shout-out goes to the Behold Israel Team— Mike, H.T. and Tara, Gale and Florene, Donalee, Joanne, Nick and Tina, Jason, Abigail, Jeff, and Kayo. Thanks for all you do to encourage, teach, pray with, and love people from all over the world. You are true servants.

Thanks to Shane for your cartography skills, and to Mike Golay and Ryan Miller for your weapons expertise. Thank you, Jean Kavich Bloom, for your edits that took this book to the next level. Finally, we owe a huge debt of gratitude to Bob Hawkins, Jr., Steve and Becky Miller, Kim Moore, and all the team at Harvest House for your hard labor and your ability to work timeline miracles.

וּלְעֵבֶר יֻלַּד שְׁנֵי בָנִים שֵׁם הָאֶחָד פֶּלֶג כִּי בְיָמָיו נִפְלְגָה הָאָרֶץ"
וְשֵׁם אָחִיו יָקְטָן: וְיָקְטָן יָלַד אֶת־אַלְמוֹדָד וְאֶת־שָׁלֶף וְאֶת־
חֲצַרְמָוֶת וְאֶת־יָרַח: וְאֶת־הֲדוֹרָם וְאֶת־אוּזָל וְאֶת־דִּקְלָה: וְאֶת־
עוֹבָל וְאֶת־אֲבִימָאֵל וְאֶת־שְׁבָא: וְאֶת־אוֹפִר וְאֶת־חֲוִילָה וְאֶת־יוֹבָב
כָּל־אֵלֶּה בְּנֵי יָקְטָן: וַיְהִי מוֹשָׁבָם מִמֵּשָׁא בֹּאֲכָה סְפָרָה הַר הַקֶּדֶם:"

To Eber were born two sons: the name of the one
was Peleg, for in his days the earth was divided,
and his brother's name was Joktan [pronounced
"Yok-tan"]. Joktan fathered Almodad, Sheleph,
Hazarmaveth, Jerah, Hadoram, Uzal, Diklah,
Obal, Abimael, Sheba, Ophir, Havilah, and
Jobab; all these were the sons of Joktan. The
territory in which they lived extended from
Mesha in the direction of Sephar to the hill
country of the east.

GENESIS 10:25-30

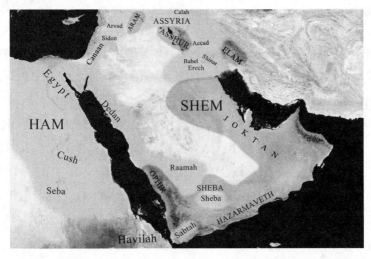

CHARACTER LIST

ISRAELIS

Dima Aronov – Kidon ops team
Avi Carmeli – Kidon ops team
Efraim Cohen – assistant deputy director of
    Caesarea
Alex Eichler – director of Caesarea
Yaron Eisenbach – Kidon ops team
Karin Friedman – assistant deputy director of
    Mossad
Yossi Hirschfield – Caesarea analyst team
Ira Katz – ramsad (head of Mossad)
Doron Mizrahi – Kidon ops team
Asher Porush – deputy director of Mossad
Liora Regev – Caesarea analyst team
Dafna Ronen – Caesarea analyst team
Lahav Tabib – Caesarea analyst team
Nir Tavor – Caesarea/Kidon team leader
Gideon Zamir – South Africa ops supervisor for
    State Security

SOUTH AFRICANS

Christiaan le Roux – brother of Nicole
Nicole le Roux – Caesarea analyst and computer
    specialist

EMIRATIS
Isa Al Maktum – agent with the Signals Intelligence Agency (SIA)
Abdullah Al Rashidi – director of the SIA
Lieutenant General Dhahi Khalfan Tamim – UAE deputy chief of police and general security, formerly Dubai chief of police

IRANIANS
Ahmad al-Qasimi (aka Mehdi Zahiri) – leader of a Dubai-based Islamic Revolutionary Guard Corps (IRGC) cell
General Esmail Qaani – commander of the Quds Force of the IRGC
General Farrokh Soltani – deputy commander of the Quds Force of the IRGC
Jamshid Taheri – member of Dubai-based IRGC cell

IRAQIS
Seif Abdel Abbas – deputy commander of Kata'ib Sayyid al-Shuhada (KSS) and head of mission
Muzahim al-Aiyubi – leader of KSS first team
Abu Mustafa al-Sheibani – commander of KSS and head of the Sheibani weapons network
Omar Ali – KSS militia soldier
Mohamed Hassan – KSS militia soldier
Falih Kazali – secretary general of KSS
Fuad Razzak – leader of KSS second team

KURDS

Lieutenant Murat Erdal – deputy commander in People's Protection Unit

Major Mustafa Nurettin – commander in People's Protection Unit

PALESTINIANS

Mahmoud al-Mabhouh – Hamas military commander and weapons buyer

Muhammad Nasr – Hamas soldier

ROMANIAN

Nicolae Filipescu – Dubai-based tech smuggler

CANADIANS

Bruce Hatcher – Wasaku Katagi's coach

Wasaku Katagi – MMA fighter

Brett Terrell – Wasaku Katagi's trainer

AMERICANS

Elliot Musser – twin

Katie Musser – mother

Nevin Musser – oldest son

Rick Musser – father

Zabe Musser – twin

CHAPTER 1

12 YEARS EARLIER—CAPE TOWN, SOUTH AFRICA
JANUARY 20, 2008—13:30 / 1:30 P.M. SAST

Even with a trained ear, it's difficult to place the origin of a single gunshot. For that reason, Nir Tavor didn't know which way to point his gun until dozens of shots joined that first volley. A glance to his left confirmed what he expected to see—Gideon Zamir, his ops supervisor, using his body as a shield over their charge.

Zamir had been a battalion commander in the 1982 Lebanon War and the First Intifada, so he had plenty of experience with bullets whizzing overhead. Nir was only 24, still fresh in public service, and he'd never fired a bullet in battle.

That was about to change.

His journey to this point flew through his mind. Only three months ago, he'd been finishing his training with the State Security System of Israel's Ministry of Foreign Affairs. One of the reasons he'd joined the MFA was to see the world, and the available postings—London, Washington, Tokyo, Paris—all seemed so glamorous. Yet as he considered those cities, they also seemed . . . predictable.

Then two words on the list caught Nir's eye,

and the sense of adventure was back. South Africa sounded exotic with a little hint of danger. It certainly wouldn't be a sleepy posting. Many in South Africa felt a kindred relationship with the Palestinians because of their perception of the refugee situation, and this had led to governmental sanctions, popular protests, and even some acts of violence. But Israel and the post-apartheid South African government under President Thabo Mbeki were just starting to thaw their frosty relationship, and despite objections, ties between the two nations continued to progress. Israel had even reopened their embassy, sending Ilan Baruch—the man Nir was here to protect—as not quite an ambassador but someone who would hopefully transition into a full-fledged holder of that position one day.

Today they were at an enormous Cape Town mansion that screamed of old apartheid money—Doric columns, a vast outdoor pool, marble everywhere, all set on a massive, lush property. Nir had even seen peacocks wandering around the garden area. Baruch was here at the invitation of the South African minister of home affairs, Nosiviwe Mapisa-Nqakula, whom he met at a diplomatic function in Johannesburg several months back. In response to her inquiry about his eye patch, he'd told her about being severely wounded in 1970 during the War of Attrition with Egypt. This event had transformed him, he told her, and he was now very much a man of peace. His views on the Palestinian situation and his criticism of his own government's policies intrigued her, and she invited him to visit the city of her birth.

Now Nir was here on the last day of a weekend excursion that had been everything he'd hoped for when he'd written *South Africa* on that assignment request form. The previous two days had seen them sailing in the Atlantic, touring the Iziko Slave Lodge, and jaunting down to the Cape of Good Hope to see the penguins. Today they were wrapping up the trip with a luncheon followed by an outdoor fashion show at what was truly one of the most beautiful properties he'd ever stepped foot on.

Blue skies, a gorgeous mansion, stunningly attractive models . . . It was the perfect day.

Until the gunfire.

Without seeing them, Nir couldn't be sure who the attackers were. But it was likely one of two groups—a Palestinian militia that had somehow found its way to Cape Town, or more probably, a local, Palestinian-sympathizing Xhosa militia that wanted to punish Israel by killing Ilan Baruch.

The assassination of Israeli diplomats wasn't unheard of. In 1982, three members of the Palestinian organization Fatah attempted to assassinate the Israeli ambassador to the UK,

Shlomo Argov, by shooting him down on the streets of London. Argov survived a bullet in the head but remained paralyzed and under constant medical care for the rest of his life. The fallout from that incident led to the 1982 Lebanon War, which left dead hundreds of Israeli soldiers and thousands of Palestinian militia and Syrian military. It also cost the lives of tens of thousands of Lebanese civilians. Nir knew his history and the potential ramifications of this attack. He would not let anything happen to Baruch.

A half-dozen members of Mapisa-Nqakula's military escort immediately opened fire, their aim the entrance of the 12-foot cement wall surrounding the property. Knowing that their Vektor R4 assault rifles would cause a lot more damage than he could pull off with his Jericho 941 9mm, Nir saved his ammunition and took stock of the situation. From where he stood at one front corner of the seating area, he could see that the hundred or so guests had all dropped to the ground, including Baruch, who'd been sitting in the row of seats next to the stage-right side of the fashion show runway. Mapisa-Nqakula was on the ground next to him, and Zamir now hovered over them both.

Nir scanned the scene looking for more hostiles. Then his gaze reached the runway and stopped short. With a fear-filled yet inquisitive stare, two ice-blue eyes held him captive. Nir sucked in a breath. The woman lying on the stage was remarkable. Beyond remarkable. Full dark brows crowned her captivating eyes. The skin on her narrow face was bronze, and her thick, pouty lips were colored a rich red. As he gawked, those lips formed two words—"Do something!"

"Stay down!" he called to her, angry that he'd allowed himself to be distracted.

The gunfire stopped. Nir turned toward the security wall figuring the South African soldiers had dealt with the shooters; all he could see was camouflage-dressed military.

A groan sounded to his left. He spotted a woman in a brightly patterned dress lying faceup near the stage, a matching traditional *iqhiya* wrapped around her head. Blood was rapidly staining the yellow fabric on her shoulder red.

He turned back to the model and reversed his instruction. "You! Come here!" He thought she might be too stunned or afraid to obey, but as he pulled off his suit coat, he was gratified to see her sliding off the raised platform, leaving her ridiculously high heels behind. Her knee-length dress looked unbearably tight, but before she ran, she tore apart the lower seam, giving her legs more freedom to move.

When he reached the injured woman, he knelt and pressed his jacket to her wound. The model's eyes revealed terror as she dropped beside him, but the rest of her expression showed resolve.

"I'm Nir."

"Nicole."

"Great. Nicole, keep pressure on this. As soon as we're clear, I'll get you, my ambassador, and the home minister into the house. Good?"

"Good." She had the type of voice he'd once heard described as smoky. Between that and her South African accent, he could spend the day listening to her read the Talmudic laws on skin diseases and be a happy man.

The things that go through your head when you're under fire.

He stood, and catching Zamir's eye, he pointed at him and gave a thumbs-up. Zamir responded with a thumbs-up of his own.

Shouting erupted from the wall, and the military soldiers began firing their weapons on full-automatic toward the gate. A SAMIL 20 military transport truck burst through the iron gateway and onto the lawn 50 meters from where Nir stood. At least a dozen poorly uniformed guerilla fighters jumped out of the back of the truck and began firing AK-47s at the military guard. It was a blood bath as both soldiers and guerillas crumpled to the ground.

Nir ran toward the truck, firing as he went. A scream sounded behind him, then he heard new gunfire erupt. Spinning around, he spotted three assailants who must have come up from the rocks leading to the ocean while everyone was

18

distracted by the new assault. They were firing directly into the crowd of people prone on the ground, and 9mm shots sounded from Nir's right as Zamir emptied his magazine at the gunmen. One of them dropped, and the other two took cover behind a large stone planter.

"Get them inside," Nir yelled at his commander. Zamir nodded, then pulled Baruch to his feet, followed by the home affairs minister. "You too," Nir shouted to Nicole. She'd already helped the injured woman up.

Ahead, one of the gunmen stepped around the planter. Nir fired seven quick shots, causing him to retreat. Quickly changing his mag, Nir dropped to one knee and scanned his surroundings. At least six people were undoubtedly dead, and several others were bleeding. While Baruch was his primary charge, there was no way he could leave these people here as sitting ducks. But if he stayed where he was, he would likely be one of those sitting ducks too.

If I've got no possibility for a solid defense, I better go on offense. And I better do it fast.

Not giving himself time for doubt, Nir sprinted toward the gunmen's cover. His only chance was to surprise them in the next five seconds, before they recognized their two-to-one advantage and came out firing.

Ten meters . . . five meters . . . two meters . . .

Both camouflage-wearing Xhosas stepped from

19

behind the planter. Nir fired three shots, which all struck one of them, and the hostile dropped to the ground. The surprise at seeing his foe so close to him stunned the second gunman long enough for Nir to launch himself full speed into his body. They both tumbled to the lawn, and Nir landed heavily on his left shoulder.

The pain caused him to lose his breath.

Rolling to his right side, he saw his opponent flying toward him. The man's full body weight landed on Nir's hurt shoulder, causing him to momentarily gray out. A hard punch to the side of his head snapped him back into full awareness. The first punch was followed by another, then another. Nir bucked his body and tried to twist, but the man just rode him out and brought his fist down on Nir's nose. He felt a sickening crunch, and his mouth filled with blood.

Hands now clenched around his neck, sealing off his windpipe. Nir gasped for air, instead getting a throat full of blood pouring from his sinuses.

Time was ticking. He bucked his legs up once, twice, and on the third time he was able to take hold of what he was grasping for. He slipped his DUSTAR Arad 7-inch blade from its ankle sheath and plunged it up under his attacker's ribs. The hands released Nir's neck as the man fumbled for the blade in his back. Nir pulled it out, then drove it in again, then one more time just to make sure.

The gunman dropped to his side as Nir sucked in a lungful of bloody air, choking and coughing as he tried to force it back out.

As he sat up, two South African police officers ran toward him. In the midst of his fight, he'd missed their arrival. Now he could see several cars with flashing lights parked on the lawn and a steady stream of them pouring through the gap in the gate.

"See if they're dead," Nir said to the men, nodding toward the three Xhosa bodies.

He'd never killed anyone before. Shooting the first guy was enough to shake him up a bit, but as he sat there, the second kill played over and over in his mind. The sound of the tearing fabric, the feel of the puncturing flesh . . .

A new picture invaded his thoughts. He had to be in shock, because what he saw in his mind's eye were the last things that should have his attention. But still, there they were.

He dropped his face into his hands, and those two inquisitive, ice-blue eyes pinned him in the darkness. Maybe he needed to find them again just so he could answer the questions behind their stare.

CHAPTER 2

The scents coming from the restaurant reached Nir even before he opened the front door. Some sort of meat was definitely roasting inside, and it was quite evident that fresh naan was baking. But the smell of curry overpowered all others.

This will be a good meal.

The Bo-Kaap district of Cape Town was like nothing he'd seen. Blocky, flat-facade houses lined the streets, each one painted more brightly than the last. All shades of blue, yellow, red, and green were represented with no apparent plan or consistent color scheme. Evidently, each homeowner simply decided what their favorite color was, then ran down to the paint store. The only common bond he could find beyond their boxy shape was the bright-white cornice that surrounded many of the houses. That simple touch was enough to give the randomness some kind of unity.

This unique neighborhood reminded him a bit of home, though. The minarets of the old mosques that reached up into the blue South African sky were familiar, and he had no doubt that the sound of *muezzins* calling the Muslims of this area to prayer would be echoing throughout the district in the next few hours. Where this experience diverged from home was that he'd keep his head on a swivel and his hand near his pistol if he was wandering alone in the Muslim quarter of Jerusalem. Here, though, he felt no need for concern. If any sort of threat from the local Muslims existed, he would have been briefed back at the office in Johannesburg.

The office. What a train wreck that place is right now.

By the evening of the day of the attack, Nir, Zamir, and Baruch were back up in the safety of their compound in the capital city. The South African government had posted some military units around the walls until a team from the Israeli Defense Forces had time to arrive, and Baruch was handling the attempt on his life with the matter-of-fact practicality expected from a battle-hardened veteran who had lived much of his life with a war injury. Being Israeli just added to his stoicism. But he wanted answers, he wanted to ensure the safety of embassy employees, and he wanted to make sure this event didn't in any way derail the progress in South African and Israeli relations.

Commander Zamir was determined to oversee

23

the security of the Johannesburg compound himself, so he sent Nir back down to Cape Town to liaison with the investigation. Nir was only too happy to go. First, it would get him away from the circus of the compound with the constant calls from cabinet ministers, members of the legislative Knesset, and the press. Second, it would let him return to where he might be able to track down a certain female he'd recently met in a distressing situation.

He'd been looking forward to this meeting ever since he'd made that phone call two days ago. After walking through the restaurant's door, he spotted her right away. Somehow she was even more gorgeous without the professionally done makeup and the fashion-forward dress.

She was seated at a table facing the doors, next to a floor-to-ceiling window that gave a view of the Bo-Kaap below and the hills beyond. As he neared, she stood.

"Nicole." He leaned forward to greet her. As his cheek briefly touched hers, the fresh smell of citrus overtook the spicy scents coming from the kitchen. "You look beautiful."

She was wearing jeans and an oversized sweater, and her dark, wavy hair hung loosely past her shoulders. She smiled as she pulled back. "I wish I could say the same for you."

Nir laughed. His face was still a mess from the hand-to-hand combat of nearly a week ago. But at least he could breathe through his nose again, and the blackish purple surrounding his eyes was beginning to fade.

"You should have seen the other guy," he said, then immediately regretted the joke. Nicole had seen the other guy as he was firing an automatic weapon at her and the rest of the crowd that day. In the military, gallows humor is standard operating procedure. Not so much with a fashion model—perhaps especially with one he'd learned was just 20 years old. "Sorry."

Nir held Nicole's chair for her as she sat, then took his place on the other side of the table.

"Honestly, I wasn't sure if you'd want to see me after everything that happened," he continued. "I was hoping to get a chance to thank you for what you did when it was all going down, but everything was so crazy, and then you were gone."

Nicole remained silent, so Nir forged forward. "I tracked down your number from our records. I've got to tell you, how you handled yourself was amazing. You likely saved that woman's life."

Still silence.

This is not going well.

Nicole pointed out the window. "That peak over there is called Lion's Head." Nir spotted the large hill a distance away from them. "The rise that comes back our way is Table Mountain.

It looks a lot like the body of a lion. Where we are is called Signal Hill. Now, if that over there is the lion's head and between us is the lion's body, then where are we?"

"Uh, the lion's backside?"

"Exactly." She smiled. "That's why another name for Signal Hill is Lion's Rump. So lunch today will be served on the lion's rump."

Message received. You don't want to talk about the attack. That's fine by me.

"Did you recommend we meet at this restaurant just so you could tell me that story?" He laughed.

"Maybe." Now she had a mischievous glint in her eyes. "That, and they serve the best bobotie in the city."

"Fair enough." Nir had tried the minced meat curry dish numerous times up in Johannesburg, and he wasn't really a fan. But that didn't matter. He'd eat fried grubs if it allowed him to get to know this woman better.

The server came and greeted them, then looked at Nir.

"I'll defer to the lady," he said. "I am completely at her mercy."

Nicole smiled her appreciation, then ordered a bobotie platter for each of them and a samosa appetizer to share. "And a sparkling mineral water for each of us," she added. When the server left, she said, "This restaurant is halal, so no wine is served."

"Are you—"

"No." She laughed. "If you saw most of the clothing designers put me in, you'd know my profession would never fit the lifestyle of a good Muslim girl. But the food here is good, the view is good, and, hopefully, the company will be good." The lift in her eyebrows caused Nir's adrenaline to kick up a notch. He couldn't believe he was sitting across the table from such a beautiful woman—someone he considered out of his league.

"Tell me about yourself, Nicole. Have you always lived in the Cape?"

"Born and raised. My family has been here for generations."

"Are you Boer, then?"

"No, the le Roux name is Cape Dutch. Two or three hundred years ago, people started migrating north from here, settling the Orange Free State and Transvaal. Those are the Boers."

Nicole continued to talk in her alto voice that sounded years older than her actual age. But she gave few details about her upbringing, deftly deflecting any probing questions Nir asked. It quickly became obvious that home was not a good place and she would rather focus on happier subjects.

The modeling had begun when she was 15. "I had no interest in school, and certainly not in higher education. I just wanted a job that gave me the time and money to do what I really love doing."

"Which is . . ."

"I'm a keyboard geek."

Nir laughed. "First, nothing about you says *geek*. Second, don't you need university to get into all that IT stuff?"

"Well, *all that IT stuff* isn't what I'm into," she whispered with the tone of a conspirator. Then grinning, she made a show of looking left, then right. "I probably shouldn't be telling you this, since you're kind of in international law enforcement—"

"I'm not law enforcement."

"Oh? Do you shoot people?"

Ouch. Too close to home. "Occasionally. So what do you do that might tempt me to arrest you?"

"Let me put it this way. The records show I passed my matriculation exam with distinction."

"Okay. Congratulations." Nir had no idea where this was going.

"Thank you. The thing is, while my exam was taking place, I was out surfing."

"Then how . . . Oh, I get it. You naughty girl. You're a hacker."

Nicole pulled back, feigning offense. "Hacker. Such an ugly name for the beauty of my craft."

This girl just keeps getting more and more intriguing.

The waiter brought the samosas, setting the plate in the middle of the table.

"You first," Nicole said.

Nir lifted a puffed triangle from the small stack and took a bite. Inside the flaky dough was a mixture of beef and onions spiced with an aromatic blend of curry, turmeric, ginger, and just enough heat to let Nir know the chef meant business.

"Do you like it?" Nicole asked.

"This is amazing."

"When I was growing up, a lady named Abaasa would stop by to visit my grandmother. Sometimes she'd bring along some groceries. She was a Cape Malay."

"Cape Malay?"

"The Cape Malays are the descendants of Muslims who moved to the Cape region back in the nineteenth century. All the colorful houses you saw as you drove in? They all belong to the Malays."

"Hence, the minarets and the halal restaurant."

"Exactly." She lifted a samosa and took a bite. "Anyway, Abaasa would sometimes bring samosas for me and my twin brother. I've loved Malay cuisine ever since."

"I can understand why." Nir took another samosa from the plate, wondering what a twin male version of Nicole would look like. "So back to your criminal activity. Just how good a, uh, keyboard artist are you?"

Nicole grinned. "Let's see. Nir Avraham Tavor. Born October 27, 1983. Father's name Avraham; mother's name Rivka. Grew up in Kibbutz Yizre'el in the Jezreel Valley. A satisfactory student, although you didn't matriculate with distinction like someone else we know. Mandatory service in the Israeli Defense Force from 2002 to 2006. Employed by the Ministry of Foreign Affairs' State Security System since 2007. Stationed in Johannesburg since November. Likes puppies, Taylor Swift music, and long walks holding hands in the rain."

"Wow, stalker much?" Nir was stunned. He didn't know if he should feel impressed or violated.

"Rude." But she'd said it with a soft grin. She looked down and began tracing circles on the rim of her water glass. "I made up that last part," she added in a tone that lacked the self-assuredness she'd had from the beginning of their conversation.

Nir realized the risk she'd just taken. She was laying herself out before him, showing him the real her. How he responded in this moment would determine whether their connection would go any further.

With a firm voice, he said, "Nicole, as a member of the State Security Service, duly authorized by Interpol and the International Court in The Hague, I place you under arrest for hacking . . .

uh, for inappropriate criminal keyboard artistry."

Nicole's relief was evident as she looked up. Then she batted her eyelashes and said in a vapid voice, "Oh no, Officer Tavor. I promise I'll never do it again. Is there anything I can do to get out of this predicament?"

He had no problem playing along. "Hmm. Let's just see how the day goes. I'm sure I can come up with something."

THREE MONTHS LATER
AROMA ESPRESSO BAR—TEL AVIV, ISRAEL—
APRIL 19, 2008—08:15 / 8:15 A.M. IST

Nir sat alone in his favorite Tel Aviv coffee bar, watching the people go by and wondering where Nicole le Roux was this morning. Home in Cape Town? Modeling somewhere? He sighed. He'd tried to put her out of his mind, but her image often formed unbidden.

After their lunch in the Bo-Kaap district, they'd spent the rest of the day together—and the next and the next. The investigation into the assassination attempt on Baruch was lengthy and detailed, keeping him in Cape Town for another three weeks. Other than the four days when Nicole had to fly to Saint-Tropez, France, for a modeling gig, they'd spent as much time together as they could.

When he was called back to Johannesburg,

they vowed to keep the relationship going. After all, it was only a two-hour flight between Cape Town and the capital. But a week later, Nir was told to go to a conference room, where he found a mystery man sitting at the long table.

He motioned for Nir to sit down on the opposite side, and then without a greeting or even an introduction he said, "I'm from the Mossad. We've heard about your performance in Cape Town, and I've come to talk to you."

MIDDLE EAST

CHAPTER 3

NEARLY TWO YEARS LATER
DAMASCUS, SYRIA—JANUARY 18, 2010—
15:45 / 3:45 P.M. EEST

Mahmoud reached under the dashboard of the Toyota Corolla. He found the battery wires, then pulled them and attached one to the other. The lights on the dashboard came on—a good sign.

"Let's go! Let's go!" his partner said.

Ignoring the prodding, Mahmoud wiped his sleeve across his forehead before the sweat could reach his eyes. He wrapped a piece of electrical tape around the wire connection, then identified the starter wire. After stripping it, he took a deep breath. What came next was the tricky part.

When he first learned how to hot-wire a car, he was a little too sure of himself. That over-confidence had earned him an electrical shock that drove his head up into the steering column so hard he'd suffered a concussion. He could still hear his trainer's laughter as he stood over Mahmoud's shaking body.

Carefully, he touched the starter wire to the combined battery wires. The Corolla started up. *Yes. Halfway there.* The car was running, but the steering column remained locked. "This is the part they don't show you in the movies," his trainer had said.

His partner, a fellow late-twenty-something Palestinian named Muhammad Nasr, handed him an old claw hammer and a dingy, yellow-handled flathead screwdriver. Mahmoud pounded the screwdriver into the keyhole. When it was well secured, he twisted it back and forth while racking the steering wheel left and right. The lock mechanism broke. Mahmoud stepped out with a satisfied smile, and Muhammad slapped him on the back before slipping into the driver's seat.

After checking to make sure his partner had arranged the boxes properly to block the driver's side of the back seat, Mahmoud walked around the car. He lifted a water bottle from on top of the trunk and drank the remaining half, then tossed the empty toward the base of a chain link fence that stood at the front of the car. The physical exertion, his nerves, and the heavy black coat he wore had him drenched in sweat. He reached up and made sure his yarmulke was still secure after rooting around under the steering wheel.

"How do I look?" he asked Muhammad, posing with his arms open and a goofy grin on his face.

"Like a Jewish dog."

"Arf." Mahmoud laughed before dropping into the passenger seat. The two men drove off, the old Corolla trailing a thin line of black smoke.

They already had their target area picked out as they left the city limits of Ashkelon. Soldiers of the Israeli Defense Forces would often hitchhike from bus stops when they were on leave. Hodiya Junction was one of those stops and stood just about five kilometers to their east, not too far north of the Gaza border. The proximity to Gaza had been preeminent in their minds when they'd chosen this location, because that was the direction they would be fleeing when this was all said and done.

As they drove, Mahmoud tried turning on the air conditioner but with no luck. He cranked his window halfway down. He was about to ask Muhammad to do the same thing, but he saw his friend staring at him and laughing.

"What are you laughing at?"

"You look ridiculous."

"You look just as bad." Mahmoud opened the mirror in the visor to look at himself.

They were dressed as ultra-Orthodox Jews, completely in black except for a white shirt under their suit jackets. Not many Jews would get into a car with two young Palestinian men who were wearing their traditional black and white *keffiyehs* wrapped around their heads. But who wouldn't trust a couple of friendly, Jewish scholars offering them a ride?

"I have never been so hot in my life," Mahmoud said. "How do they live like this?"

But instead of answering, Muhammad pointed forward. "There it is."

The intersection of two main roads was up ahead, and a covered bus stop sat on one corner. About twenty people congregated in the shade, and another ten or fifteen milled around in the sun, some holding newspapers above their heads as a makeshift screen. Mahmoud counted seven Israeli Defense Force soldiers—four gathered in a group and three others standing alone. The IDF was everywhere.

Mahmoud's heart raced, and he prayed silently. *Give me strength, Allah, to do what you have called me to do.*

Muhammad pulled the car up alongside the soldier farthest from the shelter.

After cranking the window the rest of the way down, Mahmoud asked in Hebrew, "What is your name, friend?"

"Avi."

"Where are you going?"

"Back home to Ashdod." He had a hopeful look on his face.

"Ah, just up the road." Mahmoud smiled, praying that the accent he'd been practicing would hold up. "Well, Avi, we just happen to be going that direction too. Would you like a ride?"

Avi lifted his bag from the ground. "Yes, sir. I would, very much. Thank you."

As Avi approached, Mahmoud said, "You'll have to sit behind me. We're delivering some goods, and they're taking up much of the back seat."

"No problem." Avi slid into the car and placed his bag on his lap.

Muhammad put the car in gear, then drove off.

"May I put the window down?" Avi asked.

"Of course, of course," Mahmoud cursed himself for the crack in his voice. His heart was still racing with fear and anticipation. He couldn't believe he was finally going through with this. Since the time he was young, he'd bragged that one day he would do something this bold and daring.

Three kilometers passed, and he saw Muhammad give a brief nod. Mahmoud reached down to where he'd stashed a battered 1911 .45 ACP handgun next to his seat. Turning around, he locked eyes with the IDF soldier, then fired a round into the young Jew's face. A hole opened under the young man's eye, and blood and brain matter flew out of the back of his head.

Revulsion and elation filled Mahmoud . . . until he saw that the soldier wasn't dead. He hadn't even collapsed. Instead, he smiled and reached his hand into his own bag. Panicked, Mahmoud fired again. Another hole in the soldier's face, then more gore out the back. Still, the man stayed upright. His smile turned into a condescending grin, and he began slowly shaking his head. A gun slid out of his bag, and he raised it.

Mahmoud pulled the trigger again and again and again until the slide locked back and he was out of ammunition. The soldier was pocked full of holes, but his grin remained unchanged. His gun was leveled, and Mahmoud could see down the darkness of the barrel.

"You are a foolish, foolish man," the Jewish soldier said as he racked a round into the chamber. "Don't you know that Israel never forgets?" He pulled the trigger.

Mahmoud cried out as he awoke. His clothes were soaked in sweat, and his heart was racing. The bedroom door opened, and his wife poked her head in. "Are you okay?"

It took a moment for Mahmoud to orient himself. "Yes, yes. It was just a dream." He waved her away. He was glad the lights were down so she couldn't see the fear on his face.

"I'm sorry." She held up her hands and prayed a brief *dua*. "I seek refuge for my husband in the perfect words of Allah from the evils of Satan."

"Thank you, my wife. It was time for me to get up anyway."

"Then I'll leave you." She closed the door behind her.

Mahmoud continued to lie in the cool darkness of the curtained room, staring at the ceiling. When he'd shot that Israeli boy 21 years ago, he'd fired only one bullet, after which the soldier was most definitely dead. He and Muhammad had buried him not far away from the place of his execution. Three months later, Mahmoud and some other members of Hamas had abducted another IDF soldier. He was the driver that time, so one of his Palestinian brothers had the honor of putting a bullet into that dog.

Ever since those first righteous assassinations, Mahmoud had been a marked man. Yet even though those Israeli sons of the devil had found ways to take their revenge on many of his friends, they had not caught up with him. Not that they hadn't tried; he could just see them coming. Allah had blessed him with a special ability to know when people were sneaking up on him. That's how he got the nickname "the Fox" from his comrades in Hamas.

But eventually even foxes are caught. He wasn't afraid to die a martyr's death. He'd spent his life serving Allah. Born nearly 50 years ago as Mahmoud Abdel Rauf Al-Mabhouh in the Jabalia Refugee Camp in the Gaza Strip, he'd known hardship his whole life. Gaza was a dirty, dusty wasteland filled with cement and rubble. It was a violent place where he had to learn to defend himself from an early age. Even though gangs and factions lived within the camps in Gaza, Mahmoud knew two things united him to *every* Palestinian: a love for Allah—although some loved him more than others—and a hatred of the Jews.

When he was a teenager, he joined the Muslim Brotherhood. That was where he learned what Allah expected from him. That was also where he was taught how to hurt people. He already had street-fighting skills, but then he received real combat training. He and his brothers from the Brotherhood put their violent training to use every chance they had. Sometimes they would hear about one of the houses or cafés where fellow Muslims gambled and then raid them and beat the participants. Mahmoud used sticks, ax handles, lug wrenches—anything he could get his hands on to remind those back-slidden sons of the Qur'an where their allegiance lay.

And it wasn't just gambling that triggered their righteous wrath. Any infraction—drinking, stealing, adultery . . . They all demanded some level of punishment that he and his brothers were all too happy to mete out. It was exhilarating.

In his twenties, Mahmoud was arrested by the IDF for possessing an AK-47, and the Jews had locked him up for a year. With nothing else to do, he and his fellow inmates plotted ways to carry out their revenge against the hateful Israelis. Two years after he was released, he had his opportunity, finding himself in the front of that Toyota, dressed as a religious Jew with a .45 next to his seat.

Mahmoud rose and padded across the polished cement floor to the bathroom. After snapping on the light, he looked at himself in the mirror. In one month he would turn 50. Despite the life he'd led, he felt he still looked fairly good. The hair on his head remained dark, as did his thick mustache and the small patch under his lower lip. His wife had hinted about his weight, but he wasn't at the point of worry.

He brushed his teeth, stripped out of his sweaty clothes, and stepped into the shower. Afternoon naps were not the norm for him, but he had a late evening of meetings and then tomorrow an early afternoon flight to Dubai. He would be there only a couple of days, and there were certainly worse places to go, but he was nervous anytime he left the safety of Damascus. Dubai, in particular, caused him concern. Compared to visits to Beirut or Tehran or even Istanbul, the openness of the United Arab Emirates left him vulnerable.

He rinsed his hair. *The fox will just have to keep his eyes open. Allah, please make sure those Jewish hounds stay far, far away.*

CHAPTER 4

SKIES ABOVE THE BOSPORUS STRAIT—
20:30 / 8:30 P.M. TRT

I could get used to this treatment. Nir used his knife to smear a dollop of mustard soy sauce on a piece of salmon. He lifted it to his mouth, then followed with a sip of pinot noir.

"Is everything satisfactory, Mr. McCann?"

He looked up from his tray. "Yes, Lara, it is. Thank you. And my compliments to the chef." The Swiss airline's flight attendant's blond hair and tan skin told Nir she probably spent a good amount of time skiing the slopes of Europe's world-class alpine resorts.

"I'll be sure to pass that along." Her smile said she was amused by his little quip, but her eyes belied the likely truth that she heard the same dumb joke at least five times a flight, every flight.

Lara asked Mr. Haidar, the man sitting next to the window in their two-seat, business-class row, the same question. Nir had overheard his name when the other, more matronly flight attendant greeted him as they boarded. Now Haidar grunted his satisfaction, and Lara turned her attention to the other side of the aisle.

42

"She's quite the looker, isn't she?" Nir whispered with a little nudge, sure of the response he would get.

Haidar grunted again, never looking up from his chicken breast. Nir chuckled to himself. That's the way his row mate had been ever since the beginning of the international flight. "Michael McCann," Nir had said in greeting as he sat down next to the balding middle-aged man—who appeared to be about a half-dozen rugelach away from sizing out of his suit. Haidar had responded "Good day" without looking up from the flight safety card he was reading. The man's look and French-accented English had Nir pegging him for Lebanese.

"Going to be a long flight," Nir had said to follow up.

Haidar grunted his agreement.

"Let me know if you need up at any point. I won't mind stretching my legs." Nir chuckled, but Haidar only let out a sigh, then grunted again.

Two words. That's all this guy's going to give me the whole flight. Two words! It wasn't that Nir was a big fan of small talk. He just wanted to practice his British accent. He'd been working hard on developing an estuary London sound, which falls somewhere between the traditional RP accent and cockney and would give his cover more authenticity. But Mr. Tight-Suit next to him wasn't having it. Now Nir was reduced to devising creative ways to elicit a grunt every now and again, mostly just for entertainment's sake.

"You going to eat your croissant?"

Haidar glared at him as he moved his pastry to the window side of his tray.

Wow, not even a grunt this time.

The map on the little screen in front of him updated the plane's position, showing that the Bosporus Strait was not far to the south. After crossing over Turkey, the plane would fly through Syrian and Iraqi airspace before finally reaching the Persian Gulf. As a Jew, Nir found that flying over those countries elicited a little tremor in his insides despite his traveling with a forged British passport identifying him as Michael McCann. Or maybe it was *because* he was traveling with a forged British passport. The Mossad artists were good, but were they skilled enough for it to stand up to intense scrutiny?

Actually, it wasn't completely forged. A British Michael McCann did live in Israel. *He just doesn't know I'm using his passport and that my photo happens to be on it. Thanks, Michael, wherever you are. Anyway, if this A-330 stays up in the air, I shouldn't have to worry about whose airspace it is.*

Swiss International Air Lines flight 242 was almost to the halfway point on its journey from Zürich to Dubai. Nir had been on longer flights, but this one truly seemed to be dragging. Maybe it was because *he* was dragging. He was achy and sick to death of being trapped inside a metal tube. He'd made the four-hour flight from Tel Aviv to Zürich just this morning, traveling under a different forged passport, that one Israeli.

His three-hour layover was spent taxiing from the airport to a hotel, then to a second and a third hotel, then back to the airport. All the while, he kept his eyes on the taxis' rear mirrors to see if anyone was following him. But as his body wore down, his adrenaline kept his mind alert. Even now, he was filled with nervous energy that almost made him jittery. Nir supposed that was to be expected. After all, he was traveling to Dubai to kill a man.

The matronly flight attendant took Nir's tray, then he tilted his seat back. He closed his eyes and thought about the journey that had brought him to this lethal point in his life. Two weeks after the meeting with the Mossad man in Johannesburg, Nir had returned to Israel and been immediately placed in training.

Nicole le Roux's beautiful face formed in Nir's mind. He'd had no choice but to let his barely begun relationship with her go. He never returned to Cape Town, and their last phone conversation was so strained that he'd decided not to call her again. Nicole deserved an explanation, but because he couldn't tell her the truth, it was easier to tell her nothing at all.

He'd done his best to forget the beautiful South African model with those incredible eyes, but he still felt the sacrifice. By now, she'd no doubt forgotten all about him.

He sighed and forced his mind back to his career in the Mossad.

The next six months of his life had been a blur of physical, tactical, and language preparation. He was a native speaker of Hebrew, but he'd learned English from two friends while growing up on the kibbutz. These boys' parents had made *aliyah* from Santa Monica, California, wanting to rear their children as Israelis. He helped them with their Hebrew, and they helped him with his English. The Mossad training had also greatly improved his passable Arabic, and he was given intensive instruction in French as well.

Toward the end of his preparation, Nir was told he was being assigned to Caesarea. He was ecstatic. Every Israeli boy grows up pretending he belongs to Caesarea, which they all know is pronounced with a hard *C*. Named after the city built by Herod the Great on Israel's Mediterranean coast, this division of the Mossad was responsible for much of the shady activity that gives the Israeli intelligence service its reputation as the best—and scariest—in the business.

While in training, Nir had also refreshed his knowledge about the Mossad's beginnings. In 1949, one year after the formation of the independent State of Israel, Prime Minister David Ben-Gurion decided to address the desperate need of the newly formed nation for political and military intelligence of the activities of their neighboring states, most of whom wanted to destroy the Israelis. To that end, he created the Institute for Intelligence and Special Operations. That title was quite a mouthful, so people began referring to it simply as the "Institute," which in Hebrew is *Mossad*. The motto for the organization came from the wisdom of the great King Solomon written in Proverbs 11:14: "Where no wise direction is, the people fall, but in the multitude of counsellors there is safety." This Scripture encircled the national symbol of the menorah on the Mossad's emblem.

Israeli intelligence was divided into three categories: *Aman*, which was military intelligence; *Shabak*, which focused on internal security; and *Mossad*, whose charter centered on international activities. Within the Mossad itself were eight divisions, Caesarea the one that got its hands the dirtiest.

After joining Caesarea, he was involved in several operations in Gaza, Turkey, and Italy. In each case he was mostly limited to an on-foot surveillance role—tailing a target walking the streets. Only once, in Rome, was he actually included in a car follow. But even that was short-lived. After five blocks, in order to avoid detection, he was forced to go straight while the target's vehicle turned right. Another car picked up the surveillance, and Nir never made it back into the hunt.

The international travel was exciting, as was the hint of danger, especially in Gaza. If he were being honest, though, he'd have to admit he was getting bored. Caesarea had the reputation of being the righteous outlaws of the Mossad. The most outside the law he'd ever been? Jaywalking in Istanbul.

"I saw more action guarding diplomats," he said to his Italy team leader over a couple of bottles of Peroni at an outdoor Rome café. But he was only half-joking.

"I know, I know. The intelligence game is not all glamour. Just be patient. You're in Caesarea because what you did in South Africa was noticed. Your time is coming."

That time came five weeks later when he was back in Tel Aviv and called into Alex Eichler's office. He was Caesarea's director.

"How did you feel when you killed those men in Cape Town?" Eichler had asked the question immediately after inviting him to sit down.

Nir was not expecting that. Rarely did anyone around the Mossad talk about feelings.

"Honestly? Pretty lousy. Life means something, and I took it away from those men. Not that I felt guilty or like I'd done anything wrong. I was

48

protecting innocent lives. Sometimes that means killing first those who are trying to kill you, right?"

The director answered Nir's question with another question. "What if the threat wasn't quite as imminent? Could you kill then?"

"I'm not sure I understand what you're asking, sir."

Eicher placed his elbows on his desk. "If someone was unarmed, but you knew they'd already murdered innocents and they would do it again given the chance, could you kill them?"

"You're talking about assassination, sir."

"Call it what you will. I'm asking you a question."

Nir processed for a moment, his eyes straying to the bare walls that held none of the degrees or pictures of hand-shaking moments with dignitaries and leaders that usually littered government office walls. *This is the life you've chosen for yourself. Behind the scenes. Hidden in the shadows. But there's a difference between gathering intelligence and becoming an assassin.*

He thought about whether he would have preemptively taken them all out if he'd known what the Xhosa terrorist militia had planned ahead of time. Blown up their hideout or snuck in and put a bullet in each of their heads. Then, in his mind, he saw the bloody mangled bodies lying on the grass among the chairs. He saw the men firing their AK-47s indiscriminately, trying to kill everyone they could. He saw the fear in Nicole's eyes as she pressed his jacket into the shoulder wound of a victim.

"Absolutely, sir. If someone is intent on killing others, then it's incumbent on those who can do something about it to stop them."

Eichler's eyes bored into Nir, evaluating, calculating. He was looking for something, but Nir had no idea what. He held the man's gaze.

"Tavor, I'm incorporating you into Kidon. Your work with Caesarea will continue, but I want to make you available for certain targeted operations. Are you good with that?"

"Yes, sir." Nir tried to keep his face expressionless while his insides were awhirl. Caesarea was the elite activities unit of the Mossad, and Kidon was the elite unit of Caesarea. The Hebrew word *kidon* means "bayonet." This unit was the bayonet—the tip of Mossad's spear.

Nir knew Kidon's history as well. In the early 1970s, the Palestine Liberation Organization (PLO) was carrying out terrorist attack after terrorist attack. Caesarea excelled at well-plotted, carefully designed counterterrorist operations and assassinations. It was not set up for those situations when, based on new intelligence, the Mossad had only a day or two to prepare for a targeted killing. Speed, agility, and lethality were essential. So legendary deputy head of Caesarea,

Michael Harari, created Kidon to be that lethal weapon.

Nir was startled out of his thoughts. Mr. Haidar had popped on his overhead light, then turned the air jet to max and begun flossing his teeth while watching an animated movie about meatballs raining from the sky.

Pop, went the floss. *Pop, pop, pop.*

Nir sighed and raised his seat to the upright position. He'd get no sleep on this flight.

His mind wandered back to the trajectory of his career. Following his entrance into Kidon, he'd not only worked with Caesarea but spent time exponentially expanding his training in weapons, Krav Maga—the Israeli Defense Forces' martial arts—and explosives. All the while, he knew that at any moment he could be called upon to put an end to someone's life.

That call had come two days ago. He'd spent the next 24 hours learning his legend as Michael McCann, the background and habits of the target, and the plan for taking him out. The operation was about as extensive as any he'd ever heard, involving three dozen agents. But only Nir and three others had been given the "tip of the spear" responsibility.

Taking a deep breath, he wished he could be sure the God of his people really existed, the one with all the rules he'd decided weren't for him. But in case He did exist, Nir said a silent prayer.

Let all enemies of the righteous, like the man we seek, become no threat. And help me not mess this up.

He looked back at the map on the little screen. The tiny plane had moved from over the water to land. *Less than three hours to go. I better forgo that second glass of wine.* He thought back to his assignment in Turkey six months ago. Somewhere down below him was a dark-haired, olive-complected woman with whom he'd spent a long night dancing.

Zeyna, Zehra . . . something with a *Z*. That woman had been a beauty.

He elbowed Haidar. "Turkish women, eh?"

His seatmate grunted and glared.

Nir sighed and took final stock. *Today I fly business class and eat salmon; tomorrow I kill a man. What a strange world I live in.*

CHAPTER 5

DUBAI, UAE—20:50 / 8:50 P.M. GST

The cab driver's eyes once again darted up to the rearview mirror.

Nicole scowled at the man, and his gaze returned to the road. *This fool is going to kill us both. Who thought the most dangerous part of my trip would be riding in this nasty cigarette- and sweat-smelling taxi?*

Just yesterday, Nicole was at her flat in Milan packing her bags to stay in London for a month. Fashion Week was coming up in February, and there were always plenty of modeling gigs to pick up at smaller shows leading up to the big event. But then came the call. She was needed in Dubai. So she'd pulled the sweaters and jackets out of her bag and returned them to her wardrobe, then set a small overnight bag on her raised bed and folded in clothing for a much warmer climate.

But January in Dubai wasn't quite as hot as she thought it would be. In fact, she was a little chilly this evening in her sundress. The city itself was also not what she expected. Skyscrapers were everywhere, and the whole metropolis spoke of new and wealthy. As she watched the lights as they passed by, she wondered what in the world she was doing here.

This was the first time they'd used her. Her training as an agent had been minimal—a few weeks. And half that time seemed to be just filling out paperwork and listening to lectures about the unpleasant things that would happen to her if she went rogue. She felt ill-prepared and on edge, but at least her undeniable computer skills gave her some confidence. That was good, because she'd been recruited to do nefarious things. In this case, breaking into a hotel security system.

I can do that. In fact, I have done that. It's not like I'll be dodging bullets—although I guess I've already checked that one off my bucket list.

The cabbie was staring at her again. Nicole understood why. Her straight, bright-red hair and emerald-green eyes made quite the statement. This man would probably tell his friends—and anyone else who might possibly ask—all about the good-looking, redheaded fare in a sundress he drove the short distance from the Atlantis resort on Palm Island to the Burj Al Arab. That was exactly what Nicole had intended.

She met the man's gaze, then subtly circled her finger to indicate he should put his eyes back on the road. The driver complied, then laid on the horn, no doubt taking his embarrassment and frustration out on the car in front of him. Nicole was still early in her Arabic studies, but she recognized a few of the words he used.

She smiled. *In a country where it's illegal to insult another person, I think this cabbie just earned himself seven to ten years in jail.*

The cab turned left onto a long drive, and soon the buildings to either side disappeared and the road elevated over beach and then water. Nicole marveled at the beauty of Burj Al Arab as they approached it. She'd read that the 321-meter hotel was the third tallest in the world and it was designed to resemble the sail of a ship. Rising straight up in back, the front bowed forward as if caught by the wind, giving the whole structure a sense of movement. This view of the building, set on a man-made island just off the coast, and the Persian Gulf surrounding it was unique to anything she'd ever seen.

The car orbited a large fountain before pulling up to a drop-off zone. Nicole lifted her large Christian Louboutin straw tote off the seat next to her and stepped out when the driver opened her door. She passed him the agreed-upon fare with a generous tip and walked into the hotel entryway, feeling the stares of the cabbie, the porters, and the doormen. That was good, and she shifted her walk into model mode. Being seen going in was the plan. Coming back out would be a different story.

The resort was five-star all the way—high ceilings, massive chandeliers, and an enormous cascading water feature that was truly a work of art. Nicole wished she had time to explore the luxury of this top-end hotel, but that's not why she was here. Walking to the right of the waterfall, she rode the escalator up to the main level, admiring the hundreds of tropical fish in an aquarium that ran the full length of the wall. Again, keeping to the right, she bypassed a dancing waters fountain and the check-in desk in the lobby, then entered a women's restroom.

As she'd hoped, the stalls' modesty doors were floor to ceiling. She entered the one farthest from the door and locked it behind her, then took off her wig and popped the colored contacts out of her eyes. The sundress came off, and she replaced it with a designer T-shirt, low-cut jeans, and a cropped denim jacket. She shook out a wavy blond wig before placing it on her head, and rather than messing with another pair of contact lenses, she opted for Tom Ford aviator sunglasses. Who cared that it was nighttime? Fashion meant never having to say you're sorry. The final touch was a wide-brimmed Boho wool hat, completing her transformation. With her original outfit tucked away in her bag, she flushed the toilet, then washed her hands, checked herself in the mirror, and walked out the door.

Nicole crossed the lobby and stepped onto the down escalator. *No nerves. Walk like you own the place.*

"Cars for hire?" she asked the doorman as she stepped outside.

"Would you like me to fetch you a car?" Even without the sundress, here was yet another man giving her a full body scan.

"No. Just point me the way."

She followed his finger to where a series of taxi drivers stood next to their cars. To her relief, she saw that the cabbie who had just dropped her off was not among them.

All heads turned her way as she approached.

"How much to Jumeirah Beach Hotel?" she asked the first driver, loud enough to be heard over the fountain.

"Eighty dirhams."

The fare was way overpriced for such a short trip, but she didn't want to haggle. Besides, it wasn't her money. She nodded her agreement, and the man opened the car door for her.

The hotel was within eyeshot of the Burj Al Arab, but she was determined to make use of the brief drive to rest and think. Once she arrived at her destination, she would be on the go for the next 24 hours—at least. Two years ago, her greatest goal was to make enough money to escape her life in Cape Town. Now, here she was practicing tradecraft—what her trainer had called *maslul*—while on assignment in Dubai for the Israeli Mossad.

Didn't see that coming, she thought with a

silent laugh. *Not with the background I have.*

Her mother had a one-night stand with the bass player in a band passing through Cape Town, and Nicole and her twin brother, Christiaan, were the result. But only 19 and stunningly beautiful, her mother wasn't ready to give up her partying ways. So the two siblings spent most of their time with their grandmother, who was a barely functioning alcoholic. When they were four, her mother married some shady guy she'd met at a club. Her visits became more and more rare until she pretty much disappeared.

When Nicole and Christiaan were eight, two years later, she suddenly reappeared. Nicole couldn't believe the change in her. She was incredibly thin, her beautiful skin was pocked and scabby, and her hair was matted and uneven. All her vibrancy was gone. When Nicole was older, she realized her mother had looked strung out and defeated. Thinking back to that day now, she figured if someone had put her mom on an anti-drug before-and-after poster, any teenager who saw it would have been scared clean.

When her mother opened her arms for a hug, Nicole had gone to her, but Christiaan held back. Nicole could still smell the sour odor of her body and the vomit smell on her breath when she whispered, "I love you, my little girl." Nicole hadn't replied.

The visit was short and ended in a screaming

match between their mother and grandmother over money. Mom stormed out without saying goodbye. Less than 18 months later, she was dead of a heroin overdose. Christiaan and Nicole had talked many times about that last visit, and he admitted to feeling guilty for not hugging his mother one last time when he had the opportunity. Nicole was sure that was one of the many factors that went into his own current substance abuse.

But she and her brother were always close. Nicole knew that no matter what was happening around her, at least one person loved her unconditionally. This was true even when they hit their teens and their paths diverged. Christiaan followed their mom's and grandmother's footsteps, falling into the party lifestyle. Nicole was determined to make something better of herself. She didn't want anything to do with the drinking and drugs. That life was not going to take her too.

She hadn't been a recluse. She still spent time at the skate park or out on the waves. But whenever she wasn't skating or surfing, she was in her room on her computer. It started with gaming. She was a good gamer but not great. Then an online friend told her how she could do a little recoding to a particular game that would allow her to absolutely dominate. Nicole tried it, and it worked. That was all it took; she was hooked.

What started with how to win computer games became how to game the system. She found she had an aptitude for finding or creating back doors into computer systems. The dark web introduced her to a small community of hackers who were always ready to share their new discoveries with one another. Soon Nicole found she could break into just about any system she wanted. While Christiaan found companionship at clubs and parties, Nicole's friends lived in dark-web chat rooms.

When she was 15, she saw an online ad looking for models for a show at a local mall. All her life people had been telling her she had a certain look. "You should be a model. There's just something about you." Nicole didn't see it. But if what people said about her was true, this might be the way to eventually get out of her grandmother's house and out of Cape Town for good.

By the time she'd seen the ad, she was too late for the auditions. But five minutes and a couple hundred keystrokes later, the name Nicole le Roux was on the model list. She still felt bad for a girl named Gretchen Booysen, who was mysteriously dropped from the schedule. Gretchen and her mom had raised quite a stink when they arrived at the show only to be told the girl's name was nowhere to be found.

Nicole shook herself back to the present as the cab passed from the artificial island to the bridge that traversed the water. Once they passed the beach, the car turned left.

"Go slow. I want to admire the view." In truth, she was just stalling. She was excited but scared. The terrorist assault that almost took her life had been two years back. If Nir Tavor hadn't been there to rescue her, who knows what might have happened?

Nir's olive-skinned face came to mind. After the attack, she'd been shaken. It seemed impossible to have been that close to death and then be expected to live life as usual. She was reeling, so when she got the call from Nir, she jumped at his offer for lunch. She needed to spend time with someone who would understand what she'd gone through, who had heard the bullets and seen the dead people. Christiaan tried to console her, but he just didn't quite get how it felt to have been so near to death.

She and Nir had a foxhole bond, but that wasn't all that drew them together. She'd had a couple of boyfriends in her teens, and she'd dated a little since leaving Cape Town, but those relationships had been nothing like the brief connection she'd had with Nir.

And it *was* brief. Not long after he returned to Johannesburg, he grew distant. When his communication stopped completely, she wrote the relationship off. After all, long-distance relationships rarely work. Still, it hurt, and she wanted to know what happened. She needed some kind of closure. So she did a foolish thing that changed her life forever.

Late one night, she was bored and lonely, and her thoughts drifted to Nir. *What happened that he just fell off the face of the earth? Didn't he want to be with me anymore? Did I do something wrong?* A new thought hit her. *Or couldn't he be with me anymore? After all, given his profession . . .*

There was one way to find out.

Two hours later, in the server files of the Israeli Ministry of Foreign Affairs, she'd discovered that Nir had been transferred back to Israel to work in Israeli intelligence. It took her almost to daybreak to finally gain access into the Mossad system and see that he was in training to be an agent.

Good for him. He'll be good at that. She was relieved that work—work he couldn't tell her about—had pulled him away rather than her somehow pushing him away.

The knock on her front door came three days later. Her grandmother was at work, and Christiaan hadn't been home for a week. She was surprised to see two late-middle-aged men standing on her front steps, one with a familiar face. Her stomach dropped, and she felt nauseated.

"My name is Gideon Zamir," the man said.

"I remember you." She tried to remain cool. "Please, come in."

You broke into the computer system of the world's greatest intelligence service, you fool. Of course these men are here.

Nicole invited them to sit at a small, chrome-skirted dinette table in the kitchen.

"Would you like some tea?" she asked, trying to be hospitable as her grandmother had taught her.

"Please, don't trouble yourself," Zamir said. "Come, sit. We don't want to take much of your time."

Hesitantly, Nicole pulled out a chair with a zigzag tear in the bottom cushion and sat down. She didn't know if she was about to go to prison for hacking or if these guys were just going to make her disappear.

The men sat after her.

Zamir began. "Nicole . . . May I call you Nicole?"

She nodded.

"Good, thank you. I would like to know how you're doing after you so admirably saved that woman's life during the incident here in Cape Town."

Incident? What a safe and sanitary way to describe a terrorist attack where people lost their lives.

"I'm okay. Nightmares every now and then."

"Of course. It's to be expected after so traumatic an experience." He nodded to his companion. "This is my colleague, Asher. As much as I would like to ask you more about your well-being, his time is quite limited. He has some questions for you."

"Um, fine."

Nervously, she picked at one of the pits in the table's surface. This Asher guy had the kind of dead stare that said he would likely ask her to dig her own grave before he dropped her into it.

After a short silence that seemed like an eternity, Asher said, "Nicole, I am with the Mossad. I would tell you more about who we are, but I think you already know."

And there it is. "Look, I'm sorry. I was just—"

Asher held up his hand. "I am not here to punish you. I'm here to give you a job."

Nicole burst out laughing. She wasn't sure why. Shock, relief, or maybe just the absurdity of his words. "A job?"

"Yes, a job." The left corner of his mouth lifted ever so slightly, acknowledging her amusement.

"But I already have a job. I model. That's enough to keep me busy for now. But thank you for the offer." Nicole slid her chair back to conclude the meeting.

Asher waved his hand dismissively. "Nonsense. Hear me out."

Reluctantly, Nicole scooted her chair forward again.

"First, your modeling career is one of the

reasons we want you. We can use it to put you in places where you might be beneficial to us."

Beneficial? Why would I care if I were beneficial to you? She opened her mouth to protest, but he held up his hand again.

"Second, my dear girl, you must understand that I am not *offering* you a job; I am *giving* you a job. You will be joining us at the Mossad, where you will use your connections through modeling and your remarkable computer skills—skills that allowed you to illegally break into our server, which we were always told was impenetrable, and see files that, quite frankly, you never should have seen. Yes, you will now join in our efforts to protect the security of the sovereign State of Israel."

Nicole couldn't believe what she was hearing. Was he actually blackmailing her into becoming part of Israeli intelligence?

"Is there an *or else* to your offer?" she asked, angry—and not only because he'd been so condescending.

Asher leaned back in his chair and smiled. "Talk of *or else* can get so ugly. Is it really necessary?"

"It is to me. You're making veiled threats, and I want to know what I'm being threatened with."

Asher shrugged and sighed. "Let me put it to you this way. When you broke into our computer system, you made yourself a liability. In our business, we are not comfortable with liabilities. Thus, I'm here to turn a liability into an asset."

After more back-and-forth, Nicole had accepted the job. What choice did she have?

As the two men stepped onto her front steps, Asher turned around. "I have one more thing to ask. You and Nir Tavor had a . . . romantic relationship, correct?"

"Yes." Why did she feel embarrassed?

"He is busy developing skills that could ultimately save his life. He doesn't need any . . . how should I say it . . . complications. I'm asking you to not make contact with him. To do so could distract him and ultimately put him at risk. May I count on you for that?"

Nicole thought Asher's reasoning sounded forced, but she got the sense that when Asher said he was asking, he was actually telling.

"Okay."

"Good." He turned around to walk away, but then he stopped one more time. "And, Nicole, stay out of our computers. This is a lovely city, but I don't want to have to make a return trip."

Three weeks later, she received a call from one of the more well-known modeling agencies saying they would be representing her and asking her to please make arrangements to move to Milan within the next two weeks. She was shocked; she'd never applied to any European agency. Then, just as she was trying to figure out how she could possibly afford a move to that incredibly expensive city, she received an encrypted email saying a flat had been arranged for her and a comfortable nest egg had been deposited into a bank for her expenses.

For two years she'd been establishing herself as a model in the European fashion world, the whole time waiting for a call to begin her Mossad work. That call had finally come yesterday.

The cab pulled up to the Jumeirah Beach Hotel. While the Burj Al Arab had been designed to look like a giant sail, the Jumeirah Beach resembled a wave slowly building up to its crest. It, too, was top of the line in all its amenities. Nicole walked through the lobby and took the elevator to the sixth floor. There was no need to check in; she'd done that two hours ago when she hacked into the hotel's computer system from the lobby of the Atlantis. Then she'd slipped a blank key card into a little machine tucked away at the bottom of her tote and coded it to unlock the room.

When she reached room 632 at the Jumeirah Beach, she placed the card in the door's slot, then opened the door and walked in.

CHAPTER 6

DUBAI, UAE—JANUARY 19, 2010— 00:10 / 12:10 A.M. GST

The man ahead of Nir stepped up to the booth. Inside sat an Emirati immigration agent who looked to be in his late thirties. His thick black hair was combed to one side, and he sported a narrow mustache. Nir studied him as he worked. His hair was starting to sag a bit in the front, and his uniform had lost the crispness of its seams. This was good. It meant he was likely nearing the end of his shift, so he wouldn't be quite as on top of his game as he would if he were just starting his day. Also, as he worked, he kept his head down nearly the entire time, looking up only once to compare the photo in the man's passport to the face that stood before him.

Here's a man who does not love his job. Another good sign.

The agent punched a stamp onto the passport, then turned back to his computer monitor as he lifted the document to the traveler. The man snatched his passport and hurried off.

"Next in line," he said in Arab-accented English.

Nir stepped forward and placed his passport into the agent's upraised hand.

Turning from his screen, the man gave Nir a once-over, then looked at the cover of the passport. "United Kingdom?"

"London, born and raised."

"Name?"

"McCann. Michael John Agnew McCann."

The agent's brief moment of interest in Nir quickly passed, and he turned back to his desk. Nir's passport slid through a reader, and the man's computer screen populated with information.

"Reason for your visit?"

"Business."

"Where will you be staying?"

This was a tricky question, since Nir had no good answer. Headquarters was still working out accommodation details as he was boarding his flight.

"Jumeirah . . . the Jumeirah something," he said, taking the advice of his Caesarea handler. Apparently, half the hotels in Dubai were the Jumeirah something or other. "I'm sorry, I forget the exact name. I can dig it out of my carry-on if—"

The agent interrupted with a dismissive wave of his hand.

There are few better sounds than a stamp hitting a passport, Nir thought when the man added the

Emirati seal. *Especially when that passport is . . . well, compromised.*

Nir took the booklet when it was offered and exited the immigration hall. He'd fit everything he needed into his carry-on, allowing him to bypass the baggage carousels and walk straight to customs. He'd filled out his declaration slip on the plane, and he handed the paper to a customs agent and passed through to the terminal.

No sooner had he cleared the secure area than he heard his cover name—"Michael."

The tall, thin man walking toward him had a shaved head, and his tight beard was a mix of brown and white. The smudges on his glasses told Nir he usually didn't wear any visual enhancement.

"Peter," Nir said. This man was Peter just as much as Nir was Michael, so it wouldn't do to be overheard calling him Shmuel, his actual name. This was particularly true here in an Arab Gulf state where nobody had much love for the Jews. The handler had emphasized that everyone would be using legend names on this operation the whole time, no exceptions.

Keeping those names straight for this 36-member team would likely be tough for the operation leaders, but not for Nir. The operators were broken into smaller squads, so he had only a handful of names to remember. Peter, Gail, and Kevin were the operation's three key leaders.

The fourth name belonged to his hotel roommate and fellow member on the four-person hit team, James.

"Good flight?" Peter asked.

"Ah, you know the Lebanese."

Peter wrinkled his brow at him but didn't follow up.

Speaking softly as they moved through the terminal, Peter said, "The operation is called Operation Plasma Screen, after the code name for the target. Go to the hotel and get some sleep tonight because you'll need to be rested tomorrow. James is flying in from Paris in two hours. He'll have a key card to let himself in. At 09:45 tomorrow morning, a car will be out front to take you both to a shopping mall. Kevin or Gail will meet you there. The situation is fluid now, but they'll be able to give you more information as time goes on. Any questions?"

"Where is the target staying?"

"We're working on it."

"How are we dispatching the target?"

"We're working on it."

"How will we—"

"What part of *the situation is fluid* do you not understand?"

"So asking me if I had any questions was rhetorical?" Peter had sounded exasperated, but it was frustrating to have so little information. Still, Nir figured this is how it worked in Kidon—no time for detailed plans going in. You just figured it out as you went along.

Something touched his hand, and he instinctively took hold of it. Peter said, "In this envelope is a key to your hotel room, Hilton Dubai Jumeirah, room 2910. Take a cab. In the envelope is 1,000 dirhams for expenses. Go straight to the hotel. It's late enough that any *maslul* will probably draw extra unwanted attention. Tomorrow we'll make sure no one is interested in you. Be safe."

Peter stepped away without another word.

Cold air hit Nir as he passed through the terminal doors, and he wished he'd brought a coat. The cab ride was uneventful, but the city itself was spectacular. The lights of the skyscrapers rose high into the sky, while down on the ground a surprising number of cars were out on the road for this late at night. Most of them cost far more than he could make in three years at the Mossad.

Once at the hotel, Nir bypassed the check-in desk and took the elevator to the twenty-ninth floor. He removed the key from the envelope and saw no Hilton markings on it. *Hopefully, whoever made this key did a good job. Otherwise, I'm probably sleeping on the beach tonight, because I doubt the front desk even knows I'm here.*

He slid the key into the door slot for room 2910, and the red light turned green.

As he toured the room, making sure there were no bad guys hiding in the shower or under the beds, he could see that the room was Hilton nice. Clean, well appointed—sort of like the business class flight he just took. It wasn't quite first class, but it was good enough for his tastes. After examining lamps, picture frames, and any other little crevice for listening devices or cameras, he pulled a bottle of Dos Equis from the mini-bar fridge and stepped out onto the balcony. The air was even colder at this height as the wind blew past the hotel. Nir stepped back in, then took one of the blankets in a closet and returned outside.

He tested one of the patio chairs for dryness, then positioned it so he could see the room's entrance out from the corner of his eye. Once seated, he covered his legs with the blanket. Bright lights outlined the shape of the Palm Jumeirah, the middle of three large artificial islands built in the Gulf waters. Shaped like enormous palm leaves, they were architectural and construction marvels. At the top of the Palm was the massive Atlantis resort, and beyond it lay the blackness of the Persian Gulf waters.

He put his feet up on a glass-topped table. Closer to the hotel, boats of all sizes were moored in the calm waters of the marina. Some of the yachts anchored a little farther out into the Gulf looked like they had to cost in the millions of euros.

As he sipped his beer, he thought back to when his parents had taken the whole family on a weeklong vacation to Haifa. The second day, his father had rented a sailboat. Dad had done some sailing when he was younger and wanted to teach Nir's two older brothers the basics. Nir, fourth out of the five children and the only other boy, was declared too young by his father and left out of the training. Everyone piled into the boat and Dad pushed off, but the trip was ill-fated from the beginning. Despite his bravado to his family and the marina master, Dad had forgotten more about sailing than he remembered.

Tensions escalated quickly as his father's embarrassment grew. When Nir's oldest brother, who was 13 at the time, made a joke at Dad's expense, the man swung at him with the back of his hand. His brother dropped to the ground, his mouth bloodied.

Not that getting hit by their dad was that unusual. While certainly not a daily occurrence, each of the kids would occasionally feel the brunt of his frustration, and Nir got used to the taste of blood in his mouth. Mom made excuses for him, saying he hadn't been the same since the First Lebanon War in 1982. But by trying to explain away his violent outbursts, she'd allowed them to continue.

The Haifa trip ended early, and Dad disappeared for a few days after they got home.

Nir drained the last of his beer and went back inside, dropping the bottle into a little can by the bar. *Enough reminiscing. Nothing good comes from looking backward.*

He practiced his Arabic by watching some strange TV show until James arrived. Then he took a shower before slipping into the queen bed nearest the window, eager for sleep.

CHAPTER 7

JUMEIRAH BEACH HOTEL, DUBAI, UAE— 08:45 / 8:45 A.M. GST

Nicole had been swamped all night, but now she was in hurry-up-and-wait mode.

From the moment she'd stepped into the mini-suite last evening, she'd prepared for the arrival of the rest of the team. Thirty-six agents translated to 14 squads of two, four drivers, and three leaders—Peter, Kevin, and Gail would be headquartering in the suite—plus her, the *goy* hacker.

Her first order of business had been reserving 16 rooms in five different hotels. That meant hacking into each hotel's computer system, reserving the rooms, checking into each room, and making key cards for each operator, and the clock was ticking on this enormous task. Peter's flight was to arrive at 22:35, which meant he would be at the hotel room by 23:15 for the key cards and a printout of the reservations. That had given her a little over 90 minutes to get the job done. His turnaround would have to be quick for him to get back to the airport in time to meet the other team members as they arrived.

When the knock came at 23:20, she hurried to the door. As she looked through the peephole, the man on the other side said, "Annabelle?"

The name made her cringe. When she'd seen that name on the legend dossier her handler had given her in Milan, she wasn't sure if she wanted to laugh or cry. Annabelle Crittenden Smythe sounded like a rich, self-important villain in a Jane Austen novel.

Nicole opened the door, and Peter walked in.

"Do you have the cards?" he asked after pulling a bottle of sparkling water out of the mini fridge. He twisted it open, threw the cap onto a long dresser, and took a long draw.

"Of course. Right over there."

Without pulling the bottle from his lips, Peter waved for her to bring him the materials.

Nicole took a tan envelope with the key cards and printouts to him. He put the half-empty bottle down next to the cap and opened the package. "You sure it's all here and all good?"

"I wouldn't be giving it to you if I wasn't." Her reply came with a little anger in her tone. She was tired and he was being rude, and that wasn't shaping up to be a good combination.

Peter looked up from the envelope. "I'm only asking you this because my agents' lives are depending on you not screwing up. I don't know you. I don't know anything about you, except that you're a Gentile from South Africa who's supposed to be some kind of computer genius. I look at you and wonder if you're here because some deputy director liked your skills or just your pretty face."

Nicole gave him an icy smile. "Well, my pretty face is one more asset than you have at your disposal."

Peter stared at her, then burst out laughing. He looked back into the envelope. "I think I can get to like you."

Don't do me any favors.

She'd expected this kind of attitude as an outsider coming to the Mossad. In fact, Asher had warned her about it. In a follow-up call to his initial visit, he'd told her a lot of people would be wondering what a non-Jew was doing working for the Mossad. Trust would be an issue, and her looks would only make things worse. "Just stand your ground and don't take any lip," he'd said. "Prove yourself by your work, and don't give anyone a reason to confirm their initial impression of you."

Peter wandered around the suite, looking into each of the two bedrooms. "How are you coming on the coms?"

Phones were being smuggled into the country. Any call made by these doctored devices would be routed through a bank of numbers secured in Austria. This allowed Nicole to create a centralized system through which Peter, Gail, and Kevin could monitor all communications between the operatives. Also, routing it through

Austria brought one more level of confusion to anyone who might investigate after the fact.

"Gail and Kevin will each be bringing in the phones. I'm just starting work on establishing the relay routing through the Austrian numbers."

"Excellent." Peter retrieved the water bottle, then drained the rest of its contents and stifled a carbonation belch. "Make sure the coms are ready on time. Once the team figures out where Plasma Screen is staying, they'll have to move fast. Our success or failure will depend on you. Understood?"

"Understood."

Peter set the empty bottle back on the dresser and headed out the door.

It was nearly 01:00 before Gail arrived. Nicole assumed Peter had met her at the airport because she let herself in with a key card.

Good to know the cards work, Nicole had thought.

Gail was cold toward her, but unlike Peter, she'd never warmed up. After she gave her phones to Nicole, she went into one of the bedrooms and closed the door. When Kevin arrived an hour later, he was much friendlier than the other two. But after a couple minutes of idle chit-chat, he disappeared into the other bedroom.

Nicole's adrenaline finally failed her around 05:00, and she curled up on a corner of the couch. She woke an hour later to the sound of her suitemates talking as Kevin loaded an automatic coffeemaker.

Embarrassed at being caught sleeping, Nicole got up and walked to the bathroom. She splashed water on her face and took time to clean herself up. When she came back, Gail and Kevin were sitting at the two-person kitchenette table sipping their coffee.

"Good morning, Annabelle," Kevin said.

Gail didn't even look at her.

"Good morning." Nicole vowed to track down whoever had created her legend name and do something nasty to their credit rating.

"Help yourself to the pot. It's not too bad for hotel coffee." As Kevin resumed his conversation with Gail, Nicole poured herself a cup, then went back to her laptop.

That had been two hours ago. Kevin had run out for a short time while Gail used the shower. When he came back, he had a bag of fried dough triangles filled with cheese. He called them *fatayer jibneh*, and they were delicious.

At 09:30, Gail and Kevin left, each carrying a shopping bag loaded with phones. Grateful for the quiet, Nicole poured herself more coffee. She went to the window and looked out at the waters of the Gulf. It would still be three hours before Plasma Screen's flight took off from Damascus and then another three until he landed. But once he did, the craziness would start again.

CHAPTER 8

DUBAI, UAE—09:40 / 9:40 A.M. GST

The Mossad driver, who had introduced himself as Evan, took another quick right turn, and the silver Land Rover moved inland, leaving the seacoast behind. Nir had never seen this guy before, but it was evident that he'd been doing this for a while. His tradecraft was spectacular. His intersection work and rapid turns were well-planned and choreographed to ensure that no one could follow them without detection. From his place in the back seat behind James, Nir stored away what he was learning for future use.

After driving around the city for another 45 minutes, the SUV turned into the parking lot of a massive shopping mall. Evan spoke from the front seat in his distinctly Irish brogue. "Just walk around. Pretend like you belong. Either Gail or Kevin will find you. They'll have something for you and some instructions. Then just walk the mall, kill time. I'll be back at 12:40 to pick you up from where I drop you off."

Three hours seemed like a long time to be out and exposed, but it was no use expressing his misgivings to Evan. He was just the messenger. Besides, who knew what was going on in the ops planning? There was likely a good reason they'd be here that long.

Evan left them at an entrance and drove off. James held the door for Nir, and they went in. Immediately, Nir knew why this place had been chosen for the meet. It was swarming with people from all over the world. Every ethnicity, every style of dress, every language appeared to be represented. The variety was so great that the differences blended together into one rainbow, where no one person stood out from another.

The mall was enormous, bigger than any shopping location he'd ever seen. Four stories, and it seemed to stretch out forever. Like every-thing else in Dubai, the building looked like it had just been constructed. No fading paint, no stained flooring . . . Everything simply sparkled.

"This place is insane," James said.

"No doubt. I think the kibbutz where I grew up would fit in here three times over."

They wandered for a while. Every luxury brand one could think of had a storefront here, and they were definitely doing good business. Every-one seemed to be carrying shopping bags, except for a few women whose hired help toted their purchases a respectful one-and-a-half meters behind them.

After 20 minutes or so, a young woman brushed up against Nir. "Gail is to your right," she said without looking at them, then continued on.

Nir elbowed James, and they altered their course. About 30 meters ahead was a small alcove with a number of tables. Gail sat at one of them, her back to a wall. She was pretty, with blond hair, a long, narrow face, and a ready smile.

"Michael, James," she said as they sat down. "So glad to see you."

"Hi, Gail. I like the look." Nir knew her as Eliana, a dark-haired agent from Tel Aviv.

"It's my glamour look." She laughed. "Okay, here's where we are. Plasma Screen's plane arrives at 15:30. We don't know where he'll be staying, but it's usually one of three hotels. We'll have surveillance on him from the time he lands. Also, we'll have teams watching the entrances to those hotels in case we somehow lose him from the airport."

A pair of colorfully dressed Nigerian women passed close to the table, and Gail paused. When they were gone, she picked up again. "Once he checks into the hotel, we'll get a room right by his. Obviously, we don't know his schedule, but we do know he always meets his IRGC contact for dinner the first night he's here."

"Nothing kills you faster than routine," James said.

Nir agreed. "True, but you've got to kiss the ring of your masters, especially if it's the Iranian Revolutionary Guard Corps."

Gail centered them back in. She had a script she

needed to deliver, and it didn't seem like she had time to get sidetracked. "Listen, if he does go out, we'll hit tonight. If for some reason he breaks routine, then we'll be on hold for whenever he next leaves his room. Once he's gone, we'll get you and the other team into the hotel and into his room. When he returns, you two will subdue him. From the other team, Chester will stand as backup, and David will use the device."

"Tell me about this device," Nir said.

"It's an ultrasound injection device. David will hit him with a lethal dose of suxamethonium chloride. But instead of using a needle, he'll deliver it using ultrasound waves. That way there won't be a mark."

Nir inwardly marveled. "Ultrasound waves? I didn't even know that was possible."

"Make sure they get the dose right this time," James said.

"What do you mean, *this time?*" Nir asked.

"Four months ago, right here in Dubai, they spiked Plasma Screen's drink with something. It was supposed to kill him, but instead it just gave him a bad case of the runs. I doubt he even knows he dodged a bullet. He probably thinks he just ate some bad fish."

Gail shook her head. "Come on. I need you to focus. I've got other teams to talk to. Trust me, the dosage is fine this time. You do your job, and the operation will be a success. There's a shopping bag at your feet. At the bottom of it is a phone. I know you've run through that whole drill. Just speed dial 1, and it will connect you to us."

Nir used his foot to move the bag up against his chair.

"You've got some time before Evan picks you up to take you back to the hotel. Wander around. Blend in. Go see the aquarium. Make yourself hard to tail. If it's a go tonight, we'll meet in the parking garage of whatever hotel Plasma Screen checks into. Evan will bring you. I'll let you know either way. Now, go."

Nir snatched up the bag, then he and James blended back into the crowd.

Time dragged as they roamed through the mall. In one of the food courts they found a Canadian coffee shop called Tim Horton's. There, they killed twenty minutes with lattes and a couple of bagels. Never much of a shopper, Nir felt like he was trapped in a giant luxury funhouse. To add insult to injury, when he tried to find the ski slope on a giant mall's map board, James informed him that the indoor skiing was at the Mall of the Emirates. They were at the Dubai Mall. Sad. That was the one thing he'd wanted to see.

Evan delivered them back to their hotel by 13:30. Although they weren't tired, they both tried to nap. They would need their wits and strength when it all started to go down.

CHAPTER 9

DUBAI AIRPORT, DUBAI, UAE—
15:15 / 3:15 P.M. GST

Eyes everywhere. Mahmoud could feel them. But whose eyes were they and were they looking for him?

He passed his customs form to an agent who waved him through without even looking at it. Mahmoud had long ago concluded that if you weren't bringing in a lot of luggage, the customs agents figured that whatever screening you had at passport control was good enough.

Casually scanning the airport lobby as he walked, he tried to memorize anyone who was sitting on a bench or leaning against a wall. He ruled out anyone who was obviously African or East Asian. It was the Israelis he was worried about, and the ethnicity of their agents tended toward Jew, Arab, and European. Every now and then there might be an Ethiopian or Tunisian but nothing sub-Saharan. The fox in Mahmoud had developed a sense about who was looking at him. Even if their head was buried in a newspaper or they were thumbing a text into their phone, he could tell if that was real or just a cover.

With all the people passing through the front

of the airport, only four possibilities stood out. A European-looking man talked on a pay phone, but his back was to the wall. A young Arab couple sat on a bench with a baby carrier between them. He was dressed in the traditional Emirati white *Kandura* and was leaning back with his eyes closed. She was talking to her baby in the carrier. Two fit young men leaned against another wall. They wore white, red, and blue warm-up suits with the Czech Republic logo on the sleeves. Finally, a tall, thin, balding man with a beard seemed to be taking a much longer time than usual looking at the departure board.

I'm betting it's the beard.

He diverted his course and walked into a men's room. Finding a stall, he closed the door and sat down. He knew he was being overly cautious. Who could possibly know about this trip? But the Israelis seemed to have eyes and ears everywhere, and one could never be too careful. Besides, his sources told him he was near the top of the Mossad's hit list.

The thought of his death being that important to the Israelis both frightened him and filled him with pride. It meant he was doing his job well. He was a connections man, a financial wizard, and an acquirer of goods important to certain groups of people—weapons of all kinds. Parts for the Palestinian-made Carlo submachine guns, Russian Katyusha rockets, 82mm and 120mm mortars, even the raw materials to make TATP explosives . . . He could and had bought weapons of all shapes, sizes, and calibers.

The certain groups of people for whom he purchased these weapons were mostly Hamas, the militant and nationalist Palestinian organization, and its military arm, the Izz ad-Din al-Qassam Brigades. These were his people, and one day they would push the Jewish invaders into the sea. His clientele wasn't limited to home, though. He freelanced, too, arranging deals for groups like Hezbollah, al-Qaeda, the Palestinian Islamic Jihad, and Fatah al-Islam. He'd even overseen a shipment of 2,000 AK-47s to Boko Haram in Nigeria.

It was true that his work had made him a wealthy man. But he liked to think he wasn't in it for the money. He was a servant of Allah. He did what he did so the warriors of Islam could be well prepared for battle. And if Almighty God chose to bless him with a comfortable life here on earth, it was simply recompense for the sacrifices he made.

JUMEIRAH BEACH HOTEL, DUBAI, UAE— 15:17 / 3:17 P.M. GST

The tension in the room was almost unbearable. Plasma Screen had landed, and now it was just a matter of spotting him. Nicole sat at a small desk in the suite with her laptop open. Gail and Kevin stood on either side of her.

"Team *Bet*, got him," came a female voice over the computer.

Peter, who was pacing on the other side of the room with a phone held to his ear, said, "Ident confirmed?"

"*Root*," a deeper voice confirmed.

"Is he leaving?"

"Hold on," said the second voice. "Looks like he's hitting the head."

Peter stopped his pacing. "Okay, *Bet*, I want you out. *Gimel*, you take over. Team *Vav*, you stay where you are outside so you can identify his transportation. Got it?"

"*Bet*," the first team confirmed.

"*Gimel*."

"*Vav*."

Ten minutes later, Nicole heard the team member posing as a young, French-speaking father report, "*Il quitte l'aéroport.*"

CHAPTER 10

H e's leaving the airport," Gail translated for everyone's benefit. Then she looked down at Nicole. "Are you sure you're ready?"

"I've got this."

Nicole was determined not to take offense at Gail's question. She'd decided to try to keep her teammates' perspective in mind. Peter was right. These people didn't know her. She was an outsider, and now they were being asked to trust her. If she blew it, not only could the operation bust, but they could all find themselves in an Emirati prison at the center of an international incident. She would do her part, and she would do it to perfection.

"*Vav*," came another voice through the computer. "He's hired a taxi. White with orange roof. Cab number Z708."

Peter wrote the number onto the palm of his hand. "Got it. *Zayin*, you follow the target into the city. *Het* and *Yod*, you be ready in case *Zayin* needs to break off. *Alef* through *Vav*, you are released from the airport. Go to your next assigned areas and await orders. We'll see if he goes back out tonight."

One by one and in order, the affirmations sounded through the computer.

Four minutes into the pursuit, the *Zayin* team had to break off at a traffic light. *Het* team picked up the follow.

"Turning south onto Jumeirah Beach Road."

"That's the Ritz-Carlton." Nicole quickly typed into her computer to make sure her link into their system was still active.

"*Lamed*, be ready," Peter called on the coms phone. "Looks like he's coming your way."

The minutes passed with occasional updates. Peter paced, Gail chewed at her fingernails, Kevin played with the change in his pants pocket, and Nicole did her best to ignore them all.

"They're turning east," *Het* called out. "Looks like they're getting onto the E11 and going back the way they came. I've got to break off."

"Stepping in," came the voice of *Yod*. They'd been following three blocks behind just in case of this eventuality.

"It's going to be the Al Bustan," Nicole told them.

"Why?" Gail said. "How do you know it won't be the Sheraton Grand? He's stayed at the Sheraton more often than the Al Bustan."

"I don't know how I know. I just know. It fits."

"Pardon me if your *I just know* doesn't instill a lot of confidence in me," Gail sneered.

Peter spoke from across the room. "*Khaf*, we think he's coming your way to the Al Bustan Rotana. You guys be ready."

Gail glared at Nicole and set to work on her fingernails again.

Three minutes later, *Yod*'s voice sounded in the hotel room. "We've passed the exit for the Sheraton Grand. Unless he circles around again, it's the Al Bustan."

E11 FREEWAY, DUBAI, UAE— 15:45 / 3:45 P.M. GST

Although Mahmoud would have preferred to go right to the hotel to rest before his first meeting, he still went through his evasive maneuvers. It's when you get lazy that you'll meet your end. As he watched the traffic behind the taxi, for a moment he thought he spotted a tail car. But it hadn't followed them onto the freeway, and he hadn't seen anything suspicious since.

Dubai was so different from when he'd first come in the early 1990s. The building boom had already begun, but it was nothing like today. It seemed that the city's skyline changed every time he visited. Massive cranes littered the landscape as the metropolis grew taller and taller. And the city wasn't just expanding up. With the desert hemming in development to the east, Dubai had spread to the west, into the Gulf itself.

But at what cost was all this? They'd gained riches and luxury untold, but they'd paid for it with their souls. The United Arab Emirates had courted the business and wealth of the unholy West. Such a Sunni thing to do. It might buy them short-term prosperity, but Allah was a god of justice. Eventually, they would pay for their compromise.

His taxi pulled up to the entrance of the Al Bustan Rotana hotel. He paid the fare, then let himself out of the car. The front doors opened to a large entryway, behind which was a massive circular atrium. Balconies ran its circumference, with each level holding the doors to room after room.

A friendly Filipino woman greeted him as he walked up to the front desk. Her name tag said *Rosa*.

"Reservation for Mahmoud Abdul Raouf Muhammed," he said, sliding a forged Iraqi passport across the counter.

Rosa typed on her keyboard. "Yes, sir, we have your reservation."

"Excellent. I would like a room with sealed windows and no terrace, if possible."

"Of course." She typed a little more. "Here we go. Room 230."

As she worked, Mahmoud's peripheral vision

remained active, looking for anyone who might be taking too great an interest in him. So far, his fox instincts weren't picking anything up.

After a couple of minutes, Mahmoud signed his alias, and Rosa slid him two key cards in a small envelope. "May I do anything more for you, Mr. Muhammed?"

"Yes. Please have a car and driver waiting for me at 4:20."

"Yes, of course. And if you need anything else, just call down to the front desk. Have a pleasant stay."

Mahmoud crossed the lobby to the elevators. As he stepped in, two men dressed in shorts and carrying tennis equipment joined him. They all nodded to one another, and then the men turned toward the doors. Mahmoud tried to pick up the thread of their conversation, but they spoke in one of the Central European languages. He recognized the names Federer and Djokovic, though, so they must be discussing some recent tennis tournament.

When the doors opened, the men got off the elevator first to make way for Mahmoud. As he turned left down the hall toward his room, they remained in the alcove. He slid his key card into the lock of room 230, and as he closed the door behind him, he could still hear the men carrying on their debate.

"He's in room 230," Nicole said, excited. "The rooms on either side are taken, but I can get us in across the hall."

"Do it," Peter said. "Kevin, Gail, pack up everything we may have brought in and bag up the trash. We'll take it with us."

"I've got us in room 237 for three nights."

"Excellent. Let's go."

"Wait. Give me three minutes. Let me check something."

Peter didn't seem happy about a delay, but he acquiesced. Meanwhile, surveillance team *Khaf* reported in. "We rode the elevator with him to the second floor. It's confirmed that he's in room 230."

From the corner of her eye, Nicole saw Kevin give her a thumbs-up. She couldn't help but smile as she typed.

"Let's go, Annabelle." Gail emphasized her pseudonym.

"One minute more." She typed on. "Got it! I checked the concierge's computer, and she just received an order from the front desk for a car for a Mahmoud Muhammed for 16:20. Looks like he's going out tonight."

Cheers sounded in the hotel suite. Even Gail managed to give her a "Good job."

Peter said, "Now that we know where he is and

that he's going out, let's hold here for another 30 minutes. Annabelle, we'll need ten key cards for room 237 and two for room 230. Once Plasma Screen is out of his room, we'll move in across the hall from him at the Al Bustan."

Nicole set to work on the key cards as the other three each called different teams to give them a situation report. The most important part of her job was done, but she knew she was still needed to make sure the coms stayed active and to troubleshoot anything that might go wrong. Being part of a team was a good feeling. Modeling was all about competition, and you never knew when supposed friends would cut your throat for a gig or better walking position. Sure, she had the hacker community, but this felt better. It felt cleaner. It felt right. She was doing good and making a difference. For the first time, she could honestly say she was thankful for that day the Mossad literally came knocking on her door.

CHAPTER 11

BURJUMAN MALL, DUBAI, UAE—
16:50 / 4:50 P.M. GST

The Burjuman Mall wasn't as new or fancy as some of the others in Dubai, but it was also not as big, and that was what mattered to Mahmoud. The Mall of the Emirates and the Dubai Mall were both huge and filled end to end with people. While that made it easier for him to get lost in the crowd if need be, it also made it more difficult to spot anyone who might be following him.

He still had an hour before his first meeting, so he took his time walking past the shops. Every now and then he'd stop and pretend to be examining something through a store window while using the reflection to see who was around him. So far everything seemed to be clear.

Up ahead, he saw one of the shops he wanted. He walked past the Montblanc store, then abruptly turned around and walked back. No one seemed to notice except the father of the Arab family behind him who had to dodge his sudden reversal. Mahmoud mumbled an apology and stepped in.

In a glass case, he found what he was looking for—a Montblanc Meisterstück Platinum-Coated

Classique Rollerball. This would be a gift for the banker he was about to meet.

Mahmoud had uncovered a connection to a supply of specialized surveillance equipment. Right now, other than some preteen lookouts they paid two dollars a day, Hamas was essentially blind to the Israelis' movements at the Gaza border, especially at night. If he could purchase this new gear, it would finally bring their monitoring and reconnaissance into the twenty-first century. Also included in the cache was state-of-the-art night vision equipment. Being able to see in the dark would open up a whole new set of possibilities for attacks on the Jewish border settlements through Hamas's network of underground tunnels.

But the financial cost for this gear was very high. Mahmoud had tried to haggle the sellers down to no avail. They knew how much Hamas needed the equipment, which meant Mahmoud couldn't bargain from a position of strength. That is what brought him to Dubai and to the banker. Spending five hundred dollars on this pen would be well worth it if it eased open the strings to the moneyman's purse.

Mahmoud turned left out of the Montblanc store. Two windows down, he saw an olive-complected man looking into a storefront. His tight haircut and black T-shirt covered a muscular physique. He looked familiar to Mahmoud; he was sure he'd seen him before. As Mahmoud walked by, he side-glanced into the window, but the man didn't seem to notice his passing. Still, his fox senses were tingling.

Crossing to the other side, Mahmoud walked another minute, then abruptly stopped to rummage through his Montblanc bag. Sure enough, the man was walking his direction, though still on the other side of the aisle. One store up was a Canali boutique. Mahmoud ducked in. He took his time trying on shoes, then settled on a pair of dark-brown calfskin Oxfords.

After paying, he walked out and spotted a bench. Setting the shoe bag on it, he consolidated the Montblanc pen into the Canali bag. Then he straightened up and stretched his back. This gave him the opportunity to see up and down the concourse. No muscular, olive-complected man wearing a black T-shirt. His fox senses began to calm, and a quick glance at his watch told him it was time to go.

As hopeful as he was about his first meeting tonight, he dreaded his second with one of his contacts in the Islamic Revolutionary Guard Corps. He was arranging a shipment of Katyusha rockets to Gaza.

The Katyusha was not a very effective weapon. The warheads were unreliable, and their aim was atrocious. But they were cheap, so Hamas bought them. If you launched enough rockets over the border into Israel, one of them was bound to hit something.

Thus, the purpose of the IRGC meeting was good; the man he was meeting, however, was not. All of the members of the Iranian military were obnoxious and condescending, and this particular colonel took those characteristics to the extreme. To make matters worse, he used being away from Iran as a license to partake of all the indulgences unavailable in Tehran. Because he wanted a partner with whom he could go dancing and drinking and womanizing, he would constantly pester Mahmoud to visit the many clubs in Dubai. It was like dealing with a bratty child, trying to get him to focus on his schoolwork when all he wanted was to go out and play.

It wasn't that Mahmoud was a religious zealot; he was not above a little drinking and womanizing himself. But he kept the lines separate. You work during worktime, and you play during playtime.

His driver was waiting for him when he walked out, and he opened the door for him. A chilled bottle of water waited in the center console, and Mahmoud opened it and sipped. He was happy with his shoe purchase, one of the perks of his job. Now all he wanted was to make it through his meetings, then go back to his room and sleep.

CHAPTER 12

AL BUSTAN ROTANA HOTEL, DUBAI, UAE— 17:05 / 5:05 P.M. GST

T his is *Tet*. I'm out." The voice on the computer seethed with frustration.

Peter jumped in immediately. "*Lamed*, you're on. Be careful. You're our only other asset there."

"*Lamed. Root.*"

"*Tet*, SITREP," Peter said.

Nicole thought *Tet* sounded apologetic and embarrassed when he responded. "I got too close. He was in a Montblanc store. When he walked back out, I was just two doors down out in the open. He walked past me, and he was watching me in the glass. I kept my eyes on the lingerie in the window."

"Of course Noam would be looking at lingerie." Kevin chuckled.

Peter wheeled toward him. "Legend names! We only use legend names!"

"*Ani miztaer*," Kevin said, apologizing. Then realizing his Hebrew slip, he said, "Sorry. Got it."

Peter addressed his phone again. "Were you burned?"

"I don't think so. I don't know. He's in the Canali store now."

"Get out of there! *Lamed*, he's in the Canali store."

"*Lamed. Root.*"

Peter flipped his phone closed, and for a moment he looked like he was going to throw it. "Stupid! I won't let this operation get sidelined by shoddy tradecraft. Gail, set up an appointment for me with the *Tet* team when we're back in Tel Aviv. Apparently, they need to be reminded that their job is to not be seen."

Gail, who had just arrived five minutes earlier, pulled a small black Moleskine notebook out of her purse and began jotting in it. From the look on her face to her short, quick movements, it was evident to Nicole that Gail was not doing well with the stress.

Rising from her table by the window, Nicole went to where Gail was sitting on the queen bed closest to the door.

Gail looked up. "What?"

"Hold still." Nicole reached toward her, and Gail pulled back.

"Hold still," Nicole said again.

Gail sat still but with a doubtful look on her face.

Taking Gail's wig in her hands, Nicole gave it a one-and-a-half centimeter turn to the right. Then she brushed the hair back over Gail's shoulders with her fingers.

Nicole smiled. "Better."

Gail surprised Nicole by smiling back. "Thank you."

Gail returned to her notebook, and Nicole went back to her computer. Time was ticking down. Still, it seemed like the moment of launch would never arrive.

AL BUSTAN ROTANA HOTEL, DUBAI, UAE— 18:15 / 6:15 P.M. GST

Nir sat in a white panel van in the parking garage of the Al Bustan Rotana hotel. With him were the three other members of the Kidon hit team, James, Chester, and David, along with their driver, Evan. There was no telling how soon Plasma Screen would get back to the hotel, but for Nir, he couldn't come soon enough.

Evan suddenly sat up straight. "It's Gail."

James pulled the side door open, and Gail stepped in.

"He's finished his first meeting," she said as she squatted behind the passenger seat, probably so she could keep the dust of the van floor off her white pants. "We're guessing he's now going to meet his IRGC contact. That means we're likely on in two to three hours."

"When do you want us up in the room?" David asked. Like Nir and the other two men, he was well-built and wore a T-shirt and a ball cap low on his head. Nir didn't know anything about him,

103

but he guessed he was in his mid-thirties. Chester was the lookout, Nir and James were the muscle, and David would give the injection.

"First team, I want you up there by 18:35. Second team, come five minutes later."

Gail reached into a shopping bag she'd brought with her, then pulled out a white and chrome device about the size of a fist before turning to David. "It's already loaded with the suxamethonium chloride. I know you've practiced with it enough that I don't have to tell you how to work it." She passed the device to David, and he turned it over in his hands.

Gail looked each man in the eye. "This is our one shot at this monster. If we mess it up, he'll likely go underground for a long time. Remember, he shot Avi Sasportas in the face. He and his friends shot and killed Ilan Sa'adon. Remember all the lives this man and his weapons have taken. The time has come for justice. You four are the ones called upon by God and your country to deliver it."

Nir watched as Gail stepped back out of the van, leaving the shopping bag behind. The gravity of what he was about to do weighed heavily on him. In a country with a population of seven and a half million, he and these three men were the ones given the honor and responsibility for not just avenging the deaths of those young soldiers and so many others but preventing more murders. He would not disappoint Israel. He would not disappoint the families of the murdered young men. He would not disappoint the rest of his team. Plasma Screen would die tonight. Nir would make sure it was so.

CHAPTER 13

Nicole was furiously typing on her laptop keyboard. Team *Yod*'s com system was glitching, causing it to sound like they were talking through a sock in a tunnel underwater. Peter was demanding that she resolve the problem, and she was doing her best. Unfortunately, there was a very good chance that the problem lay not on her end but with the phone itself.

There was a knock on the door, and Kevin opened it. She heard male voices greeting each other. She supposed this was the second of the Kidon teams who would be making the actual hit. She'd never seen actual assassins before, and she was curious to learn what they looked like. But she was in emergency mode, so she kept her back to them. Her curiosity could be sated once Peter could talk with Team *Yod* again.

Then she heard one of the hit men laugh, and she froze. She knew that laugh. She'd laughed along with it. That laugh had brought joy to her life. The man who owned that laugh had also disappeared from her life. She'd convinced herself she was done with him. She thought she'd moved on. But in this moment, she realized that,

106

deep down, she'd never gotten over Nir Tavor.

Come on, you knew this might happen one day. You can't lose sight of why you're here. And you absolutely cannot let him know you're in this room. He's got a job to do. If you distract him, you could get him killed. Asher warned you about that, and it was never more true than in this moment.

"Annabelle, you get the coms fixed yet?" Peter called.

She shook her head emphatically. One of the men quietly made a joke about her name, and the rest of the team, including Nir, laughed. Nicole flushed with embarrassment.

Ten minutes later, *Yod*'s coms cleared up. Peter thanked her, and she waved her hand even though she knew the fix wasn't due to anything she'd done. That's the thing about tech. Sometimes it stops working for no reason, then it remedies itself for that same no reason.

She needed an excuse not to turn around, so she allowed her fingers to frantically fly across the keyboard like she was doing something important, even though in truth she was just writing code to create a little blue and red frog that would hop across the bottom of her screen.

At 19:15, Peter announced, "I'm leaving. As some of you already know, due to previous experiences, it would be particularly unfortunate if I were apprehended here in the Gulf. Kevin is in charge. God speed to you all."

Thirty minutes later, Team *Yod* announced, "Plasma Screen has finished his meeting and is heading back in the direction of the hotel. If he takes a straight route, he'll be there in 20 minutes."

"Acknowledged." Then Kevin dialed a different number.

"Gail," came the answer.

"Is housekeeping still in the hallway?"

"Affirmative."

Five minutes ago, hotel staff had wheeled a cart to a room four doors down from the target's and begun cleaning. Gail had left room 237 and was monitoring the situation from the elevator alcove.

"Beautiful," Kevin sneered. "Well, Plasma Screen is on his way, so keep me informed."

"*Root.*"

"Get ready, guys. As soon as she's gone, you're going in."

E11 FREEWAY, DUBAI, UAE—19:50 / 7:50 P.M. GST

The evening could not have gone better. The banker had agreed to finance the surveillance equipment, albeit at a ridiculous rate of interest. But at least the deal was done. Then his Iranian contact was not feeling well, so he left dinner after the appetizers were served. Mahmoud had

108

taken the time to celebrate alone with a steak of Wagyu beef and a fine bottle of wine. He'd even ordered *Assidat Al Boubar* for dessert. The pumpkin pudding was the perfect conclusion to a great day.

"Drive me around some," he said to his driver. "Let me see the city lights."

Although lying down back in his room was all he'd wanted to do earlier, now he couldn't imagine just locking himself away. When he next met with the Hamas leadership, he would be hailed as a hero. So many think weapons are what make the difference in the fight, but often the rest of the equipment matters the most. You could have the finest rifle in the world, but it would be useless if you couldn't see where to aim it.

Because of the brilliant deal he'd just pulled off, the Izz ad-Din al-Qassam Brigades would be able to clearly spot their Jewish targets before they pulled their triggers. *What is it they call it in the West?* He smiled. *That's right. A game changer.*

Mahmoud took a sip of the San Pellegrino his driver had left in the cupholder. Admiring the lights of the city, he thought, *Next month I'll have to come back. But instead of working, I'll come to play.*

CHAPTER 14

20:00 / 8:00 P.M. GST

Hotel staff is leaving," Gail said, her voice betraying her excitement.

"I'm coming to you." Kevin turned to the hit team. "Listen for my go. Annabelle will make sure you hear."

Every one of Nir's senses was heightened, and his adrenaline was surging. He was like a greyhound in the starting box just waiting for it to burst open.

When Kevin closed the door, Nir turned his attention to Annabelle. Even though she was sitting with her back to him and wearing some kind of floppy hat, he could tell she was a tall, well-shaped blond. Kevin had whispered that she was some kind of looker, so Nir had found himself stealing peeks at her hoping to catch a look at her face. But her attention had never left her computer screen. She also hadn't said anything. Only the clicking of her keyboard and a strange croaking, followed by her pounding one of the keys over and over, came from her part of the room. The woman was a mystery.

But she's a mystery to be solved another day. He turned toward the door.

"Team, go," he heard Kevin command from down the hall.

His voice came from Annabelle's computer, and Nir instinctually turned around. Now she was facing him, and she was spectacular. The blond hair, the face, the eyes . . .

Her eyes. Her incredible ice-blue eyes.

He was stunned. "Nicole?"

The door opened behind him. He hesitated a moment, then turned and followed. His mind was in complete confusion, and he bumped into James, who was holding their room door open so it wouldn't lock behind them just in case there was a problem.

The elevator bell dinged down the hall, then Gail rounded the corner and waved them back. All four men pushed back into the room.

As soon as the door closed, Nir said, "Nicole, what are you doing here?"

She just sat there looking as stunned as he was.

A gloved hand thwacked the back of his head hard enough to make him take a step forward. He wheeled around, and David grabbed him by the shoulders. The older man pinned Nir against the wall by the bathroom door, then put his face close to Nir's.

"Listen, I don't know what's going on between you two, nor do I care. Get your head in the game! If you don't, you'll get us all killed.

Do you understand?" He'd emphasized every syllable of the last three words.

"Yes, sir," Nir answered, still confused . . . and angry.

David let him go, then turned toward the door.

James whispered to Nir, "You good, man? You got this?"

"Yeah. Yeah, I'm good." He faced the door, fuming.

Why didn't she say anything? Of course, because she knew you would react exactly as you did, you idiot. Like David said, get your head in the game. You'll have plenty of time for questions later, like what in the name of all things holy are you doing on a Mossad assassination operation in Dubai? Yeah, maybe I'll start with that.

Gail's voice came through the computer. "It's a hotel guest. Kevin is engaging him."

Two minutes passed, then Kevin's voice said, "We're clear. Make entrance."

Without looking back, Nir left the room. Chester opened the door to room 230, and the four men entered.

20:24 / 8:24 P.M. GST

The car pulled up at the front of his hotel, and a doorman opened Mahmoud's door.

Mahmoud passed his driver a bill. "Tomorrow at 10:00 in the morning, sharp?"

"Yes, sir. I will be here."

Mahmoud entered the hotel and made his way to the elevators, his shoe bag swinging in his hand. *Maybe I'll order up some champagne tonight. I can order tomorrow's breakfast at the same time.*

The elevator dinged, and he stepped inside. The ride to the second floor was quick. As he stepped out, he saw a man off to the right talking on a phone, but Mahmoud turned left toward his room.

A pretty blond women was walking toward him in the hall, also talking on a phone. As she passed him, she said, *"Salaam aleikum."*

Surprised she would speak to him, he replied, *"Waaleikum us salam."*

He stopped and watched her as she walked away, appreciating the view. Once she disappeared into the elevator alcove, he turned back around.

Shaking his head, he strolled to his door, smiling. *Maybe you do still have some of that old charm.* He slid his key card into his door, then turned the handle and pushed it open.

Hands grabbed the front of his shirt, and he was pulled in.

20:28 / 8:28 P.M. GST

Nir and James hauled Plasma Screen into the room, and he stumbled forward, off-balance,

113

dropping a bag to the carpeted floor. Nir clamped a gloved hand over the man's mouth, and James pulled one of his arms high up behind his back. Once they dragged him past the bathroom, they angled him toward the bed. But Plasma Screen wasn't ready to go down without a fight. He stomped on James's foot and twisted from their grip, then ran for the door. But Chester had already positioned himself in the flight path.

Plasma Screen hesitated, and that one moment was all Nir and James needed. Nir's hand went back over the man's mouth, and James swept his feet from under him. He tumbled toward the floor, but before he hit, Nir yanked backward on his shirt, slowing him enough for a gentle landing. Their goal was to make it look like the target died of natural causes. A broken nose from a face-plant would absolutely destroy that charade.

Nir pulled a cloth from his back pocket and tied a gag in the man's mouth. Then he took hold of both his arms, and James pinned down his legs, stopping their kicking and flailing.

"Okay, *akhat, sh'tayim, shalosh*," Nir counted, and they hefted the man up and dropped him on the bed facedown.

As he and James held their target to the mattress, David stepped in.

CHAPTER 15

20:29 / 8:29 P.M. GST

Mahmoud struggled to break free, but his attackers were too strong. His face was being pushed down into a pillow, and he wondered if they were going to suffocate him. But then he felt something being pressed to his neck, and it emitted a low hum and vibrated. *What are they doing? Are they testing me for something? Have they tagged me with an identifier?*

His breathing was approaching hyperventilation, and he tried to slow it down. *I must stay calm, think! So far I'm still alive. Maybe they won't kill me. Maybe they're kidnapping me. Maybe they'll swap me for prisoners.*

But he knew the truth. He had heard the Hebrew counting. These were the Israelis. This was the Mossad. He was a dead man; they were just killing him on their own time schedule.

Hands grabbed his arms, and he was flipped faceup. Then the men stepped back. One of them was saying something in Hebrew, but Mahmoud couldn't seem to process the words. One thing he did know—they'd just made a big mistake. No one was holding him down, and here was his chance.

He tried to make a run for the door, but his legs wouldn't move. In fact, no part of his body could move. He was completely paralyzed. He couldn't even blink.

The room began to spin, and it felt like he'd started to float. He tried to take a deep breath but found he couldn't even do that. His breathing grew more and more shallow. Darkness crept in from the corners of his vision.

What were the words of that ghost who had haunted his dreams for the past 20 years? *Foolish, foolish man. Don't you know that Israel never forgets?*

20:35 / 8:35 P.M. GST

David felt for a pulse, then put his ear to the man's chest. "He's dead. Let's get to work."

While Nir and James undressed him, Chester continued to watch by the door. David went through the room putting back to right anything that looked out of place from the struggle, and Nir and James redressed the body in pajamas, then pulled the bedding up to cover it. David set the dropped bag on a chair before pouring a half glass of water and placing it on the nightstand.

"Okay, everybody, look. Is anything out of place?" David asked.

Nir walked the room checking every detail. It all looked right to him.

"Okay, Chester and I are out first. James, Michael, you follow in five. Lock up, then head straight for the van."

Nir tried not to think about the fact that the body of a man he'd just helped kill lay four meters away from where he stood. He wanted nothing more than to get out of there. Finally, James said, "Time. Let's go."

Nir stepped into the hallway as James attached a device to the door's bolt. His hours of practice paid off, and James had the bolt slid into its slot in under ten seconds. He closed the door, and Nir hung the Do Not Disturb sign on the handle.

It felt surreal as Nir rode the elevator down. It was as if nothing had changed from the moment he'd taken the elevator up. Same elevator, same lobby, same van. Yet it was all so very different.

He'd taken lives before, down in South Africa. But that had been in a gunfight as he was saving those around him. This time he'd lain in wait, then ambushed and killed an unarmed man. Sure, he could justify it by saying Plasma Screen had killed before and his activities were killing others. But that was quite a few theoretical layers up from where he was now. Here, nothing was theoretical. It was all very real from the ache in his hands from the struggle to the place where his index finger had slipped into the man's mouth and pressed against his front teeth.

The right and wrong of what he'd done weren't

what troubled him. The change that had taken place in him was what he'd have to work through. He had no doubt that the man walking away from the hotel was very different from the man who had walked into it.

CHAPTER 16

ONE MONTH LATER
HEATHROW INTERNATIONAL AIRPORT,
LONDON, ENGLAND—FEBRUARY 15, 2010—
19:10 / 7:10 P.M. GMT

Nir spotted her immediately. Nicole was sitting on a bench with her long legs crossed, her bag and a newspaper occupying the space next to her. A smile spread wide across her face when she recognized him among the crowd exiting immigration and customs. She rose to embrace him, and he dropped his bag and wrapped his arms around her. Once again, he wondered what a woman this beautiful was doing with someone like him.

As soon as the debriefings in Tel Aviv had completed, Nir convinced a friend to look up Nicole's information in the Mossad database. His mind was still reeling. Her being in that room running the coms for a Kidon hit team was beyond absurd. On the flight to Zürich, then back home, he'd racked his brain trying to come up with logical answers. But he was at a loss.

He was hesitant when he made the call to her, but she seemed genuinely excited to hear from him. He'd pushed her for answers, but she'd said she would tell him the story only in person. So he told Omer Goren, his supervisor, he needed a few days to "process" the assassination and booked a flight to London.

Holding her now felt so familiar, so good. Her body was warm, and her hair smelled of honey and citrus. Nir was reluctant to let her go. Then Nicole turned her head and kissed him. It lasted only a few seconds, but Nir was pretty sure he would remember that kiss for the rest of his life. He realized he'd never fully gotten over her. The women in his life during the intervening years hadn't meant anything to him. They were just stand-ins for the real thing. Now that real thing was in his arms. When they finally separated, she looked at him with a coquettish smile.

"Nicole." That was all he managed to say.

"Welcome to London. How was your flight?"

"Five and a half hours breathing other people's air. Otherwise, not bad."

He stepped back and looked at her. She wore a belted gray aviator jacket, what he thought were called harem pants in a light brown, and dark-brown boots loose at the laces. Her dark hair was hanging with its natural curl, and she wore just enough makeup to smooth any rough edges that might possibly be on her face. "You look amazing."

Nicole did a practiced 360-degree spin. "Why, thank you. The perks of living in the fashion world, along with a little help from a secondary employer of mine." She winked.

"Okay, I've got to know about your *secondary employer*. How in the world—"

Nicole touched her finger to his lips. "Let's talk about it over a nice dinner."

Nir acquiesced—but reluctantly.

Nicole moved her hand to Nir's cheek and stroked his short beard. "What is this?"

"Oh, just something new. Going for the rough and rugged look."

"I like it. Quite manly." She still had that deep, alto voice. "So are you hungry? Do you want to go to a restaurant? Or would you rather just pick something up and take it to my place?"

"Option two sounds good to me." He hefted his duffel back onto his shoulder.

Nicole drove a four-door Mini Clubman, blue with white racing stripes. *A nice mix of function and flair,* Nir thought as he opened the split doors in the rear and threw in his bag. Then, after walking around to the left side of the car, he squeezed his body into the passenger seat.

Nicole laughed. "You can put that seat back."

Relieved, Nir found a button on the side and slid it backward. His legs thanked him for every new centimeter of space they gained.

The 30-minute drive into London allowed them to catch up on each other's lives. While there wasn't much to say about Nir's family, Nicole's loved ones were struggling. Her grandmother's alcoholism was catching up with her, causing a wide assortment of medical maladies. Nicole said she would be surprised if her grandma was still alive this time next year. Her twin brother, Christiaan, had his own issues to deal with. It was becoming more and more apparent that his partying had turned into addiction. Nicole's voice broke as she talked about him. Soon he would be the only family she had left. If she lost him, she'd be alone in the world.

Nir wanted to tell her he would make sure she was never alone, but in his head the words sounded trite. Besides, it was way too soon to make a promise like that. Instead, he put his hand on the back of her neck and gave her a reassuring squeeze.

As they drove, Nicole had him call ahead to Cafe TPT and order two Brisket Curry on Rice and Singapore Noodles. When they arrived near the restaurant, Nir jumped out to pick up the order while Nicole maneuvered her car on the tight street so it would face the other way. Located just past the ornately colorful Chinatown Gate, the restaurant could be approached only on foot. The brick pedestrian street was crowded with people. It was a festive atmosphere, complete with clowns making balloon animals, portable magic shows, and people dressed as Pokémon characters for photos with tourists.

Three doors past the gate, Nir found the small storefront he was looking for. The food was ready for him, and when he carried the brown bag out, he found Nicole in a dispute with a cab driver. He was refusing to move his car, which he'd left sideways in the narrow street.

"You shouldn't even be this far up," the cabbie said. "This is commercial traffic only."

"Who are you? The zoning police? Move your car so I can finish my turn." Nicole was clearly angry.

"I'm no bobby, but you're about to meet one. They're on their way, and you can just stay right there until they get here."

Nir sized up the man. He looked to be about 20 years older than him, and he was shorter and lean and wiry. His nose was a little crooked from at least one break in the past. It was also a little bulbous, which likely meant he appreciated his ale a bit too much.

This man isn't dangerous. But he might be scrappy.

"Hello, friend. What seems to be the problem?" Nir stepped into the fray.

"Well, this little tart—"

"Whoa, whoa, whoa." Nir waved his hand. "No need to be rude." He walked closer, and the man retreated a step.

Nir smiled. "Listen, I just came in from out of town to spend some time with my lady. In this

123

bag I've got some beef curry and Singapore noodles. I don't even know what a Singapore noodle is. What I do know is that if you and your sideways car make me eat cold noodles, you and I will have a problem." The smile left Nir's face, replaced with as much menace as he could muster in so ridiculous a situation. "Are we going to have a problem?"

"No, I don't suppose we are."

The man's eyes held Nir's, and Nir had to give him kudos. He'd backed down, but he'd also kept his dignity while doing it.

"Thank you, my friend." Nir's smile returned to his face. "Now, if you'll kindly remove your car, we'll be on our way."

The man complied, and Nicole pulled away. There was silence in the Mini until they'd driven a few blocks and made a right-hand turn. Nir wasn't sure if Nicole was mad at the situation, mad at him for interfering, or just embarrassed by the whole thing.

Then she broke into laughter. "I was so totally in the wrong. I had no business being there."

Nir laughed too. "Then why were we there?"

"Oh, I just didn't want you to walk too far. Besides, I can usually get away with it."

"That's your ethical standard? You can get away with it?"

"So says the professional assassin." She grinned and winked at him.

"Fair point." Though he had to admit that jab went a little deep. He was still getting used to the idea that killing people was his job.

Nicole was staying in a third-floor flat in Soho in the West End of London. It was small and looked like it had been decorated 60 years ago by someone's spinster aunt. All the furniture was straight-backed and proper, covered with flowery fabric, and designed specifically for discomfort.

"This will be a wonderful place to hold a celebration when we finally defeat Hitler and the Germans," he said.

Nicole laughed. "I know. Isn't it horrible? But it's just a two-month rental, and it's only a short bus ride to Somerset House, where they're holding Fashion Week."

Nir tried an Elizabethan chair with needlepoint upholstery. The design was so angular he almost felt like he was leaning forward. He stood. "Nope, that won't work. Is any furniture in this place comfortable?"

"Try the sofa."

Nir sat, then agreed this was the best option. As stiff, uncomfortable furniture went, the sofa seemed as if it was probably less stiff and slightly less uncomfortable than the rest. He pulled a coffee table close and put the food bag on it while Nicole gathered some plates.

"Would you mind bringing a fork too? I can do chopsticks; I just can't do them well. So I figure, why aggravate myself just to look global?"

"Makes sense to me." She brought the dinnerware, and Nir dished out the food.

"Ah, so that's a Singapore noodle," he said, twisting some thin rice noodles around his fork. The brisket was amazingly tender for takeout, and the yellow curry had just enough spice to make his nose run a little. "Good choice. This is amazing."

Nir noticed Nicole was only picking at her food. Something was going on in her head, and he had a feeling they were about to discuss it. He gave her space to work out the words.

Finally, she said, "Okay, are you ready for the story?"

Nir put down his fork, then leaned back against the perpendicular rear of the sofa. "Let's have it. What is a South African model like you doing in a Mossad like this?"

She paused but only for a moment. "I'm hesitating because I don't know how you'll take this. I don't want you thinking I'm some crazy stalker."

Nir had no idea where this was going, but he was certainly intrigued.

"So after you left for Jo-burg, we kind of lost touch. I was pretty confused, and after what happened with my mom, I guess I have some abandonment issues. I don't know. I just know I felt like you'd dumped me, and I didn't understand why."

"Listen, Nicole, I am so sorry. I didn't have a chance—"

"Stop. I know. You couldn't tell me what was going on because you weren't allowed to tell me. I know that now. I just didn't know it then. So one night I was bored and sad and kind of lonely, and I decided I needed to know what happened to you. So I kind of hacked my way through the firewall protecting the computer system of Israel's Ministry of Foreign Affairs."

"Kind of hacked your way?"

"Okay, I busted right through. Tore that wall down like it was 1989 Berlin. And I learned you'd become a part of the Mossad."

"I have to admit, you're the first woman who ever committed a felony for me." He laughed. "At least that I know about."

But Nicole wasn't laughing. She seemed genuinely embarrassed by her actions, yet Nir felt flattered over the attention.

"It gets worse, Nir."

He stopped laughing. "Worse?" He was absolutely intrigued.

"I was curious about what kind of work you were doing in the Mossad. So . . ."

"You didn't."

"I did."

"How?"

Nir's reaction seemed to be loosening Nicole up. It was as if the fact that he wasn't mad at her or hadn't made fun of her had given her huge relief.

"You really want me to explain how I hacked into the un-hackable computer system of the world's foremost intelligence service?"

"Most definitely! Just keep it simple—on my level."

"Okay, on your level. I pressed the little clicky buttons on Mr. Computer until the Mossad computer said, 'Oh, hi! Come on in.' "

Nir smiled. "Ah, makes sense. Mr. Computer is very powerful."

Nicole told him about Zamir and Asher's visit, then looked at him with hopeful eyes. "So you don't think I'm a crazy stalker?"

"Let's just say I don't think you're crazy."

Nicole laughed and threw a fringed pillow at him. "I'm not a stalker either. I just wanted to know what happened to you. We had something. At least I think we did."

Nir slid closer. "We did. And I'm hoping we still do."

Then he kissed her, the Mossad forgotten.

CHAPTER 17

The music was deafening. It was some kind of electronica, and Nir could feel the bass vibrating his internal organs. Multicolored spotlights were spinning and flashing, sometimes slipping into full-on strobe. Stage right, a DJ was dancing around trying to keep the crowd hyped. Unfortunately for him and the designers, no amount of hype could overcome bad fashion— especially with this critical crowd.

Nicole had left a ticket for him at the door. From the moment he walked in, he felt completely out of his element. From the hairstyles to the clothes to the exaggerated mannerisms, these people were just . . . weird. It's like they were aliens who had invaded from planet Loud. Nir sat in the back, ready to run if any of them tried to beam him up to their mother ship.

Judging by the conversations he couldn't help but overhear before the show started, these fashions were greatly anticipated. It was the first reveal of the collaborative work of a group of lesser-known French designers called Brûler la

Maison. But it was a disaster from the moment the first model walked onto the stage. She wore a shiny green blouse with gray trim in some sort of geometric design. Her black shorts were cut high enough to allow a peek of bare thigh before her legs were overtaken by an extremely long legwarmer. The dark leggings were held up by gray bands above and below the knee. At the ankles they morphed into stirrups tucked into plain black pumps, the ones his mother had always called "sensible."

To Nir, the poor model looked ridiculous, and he was relieved to hear the pink-haired woman next to him—she had to be a septuagenarian—break into laughter. He'd been afraid this really was good fashion and he just wasn't getting it.

Nicole was the fourth model onto the runway. As she strutted forward in a short sweater-dress and thigh-high boots, he could tell some sort of large lettering was in the folds of the design. When she was halfway down, she stretched her arms out to either side. The cut of the garment formed a sideways diamond stretching from wrist to wrist and neck to thigh. Printed in bold gray letters on the black sweater-dress was the word *STYLE*, with the tops of the *Y* serving as a collar. It looked absurd.

Nir felt terrible for Nicole. She was doing her best to work a design that not even the greatest supermodel in the world could salvage. Madame

Pink-Hair leaned toward him and said loudly in his ear, "If they have to tell you it's style, honey, it's not."

Fifteen more designs were revealed before the show abruptly ended. The spotlights shut down, the music terminated, and the DJ thanked everyone for coming.

"Bless the saints above," said Pinkie as she collected her bag from under her chair.

Nicole had told him she was scheduled for two outfits, but Nir had seen her only once. So this was obviously a premature ending. They say reputations are made and destroyed at Fashion Week. Nir figured the reputations of the fashionistas of Brûler la Maison had taken quite a hit today.

While he waited for Nicole, he people-watched from a bench in the foyer of the meeting hall. Thirty minutes later, she was walking toward him. She had a sheepish look on her face, but her eyes sparkled. Nir stood, and when she reached him, he wrapped his arms around her.

"Baby," he whispered in her ear, "all I've got to say is that you have style."

Nicole pushed back and playfully slapped him across the chest. "That's not even nice."

Nir led her to the bench, where they sat down.

"That was so bad," she said. "When the designer demonstrated how he wanted me to reveal his design, I almost called a cab. He did it like four times, and each time he made the reveal he cried out, 'Style!' Do you know how hard it was to keep a straight face?"

Nir suggested they get a little something to eat, and Nicole told him about a place nearby where they could get coffee and pastries. As they walked there, Nicole filled him in on the rest of the backstage story—the tantrums the designers threw, their blaming the models for not properly showing their clothing, and the abrupt halt to the show after one of the stylists punched a designer in the face.

A few blocks up, Nicole suddenly stopped walking. She let go of Nir's hand and almost ran to a newsstand. She pulled a bill out of her purse, then gave it to the proprietor and lifted a newspaper off a stack. When she came back, she handed the copy of the *Guardian* to Nir. Photos of Peter, Kevin, Gail, and Evan were on the front page. The headline read *Suspected Hit Squad in Mahmoud al-Mabhouh Killing*.

"Come on." Nir led Nicole through the door of a pub.

The establishment was old-school London and about half full. The bartender greeted them, and Nir said, "Two Guinness." They found a vacant wooden booth toward the back and slid in next to each other.

Before he'd left Tel Aviv, the word had already gone around that, despite their efforts to disguise the fact, the Emirati police had declared Al-Mabhouh's death a homicide. And while they'd said the Israelis were suspects, nobody at the Mossad really worried. The Israelis were always suspects. That's the good and bad of having the Mossad's reputation. But how had they moved from simple suspicion to photos of operatives on the front page of a London newspaper? All Nir could think about was Interpol coming bursting into the pub and arresting Nicole and him on the spot.

They read the article silently. The police chief of Dubai, Lieutenant General Dhahi Khalfan Tamim, had latched onto the case like a bulldog on a chew toy. After they'd determined Al-Mabhouh had not died a natural death, Tamim's team began looking at who had flown into Dubai just before the assassination and flown out right after. They put together a database of all the possibilities, then looked at closed-circuit television footage. Over time, the police chief was able to assemble a video time line from the arrival of Peter, Kevin, and Gail at the airport, to the activities of the surveillance teams, to the arrival of the hit team, to everyone fleeing the country.

The bartender set two pints on the table and asked if they needed anything else. Nir said no, and the man left them alone.

The extended coverage on the inside pages

displayed more photos. Nir didn't recognize most of the faces, although he knew five or six from Operation Plasma Screen or from Tel Aviv. All told, there were 20 photos. Neither Nir nor Nicole's faces were among them.

"I've got to see the video footage," Nicole said. "If I'm on there, my career is over."

So might be your freedom.

Nicole pulled out her phone, and the two stouts remained untouched as they watched the compiled footage on YouTube. At one point, Nir appeared with James going to the elevator in the Al-Bustan. But while James looked straight ahead, Nir kept his head down, his face protected by the bill of his cap.

"Tradecraft 101," he said. "You never know where there's a camera."

"That's exactly why I took the stairs up. I didn't want to go near that elevator."

When the video ended, both Nir and Nicole breathed sighs of relief. Neither had been seen. They were two of the 16 not identified.

"How did they let this happen?" Nicole said in an angry whisper. "This is Mossad. You're supposed to be the best there is."

"Whoa. First, I think you meant to say *we're,* because for better or for worse, you're one of us. But second, you're exactly right. This is a screwup of epic proportions. Heads are going to roll at headquarters."

"They should. This kind of stupidity can get people arrested or even killed."

Nir's phone vibrated in his pocket. He slid it out and looked at the screen. *Unavailable,* it said.

"Great," he grumbled, pressing the talk button. "Tavor."

"Are you done *processing?*" Omer Goren asked.

Nir ignored the question. "So how is your day going, Omer?"

"I really need to find a dog to kick. Do you have a dog at home I can borrow?"

"No dog. Seriously, how did this happen? It's a disaster."

"It's worse than you can imagine. We've got 20 agents burned. They'll never be able to work the field again. People are calling for Meir Dagan's head—the man who's been the Mossad's director for eight years! The UK, Ireland, France, South Africa are all condemning the operation and threatening to pull their ambassadors since their country's passports were forged. Dagan and Prime Minister Netanyahu say they might issue arrest warrants for the burned agents, but at least they'd do so under the fake names."

"Well, that's kind of worthless."

"It's an empty action that even those angry governments will see as an empty action. Now, back to my original question. Has Nicole le Roux given you enough processing yet? I've got to get you home."

Nir almost dropped the phone. "How did you know—"

"Really? You thought I wouldn't know? You work for the Mossad, you idiot."

"Yeah, which used to mean something. You gave me four days, and I'm on day two. You do the math."

"Sounds good. According to my calculation, then, I'll expect you on the first plane out tomorrow morning. I need you back, Nir. We're bleeding agents here."

"But—"

"Tavor, enough discussion. This isn't a request. I'm giving you until tomorrow, which is more than I have to. Losing those agents, one in particular, has left a gaping hole in an ongoing operation. You're going to fill it. So enjoy your time with le Roux, then say your goodbyes tomorrow. It will probably be a long time before you see each other again."

The line went dead.

"What did he say?" Nicole asked as Nir set his phone on the table.

He gave her the gist of the conversation, leaving out the part about not seeing each other for a while. He didn't want that possibility to taint the time they still had together. They slid out of the booth, and Nir left a £20 note next to their full glasses of Guinness.

Their plans to tour the city together were

136

forgotten. The next day they said their goodbyes, and Nir took the Underground to the airport and was in Tel Aviv by late afternoon. He went straight to headquarters, where Goren was waiting for him. They sat together at a conference table, and his supervisor slid a file toward him. Nir opened it and began reading.

Before long he realized the "long time" he'd be apart from Nicole would likely be measured not in months but in years.

CHAPTER 18

It was like walking through a fairy tale. Between the medieval architecture and the Christmas decorations, Nir felt like he was in one of those princess movies he sometimes observed little girls watching on plane flights. The cobblestone street was damp from a light mist, but the temperature wasn't yet cold enough to turn the moisture to ice. Every now and then he passed a bakery or restaurant where the sweet, rich aroma from the offerings inside tempted him. Breads, meats, coffees—they all sought to pull him into the shops.

But as tempted as he was, it was impossible to stop. He was following a man, and he couldn't let him get away. Actually, he was following three men. One was his target—Dr. Sa'd Hassan—the second was his target's guard, and the third was an unexpected twist getting in the way.

The Mossad knew much of what happened to Hassan, and they'd surmised the rest. A year ago he was a research professor in the study of nephrology at Mansoura University, located 175 kilometers north of Cairo in the center of the Nile Delta. Specializing in renal pathophysiology and how various pathogens might affect the kidneys, he'd published numerous journal articles and was an occasional speaker at conferences in the Arab world. Well respected by his peers and admired by his students, on the surface it looked like he'd created a comfortable life for himself. But the good doctor had a problem—one of his own making.

In the fifth surah of the Qur'an, verse 90, it is written, "O you who believe! Intoxicants and gambling, dedication of stones, and divination by arrows, are an abomination of Satan's handiwork. Eschew such abomination, that you may prosper." For Muslims, gambling, along with other vices, was strictly prohibited. In Egypt, any citizen caught gambling could be fined and imprisoned. However, that didn't mean the law forbade gaming in the nation. In fact, in the capital city of Cairo, 14 casinos offered legal gambling. But only if you weren't a citizen. If you couldn't show a foreign passport, you weren't welcome to wager.

But not to worry. If you were a citizen of Egypt and you liked to risk your money in games of chance, you weren't without options. With the rise of the internet, online gambling had taken off in the nation, and the police agencies had adopted a type of *Don't ask, don't tell* policy when it came to internet wagering.

This is where Hassan's troubles began. The good doctor was a fan of online poker, and he did fairly well . . . at first. But as so often happens, the early wins were followed by more frequent downturns, and he kept playing until his credit cards were maxed out and his savings were gone. No doubt disgusted, his wife took their two teenage children and moved back to her parents' home.

Like so many gamblers, Hassan probably thought all he needed was one big win to pay off his debts and get his family back. But he had no more credit for the online games. That's when he moved to the underground casinos. Soon, he was way over his head in even more debt.

Then, one day Hassan failed to show up for work at the university, and that one day led to another, which led to another. After two more weeks, a Mossad informant who attended Mansoura passed on the information that a research professor specializing in renal patho-gens had vanished. A BOLO notice was sent to Mossad agents throughout the Middle East and Europe to "be on the lookout" for this Dr. Hassan.

The Mossad didn't know what happened between the professor's gambling fiasco and the day he disappeared—although the casino owner he owed was known by them to have secret Shi'ite ties into Iran. But for seven months,

Hassan remained missing. That had ended four weeks ago when an agent spotted Hassan walking through Old Town Tallinn. His black hair had been dyed gray and he'd shaved his beard, but the agent had no doubt it was him. He was also accompanied by a man who was obviously a guard.

Several surveillance teams were sent, and the Mossad's considerable online assets were put to work. They soon discovered that Hassan had come to Tallinn four months earlier and was working under the Sudanese name Umar Atem in a private research lab allegedly working on therapeutic relief for chronic kidney disease. His true work, however, was far more sinister. Hassan had been recruited by the Iranian Revolutionary Guard Corps. He and his team of three assistants were diligently working on the development and dissemination of a toxin that would cause renal failure and potential death when dispersed within a controlled environment.

The team at Caesarea had passed their findings on to the leadership of the Mossad. The *ramsad*, or director, had approved a targeted assassination, and Nir was called in to carry out Operation Inside Straight. They had little doubt that Hassan's life had been threatened, perhaps his family's as well. But that didn't change the danger he presented, the choice he'd made.

When Nir heard the story, he thought it was

brilliant for the Iranians to snare this Egyptian scientist. Who would suspect a Sunni Muslim of developing a biological weapon for his hated Shi'ite enemies, who could then turn it around and use it on his own people?

Dr. Hassan didn't venture out often. A driver took him and his guard to work in the morning and drove them home at night. Their departures and returns varied, making it difficult to time a hit for when they were transitioning from one location to the other. As for dealing with Hassan at home, his house had a good alarm system that made entry not entirely impossible but certainly risky.

When Nir examined the notes from the day-to-day surveillance, the solution, though a precarious venture, became apparent. Late afternoon Sunday was the only time Hassan emerged from his home to journey to a location other than work. His driver dropped him and a guard at the bottom of the Old Town hill. Then the two walked up the cobblestone streets until they reached the town square. There, Hassan had a cup of coffee at a café. Once he had his caffeine fix, the two would find the car and go back to his home.

Nothing will kill you faster than routine, Nir had said to himself.

With just one other person with Hassan, Nir could execute a brush injection as the man was strolling through the city. But now here was his target with the guard on one side and this stranger on the other. The third man hadn't started the walk with them, and no reports of him appeared in past surveillance notes. However, two blocks ago he'd suddenly appeared strolling alongside the doctor.

I wonder if this is one of his Iranian handlers. It would explain the regular weekly walks—making himself available in case one of his masters wants to talk with him.

He gradually closed the gap between himself and the three men. The street they were on opened into a small square. A number of temporary kiosks had been erected, where vendors sold toys, mulled cider, and Christmas treats like braided, sugary breads called Kringle and *piparkoogid*— little gingerbread cookies cut in the shape of angels and stars and barnyard animals. Nir knew the route Hassan normally traveled, so he took a chance and broke off his follow. He bypassed all the delicious-smelling kiosks for one he'd spotted across the square, where he made a quick purchase. Then he hurried to catch up to Hassan and was glad to see the three men had continued on the usual path.

Again, Nir broke off the pursuit and stepped into a liquor store. He bought a bottle of Vana Tallinn, a 90 proof Estonian liqueur that had a distinct rum, spice, and citrus smell. When he was back outside, he opened the bottle, then took a deep swig and swished it around in his mouth before spitting it into a trash can. He repeated the action, then poured some into his hand, which he rubbed onto his neck and into his hair. He dropped the bottle into the garbage.

Next, he put on his kiosk purchase—a red gnome's hat and a fluffy white beard. This completed his transformation from stealthy Israeli assassin to loud, drunk Estonian dressed like *Jõuluvana*, the Baltic country's version of Santa Claus.

Hustling ahead, Nir lined himself up behind Hassan and the guard. Reaching into his right pocket, he pulled out his injection device, a quarter-size hollow disc filled with a slow-acting neurotoxin. On one side were three microneedles, and on the other was a narrow extension that allowed Nir to wedge the device between his third and fourth fingers. He'd practiced with this device countless times, and he knew he had to get the slap just right to ensure the toxin drained fully through the needles.

The gap shrank to three meters, then two, then one. Nir lunged forward into the two men in front of him, his hands slapping the backs of their necks as he slurred, *"Häid Jõule!"* He hung on to their shoulders as he laughed and stumbled along. Hassan looked shocked and spun out of Nir's grasp. The guard did one better, driving his elbow into Nir's sternum. All the air blasted out of his lungs, and he dropped to his knees. The guard was about to follow up with a kick when the third man said something in Farsi. To Nir's relief, the guard stayed his kick. But in Arabic, he did question both the purity and the species of Nir's mother.

Pushing the guard to the side, the third man threw Nir's hat to the ground, then grabbed a handful of hair and tilted his white-bearded head up. As he gasped for air, Nir tried to get a good look the man's face, but his vision was graying out from the lack of oxygen.

"*Mul on kahju*! *Mul on kahju*," Nir eked out, apologizing.

The man gave Nir a disgusted look, then released his head with a shove and walked off. The other two men followed.

Down on his knees, Nir continued to wheeze. A small crowd had gathered, and a young girl walked up and handed him his *Jõuluvana* hat. He was sure to take it from her with his left hand. "*Häid Jõule*," she said quietly. Nir smiled his appreciation, then her mother stepped forward and took the girl's hand. They hurried off.

Slowly, he stood, then staggered to a street-lamp. A quick look told him the device was empty. Hassan had received the full dose. Nir put the cap back on, then slipped the device into a nonporous envelope and into his pocket. He took out a high-strength cleanser poured into a small hand sanitizer bottle, then squeezed out the liquid and scrubbed his hands until they burned.

He felt a familiar twinge inside. It wasn't guilt; it was the gravity of what he'd just done. Hassan wouldn't feel anything tonight. Tomorrow would be a bad day for him, though. Sometime around noon he would feel light-headed, and ten minutes later his heart would stop.

It took him 20 minutes to walk to the ferry dock and two hours to cross the Gulf of Finland to Helsinki. When the ferry had reached halfway, Nir slipped the envelope from his pocket and let it drop into the dark water.

He overnighted at a hotel near the airport, and by 10:00 the next day he was back home in Antwerp. He took the rest of Monday off, but by the time Tuesday rolled around, he was back in his office.

CHAPTER 19

ONE DAY LATER
SALAHUDDIN PROVINCE, IRAQ—DECEMBER 23, 2019—19:40 / 7:40 P.M. AST

The helicopter drone lifted off the ground with a muted buzz, and quiet cheers sounded among the dozen or so onlookers. Abbas scowled at the men. This was the wilderness, after all, and sound carried. Still, even his glare couldn't silence a handful of whispered prayers.

"May God pilot you to your destination."

"Bring your wrath down on the servants of Satan."

"So shall it be for all the enemies of Allah."

With great satisfaction, Abbas watched the machine rise. If this mission was successful, he would not only gain praise from his superiors but also notice from Tehran. The latter to him was what mattered most. No matter how much the leaders of his militia might sing his praises and celebrate his victories, still they would remain in their leadership positions and he would be forced to continue to serve their wishes. Those in Tehran, however, held the true strings of power. When they decided a change in leadership was needed, there would be a change in leadership. Abbas had been working for months now to provide them a reason for that change. It wasn't that he disliked Falih Kazali or Abu Mustafa al-Sheibani; they were honorable men and led well. He just knew he, Seif Abdel Abbas, could do better.

The sky-bound unmanned aerial vehicle he piloted was called a Blowfish A2. This unusual name for the UAV came from the fact that the drone looked very much like a puffer fish at full puff that then had its belly removed. On the A2 Abbas controlled, in place of the blowfish's stomach dangled four 60mm mortar rounds looking like they were nursing off of their mother.

The UAVs had been a gift from Iran, but Abbas was well aware that these weapons of war were manufactured by Ziyan UAV in the city of Zhuhai in China's Guangdong Province. Despite heavy criticism from Western countries, including a scathing call-out by the U.S. Secretary of Defense, China had opened its UAV weapon vault to Iran. Both the Blowfish A2 and its machine-gun-carrying brother, the A3, were snatched up by Iran's Islamic Revolutionary Guard Corps. In response to their critics, China pleaded good old capitalism; their UAVs were for anyone who needed their capabilities and had the money to buy them. Hadn't they also sold some of those same drones to Sunni Saudi Arabia, Shi'ite Iran's mortal enemy? What could be more equitable and capitalistic than that?

Abbas knew those who cared about such things believed the instability caused by these unmanned weapons ultimately fed right into China's global strategy. An unstable Middle East was good for the nation, they said. It drew the attention, resources, and press coverage of the United States and Russia, while keeping them distracted from China's slow economic and political spread across the globe. But Abbas didn't care about China. He cared about his mission.

The drone lifted higher and higher until it reached an altitude of 2,000 meters. Once there, it accelerated forward. Abbas held a computer tablet and watched its progress. While he was technically piloting the drone, all he was really doing now was observing. The target and flight path had already been programmed in. Eventually, the A2 reached a cruising speed of 80 km/h. That gave it a flight time of approximately 38 minutes before it reached its destination.

While he watched, he thought about the life events that brought him here. Born in Baghdad, he'd been five years old when the Gulf War hit his country in 1985. Looking back now, he could see what a fool Saddam Hussein had been for invading Kuwait. But he'd been too young to care about who had done what wrong against whom. He only knew his whole world had fallen apart. His father, who owned a fairly successful auto repair shop, was conscripted into the army and never came home. He'd died on the first day of the Western forces' air assault without ever firing his weapon.

He could still remember the day the electricity went out. His family had huddled together in the dark, his mother singing quietly to calm them. It would be six months before the power would return. The water stopped five days after the electricity, and it was even longer before he and his brothers and sisters could stop making daily trips to the water trucks or the river.

His parents had money stashed in the house, and his mother had used that cash to feed him and his four siblings. But food was scarce, and prices soared. The life savings of these two hard-working Iraqis lasted only three weeks. Once that was gone, he and his older brother and sisters rummaged food among the dumpsters and garbage bags left uncollected on the streets. Soon, however, the competition grew too great for that resource as older children and adults forcibly stole whatever the younger children had gathered and were trying to take home. At that point, Abbas's mother abandoned their house, and they moved in with her parents.

He'd once heard it said that someone in the Western alliance boasted about bombing Iraq back into the Stone Age. Abbas knew what living in the Stone Age meant. He'd resolved that one day he would return the favor.

When the Americans returned in 2003, he saw his chance for some payback. After joining Jamaat Ansar al-Sunna, a Sunni Islamic insurgent militia, he fought against the United States and the forces of the Iraq puppet regime, seeing action in Ramadi, Husaybah, and Mosul. That had been his life ever since—always looking for the next fight and for the militia that had the best chance of doing something meaningful.

His desire for vengeance is what had led him to Kata'ib Sayyid al-Shuhada, the Masters of the Martyrs Brigade. Too many militias refused to see the big picture, so they wasted their resources fighting small. Strapping on a vest full of explosives and walking into a market barely even made the news anymore. No one could bring down the world's strongest superpowers with their unlimited resources just by thinking in that limited manner. But due to a lack of financial and military resources, neither could a militia think too big. The goal, then, was not to think big but to think smart. How does one leverage the few resources they have at their disposal in order to make the greatest impact?

That was the kind of big-picture mindset that would push him to the forefront in the eyes of the Tehran power-wielders. Kazali and Abu Mustafa were smart, but Abbas was smarter. So he would use the KSS as his platform to show those in Tehran's power positions that Seif Abdel Abbas was the man they should be standing behind.

A flash on his screen told him the Blowfish was decreasing its speed. Pressing a viewing-square set the picture from the front camera to full screen. The distant lights were growing larger, and he switched back to control mode. Three minutes later, the helicopter drone slowed to a stop, then began its descent. Hundreds of meters of empty air passed until it halted at an altitude of 500 meters. From the camera on the drone's underside, the Siniya refinery looked massive, even at this height. Smaller than the enormous Baiji refinery nearby, it still put out 20,000 barrels of oil daily. Abbas had studied the layout of the oil processing plant, and he knew if he hit it just right he could slow down or even completely halt production for a time. That ideal ground zero was precisely below where the drone hovered.

Pressing one button at a time, Abbas released each successive mortar round from the A2. The ten-second drop felt like an eternity. Then he saw the first explosion, then the second and third and fourth. Another button press sent the drone racing up in altitude to escape what should come next. A massive explosion sent a fire cloud mushrooming into the air and bulleted out debris he knew would strike for 300 meters all around.

The drone safely back at 2,000 meters, Abbas admired his handiwork through the lens of the UAV. Again, quiet cheers sounded behind him from his men, who had been watching the action on a separate monitor. This time Abbas joined them.

After the black smoke grew so thick that he could no longer see the ground, Abbas told the Blowfish to come swimming back home. While they waited, his team broke down their camp. They had a long, dark drive ahead of them. Drones of another sort would likely soon be out looking for who had carried out this attack. Those drones didn't carry mere mortars; they carried Hellfire missiles. While he was confident he would never see the fires of hell because of his work in the service of Allah, that didn't mean he was ready to see a Hellfire.

Abbas smiled at his little joke as he deposited the control tablet into a hard case. He would have to tell that one to his driver on the trip home.

CHAPTER 20

ONE WEEK LATER
ANTWERP, BELGIUM—DECEMBER 30, 2019—
15:30 / 3:30 P.M. CET

How many are there?" Luis Maes opened his loupe as he asked Nir the question. The shriveled man had a half ring of gray hair around the lower portion of his head and was wearing a rumpled suit that looked like it may have fit him long ago—when he was 30 years younger and 20 kgs heavier. Using a pair of tweezers, he lifted one of the stones and turned it in the light. Although he looked old enough to have fought in the resistance during World War II, his hand was steady as he examined the precious stone.

"Forty, as it said on the manifest." Nir answered in the same language, French. "All the same color and clarity. Various sizes, but they combine to a 94 total carat weight." He leaned back in his chair as Maes slowly set the first diamond to the side and picked up another.

It would be awhile. Nir had been doing business with this man for three years, and he'd never sold him a bad gem. But Maes was nothing if not thorough. For the kind of money Nir was

154

asking, he supposed he would carefully examine each diamond too.

"What is the origin of the stones?" Maes asked as his tweezers turned a third jewel, a stunning 3.5 carat diamond that would bring in €16,000 all by itself.

"Each one is clean. They all have their Kimberley Process certification." Named after the capital city of South Africa's Northern Cape province, the Kimberley Process Certification Scheme was created in 2003 to combat the flood of conflict diamonds, or blood diamonds. By holding to the rules of the KPCS, member nations sought to ensure that no slave labor was used in the sourcing of the gems and that no money would flow to violent rebel movements. It started out well, but as tends to happen in Africa, that goal fell apart. Loopholes were exploited and corruption dug its way in. Still, the KPCS was better than nothing. Nir knew enough about the brutality toward the workers at some of the diamond mines to recognize that even half a goat was better than no goat at all.

As he waited, Nir thought back seven years to when he'd founded his exporting company with a little help from his friends at the Mossad. It was the perfect deal at the perfect time. The intelligence agency needed an ongoing presence in Europe, and Nir wanted to do more with his life than just wait around for another person to target. So the agency fronted him enough money and provided him with some contacts, and Yael Diamonds was formed with his home base in Antwerp.

The name held special meaning for him. Study of the Hebrew Scriptures had been mandatory for all the kids on the kibbutz. Much of it he found boring. But the judges? He loved the stories of those heroes God raised up to chase away the invaders. The story of *Barak* particularly drew his attention, primarily because the action took place around his namesake, Mount *Tavor*.

Yavin, the king of Canaan, sent his great commander *Sisra* to plunder the hapless Israelites. The people cried out, and God answered. The judge and prophetess *D'vora* went to *Barak* and told him that God had chosen him to lead the men of Israel to victory against *Sisra* and his troops. But *Barak* wasn't having it. No way was he going to lead the troops by himself. The only way he would go to fight the battle, he said, was if *D'vora* went along. The prophetess agreed to go, but there was a price for her participation. She told him a woman would get credit for the victory. It was a beautiful setup to make the reader think she was talking about herself. But like all good stories, there's a twist.

Barak gathered his troops and attacked, and God gave his army the victory. The whole Canaanite army was wiped out except for one man—their commander *Sisra*. He somehow escaped, and *Barak* and his army pursued. Exhausted, *Sisra* found his way to the safety of King *Yavin*'s allies, the Kenites. He stumbled into the settlement, where *Yael*, the wife of *Hever* the Kenite, spotted him. Hurriedly, she invited him into her tent and hid him under a rug.

Sisra was parched after his flight from the battle, so he asked *Yael* for water. She did one better and gave him a fresh skin of milk. He drank his fill, then laid back down. *Yael* covered him again with the rug, and he fell asleep content in the safety of his hiding place. But he wasn't safe. The one person who knew where he was turned out to be the one person he needed to fear the most. While *Sisra* slept, *Yael* took a tent peg and a hammer and drove the spike through the commander's temple and into the ground.

That story had resonated with young Nir, and early on he'd sworn he would never be like *Barak*. The man had been a leader but without the strength of his own convictions. *Yael*, however, knew *Sisra* was bad news. She also had the wisdom to know that the tide had turned between the Canaanites and the Israelites. It was time for the Kenites to switch alliances. She'd done what was necessary to make sure *Barak* and his army would not wipe out her people in their quest to find the fleeing *Sisra*.

Imagine, Nir had thought. Yael *was going about*

her daily business when suddenly she was thrust into the position where the fate of her people depended on her actions. Rather than shy away like Barak, *she'd stepped up. She'd taken a risk and saved her tribe.* Naming his company after this strong woman was Nir's way of reminding himself that at any moment, he, too, could be called away from his everyday life and put into a position where the fate of his nation was at stake.

Once Yael Diamonds was established, it wasn't long before Nir found he had the personality and discernment necessary for this cutthroat world. He soon gained a reputation as a man who would give you a fair deal but one on whom you better not try to pull one over. Within three years he was able to pay back the agency. That was the same year he bought his Mercedes-AMG GT coupe. After another two years, he dished out €900,000 for a restored penthouse apartment in the historic district of Antwerp.

Life is good, Nir thought as he watched the old man slowly move diamonds from one pile to another. But as soon as that thought entered his mind, it was quickly chased away by a memory. Actually, more than just a memory. A name. Nicole.

"Very good," Maes declared, setting the last of the diamonds on his "looked at" stack. He put his loupe back into his bag and pulled out a small box with an electronic combination lock.

Nir politely turned away as the man punched in seven numbers, then turned back when he heard the lock disengage.

"May I help you?" Nir knew the answer but still felt obligated to offer assistance to the elderly man.

"Thank you, no."

The diamonds went into a small velvet pouch, and the pouch went into the box. Once the box was closed and locked, Maes removed a thin paper seal from his bag. He affixed it to the box, then signed his name with a fine-point felt pen. "If you will be so kind as to leave this in your safe until tomorrow, I will send a secure courier to pick it up."

"Of course." Nir got to his feet. "Anything else I might do for you today?"

"Not unless you can give me back 30 years of my life," Maes said, groaning to his feet.

Nir saw the man out, then went back to his office and gathered his things.

"I'm gone for the day," he told Mila Wooters, his receptionist.

"Put on your scarf. It's a cold one."

"Yes, Aunt Mila," Nir said, causing the woman to scowl at him playfully. Although not an actual relation, the middle-aged, childless divorcee often treated Nir like an inept nephew. It seemed that in her eyes he was always doing either too much or too little and was improperly dressed for either eventuality. But she was a wonderful baker, knew how to brew strong coffee, and was exceptionally good at her job. Best of all, she didn't ask questions when he occasionally disappeared for days at a time. That alone was worth a little clothing nag every now and then.

The wind and snow hit him in the face as he exited the building, tempting him to take a cab home.

Could you get any softer? Four minutes to the tram, a ten-minute ride under the streets, six minutes home. That won't kill you.

After wrapping his scarf over the lower half of his face, he turned to the right and began walking into the wind, imagining Aunt Mila smugly watching him from the third floor. In a city of strangers, it was good to know at least one person cared about you.

Someone to care about you. Nir's mind again went back to Nicole as he bumped through the traffic on the sidewalk. They hadn't spoken for six months, and the last conversation had ended as poorly as the previous one. In his attempt to protect her, he'd offended her, hurt her, maybe to the point where she might never forgive him. At least that's what it felt like right now.

Nir's timing was good, and after descending into an underground tunnel, he was able to step into the tram right away. The windows were fogged, and the seats were full. He took hold of a metal bar, feeling its cold through his glove. Nicole just didn't understand how close she'd come to not getting out of Iran alive. Or if she did, she wasn't taking it seriously enough. When he confronted her on her recklessness, her attitude was clear. "Well, I made it, didn't I? And I brought out the information." But that wasn't the point, was it?

Yes, the plan succeeded. Yes, the Mossad pulled off an incredible feat stealing Iran's nuclear secrets. Yes, Nicole had survived, although just barely. But he'd told her, "There's no way I'm going to let you take that kind of risk again." Wrong thing to say. Those two words—*let you*—were the ones he most wished he could have back. They hadn't sat too well with Nicole. In fact, she'd chewed him out, using language that would make an Arab goatherder blush. After finishing her vent, she'd stomped away, not giving him a chance to respond.

It was so aggravating, because Nicole simply didn't understand the true situation. Sure, maybe he said it the wrong way, but she needed to realize that she was too valuable to risk that way. Too valuable to the Mossad—and too valuable to him.

In the months leading up to the Iran operation, they'd connected every time their competing schedules allowed, which wasn't often. But the times they were together were exquisite. Then, just when it felt like their relationship was getting to the point where he was wondering if she might be *the one* for him, he almost lost her to the IRGC. And while her life was in danger, all he could do was sit in Azerbaijan and wait and wonder. She had no clue what that was like—the absolute helplessness.

I wonder if I should call her, he thought as the tram slowed for another stop. *Maybe she's finally cooled down enough to talk. Maybe we could even meet up if she's in Paris.*

Then the desperation of what he was considering hit him. Next thing you know he'd be following her to fashion shows and stalking her social media. Besides, the last thing he wanted was to deal with an angry phone call on public transportation.

The tram slowed, then stopped. Nir stepped through the doors and onto the platform. He followed the crowd up the stairs and began the short walk home. He had to put Nicole and Iran out of his mind, another story for another time. Someday when he was in the French Riviera, or better yet down in Eilat, out on the beach with a drink in his hand, he would let his mind run through that saga. But not here. Not now. Not without Nicole near him.

He turned into a local pub called *Elfde Gebod*, the Eleventh Commandment. The walls were covered with religious icons and paintings—some sacred, some sacrilegious. He ordered a takeout bowl of their Apostel's Fish Stew, a mix of mullet, sole, scampi, salmon, mussels, and young potatoes—a perfect blend despite the misspelling of its name. A pint of the pub's eponymous Bruin, a hearty brown ale, kept him busy while he waited.

Soon the bartender sat a bag holding the stew in front of him. Nir took a last draw from his glass, but before he had a chance to stand, his phone buzzed. Not his regular phone. The one with the fully encrypted line, the one he kept in his right front pants pocket at all times. He snatched the bag off the bar and hurried out the door.

If anything, the wind had picked up, and Nir's breath caught in this throat. Once he was out on the street, he looked for someplace secluded, away from prying eyes. Up ahead he saw a coffee shop and an alley next to it. He ducked into the alley, then slid out his phone and read the text.

Rome January 3.

He felt the familiar surge of excitement. It hadn't been that long since Estonia, but still he was ready for some action. He needed something to take his mind off events of the past. And more importantly, he desperately needed some action that would take his mind off a certain person from his past.

CHAPTER 21

FOUR DAYS LATER
OUTSIDE BAGHDAD, IRAQ—JANUARY 3, 2020—
00:15 / 12:15 A.M. AST

The owner of the small stone house, a father who had lost a son who'd been serving with Kata'ib Sayyid al-Shuhada, brought another tray with three cups of steaming coffee resting on it. Falih Kazali, Abu Mustafa al-Sheibani, and Abbas each took one with a word of thanks. This was their third cup since arriving over two hours ago. The plane should have touched down at the nearby Baghdad Airport soon after their arrival at the home, but for some reason it was running late. Even after the IRGC commander finally made his appearance, the leaders of the KSS would remain in their safe house until they were called. That could come in a matter of hours or not until the end of the day. When Qasem Soleimani, commander of the infamous Quds Force of the Islamic Revolutionary Guard Corps, came to town, you didn't set the agenda. You simply waited your turn.

"Why again is he coming?" Abbas asked Kazali. He could see the older man was starting to fade. Better to engage him in small talk than to let him suffer the embarrassment of his coffee cup clattering to the floor. Kazali was the secretary general of the KSS. Although his fighting days were behind him now, he looked every part the grizzled warrior. His face was well-scarred, and a patch covered where he'd lost an eye while battling against Assad in Syria seven years ago.

"He is meeting with Prime Minister Abdul-Mahdi," Kazali said, his eye brightening as he took another sip of the strong brew. "The story is that he is on a peace mission seeking help from the prime minister to help broker a rapprochement between Iran and Saudi Arabia."

Abbas swallowed a laugh. The idea that Iran would seek peace with Saudi Arabia was preposterous. Sure, the citizens of Iran might be all for it, but that's not who was running the country. The only nation the IRGC and the Iranian religious leadership hated more than Israel and the United States was Saudi Arabia. Yes, there was certainly the Shi'a versus Sunni animosity, but this went deeper. Saudi Arabia was a debaucherous country filled with lecherous sheikhs. Their faith was shallow, and their lifestyle was disgusting. The Western infidels deserved to die because they were infidels. The Saudis deserved to die because they claimed to be good Muslims.

"That is obviously not truly the case," Abbas said. "Why is he really here?"

"Soon, we will find out. His summons to us gave no reasons. Only that we must be here to meet with him."

Kazali took another sip of his coffee, then set his cup on a small wooden table. The night was cold, and the single space heater in the room was not doing a good job of boosting the temperature. Through the dimness, Abbas watched as the older man slipped a blanket from the back of his chair and draped it over his shoulders. The light of the household was intentionally kept inconveniently low, but everyone understood why. One never knew what was flying in the sky above them, searching for them, targeting them.

Abu Mustafa al-Sheibani stood, then stretched and paced. Abbas had not seen the commander of the KSS militia for several months. He was away much of the time working with a network he'd developed to smuggle arms and supplies to militias throughout Iraq. His activities were so onerous that he'd earned a $200,000 bounty on his head and a place on the Iraqi government's 41 Most Wanted List. Abu Mustafa held a particular hatred in his heart for the Americans. Thirteen years ago, his brother, Abu Yaser, had been captured by U.S. forces. He hadn't been seen since.

After circling the small room several times, Abu Mustafa stopped in front of Abbas. "You know, he mentioned you by name."

Abbas was stunned. "Who? Soleimani?"

"The same." The white of Abu Mustafa's smile showed his confidence in the low light. He was used to being recognized by those in power. Abbas was not.

"What did he say?" As soon as he said the words, Abbas chided himself for sounding a little too enthusiastic, like a teenager asking about his favorite sports hero.

"The message we received was not detailed. He just said he wanted you in the meeting because of your success with drones. I think it is likely that you will play a part in whatever he has planned next."

It was Abbas's turn to stand and pace. Exactly what he'd been hoping for was now taking place. Those in the upper echelons of power not only knew his name but recognized his skills. It would not be long before Kazali would be too old to lead the militia. Abu Mustafa, himself, was in his early sixties. How long would he have the energy to divide his time between KSS and the Sheibani Network?

The sound of jet engines this time of night pulled Abbas from his internal revelry. He and Abu Mustafa hurried to a window, while Kazali remained seated and wrapped in the blanket. Opening the shutters just enough to see outside, the two men watched as an Airbus passenger jet descended to Baghdad Airport. Abbas stepped away from the window first and resumed his pacing. He was a bundle of nerves now that he knew he'd been specifically requested. The arrival of the plane was just the next step in their *hurry up and wait* night vigil, but it was good to know that Commander Soleimani was finally here and would soon be on the ground.

Their host carried out several plates of food for his guests. The first held a stack of bread and a bowl of hummus with red peppers on top. The second carried *kubba bil burghur*, fried dough dumplings stuffed with nuts and cheese and minced meats. The final plate was covered with *dolma*, boiled chard wrapped into small fingers and stuffed with rice, meat, and spices. Wedges of lemon laid neatly around the rim.

"My friend, you do too much," Kazali said.

"It is my pleasure. Let me prepare a plate for you so you don't have to get up." The man went running back to the kitchen, then returned with three empty plates and set them next to the food. Lifting one, he began to fill it for the secretary general. "I apologize for the cold. It is now just me in the house, and I have only the one heater."

"Please do not apologize." Kazali took the proffered plate of food. "Allah has seen your sacrifice for us. Rest assured you will be rewarded on the day you are reunited with your son."

Their host left, and the meal was delicious and

satisfying. Abbas hoped there would be another round of coffee soon, because he could already feel the fatigue caused by the food enveloping his brain.

Boom!

The sound of an explosion reverberated through the stone walls of the small house. All three KSS men rushed to the window. The last of a fireball was burning itself out in the direction of the airport. Smoke plumes now roiled darkly in the night sky.

Abbas tried to work out the timing in his head. The plane had passed above them 20 minutes ago. Between the time it took to land and taxi the plane, then gather the entourage into a vehicle convoy, this would be just about the time Qasem Soleimani would be leaving the airport. Abbas hoped against hope that he was wrong and the commander was safe, but in his heart he knew. The Americans didn't go after a target that big without being assured a kill.

Qasem Soleimani, commander of the Quds Force of the IRGC, had just been assassinated by U.S. missiles.

CHAPTER 22

RISTORANTE AMBASCIATA D'ABRUZZO, ROME, ITALY—13:30 / 1:30 P.M. CET

If a meeting between Mossad agents took place in the city of Rome, chances are it was in Ristorante Ambasciata D'Abruzzo. Located in the upscale district of Parioli, the restaurant was opened six decades ago by members of the Poggi family. Over the years its reputation had only grown, and despite its being "off the beaten path," it had become a must visit for many who did their web research before visiting Italy's capital city.

But why the Mossad? Nir wasn't sure. It could be the cuisine. Abruzzo was a region in south central Italy that had developed its own style of food. Heavy on ingredients like bread, lamb, garlic, and truffles and spices such as saffron and licorice and rosemary, many identified Abruzzese cuisine as some of the best in Italy. Or it could be several other factors. It was somewhat isolated from most tourists, it tended toward noisy, and it was only a brisk ten-minute walk from Israel's embassy.

Whatever the reason, if a person were to visit the Poggi family's establishment today and see an out-of-the-way table with two men—both who had somehow managed to arrange their chairs so they were facing the front door—that person just might be looking at two agents of the Israeli Intelligence Community.

Today Nir was one of the two men angled on the corners of that out-of-the-way table with their faces toward the door. The other was Efraim Cohen, assistant deputy director of Caesarea.

"Holy mother of Mordecai, I love this place," Efraim said, excitedly opening the menu. He'd flown in that morning, and despite Nir's protests, he'd insisted on meeting at Ambasciata D'Abruzzo for lunch.

"Nothing kills you faster than routine," Nir said.

"Yeah, I know. You've only told me that about 40 times. But whoever said that never tasted Roberto Poggi's fettuccine with lamb ragout. That sauce alone is worth risking a car bomb."

Nir chuckled. He'd been pleased when he saw Efraim was the one who had come to meet with him. The man always kept him laughing, even when working in difficult situations.

The waiter came with a basket of fresh, warm bread and a bottle of Montepulciano d'Abruzzo wine. The two men started their order with a plate of spinach and ricotta ravioli and a stewed artichoke with garlic and mint to share. For their main course, Efraim ordered his precious

fettuccine while Nir went with the grilled lan-
goustines and a side of roasted potatoes.

"You know shellfish is not kosher," Efraim said
with a grin when the waiter left.

"Good thing I didn't get the wild boar. That
really would have gotten you in full-on Pharisee
mode."

"Here, let me show you something." Efraim
pulled his phone out of his pocket and leaned
toward Nir. He loaded up a video and hit Play.
The feed from a night vision CCTV camera
showed on the screen. Suddenly, in the left
corner, an explosion rose up into the air.

"Bye, bye, Soleimani?" Nir asked.

"Precisely."

"Couldn't have happened to a nicer guy. Did
we have anything to do with it?"

"Sadly, no. Or at least not much. We passed
on some intel about his whereabouts, but the
American president authorized it, and a U.S.
drone fired the missiles."

That made sense to Nir. There had been
talk in the past about putting a Kidon hit on
Soleimani. He'd even spent a long weekend in
Tel Aviv with a team working through intel and
brainstorming potential scenarios. In the end, the
Quds Forces commander was just too protected
to get to or even to reach with a car bomb.
There'd been only one plausible method for
removing this murderer of thousands of innocent

people, and the Americans had just employed it.

The waiter brought out the starters, and Nir topped off their wine glasses. "To American drones and Iranian bones," he said, lifting his glass.

"Here, here." Efraim clinked Nir's goblet with his.

The artichoke was opened like a flower and coated in a high-end olive oil and spices. The raviolis were served in a brown butter sage sauce that added an amazing, herbed toasty-ness to the dish.

"I am going to eat like a pig, then sleep all the way back to Tel Aviv." Efraim pulled a few leaves from the artichoke.

"*Achi*, you came all the way here just for one meal with me?"

"What better way to spend my brief time in Rome than with the infamous Nir Tavor?"

"Infamous Nir Tavor, my backside. Just tell me why you came." Nir sat back in his chair, hoping to digest enough room in his stomach for the main course.

"You've seen the uptick in UAV activity among the militias." Efraim also leaned back with his wine glass in his hand.

"Certainly. It looks like the Houthis have bumped up their use of aerial drones against Saudi targets, as have a lot of the Iraqi insurgents."

Efraim leaned forward again and lowered his

voice to the point that Nir had to tilt in as well so he could hear him. "Precisely. We've got two moles buried so deep in the IRGC that they could tickle the Ayatollah's bum. Only a couple of people at the very top of the agency know who they are. They're telling us that Soleimani is planning—sorry, was planning—something big in the Gulf area using drone technology. As always, Iran wouldn't dirty their own hands. They've been planning on tasking one of their proxy militias to carry out the job."

"But that's over and done with now, right? Remember? Boom, down goes Soleimani?"

Efraim set down his glass, then pulled off a piece of bread and rubbed it around in the remaining brown butter sage sauce. Before putting it into his mouth, he pointed it toward Nir to emphasize his words. "I think, *achi*, that this is much bigger than Soleimani." Then he popped the bread into his mouth before adding, "In fact, I think the Islamic leadership in Iran may use the Soleimani hit as a pretext for carrying out whatever it is they have planned. They're desperate right now to destabilize the region."

"Why is that?"

"Because of the peace accords the U.S. president's son-in-law is working on. If those go through, suddenly you'll have Oman, the UAE, Morocco, and Saudi Arabia all looking to make friends with Israel. Even now, the intelligence swaps and under-the-table business deals between us and the Saudis and the Gulf states are the worst-kept secrets in the Middle East. So Iran wants to get everybody distrustful of one another."

"Is that why we're sticking our nose into this? Normally, if an attack is going to take place, we pursue it only if we're asked, like what happens in Europe so many times."

"Exactly. Think about it. A decade ago, when someone *potentially* matching your description *allegedly* went to Dubai to *presumably* bump off a notorious bad guy, it had to be done secretively with forged passports. Now we might be invited right in if we bring viable information."

Efraim was right. It was a different world now. Former enemies were now, if not exactly friends, working acquaintances.

"Do we have any idea what they have planned?"

"No clue. But again, we think something . . . drone-y."

"Something drone-y." Nir shook his head. "And you're asking me to take that incredibly helpful word and do what?"

"Stop the attack, of course." Efraim smiled a big smile and slapped Nir's shoulder.

Nir shook his head again. "*Chai b'seret.*" The phrase that literally meant "living in a movie" but was common slang for when someone had wildly unrealistic expectations seemed appropriate.

Their main courses came, as did a second bottle of wine. Whether because of the exquisite nature of the food or the absurdity of the assignment, the two friends let the topic rest for a bit. Nir asked Efraim about his family, and Efraim asked Nir about his business.

Finally, when Nir had cracked his last langoustine and Efraim had twirled his last piece of fettuccine, they returned to business.

"I have to admit, *achi*, I don't even know where to start." Nir moved to divide the last of the second bottle of wine between their two glasses.

"That's why I'm giving you a team. You'll have four full-time operators, plus as many more guns as you'll need. You'll also have a logistics support staff of four, and one brilliant and beautiful hacker babe."

Nir stopped over his glass mid-pour. "Come again," he said, setting the bottle down.

"We need the best on this. You're our best operator. I'm giving you the best logistics team we have, and nobody is better than Nicole with computers."

"Have you talked with her about this? I'm not sure she wants to work with me right now."

"I don't care if she wants to work with you or not. I just need to know whether you can work with her. And before you try to come up with any other answer, let me tell you that the answer is yes. 'Yes, Efraim, my friend, I can put to the side

176

any schoolkid crushes and stupid emotional crap and do my job.' That's your answer."

Nir glared at the other man, but he couldn't get mad because he was absolutely right. This was about saving lives. "Yes, Efraim, *achi*, I can put to the side any schoolkid crushes and . . ." He looked for help.

"And stupid emotional crap . . ."

"And stupid emotional crap and do my job." Nir lifted his glass and drained it.

The men walked to a café a little later and talked about past missions and agency gossip. Eventually, Efraim left for the airport and his flight home.

Back at his hotel room, Nir tried to picture what it would be like when he saw Nicole for the first time in months. Would she be able to put their differences behind her? Would he be able to pretend like they didn't have a past? Any way you looked at it, it would be strange and awkward.

The next morning, he flew back to Antwerp. Efraim had some work to do to figure out the logistics of the team, but he was optimistic that while the killing of Soleimani might not stop the planned attack, it would certainly slow it down.

Nir would take that time to get his business in order. This operation might last weeks, and he wanted to ensure that Yael Diamonds was prepared to survive during his absence. Then, on January 12 he would fly to Tel Aviv, and the operation to stop "something drone-y" would begin.

CHAPTER 23

Nir closed the door to the ramsad's office and walked through the reception area. For being the hub of the most well-respected intelligence service in the world, Mossad's headquarters décor was surprisingly utilitarian. No flash, nothing ornate. Instead, everything had its purpose and its place. This was true even of the director's office. Only a few pictures hanging, a bookshelf crammed with books, binders, ring-bound packets, and a wall of file cabinets. The latter had been a surprise. Did anybody still use file cabinets in this digital age? He supposed there would be some extra-sensitive information one would not want to risk to the prying of skilled hackers, but wouldn't that kind of information be kept in a safe rather than in a bunch of 1960s-era tan metal cabinets?

The meeting with the ramsad, Ira Katz, had been brief and for the most part uninformative. Yet it was probably necessary. Katz had told Nir he had all the resources he needed, and that he and the country were counting on him.

All the *rah-rah, go get 'em* stuff that usually accompanies the start of an operation. But one interesting bit of information had come out of their time. As Efraim had, the ramsad emphasized the possibility of a peace initiative spearheaded by the son-in-law of the U.S. president. He'd stressed that it was because of this peace initiative and the groundwork between Israel and some of the Islamic states that Nir and his team were even involved in this operation. He'd also made it clear that if this attack wasn't stopped, years of geopolitical courtship could be flushed down the drain.

No pressure there, Nir thought as he strode through the halls. He checked his watch and realized he was 20 minutes late for meeting his new Caesarea team. He'd come to headquarters immediately upon his arrival in Tel Aviv yesterday afternoon. After being shown to a temporary office that would be his for the day while his team's workroom was completed, he read through the files of the men and women who'd been assigned to him. Three of the Kidon operatives had served with him on previous operations, but he didn't know any of the logistics squad. Then there was the final member of the team—Nicole.

As he skimmed through her file, he was surprised to see how many operations she'd been part of. Because her skills were with computers, she could work from anywhere she was able to set up a secure connection. That's what had allowed her modeling career to soar to such great heights even while she became the go-to hacker for a growing number of Mossad operations.

They'd spent so much time together—and for almost a decade. Nir hadn't been above seeing other women who interested him, and he assumed Nicole had seen other men. But she'd been the first and only woman who had ever made him consider combining the words *exclusive* and *relationship*. Until their disagreement, he thought she might feel the same way.

Now he was about to see her face-to-face after months of angry radio silence. If it didn't go well, he would consider sending her back to Paris and letting her work remotely. He didn't need a cancer in the squad, and bitterness was a disease that could eat its way through a team's cohesion.

Rounding a corner, he saw the open door to the workroom. Laughter was coming from inside, which was a good sign. He walked in, and the space immediately fell silent. He stared at the team, and they stared at him. On one side of a long table sat his four Kidon operators, and on the other sat the two men and two women of his logistics team. Nicole sat by herself on the far side. Her face gave nothing away. There was neither joy nor anger at seeing him. Her expression was in runway model neutral.

"Sorry I'm late, everyone. Got hung up in the ramsad's office." He walked to the head of the table.

Nobody said a word.

"I hate making people wait, but when the ramsad wants to talk, you sit there and listen."

Then he laughed.

No response. They all just impassively watched him as he sat down.

Well, this is awkward. Has Nicole been telling stories about me? Do I already have to dig myself out of a hole with this team?

"Okay, so I'd like us to introduce ourselves, then we can get to work. Who wants to start?" He knew who they all were; he'd seen their photos in their files. He just wanted to make sure they all knew each other.

They said absolutely nothing. This time, however, he did see a little glint in the eyes of Yaron, an old-school Kidon operative with whom he'd worked several times before. That's when he remembered one other fact he'd gleaned from his time in the files of these men and women. While each of them was among the best at what they did, they'd all been written up at least once for insubordination or inappropriate behavior.

Efraim, you knew me too well when you put this motley crew together.

"Okay, then, I'll start. Hi, I'm Nir Tavor, and I'm an alcoholic."

"Hi, Nir," the team responded, and then they all burst out laughing. Nir was relieved to see that Nicole was laughing with the rest.

"When the ramsad wants to talk, you sit there and listen." Avi was another Kidon member and friend, mocking him with a very poor, self-important Nir impersonation.

"I'm sensing that you have a problem with taking personal responsibility for your actions," one of the two logistics women put in. Her name was Liora.

"I'll vouch for that," Nicole said, and they all oohed and laughed.

"Okay, okay, I can see how this is going to be." He attempted to calm them. They had work to do. "Now, Efraim Cohen gave me you bunch of misfits for a reason. You think differently. You're not bound by tradition. You're innovators. That's what I want. That's what will allow us to find an unknown enemy and stop their unknown attack. I don't care what you look like—well, except for maybe you over there with the man-bun." He rolled his eyes and pointed to one of the logistics guys. "I don't care how you dress. All I ask is that you do your job to the best of your abilities and that you aren't a jerk while you do it. For the next days or weeks, we're a family. Who's your daddy? You're looking at him."

"Nothing creepy about that," Nicole mumbled just loud enough for everyone to hear.

"If you're Dad, then who's Mom?" This from the logistics guy with the man-bun—Yossi.

"I'll be Mom," the second logistics woman said, "but I'm not cooking for you. And don't get any other funny ideas." This was Dafna.

"There is no mom," Nir said. "It's an analogy."

"No mom?" Yossi shook his head. "That's kind of sad. Everyone should have a mother."

"Everyone does have a mother," Yaron said. "Otherwise, we wouldn't be here."

Nir had to gain some control. "Stop! I'm Daddy, there is no mommy, and you're all about to get time-out if you don't focus."

"Dad's kinda grumpy," Nicole said to Yossi in a loud whisper. "Must have been a tough day at the office."

Nir couldn't help but laugh with the rest. As irritating as the banter was while he was trying to lead the team, it also meant they were bonding. This kind of obnoxious talk-around would pay dividends during the high-pressure times when this odd-ball, individualistic group would have to function as one unit.

"Okay, I still want introductions. We'll go around the table. Give us your name, your specialty, and one reason you've been written up."

Words of appreciation sounded around the table as all eyes went to Yaron, a short, stocky man in his late forties.

"Yaron Eisenbach. Explosives and general mayhem. I was sent to put a bomb under a Hamas leader's car. I recognized the car of his superior, so I put the bomb under it instead. He came out, and that was the end of him."

"What about the guy you were sent to kill?" Nir asked.

"Oh, I shot him in the head when he came out to see what had happened."

"Fair enough." Heads around the table nodded in appreciation.

"I'm Avi Carmeli." This Kidon man was in his mid-twenties with black hair and the well-toned body of a triathlete. "I am general mayhem, no specialty. I once skinny-dipped in the ramsad's pool."

"Tell them the rest," Yaron said.

"With the ramsad's daughter."

The table erupted with laughter.

"Surprised you're still with us," Nir said.

The next man was also in his twenties. His head was shaved, and he had a bushy, full beard. "I'm Doron Mizrahi. I'm good with locks and coms. I had a little bit too much to drink one night and didn't want to drive home, so I came to the office, broke in, and fell asleep on Assistant Deputy Director Friedman's couch."

"Can't blame you," Dafna said. "She has a very comfortable couch." Liora enthusiastically nodded her agreement.

The last Kidon man was enormous. A Russian Jewish immigrant, he looked very much like 1980s Dolph Lundgren. In fact, his nickname around the campus was Drago.

"My name is Dima Aronov," he said with a heavy Russian accent. "I like to break things. I was written up for punching my supervisor."

"Nice," Nir said. "And just why did you feel the need to punch your supervisor?"

With a lowered voice, Dima said with a sneer, "He wanted me to call him Daddy." Laughter and applause broke out around the table as Dima punched his hand.

"Well played." Nir already loved his team. Turning toward Nicole, he said, "Next."

"I'm Nicole le Roux. I have a knack for finding my way into other people's computer files. I've been written up several times for doing unauthorized research on the agency's computer system."

"In other words, you hacked into Mossad's databank," Doron said.

"*Hacked* is such an ugly word. Like you, I just picked the digital locks until I found what I was looking for."

Liora leaned forward. "Okay, now this is going to sound weird, but didn't I see you in *Marie Claire*?"

Nicole blushed. "You probably did. That's my other job. It's what pays the bills and allows me access into places I normally couldn't go."

"I have to say, I don't totally get it." Doron's tone held a challenge.

"Don't get what?"

Nir could see Nicole's embarrassment shifting toward anger.

Avi jumped in. "We don't get why you're here, why you're doing this. You're already this international supermodel making tons of money. But even more than that, you're not even . . ."

Nir was tempted to defend Nicole, but he thought better of it. This was a battle she needed to fight and win.

Nicole's eyes flared. "Not even what? Not even Jewish? That may be true, but don't ever question my loyalty. I've proven myself more times now than I can count. I'm here because I love this country. And I'm on this team because I'm ridiculously good at what I do. Which, by the way, is how I know you left out one tiny detail in your story. You had your little *sans* swimsuit pool party the night before the ramsad's daughter's wedding."

"Drop the mic!" Yossi said, and everyone laughed and cheered. Even Avi smiled and gave Nicole a slow clap.

"Listen, team," Nir said. "I've worked with Nicole before, and her work stands on its own. She doesn't need my endorsement. But she is the best at what she does. She belongs on this team, just like the rest of you. In fact, we need her on this team. We're clear on this?"

"Yes, sir," sounded around the table. Except for Dima, who said, "*Da, Papa.*"

"Also, I want all of our communication to continue to be in English. Last I knew, Nicole's Hebrew was improving, but all of you grew up learning English, correct? I mean, except you, Dima. But your English skills are strong, are they not?"

"Me Drago. Me love break things," Dima said. When Nir didn't respond, he added, "Yeah, boss, *sababa.*"

"I'm Liora Regev." On the shorter side with shoulder-length brown hair and in her mid-twenties, Liora was the textbook definition of cute. "I'm visual surveillance and analysis. I was written up for calling my supervisor a not-nice name."

"You got written up for that?" Nir was sure there had to be more to the story.

"Well, that was after I kneed him in a not-nice place."

"I knew that guy." Dafna was another twenty-something. Her hair was dyed bright red, and her ears and nose held enough jewelry to stock her own mall kiosk. "He had it coming. I'm Dafna Ronen. I also do visual surveillance and analysis. I'm kinda the yang to Liora's yin. I was written up for making the video footage of Liora's little

188

incident disappear. And"—she turned to Nicole—"sister, if any of these meatheads hassles you about being on this team, let me know. We'll make sure they know the score."

Nicole smiled her appreciation.

Man-Bun was next. Yossi was tall and thin and had a long, well-trimmed and oiled beard. "I'm Yossi Hirschfeld. I'm research. I can find a needle in any digital haystack. It totally wasn't my fault for getting into trouble. They stationed me up in Nahariyya to watch the border. And what's in Nahariyya? Anyone? Sokolov Beach, of course. Gnarliest waves in Israel. I didn't stand a chance. They should have known better."

"You surf Sokolov?" the last man asked with genuine admiration. Lahav was in his late twenties and looked every bit the computer nerd from his thick black plastic-framed glasses to his white button-down shirt. Lifting his hand, he forced Yossi into an awkward fist bump, complete with explosion. "*Achla*, I used to boogie board down at Ha'Maravi Beach. Maybe you can teach me to surf someday."

Then a thought seemed to suddenly strike him. He turned to Nicole, looking both embarrassed and ashamed. "I'm sorry, Nicole. *Achla* means 'amazing' or 'super great.' When Dima said *sababa* earlier, he was saying he was cool with the boss's suggestion. These are both common slang words. You'll find a lot of slang terms and idioms in the Hebrew language. If you ever have trouble understanding one of these phrases, please don't hesitate to ask. I've been in situations where I feel like I'm the outsider, and it's never fun. I don't want you to feel like that. So just know that I'm there for you rain or shine. You can just call out my name, and I'll be there. That's just like that old James Taylor song. James Taylor is an American singer my mom really liked when I was growing up. She'd say his voice was so smooth, like butter. I don't know if I'd personally say smooth. But it's still really good. Really cool. But not *sababa* cool like Dima said. This is, like, cool kind of cool."

He finished with a big smile on his face, and everyone stared at him open mouthed, Nir included.

Efraim, what have you done to me?

Finally, Nicole said, "Uh, thanks."

Nir thought about this guy's file. He was the biggest wildcard among a team full of wildcards. "Lahav, thank you for your kind words to Nicole, and I'll let you and Yossi work out the logistics of your surf lessons later. For now, how about you let the rest of the team know who you are."

"Okay . . . *sababa*," he said, emphasizing the Hebrew word and giving Nicole a wink. "My name is Lahav Tabib. I'm an IT guy, and I build things. Anything you need put together, let me know. I'll make it happen. Computer systems, coms systems, portable command centers, satellite link-ups, drone surveillance—"

"Great, Lahav," Nir said. "We get the point. Tell us why you were written up."

"I shut down the power grid in Eilat."

"That was you?" Yaron's eyes widened.

"It was only for a minute. They acted like it was such a big deal. I told them it was vulnerable, and they didn't believe me. I proved them wrong."

Doron shook his head with a laugh. "*Achi*, I thought you were in prison."

"Well, I'm not." Lahav held out his arms, looking at where he was sitting in the chair. "At least not at this present moment."

Nir stepped in again. "Lahav is technically a resident of Maasiyahu Prison, but we've been granted the pleasure of his company for the foreseeable future. If he behaves and leaves the nation's power grid alone, he may not need to go back to his home away from home."

"Freedom!" Yossi called out in a Braveheart riff.

"That leaves you," Avi said. "What horrible thing have you done?"

"My name is Nir Tavor. I have for some reason been chosen the leader of this operation. Unlike you sketchy characters, I am a good boy. I have never been written up. That's because when I break the rules, I do so with a purpose. I'm a firm believer that when it comes to intelligence work, the ends quite often justify the means. So we may get rough sometimes and we may play dirty, but we *will* stop whatever the bad guys are planning."

"Do we have any idea who or what we're looking for?" Liora asked.

"Absolutely none. We're working on getting more information from our inside source, but so far there's nothing. So I want you to cull through all your HUMINT, SIGINT, and IMINT to see what's been missed. That's human intelligence, signals intelligence, and image intelligence in case any of you problem children ditched that day during training. Again, the reason you're here on this team is because you see things differently. If something is blatant or out in the open, the rest of them will find it. I want you to discover what they don't have the creativity to find. Got it?"

Affirmations sounded all around.

"Okay, they have this workroom all set up for us. But anything you need—any information, any piece of equipment, any permissions—you just ask me, and I'll make sure you get it. Let's find these people, and let's drop a missile on their heads."

CHAPTER 24

AROMA ESPRESSO BAR, TEL AVIV, ISRAEL—
17:45 / 5:45 P.M. IST

It was hard to miss Nicole even though she sat at a small, two-person table well inside of the café's glass wall, away from other patrons. The tabletop was empty, so when Nir came through the door and caught her eye, he held up two fingers. She smiled and nodded. He ordered two lattes, then carried the ceramic mugs to the table.

Nicole stood, and after he'd set the mugs down, she hugged him tightly. Surprised, Nir wrapped his arms around her too. She felt so good, so familiar, and her hair smelled even better than the Aroma coffee. Finally, they both pulled back.

"I have to apologize again . . ." Nir said the same time Nicole said, "Nir, I am so sorry . . ."

They both stopped and laughed awkwardly.

"Please." Nir said as he held her chair for her. "Let me start."

"Okay. But whatever you're about to say is completely unnecessary."

Nir sat down across from her and took a sip of his steaming latte. He breathed in deeply, then held it for a second. "Nicole, I'm sorry for disrespecting you. I let my emotions—my feelings for you—cloud my judgment. I thought I was going to lose you in Iran. I felt so helpless. Then when you came back safely, I was upset at not being able to do anything to help you. I think by telling you I would never let you get back into such a precarious position, I was trying to get my man card back. You know, by taking control."

"Wow, you've really thought this whole thing through." She smiled.

Nir shrugged. "Yeah, I don't normally get this reflective. Touchy-feely. But I spent a lot of time trying to figure out what I did wrong so that if I ever had another chance to be with you I would be sure not to do it again."

Nicole reached her hand across the table and placed it on his. "If there's anything to forgive, consider it forgiven."

Her hand was chilly, but before he had a chance to warm it with his other hand, she pulled back. "I have a couple of things to say to you too. First, an apology. Then, a story."

She looked down at her untouched coffee, then lifted her eyes to his. "When I came back from Iran, I was shaken. As you can imagine, it was terrible. I was treated roughly, but thankfully they never touched me . . . you know, inappropriately. But the threat of it was constant. Add to that the uncertainty of my future. I didn't know if I was going to be put on trial, sent to prison, maybe even executed."

Nir reached for her hand, but she quickly took hold of her coffee mug and lifted it to her lips.

Just sit back and let her talk. The only part of you she needs right now is your ear.

"So when I got back, I was a basket case. I was celebrated by the ramsad and the brass for my part in getting the nuclear information out, and I tried to put on a front on the outside, like it was no big deal. But inside I was a mess. What you said to me . . . It was the wrong thing to say at the wrong time. But I way overreacted. That's where I have to apologize to you. You didn't deserve my words that day or on the phone later. I had all this fear and rage in me, and you became the target. You didn't deserve it. I'm truly sorry."

"It's done. It's the past. Let's move on." Nir looked into Nicole's eyes, where tears were ready to spill over. He returned to the counter, where he pulled some napkins from a dispenser. But by the time he came back, her eyes were drying. She thanked him anyway and set the napkins in a wad on the table.

"That was actually the easy part." She gave a nervous laugh. "I have no idea how you'll respond to the rest of the story."

"Short of you telling me you're a spy for the IRGC, I think I can handle anything you have to say." Nir finished the rest of his latte as he waited for Nicole to begin again. She saw that his mug was empty and swapped it for hers, which was

195

still mostly full. Nicole wasn't a huge coffee drinker, and this swap had occurred often when they were together. It made Nir feel hopeful to watch her trade those mugs again.

"Soon after the whole Iran incident, not long after our last phone call, the ramsad offered me a leave of absence. Even though I thought I was putting on a strong front, he could see through the bravado."

Nir knew about this leave from reading her file, but he didn't tell her this. Besides, he was curious to find out what she'd done with her time away from the agency.

"I decided to go down to see Christiaan. Remember I told you it seemed like he was getting his life straight? I just wanted to see what was happening with him and to be around someone I knew had one hundred percent unconditional love for me. So I went home to South Africa, and it soon became apparent what had changed him. And here's where I'm not sure how you're going to react, because I know how you feel about this kind of stuff. I used to feel the same way."

Again, there was the nervous laughter.

"Come on, Nicole. You know you can tell me anything."

"Okay, then." She looked straight into his eyes. "Christiaan had found Jesus."

"Found Jesus? I didn't even know Jesus was

196

lost." As soon as he said it, he wished he could take it back. He saw the crestfallen look on Nicole's face, and he wanted to slam his head into a wall.

"You see? That's why I didn't want to say anything. I know how you feel about God and religion." She leaned back in her chair and crossed her arms.

"I'm sorry! I'm sorry! Stupid thing to say. I'm an idiot. It just slipped out before I could stop it. Please go on. I really want to hear. I've been hoping for so long that Christiaan would get his life together."

Nicole uncrossed her arms and put her hands back in her lap. "Okay. So I was skeptical, too, at first. We weren't raised with any kind of religion or church or anything. I went down there, and suddenly he's in church every Sunday and in a Christian recovery group every Wednesday and in a mini-group or family group or small group or something like that every Friday night. When I first went down there, I agreed to go with him on Sundays, but I didn't want anything to do with the rest of the stuff. I joked with him, calling him Christiaan the Christian. I wasn't being mean or anything. In fact, I was glad for him because it was the first time I'd seen him happy since we were little kids.

"Then I met Jozette, Christiaan's girlfriend. She's divorced and has a little girl, Kerina, who's four, and a two-year-old boy named Mattys. They're the cutest kids ever. We spent some time together, and she shared some of her own backstory of violence and abuse. She knew fear, but she'd also found peace."

Nicole's eyes were welling up again, and this time she took a couple of the napkins and dabbed at the tears.

"I was such a mess inside, and I didn't understand how Jozette could have so much joy in her after all she'd gone through. When I asked her, she gave me the same answer Christiaan had given me. They both said they found their hope when they gave themselves to Jesus."

Nir wanted to roll his eyes. He'd grown up with religion all around him, but it never appealed to him. He didn't see the purpose. It seemed that everyone acted exactly the same whether they went to synagogue or not. So many would spend their week lying and cheating and stealing, then light their Shabbat candles at the end of the week.

"So are you saying you're a Christian now too?"

Nicole smiled. "Yeah, that's what I'm saying."

"And . . ."

"And it's wonderful, Nir. I'm not afraid or angry anymore over what happened to me in Iran. I've forgiven my mom for killing herself with drugs, and I've forgiven Christiaan for abandoning me for his world of substance abuse.

Best of all, I feel like I've got a family again. Christiaan is about to propose to Jozette, which means I not only have my twin brother again, but I'm getting a sister and a niece and nephew too."

The joy in Nicole's words and on her face was unlike anything he'd seen in her before. They'd had a lot of laughs and some great times, but there'd always been an underlying edge to her—as if the effects of her family dynamics were always just below the surface, waiting to come out with a snide remark or a harsh word. But from what he could see now, that edge was gone, replaced by something new—peace.

"That's great, Nicole. I'm so happy for you." And he genuinely was, despite religion being the root cause of her joy. He was thrilled that she'd finally found peace and that it seemed like that peace extended to their relationship as well. Yet so many questions came with her new faith. Was she the same woman he used to know? How would this newfound belief affect her work with the Mossad? Would she still be comfortable assisting in the targeted elimination of bad guys? And what would happen if the rest of the team found out? She was already viewed as an outsider by some because she was a goy.

Most of all, what did this mean for their relationship? Was there room in her heart for both Jesus and him? Worse, would she now spend all her time trying to convert him? That was a losing proposition; he could assure her of that right from the beginning.

Nicole smiled. "I can see in your eyes that you're trying to figure out how this will work with me being a Christian, especially with you leading the team. That's why I wanted to tell you right away. If you decide the dynamics will be too weird for the team or for you, I'll totally understand your removing me."

"Do you want to stay on the team? Even if that means working for me?"

"More than anything."

Those three words did something in him—like his insides did a backflip with a half-twist. "Great, because we need you. Besides, Efraim wouldn't let me kick you off the team even if I wanted to."

"Yeah, I've got him wrapped around my little finger." She winked. Then reaching out again, she took his hands in both of hers. "I just want you to know that when Efraim told me you were the one leading this team, I jumped at the opportunity. There's no one I trust more to lead. There's no one I trust more with my safety."

She held his hands a moment longer, then released them. "I'm going to go." She stood, then reached behind her for her jacket. Nir jumped up and helped her put it on. She thanked him, then leaned forward and gave him a kiss on the cheek before walking away.

Nir signaled back to the counter for another latte, then watched Nicole through the glass walls. That had not gone at all like he'd expected. He had more questions about their relationship now than he'd had before he arrived.

All in due time. I have a much bigger issue to worry about right now.

CHAPTER 25

Despite the cold, Nir was sweating as he walked into Mossad headquarters. He'd spent the morning running drills with Yaron, Avi, Dima, and Doron. They were starting to gel as a team, and their communication was reaching peak. But Yaron, whom Nir had put in charge of their training, ran them hard. They'd started at five in the morning, and he still had them out on a trail run when Nir had to duck out to get to the office. He'd taken a shower and put on clean clothes, but the endorphins were still pumping, and the sweat kept leaking.

"Hey, all," he said to the rest of the team as he walked into their workroom. A couple mumbled greetings was all he got, which was fine with him. That meant they were working hard and didn't have time to be distracted. The team that jumped up and excitedly met you by the door had too much time on their hands.

The workroom was fairly large. The long conference table sat in the middle and was surrounded by eight workspaces up against the walls, each loaded with the latest in computer technology. Only five were currently occupied. The other three were ready in case their team needed to expand. There were no cubicles, just large desks spread around. Nir didn't want any walls dividing the players. All communication needed to be open and heard and ready to be implemented.

Nicole was stationed to the left as he walked in. She had a two-tier array of six 27-inch monitors, each filled with code that made Nir's head hurt just by looking at it. She briefly turned her head and smiled at him, her hands never even slowing on the keyboard.

They had met again, this time for dinner, but although they had a past together and their feelings were still strong in the present, they'd decided to hold off on rekindling a relationship at least until this operation was over. They didn't want anything between them to create a strange vibe in the group, and they certainly didn't need any distraction from their own work. To Nir's relief, that also put off any further discussion about Nicole's newfound faith.

Liora and Dafna had pulled their workstations together so they were working as one unit. An oversized bowl of popcorn sat on the seam between their two desks, into which they both regularly dipped their hands.

To their right was Yossi. In spite of the cold,

he was wearing shorts and sandals. His man-bun was down today, which from behind made him look like he belonged on the cover of a romance novel.

Finally, Lahav was on the far right. He was the only one who had bothered to decorate his space. His style would best be described as Star Wars chic, with various space cruisers, X-wings, and TIE fighters hanging from the ceiling. Posters hung on the walls, but only from episodes IV through IX. Each member of the team had been cornered at some point in time to hear his view as to why the prequels were an abomination. Only Liora had been kind enough to hear him out all the way.

Standing next to Lahav's desk was a full-size Chewbacca mannequin, the fur of which had seen better days. The team had decided to adopt it as a mascot, and they took turns bringing hats for Chewie to wear. It was Nir's turn today, and he pulled a pink bucket hat with *Tel Aviv Is 4* ♥*-ers* stenciled on it out of his messenger bag and placed it on the Wookie's head.

"Nice. It sets off his eyes," Liora said.

"It was a gift from my mom," Nir replied with a wink. Then he called out to the rest of the group, "Team meeting in ten minutes."

He walked past the Wookie and through a door into his office. He usually kept the door open so he wouldn't be so separated from the team, but the walls and door were essential since he'd sometimes receive calls or visits not for the whole team to hear.

He set his bag on his desk, then sat in the swivel, executive chair. The last week had been frustrating for the team. They'd chased lead after lead and come up with nothing. Also, the mysterious Iranian mole had been completely silent. Any cushion of time Soleimani's assassination had bought them would soon be gone. They needed something, and they needed it soon.

One positive note was that there hadn't been any blowback about Nicole's Christianity so far. Whether it was because nobody knew about it or nobody cared, Nir wasn't sure. He was just glad everyone was getting along.

By the time he'd responded to a series of emails, the ten minutes were up. He walked back into the workroom. "Let's bring it in, guys."

Everyone groaned but moved toward the table. Dafna tossed the metal popcorn bowl into the middle, and it came precariously close to dumping its contents as it spun. Everyone watched while it slowed and finally settled.

"Nice." Lahav grabbed two handfuls, then dumped the buttery corn directly on the table in front of him.

Nir started them off. "Let's go around the horn. Nicole?"

"As you all know, General Esmail Qaani took over as commander of Quds Force after Soleimani was particled out. There's little doubt that he knows about anything being sponsored by the IRGC. I've been trying to track down any computer signature he might have or phone I can get into, but so far I'm coming up dry."

"Okay, keep it up. Ladies?"

Liora started. "So word was that Soleimani was going to Baghdad to make peace with the Saudis, which we all know was a load of toasted goat droppings."

"That's right, girl," Dafna said.

A few days ago, the two women had stumbled across a couple of African American ladies speaking their minds on a U.S. cable news channel. They loved it and had been playing the shtick ever since.

"So we're thinking, just why did that boy go there?"

"Why indeed," Dafna echoed.

"Anytime Iran has something nasty in mind, they don't do it themselves. They get one of the militias to do their nasty."

"Nasty boys."

"What better place to meet one of their Iraqi insurgent militias than in Iraq?"

"Mmm."

"So we've been going over every piece of surveillance footage we can find in our database and in the American database, with a little help from Nicole—"

"Girl rocks."

"And we're trying to track down any known militia leaders who might have been within a ten-mile radius of Baghdad Airport."

"That's the kind of thinking I like," Nir said, laughing at their banter. "Good job. Yossi, can you help them with your needle-in-a-haystack skills?"

"Already on it, boss. The difficulty is that everyone and their left-handed *savta* has started their own militia."

"My grandmother was left-handed," Nicole said.

"Is your *savta* in Iraq?" Yossi grinned.

"Nah, she died."

"Phew, then she's probably not a militia leader."

Nicole laughed, crumpled a piece of paper, and threw it at Yossi.

"Let's rein it back in." Nir rolled his eyes. "I hate to put all of our eggs in one basket, but right now this Baghdad Airport lead is the only basket we've got. So let's go full-on with this. Lahav, what have you been working on?"

"I'm learning all I can about drones."

"Good." Nir thought back to Efraim's idea that the attack might be something "drone-y." "And what are you learning about drones?"

"If I wanted to kill you, I'd use a drone."

"And do you want to kill me?"

Lahav's creepy factor had elevated from the time the team was first formed, and some moments, like now, it full-on spiked.

"Of course not. No really good reason I can think of right now. But if I were going to launch an attack and make it big, I would not use a Katyusha rocket like the incompetents in Hamas. Their detonation is unreliable, and their aim is worthless. I also wouldn't go into someplace with guns blazing. Too many other guns around to last long. Besides, it's been done. Suicide bombs are a big yawn now. Nobody cares. If you want to make a statement, fly a drone. It's the terrorism of the future."

"Wow, Lahav, you could make a commercial for Killer Drones 'R' Us." Dafna had a point.

Lahav blushed. "Thanks."

Although said with a high level of creep, Lahav was exactly right. And what he said confirmed Efraim's earlier speculation.

"All of you, great work. Keep it going. Let me know if you come up with anything. I don't care how minuscule or seemingly irrelevant it is."

A chorus of "Okay, boss" and "You got it, Nir" rang around the table. The meeting broke up, and Nir went back to his computer. The meeting had shown him that his understanding of drone terrorism was sorely lacking. He needed to remedy that, and fast.

CHAPTER 26

TWO DAYS LATER
ABU KAMAL, SYRIA—JANUARY 23, 2020—
14:30 / 2:30 P.M. EET

The house was less than a mile from the western bank of the Euphrates. If you kept going a little further from the famous waterway, the landscape would be nothing but dirt and rocks. But here, near this ancient river, were date palms and willow trees and Syrian mesquite. Abbas could even see several rows of grapevines peeking from behind the large home.

The three men walked slowly toward the front door—Abbas and Abu Mustafa al-Sheibani holding their pace back to accommodate the short, cane-aided strides of Falih Kazali. Abbas hadn't been in Syria for several years, and this was his first time ever to be in the country without a gun in his hand. But they were here not to fight but to meet. And what a meeting it would be.

When Soleimani was murdered by the Americans, Abbas had despaired. Not only because his death was such a loss but also because Abbas worried that the plan they'd been chosen for had died with him. But then Kazali received a message. The operation was still a go. Only now it would be in honor of the great Quds commander—a tribute to his service and his sacrifice. That message was what brought them here, just across the Iraqi border into Syria. Behind that front door sat General Esmail Qaani, the new commander of the Quds Forces of the IRGC. The fact that he'd traveled all the way to this border town told Abbas all he needed to know about the gravity of this mission.

They reached the front door, which opened before they had a chance to knock. Before entering, Abbas turned and waved to the four armed men he'd left by the cars, letting them know all was well.

While not opulent, the inside of the house was nevertheless upscale for this part of the country. Gold-framed paintings hung all around, and high-quality rugs had been spread around the floor. What appeared to be marble was everywhere— the walls, the floors—but when Abbas looked closely, he could see several places with cracks and chips, which proved that what looked like marble was just an overlaid facade.

A man in a dark-blue suit led them across the entryway and through another set of doors. Seated on cushions with a feast of meats, salads, and breads in front of them were Commander Qaani, a second general wearing a Quds uniform, and two other men, one older and one younger, both dressed in civilian clothing. Qaani was telling a story in Farsi to those at the low table.

As they entered, the older man stood. Qaani, however, continued eating and telling his story, never acknowledging his visitors.

"*As-salamu 'alaykum*," said the man.

"*Wa-'alaykum salam*," Abbas and the other two men said in return.

"I am Farid Alzuhur. You are most welcome to my home." He nodded toward each of the others in the room. "The young man is my son, Karam. That is General Farrokh Soltani, deputy commander of Quds Forces. And that, of course, is General Esmail Qaani."

Still, Qaani had not looked up. Abbas tried not to let it bother him. This was standard fare when dealing with the IRGC. The Persians had a serious superiority complex. In their minds, they had developed great culture and powerful empires while the Arabs had still been living in caves and riding around on camels. Thus, they treated everyone around them as if they were mere servants. And the thing was people just took it from them, including him. He knew men, battle-hardened warriors, who would slit a man's throat for disrespecting them. Yet when a member of the IRGC talked down to them, they just took it.

Their host encouraged them to sit on three

cushions placed a small distance from the table. He did not offer them food.

Abu Mustafa and Abbas helped Kazali down to his cushion, then they took their places. Once they were situated, Qaani came to the end of his story, and the deputy commander and the host's son both laughed. Only now did the general turn toward his visitors.

"Ah, Falih Kazali, it is good to see you again after so many years." He turned to the host. "Farid, you and your son may leave us now."

Kazali bowed his head as the homeowner and his boy walked out of the room, then said, "General, it is an honor to have been invited to join you and a blessing to see your face."

"And Abu Mustafa," the general said, "you are a busy man. Your reputation precedes you, and your work for us is much appreciated."

"*Tashakkor mikonam*," Abu Mustafa replied, thanking him.

"I thank you both for coming to meet me here."

Abbas tried to ignore the general's slight against him. He was, after all, not part of the leadership of KSS—at least not yet.

Qaani continued. "I have made this trip for two reasons. First, I want to stress to you the necessity of this plan's success. If it is carried out properly, not only will the Americans and their puppet states in the Gulf be made to look like fools, but it could utterly derail the peace overtures. However, if you fail, the retaliation will be severe, and we will all feel it. Do you understand this?"

"Yes, general," Kazali said. "We will not fail you."

"The second reason I have come is so that I can hear from the mouth of this man"—he pointed at Abbas—"that he has the ability to carry out our plan."

"I, too, will not fail you. I will carry out your plan." Abbas spoke in genuine earnest.

Qaani glared at him. "Is it not foolishness to say such a thing before you have even heard the plan?"

Abbas flushed but kept his composure. "It is not foolishness, general. It is faith. I know Allah will give me what is needed to strike this blow against the apostate and the infidel. I will not let you down, because my god will not let me down."

"Hmm." Qaani assessed Abbas. "Well spoken. You, Seif Abdel Abbas, are the reason we have come to Kata'ib Sayyid al-Shuhada. Commander Soleimani, may Allah have mercy on his soul, had heard of your skills with UAV technology. Your level of expertise rivals that of some of our Houthi drone pilots."

"You are most kind, general."

"Because of the location of the attack, it would be difficult for one of my men or one of our

Yemenis to carry it out without being discovered. You may dress a lion as a sheep, but when it speaks you will still hear the roar. You and a team you will assemble, however, will have more access."

"Where will we be going, general?"

Here the general's face brightened with a wide smile. "The attack will be directly at the center of Sunni decadence—the United Arab Emirates."

Abbas's heart soared when he heard the target. He was afraid this would just be another big oil refinery or another military site. The UAE meant an attack on depravity. It meant mass casualties. It meant a place in history.

When the Arab tribes were falling behind the rest of the world economically and in technology, Allah provided them with a miracle—oil. It was this heavenly provision that allowed the Middle East to thrive and hold the Western world hostage through their dependence on OPEC crude. It was all going very well, but then the seven sheikhdoms that made up the United Arab Emirates decided to go a new direction. They took their oil money and built hotels and amusement parks and malls, all to lure in the infidels. What Allah had given them was not enough; they wanted more. So they sold their souls to the Western devils to get it. It would be a pleasure to rain fire down upon the Sunni Emiratis and their hedonistic ways.

General Soltani spoke for the first time.

Looking at Abbas, he said, "Come, let us go to where we can discuss your part of the plan."

As Abbas stood, Qaani invited Kazali and Abu Mustafa to come closer and partake of the meal.

In the next room stood a high table and two chairs. Soltani sat in one chair, and Abbas in the other. For the next 45 minutes, the general laid out the plan in detail. He explained the procedure for acquiring the necessary equipment and munitions, and he laid out the surprisingly tight time frame Abbas and the KSS had for preparation.

By the time Kazali, Abu Mustafa, and Abbas walked out the front door, Abbas's head was swimming. It would truly take a work of Allah to pull this off. But that was just the kind of situation where Allah would work his miracles.

Kazali and Abbas got in one car with two of the KSS men and headed for the Al-Qa'im border crossing. Abu Mustafa, however, was going north to Al-Hasakah along the Khabur River in Kurdish Syria. He was working on a new northern route to get weapons across Syria and down to Hezbollah in Lebanon as part of his network. He might or might not return in time for the February 14 and 15 attacks, he said. The smuggling route was for the IRGC, and they felt that Abu Mustafa's time was better spent there.

That was no mind. Success or failure depended upon Abbas—no one else.

Allah, give me the strength to carry out your will. Let us strike a great blow to those who hate you and who mock your name. Let both the apostate and the infidel feel the fires of your hell. I am your servant. Use me.

CHAPTER 27

ONE DAY LATER
MOSSAD HEADQUARTERS, TEL AVIV, ISRAEL—
JANUARY 24, 2020—11:15 / 11:15 A.M. IST

Okay, hit me," Nir said to his logistics team. They were all gathered around the conference table, and the bowl in the middle held pistachios today. A smaller bowl sat next to it for empty shells.

"We've been tracking down IRGC proxy militias who were near Baghdad Airport the night Soleimani played catch with a Hellfire," Liora began. "There must have been some kind of insurgent trade show going on there, because we counted 12 militias. Everyone from Asaib Ahl al-Haq and Hezbollah al-Nujaba to Kata'ib Sayyid al-Shuhada and the Badr Organization. I started tracing the movements of these groups to look for any intersections with the IRGC while Dafna took it from the other side."

Dafna jumped in. "I put my eye on Esmail Qaani, the motherless goat turd that took over for Soleimani."

"Motherless goat turd—that opens a whole box of questions," Yossi said.

"Exactly," Liora said. "Which is motherless? The goat or the turd?"

Lahav waved. "I know this. It has to be the turd. A goat must have a mother to exist. The turd, however, is resigned to a digestive creation process as opposed to a parental lineage. It is thereby utterly motherless."

Nir barely held back a sigh. "Fate of the world, people. Remember, we're dealing with the fate of the world. Dafna, please go on."

"Qaani has been staying close to home ever since he ascended to Quds royalty. Seems things tend to fall out of the sky when Quds commanders go to other countries. Then suddenly, yesterday, he hops on a private plane and flies to Abu Kamal."

"Syria?" Nir asked.

"That's the place. A lovely tourist destination right across the border with Iraq along the lush Euphrates River."

"It's a lovely place if you like rocks," Yossi said.

"And dirt," Lahav added.

"And goats," Liora said.

Dafna followed up. "And motherless goat—"

"Stop!" Nir looked at Nicole, who was laughing. "It's like running a day care."

"Ooh, that reminds me. Snack time." Liora reached for the bowl of pistachios. Sadly, her short arms didn't quite reach, so Dafna grabbed it and pulled it to her.

"Gotcha, girl."

"Dafna, how were you able to track him?" Nir asked. "I've got to think he keeps his movements very hush-hush."

"For that, we have our Gentile giant to thank." Liora turned to Nicole.

"And Yossi," Nicole added. "While Dafna followed Qaani's movements forward, Yossi looked backward. For every location where we could pin him down, we pulled up all the cell phone numbers that pinged the towers in that area. It was a ridiculously high number. But with each successive location, we were able to compare that list with the previous ones and cut out all the numbers that didn't match. It was surprising how quickly the possibilities shrank. Finally, after 14 locations, we had our number. We test ran it for a couple of days until we were sure it was his and it matched his known movements."

"*Achla*," Nir said.

Lahav leaned toward Nicole and said in a loud whisper, "That means 'amazing' or 'great.' "

"I know what it means."

It may have been sweet the first 15 times he'd defined Hebrew slang for her, but now it was well past the helpful point.

Nir continued. "When we're done with this operation, remind me to send that number up the chain. The bosses may want to forward the information to the Americans. See if they want to rain down on Qaani's parade someday.

So we've got Qaani in Abu Kamal. What now?"

"Oh, it doesn't end there." Liora grinned. "The militia movement information we could track down was way too thin to create any patterns. Life would be so much easier if we could just GPS chip all the terrorists like my family did to our Mini-Schnauzer."

Lahav was about to comment on that idea when Nir snapped his fingers and pointed to him. The analyst furled his brow but remained silent.

Liora continued. "Anyway, I thought maybe we could narrow the list some by looking at those who've been involved in UAV attacks. You know, something *drone-y* like Efraim said. There were four. Ashab al-Kahf, Kataib Hezbollah, Asaib Ahl al-Haq, and Kata'ib Sayyid al-Shuhada."

Dafna picked up the story again. "We're still running on speculation, but when we saw that Qaani had gone to Abu Kamal, we turned to our girl again." She used her thumb to identify Nicole as *our girl*. "Somehow using her keyboard artistry, she was able to get us a feed from the surveillance cameras at the Al-Qa'im border crossing. And who do we spot there?" She pressed a button on a remote control she must have had hiding in her lap. The huge screen hanging over their workspace lit up, and a bearded man stood next to a black car as he spoke with two members of the Syrian military.

"Oh, it's *that* guy," Nir said—with no clue who

he was looking at. "Does *that* guy have a name?"

"He sure does," Dafna said. "Abu Mustafa al-Sheibani."

"The Sheibani Network guy."

"The same. One of Iraq's 41 Most Wanted."

"Why 41?" Lahav asked.

"What?" Nir immediately regretted asking for clarification.

"Why 41? Why not 40? I could even understand 14, but 41? It's just so random. Was there a tie for fortieth place, so they added an extra one? Or did they have their 40, then they were like, 'Oh, wait, we've got to get this guy on the list too'? I kind of feel like we should do the Iraqis a favor and take one of them out so they can go back to having 40 like normal people would."

At some point I'm going to either shoot Lahav or shoot myself.

Everyone just stared at the man.

"What?" Lahav asked.

Nir shook his head, then turned to Dafna. "We've got the Sheibani Network guy at the border crossing. So what?"

"He's not just the Sheibani Network guy. If you remember, he's also Abu Mustafa, commander of the Kata'ib Sayyid al-Shuhada militia."

"Hello." A smile spread across Nir's face. "Okay, before we get too wild, did you watch for any other familiar faces at the border crossing?"

"Yes, but there were none we could see," Liora answered.

"Are there other ways across the border?"

"There are always ways across the border, but none without a lot of risk. And there would be no reason to go a different way. If General Qaani asked for someone to be let through, they would be let through."

"This could all just be coincidence," Nir said.

"But it could also be an *ays ratzon*, a favorable moment we've been given," Liora said with a smile.

Nir couldn't depend on favorable moments from God, not when lives were at stake. Still, it would be quite the coincidence.

"Liora, do we know when they left?" he asked.

"One of the two cars went back across the border three hours later. That's just long enough to hold a meeting to talk about a drone attack . . . theoretically."

"What happened to the second car?"

Yossi answered this question. "When the ladies started talking Sheibani, it triggered something in my brain. I dug through some old SIGINT I'd read, and I came across a bulletin talking about laying groundwork for a northern smuggling pipeline to get weapons from Iran through Kurdish Syria and to Hezbollah in Lebanon. Want to guess who was organizing it?"

"Abu Mustafa al-Sheibani?"

"The one and only."

"Could he have just been crossing the border there to drive up to the meeting?"

Yossi thought a moment. "I suppose he could. But that wouldn't explain the second car, and the pictures at the border show they were definitely together."

Nir tapped his pen on the table a few times. "So we think he went north while the others went back east across the border. That would make sense."

Silence settled around the table, and Nir was sure everyone's mind was racing the same as his. He started tapping his pen again—until Dafna grabbed it and threw it across the room.

An idea that was either brilliant or would get him killed was formulating in Nir's brain. Maybe both.

"You know, there's really only one way we can know if this Sheibani is involved in the attack."

"How's that?" Nicole said.

"I can ask him."

CHAPTER 28

ONE DAY LATER
NEAR BAGHDAD AIRPORT, BAGHDAD, IRAQ—
JANUARY 25, 2020—13:30 / 1:30 P.M. AST

The warehouse was less than half a mile from Baghdad Airport, which made Abbas a little nervous. Surely there was no way anyone could know about his rendezvous or the cargo he was about to pick up, but the last time he'd been here an American UAV had fired Hellfire missiles from the sky and murdered General Soleimani.

There was irony in the situation, though. He was here to pick up UAVs that would soon be employed to kill many others, and, *inshallah*, some Americans would be among them. It would be a just vengeance upon them in the name of the general.

Two of his soldiers had come with him. Mohamed Hassan was driving the battered, tan Toyota pickup, and Omar Ali rode behind Abbas in the back. Battle-tested and loyal to a fault, these two men had been with him from early on in his time with the KSS, and he trusted them completely. Wherever he went, these two men were sure to be close by.

As Hassan pulled up, one of the sliding garage doors began to ascend. An Iraqi man stepped out once it was high enough and walked toward their pickup. From his peripheral vision, Abbas watched as Hassan rested his hand on his Kalashnikov rifle. Abbas reached out and touched Hassan's arm, giving a small shake of his head. Hassan's hand withdrew.

"*As-salamu 'alaykum*," said the man upon reaching Hassan's window.

"*Wa-'alaykum salam*," said Abbas.

"I am Mohamed al-Mohamed. Hurry, please come and follow me. Our friends from the IRGC are a little testy this afternoon." The man said this with a smile and an eyeroll.

"When are they ever not?"

Ali stepped out of the truck with Abbas while Hassan remained in the driver's seat. He always stayed with the vehicle in case there was ever a need to leave quickly as there had been in the past. Numerous times.

"The delay in your arrival has them angry," al-Mohamed said. "They were talking about leaving, but I convinced them to give you a little more time."

"*Shukran*," Abbas said, grateful.

"The tall one looks the meanest, but I worry more about the short one. His eyes are dead."

Abbas just nodded as they made their way through the warehouse toward two ancient IFA

225

W50 trucks that looked like they'd seen action way back in the war with Iran. The IRGC officers stood next to the nearest truck, one bearing the rank of captain and the other first lieutenant. As al-Mohamed said, the captain was tall and the lieutenant was not.

"Why are you late?" the captain asked before al-Mohamed had an opportunity for introductions.

"We were delayed at a security checkpoint."

The captain waited as if he were expecting an apology or some groveling. Abbas wasn't giving it to him, though. For once, when dealing with the IRGC, he was actually in a position of strength. He could imagine the reaction of General Qaani if this man went back to him saying he didn't make the delivery because Abbas had delayed him by 30 minutes.

Finally, the captain said, "Follow me."

They walked to the back of the first truck, which had a large canvas tarp laid over its framework. Pulling back a flap, he revealed that the cargo area was filled with small, black, hard plastic cases.

"One hundred and fifty in this truck and a hundred in the other." The captain pulled out one case and laid it on the ledge of the bed. He flipped clasps on either end, then lifted the top. Inside was a small drone. Abbas recognized it as an Intel Shooting Star. "These are all programmed and ready to go. All you need to do is to lay them out and start the sequence."

Abbas nodded. This was all straightforward so far.

The captain then reached for another, larger case. When he opened it, Abbas saw a bigger, more intricate drone inside, this one encased in foam. Abbas had seen one of these before, but he couldn't place the name.

"This is an Aurelia X6 Standard. It can carry a 5 kilo payload. You have ten of these. Also, at the front of this first truck are two crates with a total of ten 1.4 kilo blocks of C4 surrounded by one kilo of nails and metal balls each. Each one has a detonator also. Once you power them on, they will automatically arm when they reach an altitude of 25 meters. Then, when they descend at their destination, they're programmed to go off at an elevation of 1.3 meters."

The thought both thrilled and appalled Abbas. The devastation would be horrific yet well-deserved.

As the captain closed the cases, the lieutenant gripped Abbas's arm tightly and turned him so they were face-to-face. "I don't have to tell you how important this is. Nor should I need to remind you of the consequences to you if you should fail."

"No, you shouldn't have to. But for some reason you chose to anyway."

"Listen, I don't need to hear from the smart mouth of a desert militia monkey."

"And I don't need the threats of a middle-aged lieutenant."

The officer turned bright red as he snatched the front of Abbas's desert camouflage shirt with both hands.

"Enough!" the captain shouted. "Both of you stand down."

Abbas stepped back. Inside, he was relishing the confrontation with the Iranian. *Seif Abdel Abbas is nobody's desert monkey.*

The captain approached him. "The keys are in the trucks. On this thumb drive is everything you need to know about venue, timing, and operation." He placed a small black retractable drive into Abbas's hand. "If you have any questions, there's also an email process you may employ. But do so only if completely necessary. Any communication from here on out only puts the operation more at risk. Do you have any questions?"

"I don't."

"Then *bismillah.*"

The captain turned and walked away. The lieutenant continued to glare at Abbas. But Abbas held his eyes until the Persian was forced to turn and stride off.

Ali walked up next to him. "Well, he was nice." He lit a cigarette, then offered one to

Abbas, who waved him off just as he always did.

"Persians." Abbas spit on the ground.

Al-Mohamed stepped near. "See, I told you about that short one. He's crazy." He twisted his open hand next to his head.

"You take the other truck," Abbas said. "I want the one with the explosives. That way, if I go out I'll go out with a bang."

Abbas climbed up into the cab. The truck showed every one of its more than four decades of life in its interior. The seats were covered with duct tape, and a large crack angled from the top center of the windshield all the way to the bottom of the passenger side.

Turning the key, however, he was encouraged to hear the big 4-cylinder diesel kick right to life. After a minute or two, it settled into its idle and actually sounded fairly stable. Putting it into gear, Abbas turned the truck around and exited the warehouse. A wave to Hassan brought the pickup behind Ali's truck. He'd drive third in line in case there were any problems with the IFAs along the way.

The mission was still three weeks out, and while that seemed a long time, it really wasn't. He had his team to train. Drills to run. Then there was the travel—a 1,500 km drive to Bandar Lengeh, Iran. From there, they would catch a fishing trawler that would take them across the

Persian Gulf to where they would launch the attack.

Death was coming to the United Arab Emirates. And when it did, it would come in a manner talked about for decades to come.

CHAPTER 29

The moonlit ground was a blur as it raced by 30 meters below. The air pouring through the open door of the Sikorsky UH-60 Yanshuf, the "Owl," was freezing, but Nir soaked it in. It kept him fresh, on edge, ready to go. The helicopter, called a Black Hawk most other places it was employed, was on loan from the 123 Squadron of the IDF, the Desert Birds Squadron, as was the full gear kit he wore. Normally, he liked to go more stealth—try to blend in with the population. This was not that kind of operation.

On his head was a Rabintex ceramic helmet with a Mitznefet desert camouflage covering. Because of the full moon in the cloudless sky, he thought it best that the team try to blend into the ever-present ground rather than the sporadic shadows. On his body was a Marom Dolphin semi-modular plate carrier in case a firefight broke out, but he prayed it wouldn't. On his legs were Axis kneepads, and he wore black Belleville combat boots. Because of where they were going, all flags and Hebrew writing had been removed

231

from his gear. A Jericho 941 9mm hung on his hip, and strapped to his chest was an IMI Micro Galil compact carbine rifle that carried 35 5.56x45mm NATO rounds in its magazine. The four Kidon operators from his team were similarly outfitted, as were the five *Sayeret* special forces troops he'd borrowed from the IDF. They flew in the second Yanshuf behind him.

It had been a ridiculously long journey so far, with way more complication than he'd wanted. Abu Mustafa al-Sheibani had picked the perfect place to hang out and work on his arms smuggling, because it was right on the edge of *you can't get there from here* if *here* meant Israel. It was nearly 1,600 kms to get from the Golan Heights to Al-Hasakah. Sure, they could have parachuted in, but then what? It's pretty hard to parachute back out. The best option was the Yanshuf, but fuel capacity made it impossible.

As Nir had studied a map, a solution came to mind. But a lot of people would have to buy into his idea. The ferry fuel range for a Yanshuf is 2,100 kms if it's set up with its maximum number of fuel tanks. The distance from Turkey's eastern-most Mediterranean coast to Al-Hasakah was 800 kms. Unfortunately, Turkey's President Erdogan was currently not a big fan of Israel, so it would be difficult to say, "Hey, Recep, mind if we stop in to fuel up our helicopters on our covert mission into Syria?"

There was another option, though. Nir had Yossi do a little digging, and it turned out that the *INS Hanit*, an Israeli navy 5-class corvette, was within a day's sailing to the Turkish coast. If they would move within range while still staying in international waters, then the Yanshufs could fly from the 123 Squadron's home at Palmachim Airbase near Rishon LeZion in central Israel, refuel on the *INS Hanit*, then travel east to the target. The fuel window would be tight, but it could work.

Nir took his plan to Efraim Cohen, who then took it to the deputy director, who then took it to the ramsad. Four hours later, Efraim called to let Nir know the plan had been approved. He was given the contacts in the navy and the air force to make it happen, and those contacts, though skeptical, had been fully cooperative.

A voice came through his coms unit. "Five minutes. That's five minutes."

Nir stretched his legs and shook them out. It would be tough to go from four hours of flight time to hitting the ground running, but there was no other choice. He figured they had ten minutes on the ground at the most before the world came crashing down around them.

His surveillance team hadn't left the workroom for two days, spending every moment looking at satellite images and CCTV footage, both of which were sorely lacking in this part of Syria.

But Yossi was able to keep stumbling across sources, and Nicole was ready to hack a way into each. Then Dafna had spotted Abu Mustafa on the CCTV footage from outside a bank. He was getting into a white Range Rover. Now that they had him in a particular location, they were able to use the surrounding cameras to follow his trail. Eventually, the SUV pulled into a compound on the more affluent west side of town, nearer to the river.

After some more digging, Yossi tracked down a neighbor with cameras up on the second floor of his house. The feed was uploaded to the cloud, and Nicole promptly downloaded it onto her computer. Liora and Dafna began keeping vigil. Every now and then they would see Abu Mustafa stepping out of the house for a smoke. At one point, the white Range Rover drove away, and everyone held their breath. But later in the evening it returned, and their target was once again seen in the compound with a cigarette.

"Three minutes. Three minutes."

Nir fought the urge to check his Galil again. But not only had he checked all of his equipment himself, but Yaron had also gone over it as part of their buddy check.

"Okay, men," he said, "we're here for one reason—to take Noblesse back to Israel for a little R and R time." Noblesse, an Israeli brand of cigarettes, was the code name they'd given to

234

Abu Mustafa. "He cannot die in this process or this trip is wasted. And no civilians will be killed during this operation, understood? I will have no collateral damage on my watch."

All the men acknowledged Nir's admonition as the Yanshuf rapidly descended.

"One minute. One minute to target."

Excitement and fear surged through him. Back when he was fulfilling his mandatory service, his sergeant told them, "If you don't feel a little fear, then you're not taking what you're doing seriously enough. In every engagement, there is the possibility that you will die. Use your fear as a motivator to keep you alert so that death doesn't find you or any of your comrades."

Nobody's going to die today. Nobody on my team. Nobody on their team. In and out. Quick and easy.

"Ten . . . nine . . . eight . . . seven . . . six . . . five . . . four . . . three . . . two . . . one!"

The Yanshuf hovered in place ten meters off the ground. Nir and Yaron threw rappelling ropes off the side, then wrapping his gloved hands around the rope, Nir looked Yaron in the eyes before dropping off the helicopter.

CHAPTER 30

AL-HASAKAH, SYRIA—02:40 / 2:40 A.M. EET

Yaron and Nir hit the ground, then dropped to one knee. Seconds later, Nir felt a tap on his shoulder. Dima was with them now too. Nir and the two men jogged to the front door of the house. Meanwhile, the other Yanshuf was on the home's back side dropping four of the IDF soldiers in the rear of the half-acre property. Once that helicopter pulled away, the first Yanshuf would shift to above the roof, where Avi would rappel down. Doron and one of the IDF soldiers would each remain on their respective helicopters in order to man one of the fixed 7.62mm M60 machine guns in case the raiding party received any company from the outside.

When they reached the front door, Nir held up his right hand while looking at the G-Shock watch on his left wrist. Eight seconds later, he brought his hand down and Dima slammed a battering ram into the front door. According to plan, the IDF soldiers were breaching the rear door at the same time. The first blow splintered the reinforced frame, and the second threw the door open. Immediately, the distinctive sound of an AK-47 cut through the air. Dima twisted back out as dust and debris flew from the walls and doorframe.

"Flash-bang!" Nir yelled as he and Yaron each tossed an M84 stun grenade through the open door. Nir closed his eyes, opened his mouth wide, and covered his ears.

Whoomp! Whoomp!

The three men surged through the door, Yaron going right, Dima going left, and Nir taking the center of the room. Directly in front of him was a dazed man in his twenties holding an AK. Nir shot a round into his chest, and he dropped.

So much for no one dying.

Gunfire sounded from the back of the house. The AK-47 reports told him at least one hostile was in the rear engaging the Sayeret special forces.

To his left, he heard Dima fire, then the sound of a body hitting the floor. Nir kept his eyes forward. He'd let them take care of their zones and he'd cover his.

Across the wide entryway was a long hall. To the left of the hall was an open room that looked like a library of sorts. An eating area and the kitchen beyond were to the right.

All was now silent. "SITREP," Nir said. He needed a situation report.

"Jonathan," said the leader of the IDF squad, using their operational designation. "Two hostiles down. Rear area cleared."

"David 4, all clear up top," Avi said.

"David Lead," Nir said. "We've got two hostiles down. Jonathan, proceed through the kitchen and clear through to the front." Then to Dima he said, "David 3, clear the room in front of you. David 2, let's take this hall."

Nir took the lead with Yaron on his back.

Liora's voice crackled through the com. "David Lead, be advised that the satellite is showing possible hostiles inbound mobile from the northwest."

"Dove 1, Dove 2, keep your eyes open," Nir whispered. With two clicks in his ear, the helicopter pilots acknowledged his order.

Nir twisted the handle for the first door on the right and pushed it open. Yaron spun in, gun at the ready. "Clear," he said ten seconds later.

Crossing to the left, Yaron opened that door, and Nir spun in. "Clear."

Back in the hall, Nir saw three more doors ahead.

"David 3, room is clear," Dima said from the library.

"Jonathan, we're cleared," said the second squad.

Stepping to the next room on the right, Nir turned the handle and pushed. Yaron spun in, and gunfire erupted. Yaron dropped to the ground. Nir rounded the corner and fired. An old man flew backward, the rifle he'd been holding clattering to the tile floor.

As Nir ran toward him, he said, "David 2 is down. Jonathan, clear the rest of this hall. David 3, get in here and check on the man down. I have a hostile down, and I think it's Noblesse. Identifying now."

The old Arab was stretching out with his left hand, trying to reach his rifle. His right arm lay useless next to him, the shredded shirt around his shoulder red with blood. Nir used his foot to slide the AK back to where Yaron was on the ground. The old man looked up at him, his face contorted with pain. There was no doubt; this was Noblesse. He had Abu Mustafa, and he had him alive.

As Nir rolled the man so he was facedown, Abu Mustafa cried out in pain. Nir pulled flex-cuffs from his vest and tightened them on the man's wrists. Then he rolled him back over, eliciting more cries.

"Save it, you murdering slug," Nir said in Arabic.

The man's eyes widened as he heard Nir's accent. "You're . . . you're Jews."

"God's chosen people." Nir pulled a field first aid dressing from another Velcroed pocket. "Children of Isaac, not Ishmael. God always did like us best." He pressed the gauze hard into the shoulder wound, causing Abu Mustafa to again cry out. This time his cries were accompanied by some creative curses.

"Pipe down," Nir said. He threw aside the first gauze patch and looked closer at the wound. It was through and through, but it looked like the bullet had done some decent damage on its journey. "You'll live . . . maybe. I guess that depends on how the next few hours go."

"Jonathan, house cleared." The IDF Sayeret team.

Nir linked his arm into Abu Mustafa's left arm and hauled him to his feet. When he turned, he saw that Yaron was also on his feet. He was leaning on Dima's shoulder and was holding his chest.

"You okay?" Nir asked.

"Hurts like a mother. He's a good shot for an old man. Right in the chest. Remind me to buy the IDF gear man a beer."

Machine gunfire erupted from outside the house.

"David Lead, this is Dove 1. We're taking fire. Two trucks with hostiles half a click northwest from your location. We're engaging."

"Dima, you and Yaron bring Noblesse behind, but stay clear of the action," Nir said before catching himself using real names. "David 4 and Jonathan squad, let's go!"

Nir ran out the front door with the Jonathan guys right behind him. Avi was already at the compound's front gate and had it open. They ran toward the sound of the gunfire, with too many AK-47s to be able to differentiate for a count. From above came the clatter of the 7.62mm machine guns raining down death. By the time they neared the battle, both trucks were on fire and bodies surrounded the burning hulks.

"Dove 1 and 2, SITREP," Nir said.

"Dove 1. Clear."

Dove 2 reported in. "Took some hits, but everything looks good so far."

"David 2 and 3 coming up behind with Noblesse."

Nir turned around and saw Yaron and Dima running toward him. Noblesse was over Dima's shoulders in a fireman's carry.

"Dove 1 and 2, bring it down. Let's load up."

Ninety seconds later, both UH-60s lifted off the ground.

CHAPTER 31

Once they had cleared the city, Avi had Yaron pull off his vest and shirt. A bruise was spreading on the left side of his chest. Avi felt around, eliciting a colorful remark from Yaron about his parental heritage.

"You kiss your *ima* with that mouth?" Avi asked. He turned to Nir. "He's got at least a bruised rib. Possibly a break. Can't know for sure without X-rays."

"Better than the alternative. What about him?" Nir nodded toward Noblesse.

Avi shifted over to where Abu Mustafa was buckled into a seat. The old man glared at him as he pulled the shoulder harness away from the wound. He lifted the gauze away, throwing it to the back of the cargo cabin. Abu Mustafa tensed as Avi prodded the damage.

"He'll be fine. The blood flow is slowing. Got to hurt like anything, though. Should I give him some morphine?"

"Not yet," Nir said. "Give me a sec."

A thought had been forming in Nir's mind, and he wanted to process it for a minute. The plan had been to get Noblesse back to Tel Aviv and question him there. The problem was that they were still over enemy territory. Anything could happen between here and Israel, including running out of fuel. The pilots had done all the calculations, but they'd spent nearly 15 minutes in Al-Hasakah. What if the numbers were off now? They'd risked too much, and the information that Abu Mustafa held was far too valuable to chance it.

He made the decision.

Even though he was confident that Abu Mustafa couldn't hear him over the rotor noise, Nir shifted to the opposite side of the cargo cabin.

"Base, you all still connected into our coms?"

"Check, David Lead," replied Liora.

"Okay, I want you to turn us off. I need to go dark for a few minutes."

"Wait, why? Procedure requires that we—"

"Listen, you've just had a malfunction. Do you understand? And I want you to make sure this conversation we're having right now is lost in that malfunction. Got it?"

Nicole's voice came on the coms. "David Lead, what are you planning to—"

"Please, just do as I ask."

There was a pause, then, "Going dark."

"Dove 2, I want the same from you."

"*Root*. Going dark."

Nir slid around so he could put his hand on his pilot's shoulder. "I'd appreciate you not recording what's about to happen."

"This stupid voice recorder has been given me problems all week."

Nir slapped his shoulder, then went back to the cargo pit.

"Drago, I think our friend here needs the Soviet treatment. Will you let him see how high up we are?"

"*Da*." Dima unbuckled, then walked his large frame to where Abu Mustafa sat. He leaned forward and said, "I must break you."

He unbelted the old man and dragged him to the open door of the helicopter. Then kneeling on the man's legs, he held his upper body out into the night air.

"No!" Abu Mustafa struggled to find a way to pull himself back in.

Nir let him hang out there for about 20 seconds, then nodded to Dima, who pulled him in.

"Listen, you terrorist piece of trash. I have no problem letting you take a nose dive out of this helicopter. In fact, I think it might be fun to watch you fly. But I've got a job to do, and that job is to get some information from you."

Abu Mustafa was breathing hard and looking at Nir with hate. "I will never tell you anything, Jew."

"You see, that's my concern. Is this a fool's errand? We're already short on fuel. Lightening the load by 86 kilos may make the difference between us making it or splashing into the water.

244

If you talk to me, I'd be willing to take the risk. If you say you'll never talk . . . well, then . . ."

Nir nodded at Dima, who let Abu Mustafa's upper body drop forward again, hanging free in the icy wind. After 30 seconds, Nir had him pulled back in.

But now Abu Mustafa was smiling. "Do you think I am afraid to die, you Jewish pig? I have served my god faithfully, and now I am ready to die a *shaheed*, a martyr for Allah. Go ahead, throw me out and into the arms of my god."

Nir shook his head. "You know, I was afraid you'd go this way. I didn't want to go Plan B, but Plan B it is. Dima, take him back."

On the surface, Nir was all business. He couldn't show any cracks. Underneath, though, he was a roiling sea of emotions. He'd really hoped he wouldn't have to go this direction. But Abu Mustafa had information that could save the lives of who knew how many people.

While he was training for Caesarea, his instructors drilled a quote into him. It was from a commentary on the Babylonian Talmud by the eleventh century French rabbi, Rashi. While commenting on a passage explaining Exodus 22:1, he wrote, "If someone comes to kill you, rise up and kill him first." This was the justification Nir carried with him when he executed a targeted elimination. The logic made sense to him, as did the morality. However, did *rise up and kill*

245

him first extend to what he was about to do? He wasn't so sure. But he also felt he had no other option.

He crossed to where Dima had sat Abu Mustafa down. "What are your IRGC masters asking you to do?"

Abu Mustafa spit in his face.

Nir wiped the saliva off with his sleeve. He stared in the terrorist's eyes, then pulled back and punched Abu Mustafa's wounded shoulder with all of his might. He punched a second time, then a third. He could feel the already damaged bone splintering and could see the blood starting to flow freely again.

Abu Mustafa cried out, doubling over to try to protect himself. But Nir grabbed him by the hair and lifted his head.

"Tell me, where are you going to attack?"

The man groaned and began to weep. At that moment, he didn't look like a terrorist. He just looked like somebody's grandfather. Nir felt sick to his stomach.

"Tell me, old man. Do something right in your life for once. Save lives instead of taking them."

"Go . . . to . . ."

Nir punched him in the shoulder, then again.

Abu Mustafa screamed. Nir put his hand directly on the man's wound and began to push.

"Tell me, where will you attack?"

A deep groan sounded through the old man's

gritted teeth until he finally shouted, "Abu Dhabi! The UAE! That's all I know! I promise you, that's all I know."

Nir let off the pressure. "When? What is the nature of the attack?"

"Like I said, that is all I know." He was gasping through the pain.

"Come on. They wouldn't keep you out of the details."

The old man sobbed. "I swear to you, I know no more. I went up to Al-Hasakah. The others were to make the arrangements."

"Okay, then who are the others? I know you know that much. Tell me and I'll have my friend there give you some morphine for the pain."

Suddenly, Abu Mustafa lunged forward, driving his forehead into Nir's chest. Nir stumbled backward. Before anyone had a chance to react, the old man crossed the cargo cabin and launched himself out the door.

"No!" Nir yelled.

The old man was gone. Just like that.

The men looked at one another, stunned at what had just happened.

"I'm sorry," Dima said after a moment. "It's my fault. I didn't belt him in when I took him back."

"No, it's not your fault," Nir said. "I should have noticed. I'm lead. It's on me."

He stood hunched over in the cargo area, looking at the door where a puddle of blood had accumulated, then looking at his men.

*What now? What will happen when head-
quarters hears about—*

The voice of Dove 2's pilot interrupted Nir's
thoughts. "David Lead, Dove 2. We've got a
problem."

CHAPTER 32

ur fuel loss is unusually high," Dove 2's pilot said. "When we took fire, our fuel tank must have been nicked. There's no way this bird is making it back to the nest."

Nir put his hand to the back of his neck and looked out the open door. *Is it too late for me to jump after Noblesse? This mission is turning into a fiasco.*

"How long do you have?" Nir asked the pilot.

"Consumption is steadily increasing. I'd estimate 45 minutes to an hour."

"Okay, let's just run it out, then we'll ditch your bird and all pile into this one."

"Negative, sir. That won't work. First, between the two Owls we've got 15 souls on board."

"Fourteen."

"Excuse me, sir, but we've got seven on board with us and you have eight with—"

"We've only got seven. Don't ask."

The pilot paused. "Right. Okay, that still doesn't change the numbers. Capacity on the UH-60 is 11. Even that is pushing it with the distance we're flying and the extra fuel load. Dove 1, check my math on this, but if we fly 30 more minutes, we'll have just enough fuel left in your bird to take the max passenger load of 11."

"Affirmative. Three people aren't making this trip."

Nir slammed his fist into the bulkhead. He saw the print it left and realized he still had the dead man's blood on his hand.

"Boss." Avi tossed him a bottle.

Nir poured water into his hands and then scrubbed them with a rag. He cursed to himself. *Not only am I going to lose a* Yanshuf, *but three men on my team will have to risk their lives in enemy territory for a full day until they can be retrieved after dark.*

He turned to look at his men. They all had their eyes on him.

Nir started to speak, but Avi cut him off. "Listen, Nir, you need to get back to Tel Aviv. Dima, Doron, and I will stay behind until another bird comes to pick us up."

"You're not staying without me," Yaron said, the redness of his face and mostly shaved head showing his anger at being left out. Avi reached over and slapped him on the chest, and Yaron doubled over in pain.

"Sorry, *achi*," Avi said. "This isn't your fight."

Yaron turned his head to glare at his teammate.

Nir shook his head. "Nobody is staying behind without me. This is my operation. First man off, last man on—all that tough guy military leadership stuff." When Avi and Dima started to protest, Nir held up his hand. "Listen, you guys can argue and give your reasons if it will make you feel better, but I've already decided. Avi, you take rib-man there and get him back to Tel Aviv to get looked at. Doron, you're our coms guy. I want you with me."

"*Root.*" Doron rose to start collecting the needed gear.

"Dima, I want you there in case anything needs to be broken."

Dima smiled, then also stood to pack up.

"We all good?"

Everyone gave their affirmation, although Avi looked unhappy with the decision.

"Okay, everybody listening?"

"Dove 1."

"Dove 2. By the way, you have five men here who are ready to stay behind with you."

"I wouldn't expect anything different from Sayeret. I'd take them up on it, except I want to minimize the number we're putting at risk. Here's the plan. Fifteen minutes before you have to ditch the bird, I want us down on the ground. Preferably not in some militia's backyard. Then fly the bird west as far as you can and put it down. Before you load onto Dove 1, I want you to set it up to blow in spectacular fashion. See if you can get the attention of every angry Arab in the area. I want them going that way instead of our way. Oh, that reminds me . . ." Nir turned to the pilot. "Can you get our logistics team back on?"

"*Root.*"

A moment later, he heard Liora's voice. "We're back."

Nir took a moment to lay out the situation. "We're going to need landing zones. So, as soon as they drop us, I want you guys looking at the satellite footage for three alternative LZs. We'll try to stay near where we're dropped off, but I want options in case we get company."

"Will do," Liora said.

Nir looked at Avi. "I want you in charge of the ops side. It's your job to get us back out. Base, I'm giving the goye command of logistics. We learned two things from Noblesse. First, he all but confirmed that Kata'ib Sayyid al-Shuhada is running the operation. At least he didn't deny knowledge of it, which for me is good enough. Second, we know the attack will be in Abu Dhabi. But that's all we know. Noblesse won't be giving us any more information. Run it up the chain immediately. We're going to need some high-powered liaising to see if UAE will even let us help them with this. Our friendship with them is better, but this will ask more of the relationship than they've ever given. They may let us run with it, they may relegate us to an advisory position, or they may shut us out completely."

"On it," Nicole, the goye, said, then added, "Be careful."

Nir smiled, but he wasn't sure why. He'd just lost his prisoner out the door in a 100-foot swan dive. He was about to be left behind deep inside of Syria. Yet Nicole's words of concern felt good. He looked at Dima, who was grinning at him with one eyebrow raised.

"Shut up," Nir said.

Thirty minutes later, Dove 1 touched down in the Syrian wilderness. Nir, Dima, and Doron jumped out and ran free of the rotor's wash. Immediately, the bird took off. Within 20 seconds it was out of both sight and sound.

The three men ran to a small cluster of boulders and knelt. The landscape was more wilderness than desert. White wormwood, saltbush, silver feather grass, and saltwort grew in clumps on the dirt and rock-covered ground. Here and there a tamarisk tree spread its sparsely covered branches.

At least it's slightly better than the surface of the moon.

The three men waited silently, trying to discern any noises that might be man-made. They still wore their full gear, having topped off their magazines, and they'd each added two bladders of water and a handful of energy bars.

Doron tapped Nir and pointed west. About 40 meters away sat two large stones big enough to give both cover and shade during the day. Nir nodded, tapped Dima, and the three sprinted to the rocks. Once there, they hit the ground and listened. After a minute, they felt comfortable enough to relax just a bit.

They all sat up, and Nir opened a protein bar. He thought they'd found the best cover in the area, but if anyone happened to come around, it wouldn't be too difficult to spot them. Thankfully, the blunt-nosed vipers northern Syria was famous for were one enemy they wouldn't have to worry about. The January daytime temperature wouldn't get high enough for them to come slithering out of their holes.

He finished his bar in three bites, then stuffed the wrapper back into his vest. "I'm going to go up on the rise and see if I can spot anything."

Dima shifted. "I'll come with you."

The two men ran forward in a low crouch, then up on top of the small hill, they laid flat. Thankfully, they saw no signs of life. One site made Nir's heart sink, though. A hundred yards ahead the light of the full moon revealed a road. It wasn't paved. It wasn't even fully cut. But like spotting a game trail when hunting, he saw evidence that clearly told him vehicles passed through this area—and on a regular basis.

CHAPTER 33

MOSSAD HEADQUARTERS, TEL AVIV, ISRAEL— 04:45 / 4:45 A.M. IST

Update," Nicole said to the logistics team. Even though Nir had put her in charge, she sat in her usual place, leaving his chair at the head of the conference table empty.

Liora spoke first. "Landing zones have been communicated to Avi and to Efraim. Efraim is running the LZs up the IDF chain."

Yossi was next. "I'm working on possible attack targets in Abu Dhabi that are both drone accessible and high impact. So far I have it narrowed down to about 10,000."

"Wow, good work." Dafna laughed.

"Exactly. We really need more information. A tip or an informant or a neon sign from God."

"Are we even sure it's Abu Dhabi?" Liora asked. "I don't know what Nir did to Noblesse to get the information from him, but statements under physical duress are notably unreliable."

Nicole nodded. "You're exactly right. But Nir was able to confirm that the perpetrators are Kata'ib Sayyid al-Shuhada and that Noblesse claimed the attack would be in Abu Dhabi. I don't know why we can't question Noblesse anymore. Unfortunately, right now, this is all we have."

She, too, was frustrated that Nir had lost Abu Mustafa to death or escape or whatever. But that was water under the bridge, and they had to work with what they were given. "I have to say that UAE makes sense. It fits what we've already been told. Unless Nir tipped him off that we knew about it being a Gulf State attack, Noblesse could have indicated anywhere. In fact, he likely would have said someplace else—Iraq or Saudi Arabia or even here. That he placed the attack in UAE is too serendipitous to believe he made that up."

"What is *serendipitous?*" Yossi asked.

The question took Nicole off guard. "Uh . . . fortunate, lucky."

"*Bar mazal*," Lahav said.

Yossi nodded. "Ah, got it. You throw me off with your big fancy English words, Nicole."

"Sorry." Then with a grin she added, "I'll try to speak English on a level that even you can understand."

"Ooh" sounded around the table.

"Listen, I speak Hebrew, a language with generation upon generation of culture behind it." Yossi had taken on a mock professorial tone.

"I speak English, the language of world commerce." Nicole mimicked his tone.

"Ah, but Hebrew is the language of history."

"And yet your language still hasn't evolved to having vowels."

They all laughed, with Dafna adding in a "Fair point."

"Seriously, my apologies, Yossi. Please let me know if I accidentally drop in other words like that. I'm so appreciative that you all are accommodating my weak Hebrew skills. So anyway, I think the UAE would have been too improbable for him to mention if it weren't true."

Lahav jumped in. "I just don't get Abu Dhabi, though. Dubai would make so much more sense to me, especially if they're looking to make a statement."

"Why do you say that?" asked Nicole.

"I don't know. I guess it's like the reason they went for the World Trade Center on 9/11 instead of the Empire State Building. Both would cause major damage and shake the world. But the World Trade Center represented everything the radical Islamists hate about America and the West. If you're looking just to hurt people, take out the Empire State. If you want to communicate a message, go after the World Trade Center."

"Interesting." Nicole took a moment to think about his words. Abu Dhabi had to be the team's focus, because that was the limit of their extant information. But the man's reasoning was sound. "Lahav, I want you to deep dive Dubai. I've got no direction for you except to tell you to figure out if anything is behind your hunch. Does anybody have anything else?"

Her phone rang. The contact information showed *Efraim Cohen.*

"Hang on a sec," she said to the team, then stepped away from the table. "Hi, Efraim."

"Nicole, first, the higher ups tell me we're still about three hours away from being able to contact the government of the UAE. So for now, whatever you do, do it discreetly."

"Got it."

"So we just had some interesting HUMINT come through." He indicated a human intelligence source. "One of our men at Baghdad Airport said that a cargo jet from Iran landed and pulled into a hangar four days ago. He wasn't in for the off-load, but he was told it mostly contained the usual stash—guns, mortars, rockets, all that kind of stuff. But the IRGC had everyone clear out of the hangar for one part of the cargo. Our informant said that, from his vantage point across the tarmac, he could see two vintage military trucks pull in. Fifteen minutes later, they pulled back out and everyone was allowed back in to finish the off-load."

"What does he think was loaded onto the trucks?"

"Nobody knows. But our man said he'd never seen that happen before. We've got people looking into it, and I thought you might want to look also."

"Yeah, definitely. Thanks. Oh, before I let you go, will there be any trouble getting Nir, Dima, and Doron out?" She hoped the worry didn't come through her voice too strongly.

"No, we've already got another Yanshuf on the way to the *Hanit*. Once the helicopter with Yaron and Avi refuels on the ship and takes off, this one will land on *Hanit* and wait for nightfall. As long as Nir and the guys can stay out of sight, it shouldn't be a problem."

Her relief quickly went away when she heard Efraim sigh. "But Nir has got problems when he comes back. The higher ups want to know what happened to Abu Mustafa. Do you know?"

"I don't." But she thought she probably wouldn't tell him if she did. That was Nir's purview.

"Well, if it turns out Nir took justice into his own hands, he could be facing some serious repercussions."

She was worried about what Nir had done too. Even though he'd assassinated people in the past, those operations had been sanctioned, having gone through an approval process. If he'd killed Abu Mustafa while the man was a prisoner, that felt a lot more like murder.

"Okay, thanks for letting me know about the airport."

She disconnected the call.

Lord, protect Nir. Protect him along with Dima and Doron while they wait for rescue. And protect Nir from whatever might be facing him when he comes back. And give me wisdom as I lead this team in trying to uncover this plot. I don't feel adequate for this, and You know how I struggle with the absurdity of being a South African woman serving in the Israeli Mossad. But I trust You. I trust that You have a plan and have placed me in this position for Your purposes.

When she walked back to the table, the team was in a heated debate. She was glad to hear their passion. They were really taking this seriously. Then she heard the topic.

"Oh, please," Yossi said. "He only won because of how he looks and because he shows his backside in the video."

"Duncan Laurence has an amazing voice," Liora put in.

"And an amazing backside," Dafna added.

Yossi wasn't giving up. "I can remember back when men sang like men and didn't whine their way through their songs."

Eurovision.

Nicole was sick to death of hearing about Eurovision. Once a year, 40 or more countries from Europe, Western Asia, and Northern Africa competed to find the best song of the year. The 2018 winner was Netta Barzilai from central

Israel with her song "Toy." That victory brought the next year's contest to the home country of the winner. Therefore, last May's 2019 contest was held in Tel Aviv. Now Eurovision seemed to be the topic that wouldn't go away.

"I've heard the same song with different words sung by a hundred different artists a hundred different ways." Yossi seemed determined to win this argument.

"Let's get a Gentile perspective," Dafna said.

They all looked to Nicole.

She sighed. "First, I am not going to comment on Duncan Laurence's backside. His song was fine, but it was nothing compared to Netta's. Anyone who can win a songwriting contest while clucking like a chicken . . . I've got to give the girl major props. She set the bar high, and this year's contestants didn't even try to make the jump."

"Ooh, nice analogy. Girl's got wisdom," Liora said.

"Like a female *goy* Solomon," Dafna added.

Nicole shook her head. She put up with this kind of off-topic banter because it helped keep the millennials and Gen Z's on the team sane. Too much intensity all the time can greatly damage morale and productivity. Let them have a little fun now and then and they'll work harder, longer, and more efficiently.

"Now, can we get back to business?" she asked.

She filled the team in on Efraim's news. "I want to find those trucks. I have no idea what was on them, but they could end up being our only lead to the KSS. I know our satellite footage is spotty, so I'll work on borrowing footage from our friends in the CIA, MI6, and the Guoanbu. I'll funnel it to you as soon as I get it."

"Hacking into the Chinese secret service. Oh, the irony." Dafna laughed.

"Yossi, you look for anything out there regarding KSS location, leadership, connections, patterns—everything. Lahav, like we said earlier, you take a little digital journey to Dubai and see what you come up with. *Yalla*, let's go."

They all applauded Nicole's use of Hebrew slang before leaving for their workstations. She remained at the table. It seemed nearly impossible to find where this militia was hiding in Iraq. They were looking for a compound or a camp maybe an acre square in a country that was as big as Germany with the Netherlands, Belgium, and a little bit of France and Austria thrown in. But they had no choice. They had to track them down.

You know where they are, Lord. Please, help us find them.

CHAPTER 34

KATA'IB SAYYID AL-SHUHADA HEADQUARTERS, AL DIWANIYAH, IRAQ—07:25 / 7:25 A.M. AST

It was obvious that Falih Kazali was agitated. When Abbas walked into his office, he'd found the man pacing with the aid of a gnarled mesquite cane.

Looking around, Abbas saw the room was sparsely furnished with nothing personal to the leader. But, of course, the Kata'ib Sayyid al-Shuhada headquarters in Al Diwaniyah, 195 kms south of Baghdad, was just one of a number of KSS HQs. The militia worked in well over a dozen other satellite buildings, including in Kirkuk, Najaf Ashraf, Nasiriyah, and the holy city of Karbala. For now they'd set up here because of its proximity to the capital city and its location near the main route to Basrah and the Shalamcheh border crossing just to its east that led to Iran.

"Abu Mustafa has been taken," blurted the old man.

Abbas was stunned. He dropped into a chair, trying to process the information. "What? How? By whom?"

"He was still in Al-Hasakah. Everyone else was

killed in the house, as were some of our brothers who had come to his aid. Abu Mustafa's body was never found, so the assumption is that he was taken."

"Was it the Kurds or the Americans or the Russians?"

"Why would the Russians take him? Use your brain."

"Why do the Russians do anything?" Then Abbas calmed himself. "How did it happen?"

"Witnesses said there were two UH-60 helicopters. The enemy rappelled in. There was gunfire. Meanwhile, two trucks with soldiers from the Liwa al-Imam al-Baqir militia were returning from patrol. They heard the gunfire and came to investigate. All of them perished as martyrs. The assault team ran out of the house toward the helicopters, and one of them was carrying a person over his shoulders. We can only assume that was Abu Mustafa."

"Are the witnesses sure they were UH-60s?"

"One used to be a member of the Syrian army. He recognized the aircraft."

Abbas thought for a moment. "The Kurds don't have them. Neither do the Russians. As far as I know, the only ones near us with UH-60s are the Saudis, Jordan, Americans, and some of the Gulf nations."

"Like the UAE?"

Abbas shook his head. "Yes, like the UAE, but

this is not like them. Maybe the Saudis, maybe Jordan, but this sounds more like something the Americans would do."

"Could it be the Israelis?"

"No, there's no way to get a Sikorsky from Israel to northern Syria. I would bet it was either the Americans or the Saudis. Ultimately, it is no matter. The operation is compromised. We have to abort."

"Absolutely not!" Kazali drove his cane into the floor. "We are not compromised. Abu Mustafa would not have talked."

"Everybody talks eventually. You know that. If it is the Americans, then the process might take longer because of their legislated rules. However, if it is the Saudis, then we have to assume that he has told or will soon tell them everything."

"Which is . . ." Kazali shifted to his desk and sat.

Abbas moved from his seat by the door to a sparsely padded metal chair on the desk's opposite side. "I don't follow what you're asking."

"What exactly did Abu Mustafa know? He knew there would be an attack. He knew it would be in Abu Dhabi. Beyond that, he knew nothing. He and I remained with General Qaani while you went with General Soltani into the next room for the details. Since then, Abu Mustafa has not been with us. Besides that, he was in Al-Hasakah working on his Sheibani smuggling network for the IRGC. I think it is safe to assume that he was picked up because of that work rather than the UAE attack. If they break him, it will be to gather that information."

Abbas took a moment to mull over the old man's words. What he was saying made sense. But could they still take that risk? What if, in the midst of the interrogation regarding the smuggling, he let slip about the attack?

"We need to advance our time line," he said. "We need to leave now. Once we're in Iran, we won't have to worry about some helicopters suddenly appearing over Al Diwaniyah the way they appeared over Al-Hasakah."

Kazali nodded. "Very well. I will initiate attempts to make communication with the IRGC. As you know, that is not always easy."

"Don't bother. The IRGC captain gave me an email process for contacting him in case there was a serious issue. I'd call this a serious issue."

The old man had calmed down by now, and he seemed to be gaining back his confidence. "Good, good. And what about the third truck? Weren't you supposed to retrieve it soon?"

The third truck. He hadn't thought about that. "I'll tell them I can pick it up across the border, or they can deliver it to me once I arrive in Bandar Lengeh."

Kazali shook his head. "Good luck with that.

We both know how much our Persian friends like us changing their plans."

"They will have to deal with it. We're risking our lives for them by carrying out their plan."

"Correction, my friend." Kazali leaned forward, pointing at Abbas. "We are risking our lives for Allah. And if it is for him, then it isn't really a risk. *Inshallah*, God will do what God will do." He leaned back in his chair as if to emphasize his point.

Abbas knew he was right, but it grated on him when the old man pulled out the *Inshallah* "God willing" card when he was just trying to logically think through all the possibilities and eventualities of a plan. Yes, Allah was in control. But hadn't he created them with minds to think?

Yet this was not the time to air grievances. There was too much to do. "Yes, *Inshallah*," he said, rising to his feet.

As he left Kazali's office, he began to work through a checklist of all that needed to be accomplished if they were going to pull out the next day. Despite that expanding list, he couldn't keep his mind from drifting to the fact that Abu Mustafa was gone. The second in command of the KSS had been taken, and that left an important vacancy. Who else was there to fill it if not him? And if Kazali continued on his downward health decline, could it be much longer before death or infirmity would remove him from his position?

If only Abbas could survive these next few weeks, the future he'd dreamed of would start coming together.

CHAPTER 35

Doron was on watch while Dima and Nir rested in the shade of the boulders. Although the sunshine was only occasionally blocked by the thin clouds, the temperature didn't rise far beyond its pre-dawn low when it was near freezing. Nir was thankful for every article of clothing he wore, although ultimately it still wasn't enough to keep from sporadically slipping into shivering fits.

So the one positive that came from the small arms fire suddenly sounding across the wilderness, pulling Nir from his half-asleep stupor, was that it kicked his adrenaline into high gear. For the first time since he left the helicopter, he was warm.

"I think it's coming from that direction," Doron said, pointing toward the hill that overlooked the road.

Dima scooted up next to them. "Sounds like a lot of AKs, but there are others. I would bet they're M4s."

"Kurds," Nir said.

"I'm thinking so," Doron said. "Guess they're having a slight disagreement with one of the militias or with the Syrian army."

It was obvious to Nir by the sound of the gunfire that the maybe-Kurds were outnumbered by the maybe-army-or-militia. "I want to go have a look."

Doron looked at him like he was crazy. "Why? If we keep ourselves tucked away down here, there's little chance of being discovered."

"Maybe. But what if the fight comes this direction? Or what if a squad of AK-toting bad guys decides to go for a little off-road excursion over that hill? We're sitting ducks. Worse, we're blind sitting ducks because we don't know what we're up against. More information is better than less information."

"Can't argue with that," Dima said.

"I could argue it," Doron put in. "But that's just because I'm contrary by nature."

Nir laughed. "Okay, guys, *yalla*, let's keep it low and tight."

The three men left their cover and trotted toward the hill. When they got near the top, they dropped to the ground. Once they'd belly-crawled to the crest, the situation took shape below. Nir breathed a sigh of relief. Four pickup trucks definitely not army grade government issue were parked in a line on either side of the road. He'd much rather face these militia fighters than Syrian troops. He counted 16 armed men behind the cover of the trucks and surrounding rocks. Two of the trucks had Russian-made PKM machine guns mounted in the bed. Both guns had a man pulling the trigger and another reloading. Nir knew those rifles could fire 650 rounds of 7.62x54mmR per minute, which meant they could empty their hundred-round cartridge cans in just over nine seconds.

Whoever they're firing at will get chewed up.

The ones on the receiving end of the fire were hard to make out. Nir pulled a pair of Steiner binoculars from his vest and looked down the crude road. At least three people were firing back.

"Do you recognize them?" he asked Doron, who was also looking through a pair of binoculars.

"Definitely Kurds. Trying to make out their insignia. Looks like a yellow pennant with a red star. If so, they're the People's Protection Unit."

"That means they're Democratic Union Party. Anti-Assad—"

"Depending on the day of the week," Doron said.

He was exactly right. The belief in Israel was that, like the Palestinians, the Kurds never missed an opportunity to miss an opportunity. If they would just band together, they would be a powerful force and could legitimately push for their own sovereign state. Instead, they split themselves into faction after faction—the two biggest groups the Kurdistan Democratic Party and the Patriotic Union of Kurdistan. The KDP was led by former president of the Kurdistan Region, Masoud Barzani, and was very much separatist in its leanings. The PUK was led by former Iraqi president Jalal Talabani. Many despised them, viewing them as collaborators. But these two Kurdish parties loathed each other.

This internecine conflict was the nature of much of the Middle East. In this part of the world, it was about tribes, not countries. Many of the nations didn't even exist until after World War I. That was when the European victors divided up the former Ottoman Empire, and countries like Iraq, Saudi Arabia, and Jordan were born. But no matter what lines you drew on a map, it didn't change people's loyalty to their tribes and territories. This group of Kurds in front of them was just another of the factions— another one of the tribal parties who would align themselves with you when your agenda fit theirs and shoot you when it didn't. If you wanted to know why the Kurds would likely never have their own state, it was because the biggest enemies of the Kurds were the Kurds.

"Well, one thing we do know is that today they're anti-militia," Nir said. "And it's looking like it will cost them their lives."

The three men continued watching the battle. Two of the militia fell in the fight, but judging by the rate of fire, the odds were still strongly stacked against the Kurds.

"We should help them," Dima said.

Doran responded with a quick, "It's not our fight."

After a few moments, Nir had decided. "I agree with Dima." Then when Doron gave him a dubious look, he added, "Hear me out. Listen, if these militia guys come our direction, it's three against 16 as it stands right now. Plus they've got those mounted PKMs. We'd be vulture food in seconds. But if we team up with our Kurdish friends, it will be 16 against us three plus at least four of them that I've been able to see. We've got them fully flanked, and with our element of surprise, our odds are a whole lot better."

"And what if our, as you put it, *Kurdish friends* then come after us?"

"That would be both rude and quite unfortunate for them," Nir said with a wink.

"I like it," Dima said.

"Of course you do, Drago." Doron rolled his eyes. "You get to shoot people."

Nir said, "Doron, I really think it's the smart play."

"*Sababa*, I'm in. How do you want to do it?"

"They've been firing their AKs and listening to the clatter of the PKM for at least five minutes now. They're half-deaf. Put your Galils on single shot. Let's pick our targets and snipe them when the PKM is firing and let it cover the sound of our shots. I'll be one, Doron two, and, Dima,

273

you're three. Let's start with that group behind the far truck. The far target is one, next to him is two, then three. I'll count five, then we shoot."

The men all lined up the targets in their sites. It was somewhat of a long shot, but not out of any of their ranges. The PKM opened up again.

Nir counted. "One . . . two . . . three . . . four . . . five." They depressed their triggers, and their targets dropped. None of the other militia fighters noticed the sound of their shots.

"Okay, mesquite tree is one, then boulder is two and three. Ready—one . . . two . . . three . . . four . . . five."

Three more militia met their Maker. But this time one of the fighters saw them drop. He called out to the others, and they began looking around. The Kidon agents flattened. All firing from the militia stopped. Nir assumed it was because they were trying to find the location of the new attackers. He also noticed the gunfire from the Kurds had halted too. He hoped it was because they were advancing their position as opposed to running away.

M4 shots rang out, closer than before. *There are my Kurdish* chaverim.

The AKs started firing again.

"Okay, they're obviously on to us. On five we take out the PKMs."

"*Root*," said the other two men.

"One . . . two . . . three . . . four . . . five." They

popped up to take aim, but the trucks were gone.

"Right! Right!" cried Doron. To the right, both trucks had looped around and were on their way up the hill. The three men opened fire, and the windshield of the nearest truck shattered. It swerved and began rolling sideways down the hill. The two men in the rear were thrown out. One landed in the path of the tumbling truck and was crushed. The other's life ended due to a round from Nir's rifle.

The second truck kept coming. The militia fighter manning the PKM pulled the trigger, and the gun started shooting out its large rounds. But the bumps from the moving truck kept his aim off. Suddenly, the front of his head exploded out their direction, and he dropped into the bed. Several rounds from Dima's Galil found the driver, and the truck rolled to a stop.

The three men ran toward the truck and found the loader also dead in the bed.

Let's hear it for the Kurds!

Dima and Doron jumped up into the back. Dima swiveled the machine gun around and Doron attached a new ammo box. The gun began firing, dropping fighter after fighter. Nir could see the Kurds now. There were six of them, and they were charging the militia. Soon, the last of the terrorist fighters were down.

Dima and Doron jumped out of the truck. Guns at the ready, the three made their way down to where the Kurds were looking for any threats that still existed. When they spotted the men coming toward them, they all lined up their sites on the Kidon agents.

"Drop your weapons," their commander called out in Arabic, "or I will put bullets through your heads."

CHAPTER 36

Nir kept his gun leveled at the Kurdish commander. Out of his peripheral vision, he saw Doran and Dima raise their weapons to site level.

Nir answered him in Arabic. "That's not going to happen, *sadiq*. It would be a shame for us to have to kill you after we just saved your life."

"There are more of us than of you. You would be dead before you could take us all down."

" *'Ana asif*," Nir said, his tone apologetic. "You misunderstood. When I said we would have to kill you, the *you* was singular, not plural."

The Kurd stared at Nir, then broke into laughter. "You are funny, *sadiq*. And you are right. You did come to our aid. We are thankful." He turned to his men. "Put your weapons down. We are among friends."

Once all of their weapons were lowered, Nir and his men followed suit.

"I am Major Mustafa Nurettin of the People's Protection Unit. This is my second in command, Lieutenant Murat Erdal. We were on patrol when we stumbled across this Hay'at Tahrir al-Sham trash. They had us pinned down, and it looked like we were done for. Then suddenly, Allah sent us angels from the desert. Imagine now my surprise when I learn that our angels are Israelis."

"And after I worked so hard on my Jordanian Arabic accent," Nir said.

Again, Major Nurettin laughed. "You really are funny. Now, may I ask what three Israeli soldiers are doing in the middle of northern Syria?"

"You may ask, but I'm afraid I cannot give you an answer."

"Interesting." Nurettin tapped his chin. "You are dressed as if you are IDF, but your words are cryptic like you are Mossad."

Nir gave nothing away with his face.

Nurettin smiled. "You also keep silent as if you are Mossad. But be that as it may, we are in your debt. Our camp is near here. May I invite you for some warmth and a hot meal?"

Nir looked at his men, who both shrugged their shoulders. It certainly could be a trap. But if they'd wanted to kill or capture Nir and his men, they could have attempted it while they were still approaching. Turning back, he said, "Thank you for your hospitality. We will take you up on it." *It's a risk but one hopefully worth taking.*

Nir followed the major and the lieutenant down the road to where they'd pulled a desert-camouflaged Humvee behind a low rise. The four other Kurdish soldiers stayed behind, no doubt to riffle through the bodies, collect all the weapons, and confiscate the three remaining functional pickups. Nurettin invited Nir to sit in the front passenger seat while he drove.

As they traveled down the bumpy road, the major regaled Nir with stories of his battles against the militias of the Islamic State and with his reasons why the Turks, the Iranians, the Iraqis, and the Patriotic Union of Kurdistan could never be trusted. The Americans could be trusted until they changed their minds and the Russians only when goats sprouted wings.

When they arrived at the small, tented camp, Nir was impressed with the quality of the vehicles, the weapons, and the camp equipment—all, he was sure, courtesy of the U.S. government. Two lambs were roasting over a fire pit, causing his stomach to remind him that he hadn't eaten anything of substance for almost a full day.

Major Nurettin escorted them into a large tent with cushions spread around. In the middle was a coal stove putting out quite a bit of heat. He invited the Israelis to make themselves comfortable. He excused himself momentarily, returning in seconds.

"I have to report our incident, but I have instructed my men to refer to you as nomads if anyone should ask. If I were to talk about finding three Israelis wandering in the wilderness, the next thing you know people would start expecting to find manna every morning."

Nir laughed, more because he liked this guy than due to the quality of the humor.

Nurettin continued. "Besides, massive paperwork always accompanies the word *Israel*. An incident like this would have me writing reports for the next six months."

"I appreciate your discretion," Nir said.

"May I ask you one question? Where are you going from here? Do you need to be taken someplace?"

"Thank you, but no. We have a ride coming tonight."

The major looked like he wanted to ask more, but he held back. "I'll return soon. In the meantime, please enjoy a meal."

"Your hospitality is unmatched," Nir said.

"Of course. I am Kurdish."

After the major left and the men had relaxed on the cushions, Nir put in a call to logistics headquarters.

"How are you?" Nicole asked upon answering.

"We're fine. Interesting day. I'll tell you about it when we're home. I need you to scout a new LZ for us. We are at 36°35'35"N by 39°42'24"E. I'll let our hosts know that the Yanshuf is coming in."

"Your hosts? Where are you?" she asked as the tent flaps opened and dishes of food were carried in.

"I don't know for sure. But it sure smells delicious here. Any leads there?"

"We're making progress, but it's nothing that can't wait until you're back. Keep yourself safe. We'll see you tomorrow."

"*Root*. Out."

The star of the show, the lamb, was prominently displayed and roasted to a juicy perfection. In the surrounding dishes were salads, pilaf, dolmas, and flat bread. Partway through the meal, Major Nurettin came in accompanied by Lieutenant Erdal. The lieutenant carried a tureen filled with a white concoction he called *dew*. It was a yogurt-based drink with salt and a hint of mint. Nir was dubious of it until he tried it. His first glass was followed by two more.

When the major inquired about their departure, Nir let him know about the UH-60 that would arrive a few hours after dark.

Nurettin said, "You are my guests until then. Feel free to rest or walk around. I would only ask that you refrain from entering our command tent."

"Of course. And I hope to repay your hospitality one day."

"Nonsense," scoffed the major. "It is I who am indebted to you. I will give you a way to contact me. Please do not hesitate to call should you ever need my help."

Nir thanked him, and the major and the lieutenant left the tent.

Dima ate an amazing amount of food only to outdo himself when the baklava and date cookies arrived later in the evening. Doron ate little, never fully trusting the situation they found themselves in. Nir was just glad to be out of the cold and near the coal stove.

Night fell around 18:30, and it was nearing two hours before midnight by the time they heard the rotors of the Yanshuf. With a parting salute, Nir and his men said goodbye to their hosts and climbed on board the helicopter, which had set down just outside the perimeter of the camp. It took two and a half hours to get them to the *INS Hanit* for refueling, then another three hours to get home.

By the time Nir climbed into his bed in Tel Aviv, the sun was just coming up.

CHAPTER 37

The logistics team whooped and applauded when Nir walked into the workroom. Embarrassed, Nir said, "Yeah, yeah, meeting in ten."

He felt Nicole's gaze on him before he even turned her way. Sure enough, those blue eyes were locked on him. She had a concerned smile on her face. He nodded his reassurance, then turned toward his office.

No sooner had he sat behind his desk than his phone rang.

"Nir, welcome home," Efraim said. "Sounds like you had a bit of an adventure."

"Made a few enemies, made a few friends. What's up?"

"Ramsad wants to see you at one o'clock. He won't be alone."

"Lovely."

"I know. I don't think it will be pretty. Something about prisoners jumping out of helicopter doors doesn't sit too well with the higher ups."

Nir leaned his head into his hand and rubbed his eyes. "Guess it's one of those *you had to be there* things."

"Yeah, *achi*, I don't think that's going to play with the ramsad."

"Got any other good news?"

Efraim chuckled. "Don't worry. You'll survive this. I wouldn't be surprised if old Ira has a few helicopter dives in his past. He's got to put on a show—you know, how this should never happen—but I'm guessing that deep down he wishes he'd been there holding the door open."

Ira Katz was a former Caesarea operative. Now in his late seventies, he'd been part of Operation Wrath of God. That targeted elimination program had been sanctioned by then Prime Minister Golda Meir to take out all the Black September terrorists who were involved in the massacre of 11 members of the Israeli Olympic Team at the Munich games. At heart, Katz was a warrior. But he was also one of those rare breeds able to function equally well whether their hand held a gun or a pen.

The two men ended their call, then Nir shuffled a few things around on his desk, too distracted to get any work done.

"Forget it," he said, then left his office. He walked over to Dafna and handed her a thumb drive. "Load this up and have it ready. I'll need it for the team meeting."

"You got it."

He considered walking around and checking out what everyone was doing, but then he thought better of it. He didn't want to be a distraction. Instead, he sat down at the head of the conference table and watched the clock tick its way around until the ten minutes were up.

"Bring it in," he said.

No one moved.

"Just a sec, boss," called Liora.

Then somebody did get up and walk toward the table. It was Lahav.

"Perfect," Nir said under his breath.

"Hey, boss, good to have you back. Do you know what the biggest drone in the world is? I'll tell you. It's the Ravn X. Its wingspan is more than 18 meters and it weighs 25,000 kgs. They're developing it to launch satellites. Imagine that—a drone launching a satellite. And the smallest drones are called mini-drones or micro-drones. As you can imagine, they're designed for stealth. They're even working on ones that look and move like insects. Can you believe it? You smush a mosquito, and rather than seeing blood you see a tiny microchip. That's crazy. Don't you think that's crazy?"

"Yeah, that's crazy." Nir desperately hoped the rest of the team would get there soon.

"I know. It's totally crazy. The drones the IDF uses are called the Hermes 450 and are made by Elbit Systems out of Haifa. They can be used for surveillance and communications and—"

"Welcome back, Nir," Nicole said, sitting down at the table.

"Hey, Nicole," Lahav said as Nir mouthed the words *thank you* to her, "do you know what the biggest drone in the world is? It's the—"

"The Ravn X. It's 18 meters and weighs 25,000 kgs. Much bigger than our Hermes 450s that are made by Elbit Systems out of Haifa."

Lahav's face spread into an enormous smile. "Wow! I didn't know you knew so much about drones!"

"I don't." She stared at him while he tried to figure out what she was saying. Then his smile turned into a sheepish grin.

"Was my voice carrying again?"

"Yeah, just a bit. If you could dial it back some more like we talked about, that would be great."

By now, the rest of the team was scooting up to the table.

Nir started the meeting. "Okay, everyone. First thing, the folks in the big offices have now given us a name." He nodded to Dafna, who pressed a button on her remote. *Operation Joktan* appeared on their large monitor.

"Operation Joktan," Nicole read.

Lahav jumped in. "No, Joktan is pronounced with a *Y* sound, not a *J*. You see, with the Hebrew language—"

"We don't need a full explanation," Nir said.

"Your language is so weird."

He held back a smile at Nicole's assessment.

Liora spoke up. "Says the person who speaks English, the language of the *silent letters*."

Nicole laughed. "You've got me there." She turned to Nir. "Why Joktan?"

"It's from the Torah. Somebody look it up on your phone."

Yossi raised his hand. "Already got it. It's in Genesis 10:25-30. 'And unto Eber were born two sons; the name of the one was Peleg; for in his days was the earth divided; and his brother's name was Joktan. And Joktan begot Almodad, and Sheleph, and Hazarmaveth.' And then there's a whole lot more begotting until verse 29. 'All these were the sons of Joktan. And their dwelling was from Mesha, as thou goest toward Sephar, unto the mountain of the east.' "

"So does Operation Joktan have to do with the sons or with the land?" Nicole asked.

"The land," Nir answered. "It has to do with the land. The territory of the sons of Joktan covered modern eastern Saudi Arabia and the Gulf States. Since the attack is slated for the UAE, we'll be going into the lands of Joktan."

"But are we going in?" asked Dafna. "Do we even know if the Emiratis want our help?"

"I'm going to see ramsad in about 15 minutes. Hopefully, I'll bring back an answer. Now, I don't have much time. Catch me up."

Nicole filled him in with the others jumping in

when appropriate. She told him about the Iranian cargo plane, the trucks, Yossi's deep dive into the KSS, and Lahav's hunch about Dubai. Nir was impressed with how well Nicole had slipped into her leadership role. All the others appeared to respect and follow her.

When the clock hit 12:55, Nir said, "You guys are doing great. Keep it up. I'll be back in a bit . . . if there's anything left of me once the ramsad gets done."

CHAPTER 38

13:00 / 1:00 P.M. IST

"They're ready for you," said the ramsad's administrative assistant.

Nir thanked her and went through the office door. Ira Katz sat behind his desk, and sitting in chairs on the left side of the office were Deputy Director Asher Porush and Assistant Deputy Director Karin Friedman. On the other side of the room sat Efraim Cohen and the director of Caesarea, Alex Eichler. Eichler was the one who questioned Nir before his acceptance into the Mossad. In the middle of the room stood a single empty chair. The ramsad welcomed Nir and invited him to sit in the center seat.

"He jumped right through the door, huh?" Katz began.

Well, no beating around the bush here.

"Sir, it was completely my fault that he was unharnessed."

"Why was he unharnessed?"

Nir paused, considering how to best explain what happened.

"Did it have anything to do with how you got the information about Abu Dhabi?" asked Porush.

"Indirectly, but yes." Technically, he was

289

unharnessed so Dima could hang him out the door, which turned out to be an unfruitful methodology. The mistake was forgetting to reharness him when they threw him back into his seat. But was all that information they really needed to know?

"So you were roughing him up and you unharnessed him in order to . . . what? Rough him up harder?" Porush continued.

It was obvious that the deputy director was trying to get under his skin, but Nir wasn't going to take the bait. *Keep calm and cool. Ride it out.*

"No, that wasn't it."

"Then what was it? Was the harness uncomfortable for him, so you thought you'd help him out a little? Did you offer him peanuts and a cocktail while you were at it?"

"I don't think a Muslim would have taken a cocktail." Nir saw the ramsad cover a smile with his hand.

Porush, however, was not smiling. "Do you think this is a joke? Do you know how much money and effort went into this operation? Do you know the political fallout we're dealing with from having one of our warships that close to the Turkish coastline? All that work so you could let the target jump out of the helicopter. You're lucky you're not up on charges right now. You've got no reason to be sitting there all smug when you've led one of the greatest failures in Caesarea's history."

Failure? Did he really just say failure?

"You want to know why he was unharnessed? Because I had one of my men hang him out the door to see if he would talk. When he didn't, I had him brought inside. That's when I set to work on the old man. It took only five punches to the shoulder I had personally put a bullet through no more than half an hour earlier to make him talk. You want to know why this wasn't a failure? I'll give you two words—Abu Dhabi. Out of all the cities in this world, we got it narrowed down to one. Was this a screwup? You bet it was, and I'll take the heat for it. Was it a failure? Absolutely not."

Nir glared at Porush, then turned to the ramsad. *So much for not taking the bait.* A quick glance toward Efraim saw the other man shaking his head, trying not to laugh.

"Well, that saved us about 15 minutes of interrogation." Katz gave Porush a chastising look, then turned to Nir. "I appreciate your being candid and taking responsibility for, as you yourself put it, *screwing up*. I'm sure I have nothing to say to you, no great pearl of wisdom like *always buckle the harness*—that you haven't already thought of and beat yourself up over. We all make mistakes, but only the fool doesn't learn from them. If something like this should happen again, it would be very clear to me that you are a fool. I will not tolerate fools in my Mossad. Is that understood?"

"Yes, ramsad."

"Good. Now, Director Eichler has been in touch with Abdullah Al Rashidi, director of our Emirati equivalent, the Signals Intelligence Agency or SIA. Alex, do you want to take it from here?"

Eichler—short, bald, and tending toward the round—was a man who had quite the body count behind him despite the image his appearance gave. "Al Rashidi took it to the prime minister, and then the two of them took it to the Sheikh of Abu Dhabi. Surprisingly, the Sheikh was open to our involvement and even appreciative. I think that's likely because he's heard about the rumored accords that will soon come out of Washington. Because the prime minister is very open to normalizing relations with us, most of the Sheikhs see the direction the tide is flowing. They will cooperate with us under one condition— that they're kept abreast of everything going on. Communication will be key, Nir. I need to know your every step. I will communicate with Al Rashidi, who will run it up his chain."

"Yes, sir. I understand."

"We're on the cusp of something very big right now, not just with the UAE but with other countries, like Bahrain, Morocco, Sudan—maybe even the Saudis. One wrong guy plunging out a helicopter could destroy this whole thing. But if you find a way to stop this attack, I think it's possible that we will see many new friendships. The very fact that the Emiratis are inviting us in on this investigation is a step further than we've ever seen with them."

The ramsad stepped back into the conversation. "You will have full resources at your disposal. Use them. You have ten good people on your team but thousands more to draw upon. If you feel you're in over your head, don't let pride keep you from asking for help. You're still fairly young for this responsibility, and there are those around me who want someone more experienced to lead this operation. Yet I believe since we're dealing with new technology, we need a new perspective on how to counter it. Stopping this attack will take more than a well-placed car bomb. I think you have that perspective."

"Thank you, sir. I will not let you down."

"Nir, there's one more thing," said Director Eichler. "The Emiratis are still pretty sore about the Mahmoud al-Mabhouh hit a decade ago. I had to assure Director Al Rashidi that nobody involved with that targeted elimination would be part of this operation. Do you understand what I'm saying?"

"Mahmoud Al-Mab-who?"

"Exactly. Make sure Nicole le Roux knows she's never been in the UAE either."

"Yes, sir."

"Take care. And Godspeed, Nir."

The ramsad had dismissed him, and as Nir walked back to the workroom, he felt the weight of his charge. He'd started the day trying to stop a drone attack on a foreign nation. Now it felt like he was suddenly responsible for bringing about world peace. This was when he wished he had some of that faith Nicole talked about. It would be nice to know there was some kind of higher power looking out for him, someone who would come to his aid when the going was tough.

Yeah, it'd be nice. It'd also be nice if I had lasers in my eyes and I could fly. But we're dealing with reality here. It's up to me and my team to stop this attack. And if we work hard enough and smart enough, we'll bring these terrorists down.

CHAPTER 39

I feel like we've wasted seven days we couldn't afford to waste," Nir said. "Have we made any progress anywhere?"

Nicole put her latte down without having taken a sip. They were back at Aroma, which had become their unofficial late afternoon hangout. "We've mostly just ruled things out. There's no land route for a militia to get to the UAE. They'd have to drive through Saudi Arabia, and that's not going to happen. It's possible to parachute in, but because the Saudis monitor their airspace so carefully it would have to be some sort of high-altitude airdrop. That sounds more military than militia."

"Besides, you'd have to parachute in the UAVs as well. The risk of their being damaged or getting lost on a drop like that would be way too high."

"So that leaves us with the water. The UAE navy is on high alert."

"When you say UAE navy, is that anything like saying the Palestinian air force?"

Nicole chuckled. "Actually, it's decently fortified compared to the country's size. Nine corvettes and a few dozen coastal patrol boats. Several of the corvettes will be kept in the area, and they'll be concentrating the patrol boats around Abu Dhabi."

"But smugglers have been sailing those waters for centuries. If they want to get a boat in, they'll likely be able to get a boat in."

Nicole shrugged. "Maybe."

"What's the typical range for a UAV?"

"It varies. For many of the smaller ones, you have to be within about a kilometer to control it. Larger ones can fly much farther."

"What's the distance if you want to go from Iran across the Persian Gulf to Abu Dhabi?"

"About 240 kms. Out of range of most UAVs, except for larger military grade drones."

Nir picked up his mug. "You know, you're kind of smart." He drank the last of his latte. "I mean, for a Gentile."

When he set his mug down, Nicole laughed and swapped it with hers.

"You're too good to me," he said.

"Better than you deserve."

"Isn't that the truth. So we've ruled out land, air, and most likely sea. I guess our only other option is that they've found a way for the weapons to materialize out of thin air."

"I think the only option we can completely

discredit is your *ex nihilo* hypothesis. When I say we've ruled out options, we haven't actually ruled them out fully. They may have found a way we haven't thought of yet."

Lifting up her first finger, she said, "Land. Maybe they've compromised a border guard, although it would probably have to be a full shift. Or maybe there's some smuggling route or underground tunnel system we don't know about. For instance, the IRGC is the primary backer of the Houthi rebels from Yemen who keep attacking the Saudis. Maybe terrorists B have discovered a way to help terrorists A across the border."

She put up a second finger. "Although it sounds preposterous, maybe some militia members are trained for a high-altitude parachute jump. Or maybe they have a way to mess up the Saudis' radar long enough to get choppers across the border to where they could drop a KSS team. They could then be picked up by Houthis or some Shiite sympathizers.

"Finally," she said, raising a last finger, "maybe they just need to get the boats close without having to come all the way to shore. Or, as you mentioned, maybe there's an already-established smuggling route. Still way too many questions out there."

Nir shook his head and sighed. "Great. You're essentially saying we know nothing."

"No, not really. If we were to divide it all up into three boxes, I'd say we are currently populating the ways it can't be done box and the ways it might possibly be done box. We just haven't been able to put anything into the last and most important box—ways it will be done. But I have a real peace that we'll find the answer."

Out of the corner of his eye, Nir saw three girls at a table who looked to be in their late teens. They were staring at him and whispering. *Great. This could get awkward.* While he was certainly outclassed in beauty by the woman sitting across from him, he knew he wasn't bad looking. His cropped hair and tight beard gave him a look that matched well with his naturally muscular physique that always had him playing defender in pickup football games rather than forward. The Mid-Eastern olive skin of his face was marred only by a faint scar that ran from his hairline down to the outside corner of his left eye, courtesy of a glass bottle wielded by an unhappy Moldovan in a bar fight. He'd been approached by plenty of women in the past but usually not when he was accompanied by another woman— and certainly not by girls this young.

He continued. "I know our team is good. A little nuts, but good. I just don't know them well enough yet to be able to put that much confidence in them."

"Nir, this team is great. Top of the line. But

my confidence isn't in them. Even though they might be the best there is at what they do, they're fallible just like anyone else. My confidence comes completely from God."

Nir was tempted to roll his eyes, but he stopped himself. His automatic reaction to any kind of religious talk was still dismissiveness or ridicule. Religion just seemed so fake to him. It was rituals and rules. It was saying the same prayer for the same occasion every single time. If you got the words wrong or you washed your hands the wrong way or you didn't touch the *mezuzah* when you walked into a house, God would be angry with you and maybe hit you with a plague. It had been especially bad on the kibbutz as he grew up. Rule after rule and ritual after ritual. He was constantly being told how furious God would be if he messed up.

After a while, it felt like the only one more petty than the synagogue rabbis was God Himself. The Almighty seemed more like a petulant child than the great creator of all things. *Do it My way or you're going to feel My wrath!*

But with Nicole, Nir did see something different. There had been a remarkable change in her—one definitely for the better. When they were together as a couple, there had always seemed to be an underlying anger to her. Nir figured it was from her difficult upbringing; he'd just never had the courage to ask. But that anger was gone now. She seemed so happy all the time. Well, maybe *happy* wasn't the right word, although plenty of times he would hear her laughter out in the workroom. But there was a peace about her, like no matter what you threw at her she wasn't going to break. All that hostility he'd figured she'd built up to hide an inner fragility? All that toughness and bitterness were gone.

"What? No, snarky comment?" Nicole smiled.

"Ouch! You know me too well." He laughed.

The girls at the other table were still watching him. Two of them seemed to be encouraging the third one to come say something. *Oy, please stay away.*

"I have to admit, Nicole, I don't get it. When I hear that kind of *God's peace* talk from most people, it just sounds fake. But there's no doubt that you've changed. And for the better. Not that you were bad before," he quickly added.

"I know what you're saying."

"It's just . . . I'm glad for you, Nicole. You know, glad that you've found something that has helped give you peace and confidence. It's like you're a fresh version of you, but you've still found a way to keep the best parts of the old you. You're like a new, improved model."

"I see what you did there." Nicole winked.

"Excuse me," said a female voice.

Nir realized he'd flustered himself enough that

he'd missed the approach of the girl from the table.

"Yes?" said Nicole.

Great, here it comes. How can I politely extricate myself from this girl's attention?

"Aren't you Nicole le Roux?"

Nicole smiled sweetly. "I am. What's your name?"

"Oh my goodness! My name is Shira." The girl turned to her friends and waved for them to come join her. "It's her! It's Nicole le Roux!"

As they scrambled over, Nir looked around for a box he could crawl into. Still, he grinned. *When you're with this beauty, you'll always be the beast.*

"I saw you in *Marie Claire*," said Shira. "You're beautiful. I always talk about your eyes. Don't I talk about her eyes?" She turned to her friends for affirmation.

"We all do! I'm Abigail, and this is Noya. We saw you here and thought, *That can't be her*. But it is you. What are you doing in Tel Aviv? Are you here for a shoot?"

"No, I'm just here on vacation visiting my friend." Nicole indicated Nir.

He was about to introduce himself, but Shira totally blew past him. "Would you be willing to give us your autograph? You're the first celebrity I've ever met."

"That's sweet. Of course. I'll sign whatever

301

you want." The girls each ran to get napkins. Nicole grimaced and mouthed *Sorry* to Nir, then rummaged through her purse and pulled out a pen.

Nir marveled at how cool and calm Nicole was through all this. She signed her name on three napkins and personalized each one with a little note. Then the girls gathered around her for a series of selfies, one on each of their phones. He considered offering to take a group picture for them, but he didn't think they'd even recognized his existence. It might be frightening for them to suddenly hear this male voice coming out of nowhere. They each hugged Nicole, then practically skipped back to their table.

Embarrassment was evident in Nicole's tone. "I'm so sorry. That doesn't happen often."

"Nothing to be sorry about. You handled it well."

"They were kind of rude to you. I was going to say something, but I'm still not that good at this being recognized thing."

How typical of you to be worried about me. "Again, you did great. I'm just wondering how your celebrity might affect your safety in operations. Has anyone discussed that with you?"

Nicole shook her head. "That might be because, other than what I did for the Iran operation, I'm pretty much behind the scenes."

The mention of Iran stung him, but he didn't

say anything about it. "Maybe we can work on some sort of disguise for you. Like, we could get you one of those plastic nose and glasses things."

Nicole laughed. "Listen, I pay enough to have this top lip waxed. I'm not going to have some bushy fake mustache hanging off my nose."

Nir's attention was suddenly and completely focused on Nicole's upper lip, trying to discern any kind of shadow. She laughed and covered it with her hand. "I'm joking, you dork."

"Sorry." He felt one hundred percent the dork she'd just accused him of being. "So what I was saying before, you're like Nicole 2.0. I'm just glad this Christian thing is working for you."

"It doesn't have to be just for me."

Now Nir did roll his eyes. "Come on, Nicole. You're sitting in a Jewish café in Tel Aviv, Israel. Music with Hebrew lyrics is playing in the background. Yet somehow you still manage to forget that I'm a Jew."

"What you're saying, then, is that because you're Jewish you can't be Christian."

"Hello. We've talked about this before. I'm a Jew, you're Gentile. I am of the people of Judaism, you are of the Christians. I'm Old Testament, you're New Testament."

Nicole sat back in her chair, nodding. "I finally get it. It makes perfect sense. That's why only Arabs are Muslims and only Chinese are Buddhists and only Indians are Hindu."

"That's not what I'm saying. I mean—" It dawned on him that this was exactly what he was saying.

Nicole reached across the table and put her hand on his. "I'm sorry. You paid me a sweet compliment, and I'm turning it into a battle. You're right. This is working for me, but not in the sense of it being some sort of self-help thing. It's not like I've gone on a diet or I'm starting yoga classes or I'm trying out meditation. This isn't a lifestyle change; it's a life change. The Bible says if anyone is in Christ, then he's a new creation. There's no more old because the new has come. That's what I feel like, Nir. Jesus took all the fear and anger and bitterness from me and replaced them with peace and joy and confidence. The fact that He replaced them means those things are not based on me and my abilities. They're based on Him."

"I don't know, Nicole. Again, that's great for you. I have to admit, sometimes I've kind of envied your changes. It's just . . . I don't know. I'm a Jew, and I'll always be a Jew."

Nicole smiled one of her stunning smiles. She lifted her hand from Nir's and placed it on the side of his face. "And I wouldn't want you any other way."

"Wait. You want me? Does that mean we should take the rest of the evening off?"

Nicole laughed and gave his cheek a light tap

with her hand. "Sorry, mister. Not what I meant. Besides, we have a world to save."

Nir sighed. "Ah yes, duty calls back at headquarters."

He drained the last of Nicole's latte, then they strode to his car.

CHAPTER 40

His left fist jabbed and connected. Another left, then another. The last one was followed by a right down low, hard enough to echo through the building. Next came three round kicks from the right in rapid succession—low, then mid, then high. He danced, preparing to go back in, when a voice to his left called, "Time!"

Wasaku Katagi stepped back from the punching bag, and leaned over putting his hands on his knees. His coach, Bruce Hatcher, squatted next to him.

"Good. Remember, Jerrod Keith is a striker. His focus will be upstairs. So if you can throw a high combination, he'll react. That will leave his lead leg vulnerable. He needs that lead leg if he's going to have any power behind his punches. You weaken the leg, you weaken the punch, you win the fight."

Wasaku absorbed every word Hatcher said. The man knew his stuff. A decade ago, he had been the World Fighting League middleweight belt holder. The whole reason Wasaku had come back to Vancouver was so that he could train in this man's gym.

Wasaku shot some water from a bottle into his mouth as he nodded.

"Okay, 40 gym laps, then let Brett work you over, especially your left calf. Then you can call it a day," Hatcher said.

"Thanks, Coach." Wasaku put a towel around his neck and began jogging on the small track inlaid around the perimeter of the gym. He often found that thinking back to what had brought him to this point in his life helped to keep him grounded. *"If you know where you come from, you'll better know where you are going,"* an old sensei of his had told him. He let his mind drift backwards.

Wasaku was born in Osaka 24 years ago. He was named after his great-grandfather who had died defending the island of Guam in 1944. The name Wasaku means "create harmony," a fact he played off of when he came up with his fighting nickname, Man of Harmony. As he did now, he found himself smiling at the irony every time he heard the ring announcer call out "Wasaku 'Man of Harmony' Katagi' " right before he went out and knocked out his opponent.

His dad got a job with a huge Canadian engineering firm when Wasaku was six and moved the family across the Pacific to B.C. He remembered little about Japan, but he could remember everything about growing up in Vancouver. English came quickly to him, and now only rarely did he catch an accented word slipping out of his mouth. Even then, he knew it was likely the residuals of growing up listening his parents, since he could usually in his mind hear them saying the exact same words the exact same way.

When he was ten or eleven, he really started to recognize that he looked different than most of his friends. This triggered in him a desire to learn more about his heritage. His studying led him into a fascination with the warrior culture— samurais, ninjas, martial arts. He let his folks know about his newfound passion, and, to his credit, his father found him an Aikido dojo not too far from their house. He began attending and was immediately hooked. He loved the physical workout and the discipline. But, more than that, he was good at it.

By the time he became a senior in high school, he was becoming restless with Aikido. His hard work had earned him a 1st dan black belt by his eighteenth birthday. He had great respect for his *doshu* and his *senseis*, and he thought the teachings of "the way" were a good model for how most people should live. The problem was he really wanted to punch people in the face. He had started watching MMA fights online, and something stirred inside of him. Maybe it was a calling, maybe he wanted to take out some aggression. He just knew he wanted to be in that fighting cage.

His martial arts discipline, Aikido, however, was about peace and harmony. While this connected perfectly with his name, it didn't mesh with who he was anymore. The goal of Aikido was to never use Aikido. Wasaku would never disrespect the discipline or his teachers by taking the martial art into MMA. Besides, Aikido just didn't work with mixed martial arts. Not only were many of the throws and holds and joint locks of the discipline not allowed, but its philosophy of non-violence was exactly the opposite of MMA. He once saw someone in a video say that using Aikido in MMA was akin to bringing a knife to a gunfight.

He decided to leave his dojo and the discipline. Aikido had taught him to be a master grappler. Now he needed to know how to use his fists and his feet. He found a Muay Thai dojo across town and began learning to strike.

After graduation, the problems began. Even now, the thought of this period brought a twist into his gut. His parents were insistent that he follow in his father's footsteps and become an engineer. They'd been saving his whole life so they could put their one child through the best school available. They encouraged him to check out the program at the University of Toronto, which they touted as the number one engineering school in the country. Or, if he wanted to stay at home, the University of British Columbia also had a stellar reputation. He didn't care about the reputations of either. He wanted none of it. He was a fighter. This led to several regrettable arguments, and his dad eventually put him out of the house.

As he ran, he began throwing some punches with his strides. That was the most painful time of his life. He could still see their faces as he walked out the door—his mom's sorrow and his dad's disappointment.

The next two years were difficult. He stocked groceries overnight, then spent his days training. Each day he tried to catch five or six hours of sleep in the backroom of the dojo, thanks to a very understanding sensei. He considered this his "dues paying" time. Even through the pain and struggle, he never regretted them. He knew that this was all part of preparing him for something big.

He began to be noticed around the gym, and soon he started getting fights—and winning. With each purse he took, he stashed the money away. When his savings were finally big enough, he left for Phuket, Thailand.

The next 18 months were spent training in the tropical heat and humidity among the best Muay

Thai fighters in the world. While he was there, he sent occasional letters to his parents. His mom wrote back a few times. His dad remained silent.

When his training was complete in Phuket, he returned to B.C. He tried out in front of Bruce Hatcher to be accepted into his HKP MMA gym, and Hatcher took him on. Over the next two years, Wasaku took every fight offered to him. He worked hard to develop his reputation for putting an opponent out with his fists or with a submission down on the mat. Hatcher, for his part, used his connections, and eventually Wasaku was noticed by the right people.

And now he was on his way to the big show.

Slowing to a trot, Wasaku started his fortieth lap. He took a long pull from a water bottle, then walked two more laps to cool down. Since being back in Canada, the relationship with his mom had improved. He talked with her a couple times a week on the phone and even took her out for coffee every now and then. Unfortunately, his dad was still ice cold.

He finished his last lap and cut across the gym to the trainer's room. There he found Brett Terrell sitting on a table waiting for him. Terrell jumped off, and Wasaku slid on.

"Coach said to pay special attention—" Wasaku began.

"To your left calf," finished Terrell. "Yeah, Bruce told me. I got you."

Terrell started working Wasaku's right shoulder in a way that could only be described as *hurts so good*. There were times when Wasaku wanted to squirm or pull away, but he was determined to tough it out and remain still.

"You're coming with us, right?"

Terrell moved to the left shoulder. "Yeah. Thought I was going to have to convince the Mrs., but she was all for it."

"Hmm, makes you wonder, doesn't it?"

Terrell pushed his thumb deep into a pressure point on Wasaku's deltoid. The fighter cried out in pain.

"Watch what you say about my woman," Terrel said in a mock angry voice.

Wasaku laughed. "Sorry, man."

"Anyway, it ain't like that. She's just always been really supportive of what I do."

"Sounds like you got yourself a good one."

"The best," Terrell said. He began working the neck, causing Wasaku to push his face deep down into the cradle.

"Still can't believe it. First prime time network fight. I'm going up against a baller like Jerrod Keith, and I'm doing it on Combat Island. Oh, that reminds me. My mom was asking all about contact information while we're there. You have any idea how many hours Abu Dhabi is ahead of us?"

CHAPTER 41

TWO DAYS LATER
ATLANTIS THE PALM, DUBAI, UAE—FEBRUARY 9,
2020—11:00 / 11:00 A.M. GST

Even though the website promised 65,000 fish swimming around her, Katie Musser had her eyes on only one. A black tip shark was gliding directly toward her. Her breathing increased, sweat dripped down her face, and she tasted the saltiness on her lips. Katie had read *Soul Survivor*. She felt a strong, literal attachment to both of her arms. Her body tensed, and she stood perfectly still. The shark floated past her, brushing her thigh with the black tipped fin that gave the fish its name.

Her husband, Rick, was waving at her. She turned and saw him laughing behind his protective glass. He brushed the back of his hand across the front of his helmet and mouthed *Phew*.

Seeing his joking reassurance allowed Katie to laugh along with him, although she certainly still felt a tinge of nervousness. Behind Rick was her oldest son, 16-year-old Nevin. He, too, was laughing and mimicking being scared.

"Brat," she said with a smile. He couldn't hear her, but she knew he would understand exactly what she was saying. It was her favorite word to use when her boys teased her.

Up beyond Nevin were the twins, 13-year-old Zabe and Elliot.

My four men.

Katie had always dreamed of having a daughter, and after she became pregnant for a second time, she and Rick had decided that if baby two was a boy they would go for one last shot. The discovery that baby two was actually two babies had shaken her world. After a long evening discussion, she and Rick made up their minds then and there to be satisfied with their brood of three no matter the gender. After the obstetrician confirmed they were both boys, Katie had to admit that a part of her grieved. Now, though, when she saw the four men of her family walking ahead, joy filled her heart. She'd been blessed by God—no doubt about that.

Looking around at the underwater scenery, she could hardly believe she was here. In fact, she thought that if someone had told her five years ago that she'd be swimming with the fishes she would have thought it was some veiled *Godfather* reference. But as she looked at where she was then and where she was now, there was no doubt in her mind that God was working out a very unexpected plan in their lives.

She started making her way to where her husband was waiting for her. The change in their lives began when Rick took a chance and left his steady IT job at a credit card company to join with CloudShock, a tech startup. She had to admit that she was hesitant. The company had been launched by two college friends from Duke University and was still trying to get its feet grounded. Then, just three years in, they had invited Rick to come on as an assistant vice president. But soon after he joined, the company took off, riding the cloud data revolution to become a billion-dollar entity.

Katie was so glad that after praying through the decision, they had pulled the trigger. These last five years had been amazing. The hours, though demanding, were not overwhelming. Rick was still able to be a parent-assistant for the twins' soccer team and Nevin's lacrosse. His salary was ridiculously high, and she could have quit her job if she'd wanted to. But after a lot of soul-searching, she'd decided not to. She had given up her job as a kindergarten teacher for an eight-year stretch, starting with her first pregnancy and lasting to when the twins started school. Now that she was back teaching, she didn't want to leave it again. The little kindies gave her such joy with their open minds and ready hugs. She was also able to get the "cute little girl" fix she missed living in a household full of testosterone.

It was business that had brought the family

halfway across the world. Actually, it was business that had brought Rick halfway around the world. She and the boys were just tagging along for the ride. One of the reasons that she and Rick were willing to take the chance with CloudShock was their claim to be a family-oriented company. Katie in particular was dubious, wondering if their definition of "family-oriented" was in any way similar to hers. She had been surprised and excited to find out they were.

The school of clown fish that passed in front of her dive helmet was proof of their commitment. When Rick had opened an envelope at Christmas containing the amount of his yearly bonus, there had been a sizable number printed on the paper that would be deposited into his account, as well as an invitation to bring the family on Rick's scheduled business trip to the UAE.

It was during the schoolyear, so she and Rick had wrestled with the decision—for a very brief moment—before giving an emphatic yes. They would probably never have an opportunity like this again. They had the boys talk to their teachers, she arranged a sub for her classroom, and they all hopped a plane from Durham, North Carolina, to the Middle East.

That was how she now found herself on a helmet dive in a massive aquarium with huge rays swimming above her head and what appeared to be vicious man-eating sharks brushing up against her leg.

Rick moved toward her. She read his lips. *You okay?*

She nodded, then with a smile pointed toward the boys. Even from behind she could tell they were fascinated. She didn't have to see their faces to know the exact expression they were each wearing. What an experience for them— especially for Elliot, who had talked about becoming a marine biologist ever since they'd visited one of the North Carolina Aquariums on a weekend getaway to Nags Head. Of the three boys, he was the talker, and she was sure they would all hear about each and every species of fish he saw on this 20-minute dive.

Katie slipped her hand around Rick's arm. She wanted to savor every moment of this trip. They already had tours and activities lined up for the next five days. The company had given an exorbitant per diem, and Rick and Katie had also dipped into their savings in order to ensure that this would be the trip of a lifetime, both for the boys and for themselves. After Rick's final meeting on Thursday, they would wrap up their time in Dubai by going to the show *La Perle*. The website had said it was an acrobatic and stunt performance in what was curiously called an aqua theater. Katie wasn't sure what exactly an aqua theater was, but she couldn't wait to find out.

Then on Friday, they would hire a car to take them south to Yas Island. The rest of that day would just be a chill day—a chance to get their energy up for the rest of their visit. Then the last three days would be sheer insanity. Saturday would find them riding the rides and screaming on the coasters at Warner Bros. World. Sunday was for surfing the waves and skimming down the water slides at Waterworld.

Then would come their final day, the one Rick had been geeking over ever since he first read about this place's existence—Ferrari World, home of Formula Rossa, the fastest roller coaster on the planet. Rick had read online that the coaster reached speeds of 149 mph. Although she wasn't sure how excited she was about it, she knew that the boys were going to freak out.

Katie couldn't wait to watch Rick as he walked amongst the sports cars on display at the park. He had always been a car buff. A day surrounded by Ferraris was the closest thing to heaven he would ever find on earth. Every night of the four weeks leading up to their trip, whenever she'd look over to the other side of the bed, she'd see him reading a back edition of *The Official Ferrari Magazine* on his iPad.

Those last days were going to be exhausting

but worth it. While she was excited about all the activities, she was also a little disappointed. They were going to spend all their time on Yas Island without ever making it into the city. This was sad, because she'd heard that, like Dubai, Abu Dhabi was a place of incredible beauty.

CHAPTER 42

B ut the wind is catching them. It's blowing them over," said Muzahim al-Aiyubi, leader of the first team.

Balling his hands into fists, Abbas stalked toward him. "I don't want excuses. What about the day of the attack? What if it's windy then? Should I call it off? I could get General Qaani on the phone and say, 'We were going to strike a great blow for true Islam, but Muzahim said it was a little too breezy.' "

Al-Aiyubi shook his head. "No, sir, that is not what I am saying. It's just that I don't know how we can keep the small drones from flipping."

Abbas reached the man and slapped him on the head hard enough to make him stumble back two steps. "Figure it out! That is why we're doing this! We're practicing so we can determine every potential problem and develop a solution. *I don't know* is not a solution. It's an excuse! Do I make myself clear?"

"Yes, sir."

Numerous   times   Abbas   had   considered

320

demoting al-Aiyubi and putting someone else in his place. The problem was he was still the best of this second-rate group. The KSS desperately needed new blood. Maybe with the success of this mission they would end up with enough fighters for them to choose who they kept rather than settling for whatever came through the doors.

"I will return in 15 minutes. At that time you and your squad will tell me what you have devised as a solution to the situation. Do you understand?"

"Yes, sir."

Abbas marched off in the direction of the second drone squad.

The trucks had pulled out of Al Diwaniyah, Iraq, two days after the KSS heard about the abduction of Abu Mustafa. The convoy was only three strong for the first leg of the trip. Each of the first two trucks was carrying a driver, a gunner, and drones. The third truck held the remaining 16 members of Abbas's team. It took eight and a half hours to drive from their starting point, across the Iranian border, and south to the port city of Bandar Mahshahr. There they picked up one more vehicle—the one that was supposed to have been delivered to them in Iraq.

The captain had been extremely angry after finding out about Abu Mustafa. He'd interrogated Abbas in his emails. He'd threatened him and promised severe retribution if the operation had been compromised. But Abbas had assured him that compromise had not been possible. Abu Mustafa had not known the details of the plan, and the mission was still secure. Nevertheless, he felt it essential that he leave immediately. The captain had delayed Abbas for two days in order to transport the final truck to a new location, before he finally released him for the journey to the Iranian coast.

This new truck expanded Abbas's three-truck fleet into four. Engine trouble with two of the ancient vehicles turned what should have been a long, one-day drive into a multi-day ordeal. After three more days on the road, they'd completed the final 845-km leg to Bandar Lengeh.

The last week had been all about training. The first drone set-up team he'd just walked away from worked in conjunction with the primary assault team. There was a smuggling route that would hopefully get them to the shore. Once there, they would lay out the 250 Intel Shooting Star drones, then wait for Abbas's command. In his heart, Abbas knew there was a high probability of this team being caught and likely killed. If that should come about, he was fine with it. After all, they were just the distraction.

After walking up on the second drone team, he watched their activity for a few minutes. They had their ten UAVs laid out and were readying them for launch. "Give me a report," he said.

Fuad Razzak, the leader of the second squad, said, "It all looks good. Next we'll rehearse loading the cargo onto the drones. Because we can't practice with the C4, I've created ten, two-and-a-half kilo bags of clay and metal to simulate the load."

Abbas slapped him on the back. "Now that's what I call problem-solving. I should send you over to help that group of incompetents in squad one."

These larger drones would remain at sea. The ten Aurelia X6 UAVs had longer range and would be deployed from the fishing trawler. These were the ones that mattered. When they attacked, it would be devastating. Ideally, the smaller Shooting Star drones would draw the people into the open with their light show. If they didn't, again, that would be okay. There would still be plenty of targets walking the isle. The infidel world would reel when they heard about the horror of Yas Island.

"Keep up the good work, brother. Only don't keep them out too long. Between the wind and this godforsaken Iranian landscape, it would be easy to get grit into the machinery."

"I'll ensure we give them each a thorough cleaning before we store them away."

"Very good. Carry on."

Abbas continued to watch as his men worked. The first squad would figure out their problems.

The second squad was already solid. The third squad—Abbas and his inner circle—was a whole different animal. He shivered, although he didn't know if it was from the cool wind or from thinking about this final chapter of the story Kata'ib Sayyid al-Shuhada was about to tell.

What would take place on the fourteenth would be a whisper in comparison to the scream of the fifteenth. The fourteenth would bring tears and sorrow. The fifteenth would make the world gasp and fall to its knees. People would remember the date February 15 with awe, and its devastation would stand as a testament against Sunni decadence for months if not years. The date 2/15 would rival 9/11 in the fearful impact it would have on the West and wayward Islam.

As Abbas lay on his cot each night, all the possible scenarios played out in his head. What if this attack brought down the corrupt sheikhs of the Emiratis? Maybe it would spark unrest in the other Gulf states as well—possibly even in Saudi Arabia. It was certainly time for the hedonistic Saudi royal family to meet their timely death.

Was it even possible that this one act might finally trigger the Shiite/Sunni war that he and other Shiites had prayed for so many long years now? He prayed to Allah that this would be true. Finally, Iran, Bahrain, and the militias of Iraq would have an excuse to execute judgment on the heretical Sunni dogs. If that happened, he would be a hero of historical proportions. For generations to come, people would tell stories of the great Seif Abdel Abbas with the same honor and reverence they spoke of Osama Bin Laden, Khalid Shaikh Mohammed, and Mohamed Atta today.

But don't get ahead of yourself, he thought as he made his way back to his first squad. *You still have to make this happen. As soon as you start feeling confident, mistakes will happen. Allah, bless me with the wisdom and resolve needed to carry out your will.*

CHAPTER 43

TWO DAYS LATER
MOSSAD HEADQUARTERS, TEL AVIV, ISRAEL—
FEBRUARY 12, 2020—07:30 / 7:30 A.M. IST

Yesh! Boss, I need you right now!"

Nir recognized the excitement and urgency in Liora's voice, and her enthusiasm stirred him into action. That was not the call of defeat or discouragement; that was the cry of victory. He pushed back from his desk and rushed into the workroom.

The rest of the team had already gathered around Liora and Dafna's workspaces. They opened up a place in the middle for Nir.

Liora had a big smile on her face. "*Hi-oosh*, boss. Got something seriously *achla*!"

Nir hated the cutesy new *hi-oosh* hello the logistics team had started to use. It was fine if you were a 12-year-old girl, but for people in their twenties it sounded ridiculous.

He refused to acknowledge the greeting. "Go."

"Grumpy-pants." Liora turned to her computer. "Okay, as you know, your girl has been feeding us satellite footage from just about everybody who has a piece of photographic space junk orbiting the earth." Satellite photos cycled on her monitor at about one per second.

Nir was about to protest Liora's use of the words *your girl,* but when he saw Nicole standing next to him, she just smiled and rolled her eyes. *Nicole's right. Let it go. We've got more important issues. Besides, if she's good being called 'my girl,' I certainly shouldn't be complaining.*

Liora continued. "The bad guys did us a favor by driving those W50 trucks. They're so old I'm surprised they don't have horses pulling them."

Dafna punched a couple of keys on her board, and a photo of an old truck popped up. "As you can see, they're pretty distinctive in their look. Shallow cab, small hood, very rectangular in shape."

Liora took back the stage. "This means they give a distinct silhouette from the sky. That's fashion terminology." She winked at Nicole. "It means what its shape looks like when viewed—"

"I know the word," said Nir. "Go on."

"Wow, you are testy today." Dafna added a *tsk, tsk* to her assessment.

"Listen, everybody, we're at our 90-second attention span limit, and I know someone is about to go off on a ridiculous tangent. So just for today, let's keep focused. Now, pretty please, go on."

"*Sababa.* I'll keep us on target," Liora said. "So Daf and I have been looking for these trucks. Here's the first picture we got of them exiting the hangar at Baghdad Airport. Here they are leaving the airport grounds. Unfortunately, not long after, we lost them south of Baghdad. The thing is, even though these W50s are from the late Triassic Period, a lot of them are still around. Fewer than most other models but enough to lead us on a lot of false leads. Sadly for them, they can run, but they can't hide. Show him our gift from China, *achoti*."

Dafna spoke as she typed. "The lovely Miss le Roux hit us with a feed from one of the Chinese satellites. This camera was amazing. It could show a birthmark on a beetle's butt."

"A beetle's butt wouldn't have a birthmark." Everyone turned toward Lahav. "What? A beetle doesn't have skin like us. It has an exoskeleton made of a substance called chitin. Therefore, it would not be susceptible to birthmarks or other skin-related issues."

Nir shook his head. "Remember when I mentioned ridiculous tangents?"

"I just thought it was an important clarification."

"It wasn't."

A new photo appeared on one of Dafna's screens. "By synching this satellite's orbit with the time line we created for the trucks, we were able to discover this. Take a look." She picked up a stylus and drew on a pad sitting next to her keyboard. A circle appeared on the picture.

"Notice this white mark on the green canva, the truck bed? It looks like it's a bleach fa, some sort of chemical stain. We measured 1 48cm long and 33cm at its widest."

Although the photo was somewhat pixelated, it was still remarkably clear for a satellite shot. "Are you sure it isn't a picture blemish or lens infraction?"

"We wondered the same thing." Two more monitors lit up. On each was a wide shot and a picture zoomed in. Dafna circled the same stain on both. "Each is at a different place on the screen yet on the same place on the truck, so it's not a lens or a processing issue. You can even see that the shape is slightly altered, accounted for by the movement of the canvas as the truck travels."

"Excellent work." Nir was proud. "Now we just need to find this stained truck."

Liora turned and smiled. "Prepare to have your mind blown." She pulled her hands away from her head and made an explosion sound.

Yossi, who was standing next to Nir, let out a loud "Whoop!" making Nir jump. He was bouncing up and down, totally invested in what was going on. Turning to Nir with a wide grin, he patted him on the back several times before turning back to the screens.

Millennials, thought Nir. Although he had to admit his own excitement was building.

Yossi shouted, "*Nu, achla*! Show me those pictures!"

Liora laughed and turned back to her monitors. "Once we had that identifying mark, it hugely sped up our process of elimination. We were able to expand our radius much more rapidly. Three hours ago, we spotted this." A picture of three IFA W50 trucks popped up. They were driving down a road in a single file line. "This was taken January 30 on the southern outskirts of Al Diwaniyah, Iraq." Zooming in, she said, "Notice the mark?" The picture was much grainier than the Chinese satellite photo, but there was no doubt that the white stain was there.

Again, Dafna took over. "The truck was going southeast down Highway 1. That means one of three destinations. First, Kuwait, then into Saudi Arabia. But there's no way a terrorist militia can get a three-truck convoy across two borders and into the Kingdom. The second destination is the Persian Gulf."

"Um Qasr or Al-Faw," Nir said.

"Exactly. So we deep dived both locations, although I was thinking it would more likely be Al-Faw. But we drew blanks at both."

"So you turned to Iran?"

"We turned to Iran. And what do you know?" Dafna clicked her mouse, and a photo popped up. "Yossi found this."

"You bet I did." Yossi's looser-than-usual

man-bun bounced around with every emphatic word. "My sister from a Gentile mother somehow accessed the CCTV footage for the border crossings at Chazabeh and Shalamcheh. I figured Chazabeh was a little far north. It would have meant that they were trying to fake out some pursuers by going south on Highway 1, then backtracking north. It may be good tradecraft but a little too refined for these militia Neanderthals. So Shalamcheh it was. And, lo and behold, what do I find there? Our trucks."

Liora clicked her mouse, and a picture of the three-truck convoy appeared.

These guys are so good. Efraim was right about them. "So they're in Iran. Makes sense. But where to? Has to be a coastal town."

"Bandar Lengeh was the logical choice," Nicole said. "It's right across the Persian Gulf from Abu Dhabi. Regular ferries go from Bandar Lengeh to Dubai. It's about a half-day trip. Very easy to blend in."

"And . . ."

Dafna clicked another picture up on the screen. "BL isn't just a tiny settlement. It has over 30,000 people and it's a big trade city, so it's fairly modernized. Which means traffic cameras— greatest inventions known to man. This view is from a camera as you enter the city." She clicked a button, and an eight-second series of pictures began looping. "Those are our trucks, confirmed by comparisons to the CCTV border crossing photos. But notice something new."

Nir watched the loop a couple of times. "Is that a fourth truck?"

"It is," Nicole said. "Somewhere along the way they picked up a friend."

"But how do we know it's not just traffic?"

Dafna clicked again, and eight-second loops appeared on two more monitors. "These were taken from a couple other places in the city widely separated from one other. Each one shows the same four trucks moving past together."

"That fourth truck isn't as big as the other two. Wonder why it was separated out from the others."

"Lahav and I talked about that," Nicole said. "Either there was some kind of failure of part of whatever was in those first two trucks, or what's in that last truck is something else entirely."

"Which goes back to my Dubai theory," said Lahav.

Ugh, Lahav and his Dubai attack. "Hold off on that a second. Now that we know where the attack is coming from, let's focus on the when."

"I've been thinking about that," Lahav said.

Nir groaned inside. "Okay, let's hear it."

"First, let me say that I still think there's more going on. I know you don't want to hear it right now, but we've got to talk it through. This first attack can be big, but I think the bigger fish is

Dubai. Half the people in the world don't even know where Abu Dhabi is. They think it's some made-up place in a Disney movie or something."

"Duly noted. *Para para.*"

Lahav turned to Nicole. "*Para para* literally means 'cow, cow.' It's one of our stranger idioms and refers to *first things first* or *one thing at a time.* So when Nir wants to hear about Abu Dhabi, and I instead talk about Dubai—"

"Lahav, *para para.* Let's deal with Abu Dhabi," Nicole told him.

Lahav's face showed pure joy. "Brava, Nicole. You're really catching on."

"*Achi, nu,* Abu Dhabi!" Nir said.

"Right. The attack will be someplace where it hits a lot of international visitors. If a bunch of Emiratis are killed, the West will yawn, say 'Bless their hearts,' and move on to the next thing. But if KSS wants to make a statement, they need to take out a bunch of westerners."

"Yas Island," Nir said.

"Precisely. And I figure it will need to be soon. The longer they wait, the greater the chance of getting caught. Now, what's on Yas Island that will draw people in, especially this weekend?"

"Is there a Ferrari event or some kind of Warner premier?" asked Liora.

"Nope," Nir said. "World Fighting League pay-per-view Light Heavyweight title fight between

Vladimir Nuranov and Dennis Robbins. I was hoping to be around to watch it."

Lahav's nod was emphatic. "Exactly. Now, you could do it during the fight, but the drone attack would have to bring down the Combat Island arena. Not easy to do. They could carry it out as the crowds exit, which I think makes a lot of sense. However, they could also do it the day before. You'd have the usual crowds, plus 25,000 more there for the fight from all around the world. That would make a statement heard loud and clear. Not as clear as Dubai, but—"

Nir waved him off. "We get Dubai. Keep looking into it. But I think you've nailed it. I've got to get to Efraim." He backed away from the group. "After I talk with him, I'm taking the ops team to Abu Dhabi. Nicole, I want you with us."

A chorus of oohs and kissing sounds erupted from the team. *It's like working with teenagers,* Nir thought, shaking his head. *But thankfully, they're really smart teenagers. We just might stop this thing after all.*

CHAPTER 44

TWO DAYS LATER
YAS MARINA CIRCUIT, ABU DHABI, UAE—
FEBRUARY 14, 2020—09:00 / 9:00 A.M. GST

Wasaku Katagi figured his pace was about 175 mph less than the typical speed of those who traveled this roadway. To his side were pits, and beyond those were grandstands. He imagined the noise and the flash of the cars as he jogged under the start/finish bridge. Next to him ran Brett Terrell. Always a race fan, he was freaking out even more than Wasaku as they took the first of their two laps around the Yas Marina Formula 1 circuit.

Cardio was key for his match against Jerrod Keith. Keith was strong, but the tapes Wasaku and Bruce Hatcher had watched showed that his age was starting to catch up to him. If Wasaku could survive the first two rounds, it was very possible that Keith might gas out. If that happened, then Wasaku could put him away. Of course, that was Plan B. Plan A was throwing a kick to his dome in the first round, then hammer fisting him on the canvas until the ref jumped in to stop the bout.

Because he wanted to focus on his fighter's cardio, Hatcher sent him off on a run with Terrell.

Wasaku was surprised when they got into a hired car upon leaving the hotel. Terrell refused to say where they were going, responding to any and all questions with silence and a beaming smile. When they pulled up to the track, Wasaku's jaw dropped. It was beautiful. Everything was modern and sleek and spoke of speed.

"But what about our run?" he'd asked.

"Just trust me." Terrell had replied with a sly look in his eye.

He led Wasaku through a series of stretches. All the while, he was wondering if they were going to run around the parking lot or maybe down along the water of the Gulf that was just beyond the track.

"Okay, Man of Harmony, let's go get in tune with our need for speed." Terrell headed toward the gates. After paying an entrance fee, he led Wasaku through to the track. A number of cyclists and a few joggers were already on the asphalt, making their way around the circuit. "This is 5.5 kilometers, just under three-and-a-half miles. Two laps around and we're good."

"Wait, we can just—" But before he could finish his sentence, Terrell set off.

Wasaku hurried to catch up with him, and they settled into a steady pace. All along the way, Terrell pointed out interesting elements of the track. There was the start area where, unlike NASCAR and Indy racing, the Formula

1 cars began the race from a complete stop. He showed him the rubber marks that covered the curbs on the turns. "Curbs are just suggestions in Formula 1," he said.

Terrell also explained the DRS areas where if a pursuing car was within a second of the car in front of it, the driver could employ his car's Drag Reduction System, adjusting the wing of the car to give it less drag, allowing his car to pass. But when he began describing all the rules surrounding the DRS, Wasaku tuned him out.

How does an immigrant kid like me get to a point like this? He marveled at his good fortune. But it wasn't just good fortune. This hadn't all just fallen into his lap. He'd worked hard for everything he had. There had been a lot of blood and even more sweat. But not a lot of tears. He didn't regret much in his life. In fact, the only thing he wished he could change was his relationship with his parents, especially his dad. When he'd video-chatted with them to let them know about his upcoming televised fight, his mom had been encouraging. His dad had mumbled a "Congratulations," then left the screen.

Terrell had fallen silent as they plodded along. He was usually in tune with Wasaku's moods, so maybe he'd realized his friend and charge was in a contemplative mood. They continued on, one foot rolling heel-to-toe on the ground after the other.

Maybe a good showing at the fight would soften the relationship with his folks. He wished his dad could see what an amazing accomplishment it was just to get here. Sure, he was in the first fight of the main card, but at least he wasn't in the preliminary bouts. He'd made the big show.

Why can't he be happy that I'm fulfilling my own dreams rather than being disappointed that I'm not fulfilling his dreams? He jogged a while farther, brooding about his dad, then realized what he was doing. *Enough of that. Coach said it's dangerous to get too much in your own head before a fight. I'm on a Formula 1 track. How cool is that?*

Elbowing Terrell in the arm, he picked up the pace.

"Hey, Was, slow down. This is supposed to be a casual jog."

But Wasaku wasn't listening to him. He was on a racetrack. This wasn't a place to saunter along. It was time for a little speed.

After a half mile with his turbos on, he slowed back down to a comfortable jog. The start/finish bridge loomed ahead on the straightaway, marking the completion of their first lap. Ahead and to his right, a family of five was waving to him. The father and tallest son were enthusiastic, but the rest looked like they had no clue who he was. This was one part of fighting he'd yet to get used to—the fact that he could no longer live an anonymous life. It wasn't like he was Russell Wilson or Tiger Woods, with everybody recognizing him. But especially in Vancouver, he had enough of the hometown boy makes good publicity that he tried to always remember that his actions were constantly on display. He smiled and gave a nod and a little wave as he and Terrell jogged past.

Hatcher had already laid out the rest of Wasaku's day. After the run, he'd work him out for an hour punching and kicking. No weights today; this afternoon would be the weigh-in. Then tonight they were all going to grab a light dinner out on the island. Hatcher had heard there was a light show over the island every weekend evening just after dark. But rather than with spotlights or lasers, this show was done with hundreds of synchronized drones.

He was not going to miss that.

CHAPTER 45

YAS MARINA CIRCUIT, ABU DHABI, UAE— 09:35 / 9:35 A.M. GST

"Dad, that's Wasaku Katagi right there!" Nevin was pointing at two men jogging around the track. "I'm serious! That's him!"

Katie knew Nevin had begged his dad for tickets when he learned the World Fighting League was holding a bout on Combat Island. Both father and son loved MMA. Every Saturday night that a fight was televised, they were there on the couch watching. Zabe and Elliot were starting to get into it a little more, but they typically got bored once the fights went to the mat. Apparently, for the novice, punches and kicks were much more exciting than grappling and submission.

Although Rick had learned about the fights well before their trip, by the time he inquired about tickets the arena was sold out. He could have scored some from one of those online services, but their prices started at $1,250 a seat. He'd told her that was far more than he could justify. Nevin had understood, but he was definitely disappointed. Now, however, to see this guy he'd told her was the most exciting up-and-comer live and in person . . . This moment just might turn out to be the highlight of their 16-year-old's trip.

"Mom, Mom, that's Wasaku," Nevin said, starting to wave at the passing men. "Wave, everybody! Maybe he'll see us!"

Katie didn't understand what Rick and Nevin saw in MMA. Every time she watched with them, blood started pouring out of somebody's head or their nose would get smushed. Then, when the next fighters came out, they would have to fight on the same blood-stained mat. Sure, someone had cleaned it up, but the red splatters remained. She thought it was stupid, violent, and just plain gross.

Yet Rick and Nevin, who would be going off to college in just a couple of years, held the interest in common. So she supported it all she could, always making sure their popcorn bowl was full and their sodas were topped off. That bond between her men was what had her waving her hand at a complete stranger like a crazy woman. It certainly wasn't the fighter himself. She knew full well that he would answer a bell the next night and do all he could to knock his opponent senseless.

Once the two men were past, Nevin launched. "That was Wasaku 'Man of Harmony' Katagi. He's a lightweight."

"That's not very nice," Katie said, baiting her son.

"No, Mom, that's his weight class. That means he's 146 to 155 pounds."

"Why do they call him Man of Harmony? Doesn't really fit being a fighter." Katie could see Rick smirking at her behind Nevin's back. He knew exactly what she was doing.

"I don't know. I think it's something about his name. He's Japanese, you know. But now he's from Vancouver."

Katie pretended to think deeply. "Japanese, you say. With a name like Wasaku Katagi, whoda thunk?"

Nevin finally caught on that his mom was playing with him. He shook his head and turned his attention to his brothers, telling them all he knew about Katagi's fighting history.

"And you call us brats," Rick said, putting his arm around her shoulders as they began walking a circuit around the racetrack.

"It's because you are. Besides, I'm just having a little fun." She leaned into him.

Their plane had arrived from Dubai about an hour ago. They couldn't check into their hotel for another few hours, so they looked for something to do. Back home in North Carolina, one of their favorite activities was hiking. On their way to store their bags at the hotel until check-in, they'd asked their driver where he would recommend they go to get a good walk in. He mentioned several beaches and some parks around downtown, then the Formula 1 circuit. He didn't need to say anything after that. Rick and the boys were one hundred percent sold.

"I can't believe our time here is almost done," she said, watching her sons as they walked ahead. "Think they've had fun?"

"They'll remember this trip for the rest of their lives." Rick gave her shoulders a squeeze. "And don't start talking about the trip being over yet. We still have three more days."

"Oh, I know. It's just that sometimes it's strange to think that while we're here, life is going on as usual back home. And soon we'll be back doing the usual again. This trip will be in the past, and we'll be no different. It's like that old Talking Heads song, remember? Something about being the same as it ever was?"

Rick pulled his arm off of her shoulders and started making chopping motions down his arm.

"What is that?"

"You don't remember? The 'Once in a Lifetime' video? That's the song that lyric is from. He did that chopping motion down his arm."

"Is that the one where the guy is wearing the giant gray suit?"

" 'That guy' was David Byrne, and you're thinking of the suit he wore in the Talking Heads' concert video, 'Stop Making Sense.' "

Katie halted and looked at Rick. "You really are such a geek. Only you would know that."

Rick laughed, then they started walking again. "The absent-minded professor. I can tell you the order of songs off of Boston's first album, but I can't remember to take my keys when I walk out the door."

Grabbing her husband's arm with both of her hands, she gave it a loving squeeze. "You're an odd duck, but you're my odd duck and I love you." She tucked her arm around his as they continued.

"You should. How many gals got their guys celebrating Valentine's Day by taking them to a Formula 1 track?"

Katie laughed. "Yeah, it's a dream come true."

Up ahead, they heard Nevin say, "Go!" The twins took off racing as fast as they could down the Formula 1 straightaway.

"God's been good to us," Katie said.

"That He has. Everything we are, everything we have—it's all thanks to Him."

"Amen, sweetie. Hard to believe we would end up here when you and your mom picked me up for that first prom."

"Truth."

"Come to think of it, you kind of looked like David Byrne wearing that oversized suit."

Rick laughed. "Hey, we couldn't afford to buy me a new one, so I had to borrow my dad's. Any money I had I put into that ratty little corsage I got for you."

Katie punched his shoulder. "Watch your mouth. It was beautiful. Do you know I still have it? Pressed into the pages of that hardbound copy of *Pride and Prejudice* I always keep on the shelf of my bedstand."

Rick's smile was wide. "Nineteen years of marriage, and I never knew that. What other secrets are you keeping from me?"

"If I tell you, they won't be secrets." She gave him another squeeze and a grin.

Rick lifted his arm back around her shoulders, and they walked in silence for a while. Eventually, he said, "So after we make a lap around, you'll call to see about the early check-in, right? Meanwhile, I'll call the concierge to find out about tonight. If we can get some good rest this afternoon, and if it's just an open show for everyone out on the island, I'd love for us to check out that lighted drone thing. The online video for it looked amazing."

"Sounds like a great plan."

Rick dropped his arm and took her hand as they rounded what he explained was the first of the 21 turns and chicanes that made up one lap around the circuit.

CHAPTER 46

I don't care what you have to do, Efraim. Go to the ramsad, go to the prime minister, I just need these people to back off."

Nicole could hear only Nir's side of the phone call, but she was guessing that Efraim's side was just as passionate. They were sitting in the Abu Dhabi headquarters of the Emirati SIA. So far their hosts had been accommodating and polite. Abdullah Al Rashidi himself had met them at the airport hangar where their Gulfstream had taxied, something that would have been unheard of given the relationship between the two countries when Nir and Nicole were last here, ten years ago. The UAE director had promised them all the access and resources they would need, and he'd been true to that commitment. Yet everything moved so slowly.

Nicole had needed a computer terminal with internet access. She'd received one . . . after 45 minutes of waiting. Even then the speed was way too slow, which, she suspected, was due to heavy monitoring of her work. Nir had needed a large garage or small warehouse where his ops team could prep their equipment, clean their guns, and run drills. Three hours later they'd been given a space that was too small and too hot and had a half-dozen members of the Emirati military watching their every move.

Every move they made was watched and recorded. Isa Al Maktum, one of Al Rashidi's assistant deputy directors, sat in this room where Nir and Nicole were working. Every time they made a phone call or talked to each other, he would jot down notes.

"Nicole needs internet speed. She needs to not be monitored. We're talking techniques she knows but we don't necessarily want to get around," Nir said into the phone while looking at Nicole. She nodded toward Al Maktum. Nir switched to Hebrew and continued the conversation. Their minder, however, still took notes.

That's an interesting development. I don't understand what Nir is saying, but apparently, he does. Still, two can play at this game.

Nicole left her computer and sat down next to the Emirati. While he'd given her a pleasant greeting, most of his attention had been toward Nir. Al Maktum seemed to view her as Nir's assistant or secretary, something she'd become used to when dealing with the Arab world over the years. This was true whether she was wearing her Mossad hat or her modeling hat.

"Your name is Isa Al Maktum, correct?" She asked knowing full well the answer.

He grunted his affirmation, never taking his attention away from Nir.

Nicole crossed her legs, then leaned toward him and placed her hand on his arm. "I was wondering if you could help me, since you seem to know so much."

The touch caused Al Maktum to turn toward her. She smiled an embarrassed smile and gave her eyebrows a hopeful lift. It took only a moment for the man to not only be hooked but reeled in and flopping in the boat.

Men are so easy. It always made her somewhat uncomfortable to use her looks to manipulate others. But when situations could be life or death, you had to use whatever gifts or abilities God gave you. When she was younger, she wrestled with her appearance—sometimes feeling blessed by it and sometimes feeling cursed. Now she recognized it for what it was, a gift from God for her to use to accomplish His will and do good in the world. She didn't make herself look like this. She could accept no accolades. God gave this face to her, and He could take it away just as quickly.

Al Maktum smiled. "Of course. I am here to help. What can I do for you?"

"You are from Abu Dhabi, are you not?"

"I have lived here my entire life. Other than my

time in the military and fighting in the Libyan Civil Wars, Abu Dhabi has been my home." He said this with pride.

"You must love this city, then."

The man beamed. "It is like my mother. I feel as if it has given me my life."

"Wow, so beautifully said. You know, you are exactly the man I need right now." She gave his arm a squeeze. His chest perceptibly puffed up, and she stifled an eyeroll. "Imagine you have a bunch of UAVs—maybe a hundred or more. Where would you send them?"

The Operation Joktan team was operating off of the theory that a massive number of drones could be involved in the attack. Otherwise, what would have been the need for all the trucks? They had to be filled with something.

"Hmm." Al Maktum made a show of his hard thought. "There is the Festival in the Park concert series at Umm Al Emarat Park. That's held in conjunction with the Abu Dhabi Festival."

"Interesting. Where is the Abu Dhabi Festival taking place?"

"Various locations throughout the city. It's really about a seven- or eight-month series. Most of the venues are indoors, but many attend and would be susceptible to drone attack upon leaving. Of course, there is also the mixed martial arts fight tomorrow. The same is true for that. Many people will be congregated together when the event is over. Then there's the World of Warner. They could try to attack the roof, rain down damage. Did you know it is the world's largest indoor amusement park?" He again spoke with pride.

"Wow! I didn't. Very good ideas. I knew I could count on you." She knew how to use flattery to keep the flopping fish in the boat. "A large number of drones would take space to set up and launch, though. Also, the noise of a typical drone is louder than most think."

"You are correct. You, too, have very good insights."

This time he'd spoke condescendingly, but Nicole just giggled as a new thought began forming. "Now, I know your military is prepared to shoot any drones you see out of the sky, so a sneak attack would be difficult. My thought—and here is where I really need your wisdom—is based on the idea that sometimes the best place to hide is in broad daylight."

"I'm afraid I don't understand." He had a confused look on his face.

Nicole was just processing the idea herself. It felt like a sudden dose of inspiration was being poured into her. "I just mean we're looking for hidden drones right now. When the time comes, they will suddenly make an appearance from their hiding place and try to make a sneak attack despite the noise and the spectacle they will make. But what if, instead, they somehow came in a way everyone was already expecting to see them? It's like most murders are carried out by people the victim knows. Why? Because of the access. The victim lets the murderer in the door. Their guard is down because they know the person. Then, bang! That person they thought they could trust shoots them."

"Ah, I understand what you are saying." He turned his face toward the floor. For the first time Nicole felt like he was actually more interested in the conversation than in her. She allowed him silence in order to think.

"There is one event," he finally said. "It takes place every weekend night out on Yas Island. Let me pull it up and show it to you."

Excitement pulsed through Nicole's body as Al Maktum worked on his phone. This felt like it could be it. Of course, it could also be another dead end. But it felt different from all her other theories.

"Here we go." Al Maktum leaned toward her with his phone, and there was no creepiness about his actions this time. He was feeling the excitement too.

A banner showed at the beginning of a video. It read Yas Island Drone Show. Then the shot cut to a black night sky before the camera quickly pointed down to where a huge number of people were crowded together with their heads turned upward. When the camera tilted back up, hundreds of pinprick lights appeared. They started moving around, darting in and out, making shapes and spelling out words.

Right away, Nicole thought of the opening ceremonies at the 2018 PyeongChang Olympics. She'd never seen a drone light show before, and she remembered wondering how they were able to make those shapes and letters in the sky. Then the commentator mentioned drones, and she'd been even more blown away that someone was actually able to pull off a show that spectacular.

"May I?" she said to Al Maktum, excited. She snatched his phone away before he had a chance to protest.

"Hang up," she called across the room to Nir as she made her way toward him. He pointed to his phone and mouthed *Director Eichler*.

"I don't care who it is. Hang up."

Nir said something in Hebrew, then ended his call. He was noticeably irritated. "What?"

"Look at this." She handed Maktum's phone to him.

He watched the video for a few seconds. "What am I looking at?" he asked without taking his eyes off the screen.

"Lighted drone show. Above Yas Island."

Nir looked up at her, his eyes big. "Is this going to happen again?"

"It is."

"When?"

"Tonight."

CHAPTER 47

HALAT HANYURAH ISLAND, ABU DHABI, UAE—
13:50 / 1:50 P.M. GST

The boat noiselessly slid into the slip, its port side kissing up against the wood. The voyage across the Persian Gulf had been smooth, particularly for February. The winds were low, which kept the waves to a minimum, and the boat's pilot had a deft hand having smuggled goods in and out of Abu Dhabi for decades. As the mooring ropes were tied to the bollards, Muzahim al-Aiyubi breathed in deeply of the mild, humid air. The boat secured, he stepped off and began directing the unloading.

Even though they were padded inside, the cases were still handled carefully as they were moved from the cargo hold to the three panel trucks waiting at the end of the dock. During training, al-Aiyubi had received the brunt of Seif Abdel Abbas's vitriol. Many times the proud warrior had to bite his tongue as he was humiliated for the failures of others. Rather than let it break him, though, he'd used it as motivation. With Abu Mustafa gone, Abbas was destined to be the next leader of Kata'ib Sayyid al-Shuhada. That meant al-Aiyubi's future lay in that man's hands.

He was determined to not let this back-country rabble he was overseeing mess up his reputation in Abbas's eyes.

Al-Aiyubi thought about where he and the 13 men on his team found themselves. The eastern coast of the United Arab Emirates was solid coastal land. The west coast, however, was made up of hundreds of islands. Abu Dhabi itself was an archipelago of more than 200—some large, some small, some built up and inhabited, some barren and covered in sand. One of these islands, located almost halfway between Dubai and Abu Dhabi, was Halat Hanyurah. At its western end was a long peninsula, and built onto this peninsula was the dock the men were on.

Halat Hanyurah had been used by smugglers for many years but usually at night. The arguments Abbas had made for traveling by day were understandable, but for al-Aiyubi they were not compelling. Yes, the navy would be expecting them to cross at night. Traffic in the Gulf was much greater during the day. Traveling the day of the attack gave the drones less time away from the safety of Iran. All strong reasons. Still, daylight was the enemy of stealth, and he prayed that the integrity of the mission wouldn't be compromised by a random patrol boat or local fisherman who just happened to be passing by.

Once the cases had all been transferred to the trucks, al-Aiyubi checked to make sure they were secure. Two trucks held 100 small cases each. The truck he would be driving with three of his men held only 50. The extra space would be needed for a secondary cargo they would pick up soon.

Now he spoke to his men. "Remember, we will meet at the warehouse off Channel Street at 6:30 p.m. That will give us 90 minutes to set up. This is not where the show is usually launched from, so people may wonder why there is activity there after business hours. If anyone stops you, just act like you belong there. If that doesn't work, send them to me. The only way this will fail is if somebody panics. Tawfiq, you leave five minutes after me. Arshad, you leave five minutes after that. Go straight to the parking garages and wait for the right time to leave. Do not leave your truck. Do not go get something to eat. Do not walk around to stretch your legs. If you have to pee, use a bottle. No one is to leave the truck. Am I understood?"

Nods all around.

One of these idiots is going to step out, even if just to look around. I have no doubt. Allah, strike down the fool who compromises the mission.

"Okay, my brothers, we are about to be part of something big. *Inshallah*, we will survive to fight another day. However, if we do not, we know that we will die *shaheed*, martyrs for Islam. In your quiet times of waiting inside the truck, pray that

Allah will give us success and that we will strike a great blow in his name."

Al-Aiyubi saluted his men, trying to convey a confidence in them he didn't feel. They saluted back, and he wondered if they felt the same lack of confidence in his leadership. Ultimately, it didn't matter. It was too late to do anything about it. These were his men, and he was their commander. He felt sure that, at least when it came to his part, he would serve his god faithfully and would bring honor to his family's name.

CHAPTER 48

SIA HEADQUARTERS, ABU DHABI, UAE—
14:35 / 2:35 P.M. GST

It's been three hours since we asked permission to hit the warehouse! Three hours, Efraim!" The only thing that aggravated Nir almost as much as incompetence was unnecessary delay. It was stupid. It was pointless. It would get people killed.

Using his cool and tranquil voice, Efraim said, "Take a deep breath, then count to 50."

"Tell me to take a deep breath again and I'm going to hop the next plane back to Tel Aviv and shoot you myself."

"*Achi*, hostile much? Listen, we now know what's holding everything up. Apparently, the UAE deputy chief of police and general security, Lieutenant General Dhahi Khalfan Tamim, caught wind of us being here. He was the Dubai chief of police during the Mahmoud al-Mabhouh assassination and personally led the investigation. He saw your file, and it seems he thinks he saw your face on one of the CCTV cameras at the airport after the hit."

Oh, that's just beautiful. With feigned surprise, Nir said, "Oh, come on. You told them that was

ridiculous, didn't you? The first three months of 2010 I was in Brazil." He said it for the sake of the extra sets of ears he knew were tuned into his conversation. Neither Nir nor Nicole had been allowed access to their cell phones while working in the SIA headquarters. They were told it was for security; Nir knew it was so every word they said could be monitored. Their football field, their rules. At least they'd been able to get rid of their in-room monitor and his ever-present notebook.

"Of course I told them that. But Tamim wants either a full investigation into you and your role in the assassination or for another team to be brought in."

"Brilliant. Either should be concluded some-where around the time the next terrorist group decides to attack the UAE. Can someone please explain to him that as talented an agent as I am, I cannot be on two continents at the same time? And can you please let them know that I need to get to the warehouse now?"

"I told them about the warehouse. They said if you give them the location, they'll be happy to send a police car over to check it out."

Nir dropped into a desk chair, causing it to roll back on the tile floor. He squeezed the phone's handset until he heard a crack. "No, Efraim. It's got to be me and my team. They can include some of their people if they want, but I won't have some random patrolman stumbling onto the militia and tipping them off that we're on to them. And by the way, likely getting himself killed in the process."

Frustration was starting to show in Efraim's voice as well. He sighed. "I'll talk to the ramsad, see if he can help. But if he says to tell them *achi*, then you have to tell them."

"If the ramsad says to tell them that, then he's not the strategist I thought he was." Nir slammed down the phone.

"That seemed to go well," Nicole said from across the room.

Nir turned toward her with a scowl, then saw her sarcastic smile. He gave a bitter laugh and a shake of the head.

"Remember when I talked about trusting God?"

Great, the last thing I need. "Please, Nicole, not now," he said quietly.

"I know, I know." Her smile was softer now—and genuine. "I'm just saying you're putting this whole event on your own shoulders. That's too much for anyone to carry, especially if this doesn't turn out how we want. If you give it over to God, trust Him to be responsible for the situation, He'll give you peace that He'll take care of it."

Her words sounded nice but also like a bit of a cop-out. If he couldn't handle the stress, then what was he doing in this job? Still, if what she said was true, it could possibly help him. Any

360

higher frustration level, and it was going to start clouding his decision-making. He was liable to start saying and doing things he would later regret.

"Okay, I'm game. Tell me how to get this peace."

"The Bible says we just pray and ask for it. When we do, it says—and I quote—that 'the peace of God, which transcends all understanding, will guard your hearts and minds in Christ Jesus.' "

"Yeah, well there's the rub," Nir said, again quietly. "How is my heart and mind guarded in Christ Jesus if I don't even believe in Christ Jesus?"

"You don't believe in a historical Jesus?" Nicole sounded surprised.

"No. I mean, yes, I believe there was a guy named Jesus. But was He the Messiah? No. I doubt there even is a real Messiah. It's kind of like waiting for Superman to come along and solve all your problems for you. Sometimes you've just got to go out and battle Lex Luther all by yourself."

"Wow, you really are a geek," she said with a laugh.

Yeah, I walked into that one. "So, computer nerd, back to my question. How do I get the peace of Jesus if I don't believe in Jesus?"

He was unsettled to see tears form in Nicole's

eyes. She started to say something, then stopped. Finally, she said with a sad laugh, "I don't know, Nir. I'm sorry. I'm still new at this, and I'm not very good. I'm trying to learn more, but I don't have all the answers."

Nir walked over to her, and when she stood, he wrapped her in his arms. Just holding her calmed him down. "I appreciate what you're doing," he said softly in her ear. "I promise, I hear everything you tell me. I'm not ready to buy what you're selling, but keep praying for me. There may be hope for this geek yet."

The phone rang, and Nicole stepped away to get it. Lifting the receiver, she passed it to Nir.

"Tavor," he said.

It was Efraim. "Get your guys together. It's a go. They wanted you to go unarmed, just as observers, but the ramsad had a conniption. So gear up. You'll have ten of the elite Presidential Guards unit going with you."

"Efraim, you are a beautiful man!"

"Thanks, *achi*. That's what my mom—" Nir hung up before he could finish.

"It's on," he said to Nicole as he moved toward the door. "Now that they've caved on this, demand your cell phone back and insist on using your own laptop with your most secure VPN. If they push back, have Efraim get the ramsad involved again. Let's run with the advantage while we have it."

Ten minutes later, he was in one of two BAE Caiman MRAP transport vehicles racing toward the Royal Falcon Drones warehouse, hoping he would find himself some terrorists to swoop down on.

CHAPTER 49

ROYAL FALCON DRONES WAREHOUSE, ABU DHABI, UAE—14:55 / 2:55 P.M. GST

The first exit of the roundabout led to the Rashid bin Saeed Al Maktoum Naval College, named after the second prime minister of the UAE who led the country for 32 years until his death in 1990. The one responsible for the change in the economic philosophy of the nation, he was reported to have once said, "My grandfather rode a camel, my father rode a camel, I drive a Mercedes, my son drives a Land Rover, his son will drive a Land Rover, but his son will ride a camel." This foresight in recognizing that an oil economy cannot last forever led Sheikh Rashid to focus on business, trade, and tourism. When anyone looked at what the UAE was today, they couldn't help but find the Sheikh's fingerprints.

But what did Muzahim al-Aiyubi care about that now? "Keep going straight," he said as he took his place in the passenger seat. "At the next roundabout, we'll go right toward the water." He'd just finished changing from his soldier camouflage to a white *kandura*, the traditional long robe worn by Emirati men. On his head was a *ghutrah*, a white headscarf held in place by a

364

black band called an *agal*. The two men in the back of the truck had also replaced their uniforms with *kanduras*. The driver, who would remain in the truck with the precious cargo, remained as is.

Three minutes later, the panel truck pulled up outside an old warehouse. The fresh coat of paint couldn't hide the toll the humidity of the nearby Gulf waters had taken on the sheet metal. Across the street stood the walls of the Al-Sadr maximum security prison, notorious for its harsh conditions and torture of prisoners. An image of being behind those walls chained to a chair in a dank cement room while the Emirati police violently interrogated him flashed in al-Aiyubi's mind. That was not going to happen to him. It was either success or death. He would not allow himself to be caught.

The three men exited the van and walked to a door set with three deadbolts. Hanging on the wall by the entrance was a sign on which was painted a silhouette of a UAV and the Arabic words *Royal Falcon Drones*. Trying the knob, al-Aiyubi found it locked. He pushed a button set on the frame and heard a buzzer go off inside.

The men waited, and al-Aiyubi was about to push it again when he heard the locks disengaging. The door opened, and a tall, weather-worn man with a salt-and-pepper beard and wearing the traditional white greeted them. "*As-salaam 'alaykum.*"

"*Wa'alaykum as-salaam,*" replied al-Aiyubi.

"How may I help you, friends?"

Al-Aiyubi brought his hand from behind his back. In it was a 9mm Glock 17 with a suppressor threaded onto its barrel. He pulled the trigger one time, and the back of the man's head exploded outward in a red mist. As the body crumpled to the floor, al-Aiyubi and his men listened to hear if the snap of the shot had drawn anyone's attention. Contrary to Hollywood's usual portrayal, silencers don't silence gunshots; they muffle them. Rather than the typical blast, there's a distinctive snap or pop. However, unless someone is accustomed to the sound, they won't take it for a gunshot. So far, that seemed to be the case in the warehouse.

Abbas had said to expect three to seven people. With guns down at their sides, the three men stepped over the body and entered the building. To the left, a man holding a clipboard exited an office. He was dropped by one of al-Aiyubi's men with a shot to the chest, then one to the head. The other member of the team entered an office to the right. Al-Aiyubi heard a suppressed double-tap come from that direction.

That's three. Who else is here?

Enough shots had been fired that the element of surprise was likely gone. Anyone left in the warehouse would have recognized that something strange was going on. Al-Aiyubi's persona shifted from curious businessman to stalking soldier, his walk stealthy and his gun no longer remaining at his side but up at the ready. He stopped and waited at the transition from the offices to the main warehouse. Inside were hundreds of black cases. Workstations were set all around, each with small drones in various states of repair.

He sensed the movement behind him even before he heard the soft voice. "Offices are cleared."

With the index finger of his left hand, he indicated that he wanted his men to proceed around the perimeter of the warehouse—one down one side, one down the other. He'd go up the middle. They walked slowly forward, legs moving and eyes scanning but their upper bodies never shifting position.

Two suppressed shots sounded to the right, and he heard a table clatter to its side. Up ahead, he heard a scraping, like a shoe on the cement floor. Step by step he moved forward until he came to a series of six tall shelving units. He put his back against the end of one set, then turned and stepped into the first aisle, gun raised.

Empty.

He readied himself at the second unit, then spun.

Empty.

The third aisle was empty also.

He was about to leave the fourth aisle when he

saw movement. The toe of a sneaker stuck out from behind a box. Al-Aiyubi inched forward, gun at the ready. When he reached the box, he kicked it off the low shelf. A voice cried out. There, tucked on the wooden base, was a boy in his early teens. He was shaking, and tears ran down his face.

The reality of what he was doing came home to al-Aiyubi, and he lowered his gun. He thought of his own little brother back home, the youngest of five children. This young man was just starting his life. He'd done nothing wrong, nothing deserving this kind of death. Yet the mission had to be accomplished. Any witness was a risk.

"The warehouse is cleared."

Al-Aiyubi looked to his right and saw his men standing at the end of the aisle. Turning back to the cowering teen, he raised his gun and fired two shots in quick succession.

CHAPTER 50

The MRAPs skidded to a halt in front of the warehouse. Nir was the first out, followed by Yaron, Avi, Dima, and Doron. They were already running for the door by the time the Presidential Guards had exited the vehicles. On the way over, Nir had made it clear to their commander that he was extremely thankful for their assistance but he was the one in charge. The commander had easily acquiesced, much to Nir's surprise. It was obvious that the commander's commander must have told him this was the way it would be. Nir couldn't imagine himself ever consenting to that kind of leadership structure in his home country.

Signaling with his fingers, he sent three of the Emirati special forces around the warehouse to the right and three to left. Twisting the door handle, he found it unlocked. *Strange when you've got three deadbolts on the door.* He held up his hand and counted down from three.

Nir went in first, followed by his men. An aroma instantly hit him. It was the smell of violent death—gunfire, blood, and human waste. Avi grimaced at him. It was obvious that he smelled it too. Something had gone down here, and it hadn't been pretty.

He signaled for his team to keep their eyes open. As they cleared the warehouse, it was evident that they'd come too late. Blood smeared across a desk, a table in the warehouse looking like its contents had hastily been piled on, a dark stain on a wooden shelf . . . All pointed to lives lost.

Once it was evident that the warehouse was empty, Nir instructed the full team to begin the investigation. Quickly, they ruled out robbery. A safe remained untouched, and one of the Presidential Guards found a petty cash bag in a desk drawer with nearly 2,500 dirhams. Nir hadn't expected a robbery motive for what had taken place there, but one can't begin with the conclusion of terrorism. Other reasons have to be ruled out or you find yourself discovering terrorists under every rock and behind every tree. Every now and then you'll come across a genuine coincidence, and chance flukes like that could cost both time and lives.

The money may have still been there, but two things were missing—perpetrators and victims. The bodies had all been removed, and judging by the smell, not long ago. The nitroglycerin smell of gunshots is typically the first odor to fade. The fact that he could still detect it told Nir they'd missed them by ten minutes, fifteen max.

Stepping outside, he placed a call to Nicole.

"Everyone from Royal Falcon Drones is gone and we're presuming dead."

"That's terrible."

Nir walked as he spoke. He was so aggravated he wanted to punch something. Without the unnecessary delay these people would still be alive, and they would have caught some terrorists. They probably would have been able to extract a lot of information too. Instead, they had nothing. "I think we just missed the KSS. See if you can get any satellite or CCTV footage to find a vehicle at this location within the last 30 minutes." He stopped suddenly, looking toward the ground. "Hang on a sec."

Nir knelt next to where one of the MRAPs had stopped. In the scattered dirt was the remnant of a tire track. This one ran parallel to the transport's path. He quickly snapped a photo, then sent it to Nicole. "I just sent you a pic. It's a portion of a tire track."

"I have it. Not much there."

"Yeah, the cowboys driving these transports like to go fast and stop hard. Send it on to Yossi and see what he can find out about it, whether it's standard issue for any type of car or truck—that sort of stuff."

"It's on its way."

"Do we know where Royal Falcon usually launches their show?"

"Yes. I was just talking with someone here about that. There's an open space between a place called the Al Zeina building and Yas Drive Street. That's where they set up."

"Excellent. So we know the one place in Abu Dhabi we absolutely will not find these guys tonight."

"Yeah, you're probably right. Also, remember that the range on these smaller drones is limited, so they can't be too far from Yas Marina. The show takes place over Al Raha Creek, right by the marina and the Yas Bay Waterfront. That gives a much smaller radius."

"Yeah, that makes sense."

Nicole paused, then said, "Nir, how are you doing?"

How am I doing? He hadn't really had time to stop and think about it. Nor did he want to. Ops isn't about self-evaluation and feelings. It's about the moment. It's about training. It's about instinct. Once you start slipping into personal assessment, you lose your edge.

I'll have to talk with Nicole about that when this is done. Ask me how I am before and after. But during? Only one answer for that.

"I'm fine."

"Are you sure? The stress isn't—"

"Nicole, I'm fine." He'd said it more sternly than he'd intended. "Now, do me a favor. Get me an Escalade or a Suburban or something else that doesn't scream military. If they insist on a driver, I'll take one of those. But no more than one. We've already got five of us. I don't want to drive around sitting on Dima's lap."

"Will do."

"And let me know what Yossi says about the tires. Thanks, Nicole." He ended the call and turned to walk inside. The hurt in Nicole's "Will do" was obvious, but he couldn't worry about that now. This was why Mossad didn't usually pair agents who were in a relationship.

Head in the game, achi. *You have lives to save and people to kill.*

CHAPTER 51

Her soapy hands had just gone under the bathroom faucet when Nicole's cell phone rang.

Seriously? Quickly, she rinsed, then lifted the phone with her wet hand. It took three stabs with her dripping finger to answer.

"This is Nicole," then, "Hello? Hello?" The lock screen on her phone showed a missed call. Aggravated, she dropped the phone on the counter. The paper towel dispenser was empty, so she dried her hands on her pants.

When the phone rang again. She slid the green dot to the right and answered the call. "This is Nicole."

"We've figured it out." Liora sounded excited.

Adrenaline raced through her body despite the tremendously vague statement. She hurried from the bathroom toward her temporary office. "What part?"

"We've figured out how to find the drones. Well, actually, Lahav figured it out. He'll need to explain it to you, so you better sit down and get comfortable."

"Hey, that's kind of rude," she heard Lahav say. Then, "How's it going, Nicole?"

She could picture them all sitting around the conference table—Liora and Dafna on one side, Yossi and Lahav on the other, and the Wookie standing across the room.

"It's good. Thanks, Lahav. Now, with the utmost succinctness, please let me know what you discovered." She dropped into her desk chair and slid a pen and pad close.

"Okay, so you know I've been splitting my time between drones and Dubai—which, by the way, we still need to look at. I don't know how, but I really think Dubai will fit in somehow."

"Cow, cow," she said, realizing as soon as the words left her mouth that the English translation of *para para* just didn't have the same feel. Judging by the groans coming from the other end of the phone, her misgivings were well-founded. "Sorry, guys. Bad case of trying too hard. Lahav, one thing at a time."

"Whatever." His voice resonated with disappointment. "Okay, so did you ever wonder how people control their drones?"

She hadn't, but she played along. "Sure. Isn't it with controllers? Sort of like a fancy RC car."

"Exactly. It's all radio controlled. Smaller RC cars typically run a frequency of around 27 MHz. Sometimes higher. Now, when you get to RC planes and boats, the frequency range is typically much higher, usually around 400 MHz or 900 MHz, even up to 2.4 GHz."

One day Lahav would begin a conversation and then get right to the point and Nicole would fall backward off of her chair. Obviously, today was not that day. "Okay, kind of interesting so far. Let's skip over RC helicopters, rockets, and UFOs and get right to UAVs."

"Okay, UAVs. For basic drones, the frequency range falls around that same 900 MHz or 2.4 GHz. The 2.4 G is usually for more complicated drones or ones that are videoing or taking pictures. Those sometimes run up to 5.8 GHz. For instance, the Draco drones Royal Falcon uses for their shows have to be super precise, so they run at 5.8 GHz."

"Where is this leading, Lahav?" Nicole was getting antsy waiting for the punch line.

"If we can track down the controller's radio signals, we can find the drone and the operator."

Nicole sat up, her heart racing. "Can we do that? I mean, is there a way to track down the radio signals?"

Lahav was in his element now. She could hear pride in his voice, and it was obvious that he loved having a captive audience. "So there's something called a Radio Frequency Sensor, or an RF sensor. The controller and the drone send what are known as data packets back and forth. The sequence of these packets is called a protocol. The RF sensor sits and listens for radio frequencies around certain bandwidths. When it detects the signal, it analyzes the communication protocol."

"The point, Lahav! Please, get to the point!"

"I was trying. In short, by analyzing communication protocols, the RF sensor can determine the brand of drone, the GPS coordinates of both the drone and the controller, the speed of the drone, its altitude . . . Really, any information you want."

Nicole was back on her feet. Then a thought hit her. "But aren't millions of radio signals passing through the air all the time? How can we nail down the one signal we want?"

Dafna jumped in. "Sorry, Lahav. We need to finish this sometime before the polar ice caps melt and we're all drowned with the polar bears. So, Nicole, we have two huge advantages. First, we know the range of frequencies we're looking for. Second, we aren't just trying to nail down one signal. Think about it. This is a drone show with hundreds of drones. We just need to have an RF sensor looking for this massive block of matching radio signals. When we find that, we can find our villains."

Nicole was elated. "You guys are brilliant! Get Nir on the line and fill him in on—"

Liora interrupted. "Hold on, Nicole. It's not

all duckies and bunnies. We've got three big problems."

Nicole deflated. Those were not the words she wanted to hear. Her backside found the chair again, and she said, "Okay, let's hear them."

"First, hacking the communication protocols is illegal in most countries."

"Um, we're the Mossad. Second problem?"

"Second problem, the RF sensor is a specialized piece of equipment. You will not be able to pick it up at the corner RF sensor store."

That was huge. What good is a plan if you don't have the equipment to implement it? "Okay, so give me your solution to problem two."

Lahav spoke up. "First, it's possible that the UAE police or military might have an RF sensor. If not, I know a guy . . . Actually, I know a guy who knows a guy. He lives in the UAE and deals with, let's say, the shadier side of import/export, particularly black-market tech. I would be surprised if he didn't have an RF sensor lying around somewhere since it's an up-and-coming technology."

Nicole's heart started lifting again. "Awesome, Lahav. I keep forgetting you're a criminal. Just doesn't match your personality."

"Aw, thanks, Nicole."

"*Achi*, you're blushing," Nicole heard Yossi say. "You're actually blushing."

"I am not."

"Okay, let's not lose track," Nicole said. "Liora, problem three."

"The RF sensor will read the radio signals of the controller to the UAV and vice versa. So that means . . ."

Nicole thought for a moment, then the realization hit her. "It means they're already flying. You're saying we can only stop the attack once it's launched."

"Exactly."

Nicole tilted her head back and covered her eyes with her free hand. "So we need to be ready for the drones to launch, which will be around 20:00 if they keep to the same schedule. Once we catch the signal, we track it, swoop in, and take out the bad guys controlling the show."

Yossi said, "Actually, the show will already be programmed. The controllers are what need to be destroyed. The people are extraneous."

Dafna jumped in again. "I need to say one more thing. It's really bugging me, and you probably won't like hearing it, but these are show drones. Small drones built for aerial precision, not for payload. At most, maybe you could strap a rusty nail to the bottom of each, crash them into the onlookers, and hope everyone dies of tetanus. I think there's more going on. I have a feeling these little ones are either a decoy or just there to draw people into the open. We need to have the UAE police checking out the typical view sites

379

around Yas Marina for bombs or some sort of ground attack. Meanwhile, we have to be looking for more than just the show signals. I think there might be more drones out there."

It made perfect sense. Take out the purveyors of the usual show and launch your own. That way you can ensure the timing and eliminate the possibility that the show would be canceled for some particular reason. By the time any regular watcher noticed the difference, it would be too late. Pretty lights in the sky would draw people out in the open, where you could hit them while they were congregated. A nasty, horribly brilliant plan.

"Okay," Nicole said. "I'll talk with the Emiratis. Lahav, get hold of your criminal friend. Offer him as much money as he wants; these guys here are sheikh-level rich. Liora, fill Nir in. It's 18:05 now. Time is running. Let's go."

CHAPTER 52

The weigh-in had gone smoothly, and both he and Jerrod Keith easily made their 155-pound limit. When they squared off afterward, Keith leaned in and lightly bumped Wasaku with his forehead. Wasaku had reacted by reaching out for Keith's long, curly hair, barely missing it. The two proceeded to verbally assault each other while their respective teams held them back.

Minutes later, backstage, they were laughing and giving each other the bro handshake/hug. MMA was all about respect and show. As long as both he and Keith fought their best, they would leave the cage as friends and the WFL honchos would be looking to book them again.

After the weigh-in, Wasaku took a nap. Later, he, Terrell, and Hatcher went to dinner at the Aquarium Seafood Restaurant on Yas Island. Wasaku and Terrell both opted for miso soup and sushi, partaking of some exotic rolls and incredibly fresh nigiri. Hatcher, not a fan of anything uncooked, took the option of choosing his own sailfish filet from the fresh fish market. The chefs at the restaurant grilled it and served it with a garlic lemon sauce and a side of steamed vegetables. They all walked away satisfied but, they agreed, not overstuffed.

Following dinner, Wasaku and the other men strolled along the marina, enjoying the cool Gulf air and looking across the water to the lights of the city. Wasaku's nerves were up, just as they always were the night before a fight. But the evening walk would help keep his mind clear and his stress managed.

Eventually, they positioned themselves along the waterfront facing Al Raha Creek. More of a deep canal than an actual creek, Al Raha ran along the eastern side of Yas Island, separating it from Abu Dhabi's mainland.

Directly across the water, lights sparkled from the hotels and apartment high-rises of what Wasaku knew was the Al Muneera neighborhood. He'd read some stats about it online before leaving Vancouver, but he couldn't remember the exact numbers. He just knew he would have to win a lot of fights to afford a decent place on that little island.

"What do you think about me bringing Julie and the girls here with my cut of the purse?" Terrell asked, leaning forward with his elbows on a white metal handrail.

"You could certainly go to worse places," Wasaku answered.

"That's for sure. I know she was hoping to redo

the kitchen, but you don't make memories by redoing a kitchen."

"Spoken like a true anti-pragmatist."

"You know what I'm going to do with my cut?" asked Hatcher.

"No. What, coach?"

Hatcher shrugged. "I was hoping you guys knew. Amber hasn't told me yet."

They all laughed. Wasaku was the only one of the three not married, and he was content to keep it that way—at least for now. The time would come. In the meantime, a relationship would just complicate his life. If he was going to win the belt someday, he had to be laser focused. That just didn't leave time for women and relationships.

"Mr. Katagi!"

Wasaku turned toward where he heard his name and recognized the family from the racetrack. The older boy was running toward him, followed by his younger brothers, who other than being dressed differently could be the same person. Behind them, their father and mother were both calling out. "Wait!"

"Hi, Mr. Katagi. My name is Nevin, and I'm, like, your hugest fan. We saw you earlier today at the racetrack, and I thought, *Oh my gosh, I can't believe I just saw Wasaku Katagi.* And now here you are again, and I remember watching you knock out Casey Higgins with a kick to his side. *Whoomp!* And he crumbled like a bunch of broccoli. That's from *Young Frankenstein*. My dad and I always say that when someone gets knocked out—*Whoomp,* and he crumbled like a bunch of broccoli."

All during the rapid-fire monologue, Wasaku was thinking, *This kid is great! This is why I do this, to inspire kids like him.* The younger ones were also talking, but both height and volume gave the advantage to the older brother.

The dad finally arrived with Mom close behind.

"Nevin, take a breath," his father said. "You just barged in on Mr. Katagi's personal space without saying, 'Excuse me' or seeing if he was already in another conversation." His dad was scolding him . . . but gently. It was evident that he wanted to get his point across without embarrassing his son.

Nevin's eyes got big. "I'm sorry, sir."

Wasaku put his hand on the boy's shoulder. "No sweat, Nevin. Now, please, no *sir* or *Mr. Katagi*. Those are for my grandfather and my dad, respectively. Just call me Wasaku."

He reached out his hand, and Nevin took it, squeezing it firmly and looking him in the eye.

Dad's taught this boy well.

"And who are you?" he asked, turning toward the twins.

"I'm Zabe," the first boy said with a wave.

"And I'm Elliot," said the second, matching the wave.

Wasaku had the impression that they'd been asked that question so many times they automatically fell into their routine. It was also obvious by their handshakes and eye contact that Dad started his training young.

"I'm Rick." The dad held out his hand. "And this is my wife, Katie."

"I'm so sorry," she said, also shaking his hand. "We tried to stop them."

"It's perfectly fine. I have to admit it's nice to hear some fellow English-speakers."

"We've been speaking English our whole lives," said Elliot, whose pale skin instantly colored when he realized what he'd said.

Wasaku put out his hand for a fist bump. "Awesome. Then we've got something in common." Elliot bumped him, wearing a big smile, then pulled his hand back for an imagined explosion.

An *ahem* behind him caused the fighter to turn around. "Oh crap . . . I mean, stink. This is Brett Terrell. He's my sports medicine and physical therapy guy. And this one is—"

"Bruce Hatcher," Nevin said. "Everyone knows Bruce Hatcher."

There were handshakes all around.

"You going to the fights tomorrow?" Wasaku asked Nevin.

"Nah. We couldn't get tickets."

Wasaku detected a bit of hopefulness in the

teen's voice. Best to shut that door right away. "That's a bummer. Wish I could get you in, but it's sold out, and I've got no tickets to give away."

The disappointment was evident, but Nevin held it in well. "So Jerrod Keith has those stone fists. Do you have a strategy to take him out?"

Wasaku took a quick glance around. Terrell was talking with the mom about the Canadian education system. *Crud, I've already forgotten her name. I've got to get better about that.* Rick and Coach were in a discussion about Ferraris and old American muscle cars. The twins had tired of the whole scene and were looking over the white metal railing into the water.

He turned back to Nevin and adopted a serious look. "You're not a spy for Jerrod Keith's camp, are you?"

"No way, Wasaku! That's not the kind of guy I am. I would never— Wait, you're messing with me, aren't you?"

Wasaku laughed. "Yeah, I'm messing with you. So Keith is a striker. Like you said, stone fists. What would you do?"

"I don't know." Nevin looked to the ground and started chewing on his lower lip. Then he looked up. "You need legs to punch. I remember hearing a commentator say that once. Maybe you should use your kicks to wear out his lead leg?"

Wasaku high-fived him. "You're a smart kid. Here's the plan."

As Wasaku laid out the strategy, time ticked down. Gradually, like that period just before the beginning of a fireworks display, Wasaku noticed eyes looking up. Soon even he and his fan were talking out of the sides of their mouths as they scanned the sky for the pinpricks of light that would signal the start of the show.

CHAPTER 53

The black Suburban was cruising slowly along Hada-Aiq Al Raha Street. Inside, Nir and his team were in a holding pattern, awaiting more information. Following close behind was a second Suburban with an assault team from the Emirati Presidential Guards. Director Al Rashidi of the SIA had assured Nir that a dozen more loaded SUVs were cruising the streets within a mile of Al Raha Creek, Yas Marina, and Yas Bay Waterfront.

The drone swarm should be taking off at any moment, and Nir and his men were diligently scanning the sky, looking for movement. The only eyes not looking up belonged to the PG driver and the Romanian who sat in the second row, wedged between Avi and Dima.

The SIA had tracked down an RF sensor in Dubai. Located 150 km north, there would have been time to fly it down to the team. However, a battle began over who would control it. The police held ownership of it, and Tamim still wasn't thrilled about working with the Israelis. He would loan it out only on the condition that it remained in the control of the Abu Dhabi police department.

388

Meanwhile, Lahav had been busy tracking down his "friend of a friend," finally locating him through a dark-web connection. The man was normally resistant to helping any governmental authority, but Lahav had found success by appealing to his humanity, which surprisingly, the technology smuggler still possessed. It also helped that the Emirati equivalent of $200,000 USD was thrown into the mix. Given the option between having a Dubai police device that would remain one step removed from his control and carrying an RF sensor in the vehicle with him, Nir had told Efraim to tell Tamim where he could shove his sensor and gone with option B.

Nir thought Nicolae Filipescu looked like a mishmash of every Hollywood Eastern European organized crime syndicate stereotype. His hair was perfectly quaffed and held in place with a healthy dose of gel, his beard was full and slightly unkempt, and his dark-blue tracksuit was zipped down far enough at the neck to reveal a heavy gold chain and medallion resting on a full chest of hair. Despite living in the UAE, the man's Arabic was limited. However, like many Romanians, he spoke fluent Russian. Therefore, Nir had tapped Dima to be their translator. A laptop rested on the smuggler's legs, and he had Dima and Avi each holding an elaborate antenna out the windows on either side of the truck.

"Ask him again, Dima," Nir said.

Dima asked Filipescu whether he'd seen anything yet.

"*Nyet.*"

Nir turned to the front window. It was already past time, and he was beginning to worry that this RF sensor business was just a wild goose chase. He knew part of the reason for his doubt was that he didn't really understand the whole thing. But ultimately, that laptop Filipescu held was their one basket, and in it were all of their eggs.

20:10 / 8:10 P.M. GST

Completing one last walk-though to confirm that every drone was laid out properly and powered-up, Muzahim al-Aiyubi sat down at a table. Resting on it was one row of 12 RC controllers and one row of 13. Each individual controller was linked to a mini-swarm of ten drones. The little boxes themselves were wired to one master controller. Before this piece of equipment was where al-Aiyubi sat. The switch made a satisfying click as he powered up the device.

Turning toward his men, he could see they were excited and nervous. "You have done well, my brothers. We have carried out our part of Allah's plan for righteous vengeance. Let us pray that he will bless our efforts as we strike this blow against the infidel."

"*Amin,*" they all responded.

The flip of another switch started the propellors on the drones. The volume went from silent to deafening inside the warehouse, as the UAVs immediately jumped to idle speed. Al-Aiyubi signaled to two men stationed next to large sliding doors. They pulled them open, then stepped back.

Al-Aiyubi turned his attention to a laptop that held a firewire connection to the main controller. When he tapped in a key code, the blade speed of the drones increased even more. Then row by row the UAVs lifted off the floor and moved toward the open door. It was an awe-inspiring sight. A full two minutes passed before all 25 rows had exited the warehouse. As soon as the last drone was through, the two men slammed the doors closed again.

Turning his attention back to the computer screen, al-Aiyubi saw an array of 250 dots. Now this would be the only view he would have of the show. He had no cameras set up, no video feed beaming in. But he knew that as long as the dots remained on his screen and went through their programmed acrobatics, his part of the mission would be a success.

20:15 / 8:15 P.M. GST

"There they are!" Zabe was the first to spot the lights in the sky. Wasaku and the rest of the onlookers had been looking a little too far to the right. But they all adjusted their perspective in time to see the UAVs begin their first movement. White lights flashed in a synchronized pattern that appeared to be simulating the tide rushing in and out—once, twice, three times. Then suddenly the sky filled with lights that arced up like a giant wave, then came crashing down, spreading in every direction. Wasaku heard the crowd ooh and aah.

Next the lights formed two Arabic words, one on top of the other, and they slowly spun in the sky. Maybe *Abu Dhabi*. Maybe *Emiratis Rock*. Maybe *Eat at Joe's Crab Shack*, although that was probably too many words. Wasaku had no clue. Suddenly, the lights went out. Moments later, they reappeared spread across the night sky. The drones spun and arced and eventually coalesced into a falcon, the national symbol of the UAE. Amazingly, the wings began to pump up and down, and the huge bird flew across the sky.

Wasaku was entranced. Taking a moment to pull his eyes away from the sky to the throng around him, his heart lifted. Looks of joy and wonder were on every child's face, and every adult was smiling ear to ear.

Nevin caught him looking, and, beaming, he said, "Amazing."

"You got that right, brother. I've never seen anything like it."

CHAPTER 54

20:15 / 8:15 P.M. GST

W hat is happening?" Nir yelled from the ↑
seat. He could see all the lights in the
less than a mile from their location. "Dima,
him—"

"*Zamolchi*!"

That was one of the few Russian words N
knew. "You tell him I will not shut up. The shov
has started. Does he even know how to work tha
thing?"

"Aha!" Filipescu gave them a triumphant smile,
then spoke to Nir with Dima translating. "I have
the signals. There are many. It has to be them. We
are half a kilometer away from the controllers.
Location 24°26′56″N by 54°36′25″E."

"Yossi," Nir called into his coms. "Find this
location." He repeated the coordinates.

"Keep traveling east," Dima said for Filipescu.

The driver punched the accelerator.

"Got it," Yossi said. "It's a warehouse off Al
Raha Street and the bridge that connects it to
Channel Street. Tell your driver the bridge is
the one that runs directly perpendicular to Al
Muneera. He'll know the one."

Nir did so, then out of obligation he let the SIA know.

"Yossi, tell Efraim and have him pass the info up the chain."

Efraim, himself, answered back, "Will do."

Nir hadn't known he was listening in.

"Next corner," said the driver.

"Pull over here," Nir told him. "I don't want them to know we're coming."

The Suburban stopped along the side of the road, and the Presidential Guard vehicle trailing them did the same. The SUVs emptied out except for the drivers and Filipescu, and all gathered around Nir. Each of the men was geared up and ready for a fight. Nir had borrowed armored vests for his team, and they each carried their Jericho 941 9mms. Four of them had IMI Micro Galils, but Dima had opted for an Armsel Striker 12-gauge shotgun with a 12-round revolving cylinder.

Like with the assault on the Royal Falcon warehouse, Nir instructed the PG team to go around to the rear. "When you hear the shooting start, come in."

The ten men moved up the block toward the warehouse. "All other units, hold up until further instruction." The last thing he wanted was one of the cowboy PG drivers to come tearing in while they were preparing to breach.

Reaching the front door, Nir tried the knob,

finding it locked as expected. Signaling to Dima, he stepped back. Dima came forward, and with two blasts of the shotgun he obliterated the door's hinges.

"Breach! Breach!" called Nir as he kicked the door down and tossed an M26A1 fragmentation grenade through the door. Avi and Doron did the same. They weren't looking for prisoners this time. Today they were hunting to kill.

20:20 / 8:20 P.M. GST

The patterns and shapes spinning on the laptop were hypnotic. Al-Aiyubi couldn't pull his eyes away. This was turning into an absolute success. He could already hear the praise Abbas would lavish upon him. Who knew? Maybe even General Qaani would hear his name.

A blast pulled him from his revelry. *What was that?* He scrambled for his rifle. A second blast moments later identified the sound as the report of a shotgun.

"Grab your weapons," he cried as he heard the metal front door clatter to the floor. Then several metallic bounces pinged across the cement surface. Movement caught his eye, and a green object shaped like a lemon rolled toward him. Before he could call out a warning to his men, the grenade exploded at his feet.

The dancing lights disappeared. Wasaku was as enraptured as he'd been when the show had first begun. He couldn't wait to see the new formation the drones would take when they lit back up.

But they didn't light back up. Instead, a few moments later he heard splashes—just a few at first, then dozens. The lights from the marina walk illuminated drone after drone crashing into the water. Then something smashed to the cement nearby. He didn't have to see it to know what it was. Cries of pain echoed, and people began screaming.

"Cover the boys," he yelled to Rick Musser, who was already doing that very thing. "Get down on your knees," he commanded Nevin. The scared teenager immediately complied, and Wasaku covered him with his body.

As quickly as it started, the rain of drones played itself out. Wasaku looked around, and when he was sure there were no more, he stood and helped Nevin back to his feet. Scattered across the ground were hundreds of shattered drone pieces—propellors, skids, random pieces of black plastic. Freaked out a bit, but not really scared, Wasaku figured that somehow, some-where the technology had failed. Screaming was still coming from the crowd, and people were in a hurry to clear out. At least it hadn't turned into a full-blown stampede as he'd first worried it would.

Nevin bolted to his dad, who was checking to see that his wife and the twins were unharmed. Rick wrapped his son in his arms.

"You guys okay?" Wasaku asked Terrell and Hatcher.

"Yeah, we're good," Hatcher said. "What was that?"

"Good technology gone bad," said Terrell. "I'm smelling a really big lawsuit."

Hatcher nodded his agreement. "Guys, we best clear ourselves out."

"Agreed," Wasaku said. This had turned into a really weird night, and he had a fight tomorrow. "Just give me a moment. I want to check on the family."

20:21 / 8:21 P.M. GST

Nir and his team rushed through the entrance, hoping to take advantage of the grenade blasts. Two men with rifles raised stood by the large sliding doors. A shot from Avi's Galil dropped the first one; Nir took care of the second. Up and to the left, the mangled bodies of at least six militia soldiers lay dead from the grenades. Shattered pieces of RC controllers littered the floor. They must have all been gathered around to watch the light show. These guys were either really stupid or overly confident, not that there was much difference between the two.

A series of shots sounded from the opposite end of the warehouse. The voice of the PG team leader announced, "Two down."

From behind Nir, a bang echoed into the warehouse. He spun ready to shoot and spotted Filipescu. The man had just stepped on the broken metal door and was sprinting toward Nir, carrying his laptop.

"Dima!" Nir called, running in a low crouch toward the Romanian. He heard Dima's heavy footsteps following behind him. Filipescu was yelling something, but at the moment Nir didn't really care what he was saying. This idiot was running into an active scene and was liable to get a bullet drilled into his head.

When he reached the man, Nir grabbed his laptop with one hand and pushed Filipescu hard toward Dima with the other. The Russian scooped the man up and threw him over his shoulder.

The teammates ran out the door and into the salty night air, not stopping until they were 30 meters away. Nir saw that four more SUVs had pulled up and were waiting out front. He signaled for them to go in.

"Sending in four more teams," he informed those inside the building. Several shots sounded from inside. Either some bad guys were left or some of the injured were still fighting back.

He turned his attention to Filipescu. "What is wrong with you? That was an active scene. You could have gotten yourself killed!" Nir didn't care that the man couldn't understand him.

"Nir, shut up," Dima said. "He's saying something."

The two went back and forth while Nir impatiently waited. Finally, Dima turned toward him. "Boss, he says when that huge block of signals disappeared, it uncluttered the sensor's display. Another series of signals was being blocked by the show drones. They're coming from the direction of the Gulf, and they're getting close."

CHAPTER 55

The nets had been hauled up, and Fuad Razzak stared at his wrist as his watch counted down the minutes. The fishing trawler had been laying low 30 km off the Abu Dhabi coastline, safely in international waters. The captain had informed him that coastal patrol activity seemed to be heightened. That was not good. As much as Commander Abbas had assured him that it was impossible for the enemy to know about the attack, this was too much of a coincidence for Razzak's taste.

Still, there was no turning back. They would either be successful or die trying. Or more likely, they would be successful and die trying. That was okay. He'd lived a difficult, violent life, most of it spent sleeping in uncomfortable places, surviving on not enough food, and constantly feeling the threat that at any moment a missile could come screaming out of the sky and end his miserable existence on this earth. He was ready for some peace, a little comfort, and most of all, some rest. *Although, who can rest surrounded by 72 virgins,* he thought with a laugh.

The second hand made one last circle, and Razzak touched the back of the captain, who also happened to be a first lieutenant in the IRGC. "It is time, my friend."

The captain's hand was already on the throttle. He eased it forward, and the boat began to glide through the calm waters. Eventually, it settled at 9 knots. This was fast for the trawler but well shy of its maximum speed. No need to draw unwanted attention by racing toward the coast.

At this pace, it would take nearly 90 minutes to reach their launch point 5 km offshore. Normally, the maximum control distance for an Aurelia X6 Standard drone was 2.4 km, but these were operated by a Herelink controller, which doubled their range. Razzak didn't fully understand the technology; he just knew where he needed to go and when he needed to be there.

Time passed. The captain kept a monitor on the coastal patrol boats, and for now it looked like they would hit a window in the coverage. But they could be spotted from the water or from the shore and intercepted at any moment. If that were to happen, Razzak had instructed the captain to stay off the radio and keep pushing forward. He and his men would have everything ready; he just needed to get in range. The hope was that in the confusion of what to do about this silent, Iranian-flagged trawler, he would have enough time to launch. If that were to happen, then from what he understood, it didn't really matter what the Emiratis would do. By the time they were boarded and arrested, it would be too late.

"We are five minutes out," the captain informed him.

"*Jazakallaho ahsanal jaza.*" Razzak thanked the captain, wishing Allah's best on him with one last slap on his shoulder.

He left the bridge. The cold wind from the sea air jarred him after spending the last hour inside with the captain and his space heater. At the bottom of a set of stairs, he found his men waiting.

"This is our time, my brothers. Let's go!"

They all sprang into action. He'd drilled them over and over for this very moment. Each man knew exactly what to do.

The ten cases were opened.

Drones were set out.

Detonators were inserted into each package of C4, attached to the underside of the drones, then powered on.

Once the drones reached an elevation of 25 meters, the detonators would automatically be armed. When they once again descended to 1.3 meters, a shock wave would trigger in the detonator, causing the C4 to explode and shoot out the surrounding nails and metal balls at the speed he'd been told—8,092 meters per second. All they needed was nine minutes after they launched—just a nine-minute flight time and they would achieve success.

Razzak watched his men closely as they worked. He wasn't concerned about them getting anything wrong. Still, he couldn't help analyzing their every move.

The captain's voice came over the loudspeaker. "We have a rapidly approaching patrol boat from the south. Intercept time approximately four minutes."

"What is our ETA to launch?" Razzak yelled back.

"About the same."

Razzak's insides clenched. They had to get this launch off, and they couldn't be seen doing it. The only absolutely ensured success was a secret attack that would not be detected until the bombs started exploding. "Go full throttle! Buy me a minute! That's all I need!"

The rumble from the engine increased, and Razzak could feel the acceleration.

"Power up the drones," Razzak commanded his men as he ran into the cabin where he'd set up his control station. On his computer monitor, he saw the drones come online one by one.

"One minute," called the captain.

The engine was whining, and Razzak could feel the boat slapping the water. Running back to the door, he yelled, "Stabilize the drones! Don't let go of them until I tell you." Looking to the left, he could see the lights of the patrol boat drawing near.

Allah, give us time!

"Now!" shouted the captain.

"Step away!" Razzak yelled to his men as he turned and ran into the cabin. He punched four computer keys, and then he could hear the drone engines spin to life.

"They're hailing me on the radio," called the captain.

"Ten more seconds," Razzak shouted back.

When he saw that all the drones were fully accelerated, he pressed Return, activating the programmed sequence. The sound from outside the cabin door quickly diminished, then disappeared as the drones lifted and began their flight to shore.

Light suddenly flooded the cabin. A voice in Arabic called out over a loudspeaker. "Fishing vessel, identify yourself immediately or you will be boarded."

Razzak smiled to himself. *You're too late, my friends. What's done is done, and you can't stop it.*

CHAPTER 56

20:25 / 8:25 P.M. GST

Give me coordinates—now!" Nir yelled to Filipescu. Through his com, he said, "Nicole, get to Al Rashidi immediately."

"He's with me now. What's going on? He's not happy about you not using their RF sensor, so he's a bit—"

"We've got a second wave of drones."

"Where? How close?"

"We're determining that. Tell Al Rashidi to have one of his corvettes ready with a missile. When I give you the coordinates, he needs to fire. No questions asked. There's no time. Do it."

Nir paced. "Dima, what's he doing?"

"Patience, boss. He's working on it."

"There's no time for patience."

Al Rashidi's voice came on the coms. "Fire a missile? Are you crazy? You are not the admiral of the UAE navy! You are simply visitors in our country!"

"Director, I don't have time for a jurisdictional debate. Armed drones are heading for Yas Marina, and the only chance we have that might stop them is to destroy the controllers. The only

405

way to do that is to blow a boat out of the water."

"You are insane! Where is this boat? And what do you mean by *might* stop?"

Nir blew out an exasperated breath. *Just do what I ask and quit with the questions.* "I don't know where the boat is yet, and *might* stop means just that. I don't know if destroying their control systems will stop them. It did for the light show drones, but for these—"

Dima was waving for his attention. "Hold on."

Filipescu was saying something to Dima, who was trying to communicate the message to Nir. But Al Rashidi's furious yelling was drowning everything out. Nir popped the coms unit out of his ear.

"He's found the location of the controllers," Dima said. "The coordinates are—"

"Stop. Don't tell me. Send them to Nicole, and make sure you have the numbers right. Show them to Filipescu before you hit Send."

Popping his earpiece back in, he heard silence. Al Rashidi must have figured Nir had tuned him out.

"Director, are you there?"

"What?" Al Rashidi's anger was evident.

"We have the location. Nicole is receiving it now. Please, we have no time. Hundreds if not thousands will die if you don't act immediately. Blow up this boat."

Al Rashidi sighed. "One moment."

The wait was only 30 seconds, but it felt like forever. Nir was standing next to one of the Presidential Guard Suburbans with his forehead on the cool window glass.

Al Rashidi came back on. "One of our patrol boats has a fishing trawler stopped at these coordinates. They are preparing to board."

Nir slammed his fist into the window. "No! There's no time. Get your boat out of there and fire the missile! You have to do it now!"

20:28 / 8:28 P.M. GST

The spotlight was blinding as Razzak and his team stood on the deck with the captain and his small crew lined up next to them. The patrol boat was drifting toward the trawler, ready to tie up and commence boarding. Razzak had guns on board, but he'd decided not to use them. What good would it do? Patrol boats and navy corvettes traveled throughout these waters. They'd be caught soon enough.

Suddenly, the light turned off, and the engines of the patrol boat engaged. It made a hard port turn and raced off. His men looked at one another in confusion, but Razzak knew exactly what was happening. He smiled to himself. *Finally, my rest has come.*

Thirty seconds later, Razzak heard a brief, high-pitched *whoosh.*

"He says the RC signals are gone," an excited Dima said.

Filipescu was laughing and dancing. He broke into a celebratory song that sounded like it had been sung at joyous times in Romania for generations.

Relief flooded Nir. "I can't believe he did it," he said to Dima. "Seriously, I didn't think there was any way Al Rashidi would fire that missile." He was laughing now and went to join Filipescu in his dance. But the smuggler had suddenly stopped, a look of incredulousness on his face.

"*Nu. Nu! Nu, nu, nu!*" The Romanian began shouting something to Dima in his own language.

"*Russkiy! Russkiy!*" Dima reminded him. The man changed his words to Russian, and Dima's countenance fell. Turning to Nir, he said, "There's one signal left. One of the drones is still coming."

"I don't give this number out to hardly anyone, so use it wisely and don't share it."

"Don't worry, Wasaku." Nevin brought up the electronic contact card on his phone. "I won't share it with anybody, and I promise not to go all stalker on you."

Wasaku laughed. "Good man. Now, if your folks give you permission, I can set you up with some guys I know down in Durham who have a good gym. They'd work you hard, but if you're committed, you'll do well."

"Wow, that'd be awesome."

"And next time the WFL is down south someplace you guys can visit, hit me up. I'll see if I can score you some tickets."

He put out his hand for a fist bump, which Nevin happily tapped. Behind the teen, Rick, who'd been listening in, mouthed *Thank you.* Wasaku smiled his response.

"What is that?" asked Terrell. For a guy who was so laid back, his voice had a concerned edge to it.

Wasaku turned and followed where he was pointing. About 30 feet away, a drone was descending. It looked bigger than the tiny show ones that came crashing down earlier. He wondered if it was a security drone or a news drone, but he couldn't see a camera on it. The only thing visible was a block of something secured underneath with tan-colored tape.

That's weird. He wasn't normally skittish, but this was creeping him out a bit.

The drone continued its descent.

"Hey, everybody, I don't know what that is, but I think we might want to get going," he said. They all turned to go, and Wasaku was sure to put his body between the drone and his new teenage friend.

They'd taken only two steps when he heard an explosion. Everyone and everything close to them lifted off the ground and flew through the air. Thousands of projectiles rocketed into and through all that was in their paths, the staccato, metallic din of hits and ricochets coalescing into one constant sound.

Wasaku felt like a thousand punches had hit him from very tiny yet very powerful fists. He flew forward, landing on top of Nevin. Seconds later, the pain burst throughout his body as each new hole screamed for attention. He cried out, but no sound came. The air in his lungs was all gone.

Panic set in, but it was soon replaced by peace as he gave himself over to what he knew to be inevitable.

CHAPTER 57

SIA HEADQUARTERS, ABU DHABI, UAE—
FEBRUARY 15, 2020—00:15 / 12:15 A.M. GST

It was mayhem outside the office where Nir and Nicole sat. SIA agents moved from room to room, had impromptu discussions in the hallways, and talked loudly on cell phones trying to be heard over everybody else.

Nir had asked for the early reports and was told at least 27 people were dead and local hospitals had taken in more than 60 wounded. Too many of those injured might not see the morning light. As members of the security agency passed the glass office walls, they often glanced in. It was hard to gauge what was behind their looks. Appreciation? Accusation? If there truly was indictment in their looks, Nir certainly couldn't blame them. Those bodies were on his watch; they belonged on his tally sheet.

With a sigh, he leaned back in his chair and looked to the ceiling. He'd turned off the overhead fluorescents a while ago—the glare of the fake light had been giving him a headache ever since he'd returned from that warehouse.

Despite their protests, he'd sent his ops guys to another part of the SIA headquarters,

411

where the Emirati agents retreated when they needed a quick hour or two of sleep during those occasional days-long crises. It was set up with food, beds, and showers. Nir needed his men fresh just in case. Even though everything appeared to be over, appearances were often deceptive.

He closed his eyes, and in his mind's eye he saw nets, gear, electronics, and body parts flinging high into the air when the missile hit that boat. Some pieces dropping right away, some floating, caught up in the light winds at elevation, but eventually, all the pieces returning to the water.

How had that one controller survived? There's no way—it's utterly impossible. Did it land on some floating debris or get driven into a stack of life preservers? It makes no sense! But somehow it happened. Somehow, however much it was mangled, one controller maintained its power. It kept its connection to the drone. And now dozens are dead, and dozens more will never be the same.

Someone bumped into the glass wall, causing Nir to start. Looking for the source of the noise, he caught sight of Nicole typing away on a keyboard. He had no idea what she was working on, and he couldn't summon the energy to ask. Lifting his feet onto his temporary desk, he closed his eyes and sighed once again.

"It's not your fault."

Nir opened his eyes. Nicole had swiveled her chair toward him. Without answering, he tilted his head back toward the ceiling and closed his eyes for the third time. He didn't want this conversation right now. He was at fault, and he wanted to feel every bit of his failure. The last thing he needed right now was her raining on his guilt parade.

"Think how many more would be dead right now if not for our intervention."

Without opening his eyes, he said, "Isn't that sort of like telling the judge, 'You should be happy with me. So I killed those people. Think of all the other people I didn't kill.'"

"That's about the stupidest analogy I've ever heard."

That reply got Nir to open his eyes.

Nicole went on. "You killed no one. Well, no one who wasn't trying to kill other people. They did the killing. You saved lives."

"Not enough."

"As many as you could."

Nir brought his feet down and hit the desk with his hand hard enough to cause people passing by to look in. "Tell that to the family of eight that was wiped out, Nicole. Tell it to that teenage kid who lost his parents and twin brothers. Tell that to the honeymooning guy who lost his new wife and both of his legs in one fell swoop. 'Hey, sorry. I did what I could. Guess it just sucks to be you.' "

Nicole's face reddened, but she found the strength to remain in control. "Nir, quit making this about you."

His anger flared. He opened his mouth to lash out, but then he closed it again. Leaning back, he returned his feet to the desktop, tilted his head up toward the ceiling, and once again closed his eyes. *Man, how I hate it when she's right.*

"You can't save everyone, Nir. You're not God."

That triggered a thought, and he looked at her. "Which begs this question, my dear. Where was God?"

He could see that her mind had started racing, and there was anxiety in her eyes. She'd just stepped into a trap of her own making. The nice thing would be to back off. But he wasn't feeling all that nice tonight. Besides, maybe he could finally put this whole God thing to bed once and for all.

"Seriously, Nicole, where was God? I know you'd been praying. Why didn't He save them? What had all those dead people done to deserve being shredded by nails and ball bearings? Were they the bad people and the ones who were saved were the good ones?"

"I don't think they were the bad ones."

"Then were they the good ones?" He leaned

back in his chair, feeling in complete control of the debate now. "That would make it even worse. What use is it being good if that just makes God want to stick it to you even more?"

Nicole sat silently processing her answer. Normally, she was very confident, but Nir could see she felt totally outgunned. A twinge of guilt passed through him, but, still, he pressed on.

"If you think it was God's intervention that saved all those lives, then why didn't He save everybody?"

Nicole closed her eyes. Thirty seconds passed. Then a minute. Nir was really starting to feel like a jerk. He wasn't being fair to her. He was about to let her off the hook, but then she opened her eyes and spoke, her tone soft but firm.

"When I went to see Christiaan after Iran, he and I were talking about all the changes he'd gone through. I didn't get it, so I asked him basically the same question you just asked me. But I was asking in the context of salvation—you know, forgiveness of sins and eternal life and that sort of thing. I didn't think it was fair that God wouldn't save everybody so that everyone could go to heaven. It's weird how clearly I can picture this. We were sitting on the couch in his living room. Jozette had taken the kids back home, so it was just Christiaan and me. I remember what I asked him word-for-word. 'If God is so loving, then why doesn't He save everybody?' You know what his response was?"

Nir let the question hang.

"He said, 'You're asking the wrong question, Nicole. The question isn't why He doesn't save everybody. The question is why He saves anybody.' "

Nicole paused to let the question sink in. Nir wondered if she was expecting him to respond, but she looked like she wanted to continue. He waited her out.

"Christiaan went on to say that most of us view God like some kind of genie in a lamp. When we're in trouble, we rub, rub, rub on the lamp, then out He pops. We tell Him what we want, and we expect Him to do exactly what we ask. But if that were true, who would be running this universe? God or us?"

"Us," Nir answered, surprised at his sudden interest in the conversation.

"Exactly, which wouldn't go too well." She looked to the floor and smiled. "Christiaan said if he were the one running the universe, the earth would have already flown off its orbit, bounced off of a bunch of other planets like a pinball, and gone rolling into a black hole."

Nir chuckled at the illustration. He liked this guy. "I need to meet your brother someday. Sounds like he and I are a lot alike."

"You kind of are. Anyway, the point is that the world would be a huge mess if we made all the decisions. So we trust those decisions to God. There are both pros and cons to that. The biggest con is that He won't always do things the way we think He should. The number one pro is that because He's a perfect God, whatever He does is always right, even when it doesn't feel like it to us."

Here's where he always began floundering with God. That sounded like the same old angry, petty Creator. "If I understand what you're saying, essentially God's answer to why He didn't save everybody is 'Shut up. I'm God.' Sounds a lot like what I remember hearing about Job, growing up."

Nicole grimaced. "Yeah, the way I said it does kind of sound like that. Give me a second to think."

Nir gave her some space. What she was saying was pretty thought-provoking, but, again, it sounded a lot like what he'd heard his whole life. It was God's way or the highway. He set the rules, and He just waits for someone to break them. God is happiest when He has a butt to kick.

Nicole interrupted his train of thought. "Where what you said is off, I think, is that it doesn't take into account God's love. Somewhere in the New Testament it says that God is love. He doesn't just love; He is love. That's what brings us back to Christiaan's original question. Why does God save anybody? He doesn't have to. He survived fine without us before. He could survive fine without us again. But He doesn't want to. Why? Because God is love, and He wants someone to pour out that love on. That someone is us."

For the first time in his life, he'd heard an answer to his questions that made sense. "Okay, I'm getting it a little more. But the question still remains, why does He save some and not others?"

"That's what I was finally coming around to. I just had to remember how Christiaan got there. Because God is love, everything He does stems from that love. So rather than Him answering our questions with 'Shut up. I'm God,' He answers with 'Trust Me. I love you.' "

Nir mulled over her words. He liked what she had to say, but it was still hard to accept. It was bumping up against everything he'd ever understood about who God was.

"Nicole, I'm a Jew."

"Wait, what?"

Nir laughed. "Very funny. What I mean is, as a Jew, I know the God of punishment, vengeance, and wrath. This lovey-dovey, touchy-feely God is a New Testament invention. It's like He went to an anger management class and has been reformed from His old ways."

It was Nicole's turn to laugh. "I like that picture. Sounds like it could be an old *Far Side* cartoon. One day I watched this preacher on YouTube. His message title was something like

'Reforming the God of the Old Testament' or 'A New Look at the God of the Old Testament' or something like that. But what he said was interesting. He said that whole thing about the God of the Old Testament being the angry God and the God of the New Testament being the loving God is a bunch of crap—not his exact word. But when you look at the prophets, sure, there's a lot of judgment there because the people were being nasty and sinful. Like a parent with a kid, there needed to be discipline.

"But here's the other thing he said you find, especially with those same prophets. When there was a promise of major discipline, there was usually a promise of forgiveness and reconciliation and restoration as well. Again, just like with a kid. You discipline them, but you never stop loving them."

There was a knock on the door, and Nir waved in a man in a *kandura*.

"I apologize for the interruption. Director Al Rashidi has asked that you both join him in his office."

"Of course." Nir stood with a groan. His body was exhausted, and his legs were stiff. Nicole stood as well but much more gracefully.

He took her arm. "Thank you. I was in a dark place and needed a little perspective. What you said makes a lot of sense. I promise I'll keep thinking on it."

"That's all I can ask." Then she leaned into him for a brief moment.

"Please," the Emirati said, inviting them out with his hand.

CHAPTER 58

SHARJAH, UAE—02:50 / 2:50 A.M. GST

The dock drew close, which both excited and worried Abbas. "How do we know Emirati police won't be waiting for us?" he asked the boat's captain.

"First, everything about us is legit. We're just a fishing boat that's been out fishing. We may be unloading our catch at an unorthodox location, but that's what our client wanted. Or at least that's what I'll tell any coastal patrol who may be tracking our course.

"The second reason I know we're safe is because earlier this evening our men visited the home of the dock manager for the company who owns this property. While two of our IRGC brethren wait at the house with the wife and children, he will be here with two others making sure your path is cleared for unloading and departure."

That certainly gave Abbas some peace. But still . . . "Won't he be a loose end? He'll just go to the police when he's set free."

The captain smiled. "There will be no loose ends, neither here at the dock nor at the manager's house."

"Excellent." Abbas felt relief. He'd known there had to be an IRGC presence here in the UAE, just as there was in most other nations worthy of their interest. He was glad to know they were involved.

But the positive feelings he'd been experiencing were quickly wiped away when he thought again about Abu Dhabi. While not a complete failure, it was close enough. How had the Emiratis known? The drone show team was not a surprise; al-Aiyubi had always been a fool. But what had happened with Razzak? How could they have possibly tracked down that boat?

It was a blessing to have already disembarked from the cargo ship for the boat he was on now. Here, he was under radio silence, which meant Qaani and all his people couldn't contact him. Once Abbas finished in Dubai, the failure of Abu Dhabi would be forgotten.

The boat pulled alongside the dock, where a man dressed all in black and wearing a black balaclava waited to tie the rope to the bollard. Abbas jumped to the cement dock and said, "*As-salaam 'alaykum.*"

"*Yalla, yalla!*" the man replied from behind his mask, hurrying him in Persian-accented Arabic. He jumped onto the boat, and Abbas followed behind him seething at the IRGC soldier's rudeness.

Two of the boat's crew members were lifting

the heavy cases out of the hold and setting them on the deck. Mohamed Hassan and Omar Ali each took a side of the first one and hauled it off the boat. Abbas and the unnamed soldier took the next. They stepped onto the dock and walked the case ten meters to where a large moving truck stood with its rear door already open. Twenty meters beyond the truck knelt a man. His head was covered in a hood, and the barrel of a pistol was pressed against it. Blood stained the front of his shirt. Standing behind him holding the gun was a second IRGC soldier dressed identically to the man helping Abbas unload.

Ah, that must be the dock manager—the loose end that will soon be "tied up."

After hefting the case into the back of the truck, the two men returned to the boat. A dozen times they made the round trip while Hassan and Ali made it one more. Then they moved on to the crates. The four boxes Abbas estimated to weigh 60 kg each had him wishing they'd started with them. He was exhausted and nearly stumbled several times, each shift of the weight eliciting a hard look from the eyes of his balaclava-wearing partner.

By the time they'd tied down the cases in the rear of the truck and walked back out into the cool air, the boat was already gone. The IRGC soldier approached Abbas and handed him a set of keys. After Abbas took them, the soldier swung hard toward his face. The blow connected, and Abbas dropped to the ground. Behind him, he heard Hassan and Ali racking their pistols.

"Wait! Put down your guns!" he said, the coppery taste of blood in his mouth.

The Persian soldier stepped forward so that he was towering over Abbas. "Do not fail like you did in Abu Dhabi. If you do, we will not only ensure your slow death but utterly destroy every last remnant of your little militia, starting with your tottering leader Falih Kazali. Do you understand?"

Abbas spit blood onto the dock, then looked up at the man. "I will not fail."

"You best not. Because you cannot be fully trusted, I will be there for the launch to ensure that everything is prepared properly. Do not initiate before I arrive." The man kicked him in the ribs, lifting Abbas's mid-section off the ground. Then he turned and walked away.

Ali rushed forward to help, but Abbas pushed him away. "Iranian filth," he said quietly as he stood. Then he slowly walked to the truck.

Ali jumped in first and slid to the middle. Hassan got behind the wheel, and Abbas closed the passenger door after painfully pulling himself up into the cab.

"Want me to run them down?" Hassan winked. He nodded his head to where the four IRGC men were gathered around the kneeling dock manager.

Abbas laughed, sending another wave of pa. through his side. "Let's just go."

Hassan started the truck and put it in gear. As they neared the gates, they heard a single gunshot from the direction of the dock.

MOSSAD HEADQUARTERS, TEL AVIV, ISRAEL— 02:10 / 2:10 A.M. IST

This could be big. Maybe. Yossi was excited— but cautiously so.

"Hey, everybody! Come here!"

Liora and Dafna stood and shuffled over. None of them had slept more than two hours in the last three days—except for Lahav, whose head was currently on his keyboard. An ever-expanding repetition of the letter *L* ran across his monitor. He'd been asleep long enough that duplicates of the letter likely numbered in the tens of thousands.

"Apparently, he's used to a better sleeping schedule in prison." Yossi tossed an empty Coke can that bounced off of Lahav's left ear.

"Ow." Lahav lifted his head and looked around. "*Yalla, achi.*"

"What? Now? Come on, I can't live like this. I've got to sleep." When he got no sympathy and no reprieve, he reluctantly stood.

"It's about Dubai," Yossi told him.

As though a switch had been flipped, Lahav was fully energized. He rushed the rest of the

way to Yossi's station, almost knocking over his Wookie in the process. "*Achla*, I told you! I told you!"

"Slow down, *achi*. I'm not even sure if it's anything yet."

Yossi clicked a button on his computer screen, and a split-screen map of the Persian Gulf appeared. Shapes of various sizes and colors littered the waters. "Okay, this is a live map of all the active shipping in the Gulf. Each one of these shapes represents a boat. The bigger ones are tankers." He clicked a red arrow, and a picture of the *New Hellas* popped up. The information included stated it was a crude oil tanker flagged in Greece. It was currently underway using its own engine and was traveling at 11.7 knots on a 130° course.

"That's cool," Liora said. "Does it work for, like, yachts and non-commercial boats too?"

"All traffic." Yossi clicked on a purple dot. "It says here that this is the *Samach*, a class B pleasure boat flagged out of Japan."

"Dubai, *achi*. Let's get to Dubai," Lahav said.

"Patience. Okay, so, Dafna, ever since you tracked that boat that got missiled back to Bandar Lengeh, I've been checking into every ship and boat that's sailed from there to the UAE in the last week. So far they're all legit. But then I got thinking. What about any that sailed from BL but not to the UAE?"

"Seems like that would be less than helpful." Dafna popped a handful of seeds into her mouth.

"Normally, yes. Especially if we were looking at any other country."

Liora started bouncing in her seat. "Ooh, I know where you're going with this."

"Don't steal my thunder." He smiled. "One thing we've learned about our Iranian friends is that when they want to do something shady with their ships—you know, drop an arms shipment here, launch a raiding party there—they shut off their automatic identification system. They'll be on a map like we have here, then suddenly, *abracadabra*, they disappear. A little while later they'll reappear saying, 'Sorry, our AIS went out. But we have it fixed now.'"

"Exactly." Apparently, Liora couldn't keep herself out of the conversation. "I was part of the team that tracked an Iranian cargo ship last year when it went dark in international waters near Haifa. When it reappeared, it was all the way up by Syria. We never did figure out what they were doing."

Yossi continued. "So I went digging around, and wouldn't you know? Yesterday evening the Iranian-flagged cargo ship *Samia* suddenly disappeared in the Persian Gulf . . . near where?"

"Dubai!" shouted Lahav.

"Well, almost but not quite. It was just past

427

Greater Tunb Island, which is about 130 km north from Dubai."

"When will you get to Dubai?" Lahav's impatience was on full display.

"Wait for it, young Padawan. From where *Samia* went dark, it's about an eight- or nine-hour trip to Dubai. So I looked for any vessel that was around Greater Tunb Island at the time the *Samia* disappeared that then headed right for shore. And once again, wouldn't you know, the UAE-flagged *Murban*, which had been fishing off the island, just pulled into dock in Sharjah, a suburb of . . ." He signaled to Lahav.

"Dubai!"

"Exactly! It landed about 25 minutes ago, which is exactly eight hours and 45 minutes after the *Samia* vanished into thin air. And what's doubly odd is that the dock it pulled into isn't a fishing port. It's owned by an import/export company called Ultra."

"I told you it was Dubai! I told you!"

"Yes, you did, Lahav. As a reward, I promise to put 150 shekels on your canteen account when you go back to prison."

"*Sababa, achi!*" Lahav gave him a huge smile.

Liora stepped in. "Yossi, get Nir and Nicole on the line right away. Fill them in. Dafna and I will try to find some footage around Ultra. We'll see if we can figure out what they're driving. Make sure to let Nicole know we'll prob-

428

ably need her help. And, Yossi, great work!"

She leaned around him and gave him a peck on the cheek. Yossi swiveled his chair just in time to see Lahav standing next to her with his lips puckered.

"Ew. No." She skirted around him.

"What? I came up with Dubai. Dubai was all me. Doesn't that deserve at least something? A hug? A handshake?"

"Or this?" Dafna punched him in the arm. "There you go. Enjoy it."

CHAPTER 59

The call from Yossi came while Nir and Nicole were still with IRGC director Al Rashidi. Nicole switched her phone to speaker as he began explaining what he'd found. While the evidence seemed solid to Nir, Al Rashidi's response was tepid. Too much speculation, he claimed. You can't build a case on coincidence. Still, he promised to alert Lieutenant General Tamim and to have his SIA teams on the lookout around the city.

Nir was unimpressed.

"Okay, but at least let me get my team up to Dubai. I just need a vehicle."

He was banking on the hope that Al Rashidi was tiring of their presence and was ready to get them out of his headquarters. He was pleased to hear him say, "I'll have a driver waiting for you out front in ten minutes." Not quite what he wanted but a good first step.

"No. I appreciate your kind offer, but, like you said, it's probably nothing. I don't want to pull away another of your agents just to chauffer us around. All I need is a Suburban or something and we'll get ourselves there."

As a man who had spent years in intelligence work, Al Rashidi knew a blow off when he heard it. The next half hour saw a negotiation between the men that at times got quite heated. Finally, the director offered to let them have the SUV but with the condition that they would check in with the Dubai branch of the SIA as soon as they arrived.

Nir had quickly promised their cooperation. "Absolutely. As soon as we get there."

He and Nicole packed up their stuff, then roused the ops guys from their cat naps. True to his word, Al Rashidi had a Suburban waiting for them. As soon as they pulled away from the curb, Nir asked Dima to call Filipescu and ask him to join them with his RF sensor. He also wanted him to bring one more piece of equipment he had a hunch they'd need. The Romanian readily agreed. His part in the evening's activities had left him shaken and angry. He was sad and hurt and wanted revenge.

Filipescu was waiting outside when they pulled up in front of his walled compound. He climbed in next to Nicole, and the SUV zigzagged through the Abu Dhabi streets for a quarter of an hour. Then, spotting a parking garage for a high-rise apartment complex, Yaron pulled in. He circled up the ramp until they reached the third floor.

Prowling through the aisles, they focused on the SUVs. When Yaron stopped, Avi passed a screwdriver up the rows, and Filipescu, Yaron, and Nir climbed out. While Yaron used the tool to swap plates with a parked white Suburban, Filipescu ran the signal-tracing device Nir had asked him to bring around their SUV. Beeps sounded in two separate places under the vehicle. Nir slid beneath the frame and pulled a magnetic tracking device from each location. Exactly what he'd suspected they'd find.

"Guess they wanted to be thorough," he said, tossing them up and down in his hand. Even though Filipescu couldn't understand his words, his smile said he got the drift.

The three men climbed back in, and Yaron got them back on the road for the 90-minute drive to Dubai—Yaron and Nir in the front; Nicole and Filipescu behind them, each with computers open on their laps; and Dima, Doron, and Avi squeezed tightly into the final row, busy ensuring that each gun was clean and every magazine was full. After they'd traveled for 15 minutes, Nir opened his window and dropped the tracking devices to the ground.

The debate with Al Rashidi over requisitioning a vehicle had solidified a thought that had been germinating in Nir's mind for a while. They were better off on their own. Sure, it might upset some folks, both in the UAE and in Tel Aviv, but it was better to ask forgiveness than to ask permission. He'd weathered the chain-of-command storm before and survived. He would likely survive this one too.

Another 20 minutes' worth of road passed under the tires before his phone rang. "Tavor."

"It's Efraim."

"Hey, *achi*, what are you doing awake?"

"Same thing you are—trying to save the world." A lilt in the man's voice told Nir he would likely enjoy this conversation. Efraim was a good guy, and Nir and the team were lucky to have him as their liaison. "Got a strange question for you."

Nir knew what was coming. "Shoot."

"Did you happen to borrow an SUV from the SIA?"

"I did. My friend Director Al Rashidi acquired it for me."

"And did you happen to remove a tracking device from said SUV?"

"What? *Me?* Come now, Efraim. You know me better than that. Besides, why would tracking devices be on an SUV they let me borrow?"

"Interesting that you said *devices, achi.* I mentioned only one."

Nir remained silent, trying to suppress his grin.

"Anyway, it seems Al Rashidi is having kittens, claiming you've gone rogue. He's threatening to have you arrested."

Nir rolled his eyes. He hated sore losers. "How's he going to find us if he has no trackers?

Listen, tell him I can't help it if the SIA uses *schlock* tracking devices. Maybe you can offer to sell him some high-quality, Israeli-made spy gear."

Efraim laughed. "Listen, I promised him I'd tell you to check in when you get to Dubai."

"Promise fulfilled. I'll see if I can fit it in."

Now Caesarea's assistant deputy director's tone changed. "Listen, Nir. I need to tell you something that no one on your team is authorized to know. I'm telling you only because I got special permission from the ramsad himself, and because I've got le Roux–level encryption on this line."

"I'm listening." Nir leaned forward and toward the passenger window.

"Caesarea has an asset in Dubai with connections to the underground IRGC presence. This person said there'd been rumblings that something big was coming, and their assumption was that it was about Abu Dhabi. But rather than slow down now that the attack is over, the rumblings are still going—even ramping up. But it's just internal speculation based on various soldiers' takes on their superiors' moods. Absolutely nothing concrete."

"Nothing concrete is more than we have now."

"Exactly. So our asset is fairly confident that whatever's happening, the local IRGC commander is connected in some way. Whether it's full involvement or not, he doesn't know."

As Efraim gave him the commander's two names, both alias and true, Nir grew excited about the plan forming in his mind. "Do you have a location on him?"

"Listen, Nir, I know what you're thinking." Efraim spoke with a new firmness. "You want to snatch him up and interrogate him, maybe throw him out of a helicopter."

"Cheap shot."

"Cry me a river. What I'm telling you is *Do not do that*. Let me say that again. Do not apprehend the IRGC commander. Picking him up would likely compromise our asset. I can't tell you why; just trust me that it would. We cannot lose that information pipeline. You're authorized by the ramsad to follow him but that is all. Are we clear about that?"

"We're clear."

"Good. Because if you act contrary to this order, you will certainly lose your job and will probably be brought up on charges."

"We're clear, we're clear." He was frustrated by the order but understood it perfectly. When in the field, his safety was dependent on the discretion of his fellow agents. He would never unnecessarily put an asset at risk.

Efraim continued. "I'm sending you an address. Keep your team working on finding the KSS militia. I'll check in with you soon."

"Got it. Thanks, Efraim." His friend may not

have been a wealth of information, but what he'd shared was enough to hone their plan from *go to Dubai and figure it out* to actually having a lead to pursue.

The kilometers passed, and soon the lights of the city appeared in the pre-dawn skyline. A feeling of déjà vu caused some edginess on Nir's part. The last time he was in Dubai, he'd killed someone. Now he was back to do the same.

CHAPTER 60

Though reluctant to do so, Abbas had to admit the Burj Khalifa was a marvel. In preparation for what he was about to do, he had learned all he could about the structure.

Reaching 828 meters into the sky, the building was over half a mile from base to tip. No other man-made structure on the face of the earth came close to its reach. The second-highest building in the world, Taipei 101 in Taiwan, wasn't even two thirds of its height. But more than just the elevation of its penthouse made the structure a wonder. One could build a half-mile-tall cement block and people would say, "*Meh,* it's big, but . . ." What made the Burj Khalifa a one-of-a-kind work of art was its sheer beauty.

Built upon a Y-shaped base and surrounded with an 11-hectare lush green oasis, the architectural style of the Burj was taken from its culture. Reminiscent of a glass minaret, it was designed as a tribute to the religion and the god of the nation's people. Not only was its design homage to Islam, but the nearly 26,000 hand-cut glass panels of its exterior reflected its affluent surroundings, its bustling citizenry, and the rich, blue waters of the Gulf. Then, when night fell, the Burj offered a visual echo of the magnificent lights of a glistening city that sprouted, then bloomed, in the desert.

But while the outside may have pictured a desire to reach up to heaven, the inside was old-school capitalism at its finest. And it was what was inside that made it deserving of its fate. The 5.67 million square feet were separated into more than 200 floors, each one designed with quality and opulence in mind. The top 37 floors were corporate, with the three highest floors merged into one over-the-top office suite. Below these were 900 residences spread over nearly 80 levels and priced between very expensive and *if you have to ask, you can't afford it.*

At the base, the first 16 floors were graced by a collaborative effort between Italian fashion icon Giorgio Armani and Emirati integrated lifestyle developers Emaar, both known for their exquisite style and creativity. The Armani Hotel filled the first eight floors, with the next eight holding the 144 suites of the Armani Residences. The remaining floors scattered throughout the building held restaurants, shopping, a cigar bar, five swimming pools, numerous health clubs, a library, and three observation levels.

The Burj Khalifa was a tribute to what the ingenuity of mankind can accomplish—a marvel of architecture, design, and engineering. It was an idol that rose high into the sky, and it drew the worship of Western infidels and apostate Muslims. That's why today he would fly 227 kilograms of C4 explosives directly into it.

After unloading the cargo into the warehouse, Abbas and his two men had climbed up into the empty moving truck and slept. It was only for a few hours, but it was an essential break. Now that they were once again awake, all three were energized. Today they would make history.

The IRGC soldiers had left bottles of water in the truck along with some pita bread that chewed like it had been baked weeks ago. But it was better than nothing, and the men appreciated the meal. Now it was time to get to work.

Opening the first of the cases, Abbas smiled. It was like reuniting with an old, ugly, odd-shaped friend. Along with Ali, he reached in and lifted the Blowfish A2 UAV out of its case. He hadn't flown one since he'd dropped the mortars on the oil refinery. The drone wasn't really all that heavy, weighing in at only 13.4 kg. It was just awkward with its wide-reaching legs and 2.1-meter main rotor. Tucked into foam in the corner of the case was a large battery. The power supply and UAV together tipped the scale at 23.7 kg.

As Abbas and Ali moved to the next case, Hassan placed an M183 demolition charge assembly next to the first drone. The M183 was a package of 16 M112 C4 demo blocks. Each demo

439

block contained .57 kg of explosive. Often used by the military for satchel charges, the M183 was powerful enough to destroy large structures. Not surprisingly, though, "large structures" did not mean Burj Khalifa large. Bringing down a building like that would take a full-scale military attack.

This would not be a 9/11-style demolition. The goal of this assault was to cause maximum damage to the psyche of the Sunni fools and the West. And unlike 9/11, this was not to be an onslaught on capitalism and the West; it was purely Shi'a versus Sunni.

That was why the attack was to be today, on a Saturday, instead of tomorrow, the first day of the workweek. This target was not businesses but the people themselves. The drones weren't programmed to hit the weekend-unoccupied upper corporate floors; they were directed at the residences and the hotel and the restaurants, all the levels that would be teeming with souls on a Saturday. The carnage would be great, and it would be personal. People would be blown to pieces not at their places of business but in their very homes.

Abbas could already picture the ostentatious building with massive holes in the glass, smoke pouring out, hundreds—even thousands—of bodies littering the inside of the building and the oasis around its base. It would be demoralizing and would stand for months as a testimony to Allah's disfavor toward those Muslims who heretically claimed Abu Bakr to be the successor to Muhammad—*peace be upon him.*

A wave of reverence passed through Abbas. More than ever, he believed he was doing the work of Allah. He was a servant, and he could feel his master's favor, his smile shining down upon him.

CHAPTER 61

10:00 / 10:00 A.M. GST

Nir." Nicole punched the back of his seat.

He set the pen he'd been tapping against the window on the dashboard. "Sorry."

Three minutes later he had the pen again, tapping the back of his hand.

"Yaron." Nicole heaved a sigh.

Yaron snatched the pen out of Nir's hand, snapped it in half, and dropped it into the center console.

"I lose more pens that way."

Stakeouts were the worst. You hurry to get to your location, then you sit outside and wait, then you wait, and after that you wait some more.

The team had wanted to know why Nir chose to stake out the home of Ahmad al-Qasimi, but the only response he could give was "Trust me." No one else was cleared to know this al-Qasimi was actually Mehdi Zahiri, leader of a Dubai-based IRGC cell—a fact the Mossad knew only through the daring intelligence work of a mole who was so far undercover that not even Nir was supposed to know his identity.

Liora's chipper voice came through the com system connected to everyone's ears except

442

Filipescu's. "Let me give you an update on the truck situation. As you know, using a highway camera Nicole found, we identified that moving truck driving away from the area of the Ultra dock at just the right time to fit our time line. Being the middle of the night, it wasn't hard to spot. We were able to track it for several kilometers, but then we hit a blind zone. So we created a radius and looked for similar trucks. These Emiratis love their moving trucks. We identified 13 possibles. Eight of them stayed in Sharjah, and five drove to Dubai."

"You have addresses for their destinations?" Nicole asked.

"We do for all the Sharjah trucks and three of the Dubai. Do you want me to send them to you?"

"Sure. Good work."

"Boss." Yaron pointed to the gate of the compound. The metal doors slid sideways, and a white Land Rover drove out. Nir snatched an SLR camera from his lap and took the lens to its longest end. He rapid-fired shots until the SUV had driven past.

"Follow him, Yaron, but be careful. We cannot get made."

The Suburban pulled out, and Nir angled up the screen on the back of the camera.

Nicole leaned forward to look, putting her hand on his arm to let him know she was there.

"South on Al Mustaqbal Street," Yaron said.

"Got it," Dafna said from the Tel Aviv workroom.

Nir sped through the photos until he came to one that had a clear view of the Land Rover's front seat.

"West on Al Safa Street."

Again, Dafna acknowledged Yaron's direction.

"Pull up a picture of al-Qasimi," Nir said to Nicole. A couple of clicks later, she handed her laptop forward. He set the camera next to the screen. "No doubt. That's him."

"We're on the ramp for northbound E11."

Nir shifted his attention to Yaron. "What's with all the turns? Has he made us already?"

"Don't think so. They're just the fastest route to get to the freeway."

Nir slapped Yaron on the shoulder. "Good. Be careful." Then turning around, he said, "Dima, ask Filipescu if he's picked up anything."

Dima spoke to the Romanian, who let out an exasperated rant.

"He says nothing but single drones. Low frequency. He'll tell you if he finds anything."

"Sounds like he said a few other things." Nir raised his eyebrows.

"He did, but I edited."

The SUVs drove on, with Yaron staying eight to ten car lengths behind. After they'd traveled five kilometers, the Land Rover exited the freeway.

Nir sat up straight. Maybe this was it. "He's getting off onto Tariq bin Zayad Road. Liora, tell me which of the moving trucks is in this area."

He heard the sound of typing, then Liora's voice. "I got a blank, boss. It could be one of the trucks we lost, but nothing we've identified is around your location."

Nir started tapping the side of the door with his thumb. This time it was Filipescu who angrily pleaded with him to stop.

On they drove. Sometimes Nir felt like Yaron was getting too close. Other times it felt like he'd fallen back so far that he was bound to lose them. But somehow the agent was always proven to be at just the right distance at just the right time.

They passed the Palace of His Highness Sheikh Ahmed the Emir of Qatar, then crossed over Dubai Creek on the Al Maktoum bridge. Finally, when they reached the Deira Clocktower roundabout, they followed the white SUV to the east. This led them back onto the E11 freeway at the airport and north.

"What's with the tradecraft? Yaron, you're sure you're not made?"

Yaron shrugged. "How can I be sure of anything except the rising of the sun and my love for my children? But I would bet against it."

Nir laughed. "Truly a philosopher."

It looked as if they'd end up in Sharjah after all. Another ten minutes had passed when the Land

Rover exited the freeway. "Liora, he just got off on D95. Do we have anything there? I don't think we're in Sharjah yet."

"Wait . . ." More typing. *For a tiny girl, she's got some powerful fingers,* Nir thought randomly. "I got one. It's right on the mushy line between Dubai and Sharjah. Let me know if he turns on 204th. If so, we've hit jackpot."

Two minutes later, the SUV made a left onto 204th Road.

"Keep going straight. No need to follow from here. We've got him pegged. Liora, give me an address."

She fed him the location of a warehouse on nearby 11th Street.

Nir lifted his phone from the console and dialed Efraim.

"What's up, Nir?"

"We've got the location." He filled him in on the details. "I'm requesting permission to take a look."

"Nice work! Hold on."

"You guys ready to roll?" Nir called back to his team.

"Say the word," Avi said.

A minute turned into two, which turned into five. The activity in the Suburban slowed, then stopped. This was not a good sign.

Finally, Efraim came back on. "Hold your position. Remain on watch." He sounded angry.

446

Nir couldn't believe his ears. "What? Are you serious? We're right here. We can stop this thing now."

"If it's the right location."

"What do you mean *if it's the right location?* You heard what we've got, Efraim. The sooner we go in, the better chance we have to stop this before it starts."

When Efraim spoke again, Nir recognized by his tone this was definitely not his call. "The brass is worried that we'll burn our asset if this isn't the right place."

"But . . . I mean, come on . . ." But arguing with his friend was arguing with the wrong person.

"Understood," he said, then disconnected the call and turned to the team. "Stand down."

Angry cries sounded throughout the SUV.

"I said stand down! Yaron, get us within view of the warehouse. We'll watch it until we're given a reason to move. But if we do get that reason, we're going in hot."

CHAPTER 62

The rattle at the warehouse door had all three men jumping for their guns. Sunlight streamed in, and two silhouettes entered. Abbas sighted up the figures. The door closed, and Abbas saw two men in traditional Emirati clothing. One was striding toward him while the other remained by the door.

"Stop where you are." Abbas had his AK-74 leveled at the lead man's chest.

The stranger didn't slow. "Put down your gun, you fool."

Abbas recognized the voice. He angled the barrel of his rifle toward the floor. "Who are you? Tell me your name."

Ignoring the question, the man continued his approach. When he was within three meters, he removed his sunglasses. His eyes sent shivers through Abbas. Those dark, dead orbs had glared at him from behind a black balaclava as he'd lain on the ground earlier that morning, trying to regain his wits. They were the eyes of the man who had humiliated him in front of his own men. The temptation to raise his rifle and regain

448

his pride was great. But he knew that would be foolhardy. Higher stakes were at play today—much bigger than his ego.

"My name is Ahmad al-Qasimi. I was part of your greeting party this morning."

"I remember." The inside of his mouth was still raw, and his ribs hurt whenever he breathed too deeply. He had no doubt that al-Qasimi was not this man's real name. This was no Emirati. He was IRGC through and through.

"Then we can dispense with the pleasantries. Show me what you have done." Without waiting for Abbas to lead him, al-Qasimi marched to where the Blowfish drones were laid out. Abbas hurried to catch up.

The UAVs were set in five rows of five. Al-Qasimi stopped next to the first one, then squatted and examined it closely. "Talk."

"As you can see, the batteries have all been tested for full charge and attached. Secured under every drone is an M183 demolition charge. Into each has been inserted a four-detonator bundle. And as you know, they have been programmed to detonate six meters from the building so that the blast radius can expand and not be limited to one or two floors."

Al-Qasimi nodded in appreciation, and Abbas thought it was probably the closest to a compliment he'd ever dished out. "So you are saying that everything is prepared?"

"It is." Abbas said it with pride. "At 11:30 we will commence."

Al-Qasimi checked out the drones once again, then turned to the control station, which held 25 transmitters with wires bundled together and connected to a laptop. A look of stern resolve came across his face. "No need to wait. We will begin the start sequence now."

10:45 / 10:45 A.M. GST

"This is stupid." Yossi's voice came through the coms. "In fact, this is stupider than stupid. It's like the highest level of stupid that stupid can get."

Nir had to agree. Just beyond those warehouse doors was probably everything needed to launch a major terrorist attack. Yet here they were outside, sitting on their hands. Time was wasting, and a greater likelihood that more people would die came with every second that passed.

Time is a precious commodity when it comes to operations. It's a sin to waste it. Besides, sitting and doing nothing is completely against my nature. Okay, then. Let's make use of this time.

"Everyone, listen up. We've all figured out that a terrorist drone attack is about to happen in Dubai. What we don't know is what the target is."

"The Burj Khalifa, of course."

"Okay, Lahav. Why do you say that?"

The man gave an exasperated sigh. "Because I'm not an idiot."

"Remember our talk about people skills and respecting authority, Lahav?" Nicole said.

"Right. Sorry. Because I'm not an idiot, sir."

Nir turned to look at Nicole. She just rolled her eyes.

"Elaborate," said Nir. "Maybe with a little more substance."

Liora interrupted. "The Burj is an obvious target. Our socially graceless friend here has been going on about the terrorists wanting to make a big statement, which makes perfect sense. And what bigger statement can you make than the Burj Khalifa? If you attack the Atlantis or the Burj Al Arab, you're essentially duplicating what you did in Abu Dhabi."

Dafna took over. "Exactly. Our whole premise is that Yas Island was to be a distraction from a bigger attack. Get everybody looking south so you can make the bigger hit to the north. The only thing bigger and more psycho than what they already did is to go after the Burj."

Nir understood what they were saying, but something still didn't make sense. "Okay, the Burj. But what can they do to it? It's not like they can drone the thing into the ground. A UAV is not a 767."

Only silence came across the coms.

Finally, Nicole spoke up. "While it would be nice to know the why, I don't think we have enough information to figure that out. Logically speaking, we can pretty well assume the target—the Burj Khalifa. But even that isn't what really matters. We're not going to stop this attack at its destination but at its source—right here at this warehouse."

"Which we can't do just sitting out here and observing," Nir grumbled.

"Shh." Avi was suddenly animated. "Nicole, put your window down. Yaron, turn off the engine."

Both complied. Avi leaned over the seat into Nicole's personal space, and she scooted to the left to give him some room.

"You guys hear that?"

Nir closed his eyes and put his head out the window. At first, all he could hear were the sounds coming from a nearby construction yard. Then there it was. Very subtle, like a long bass note underlying the busyness of the rest of the orchestra.

"What do you hear?" Dafna asked from Tel Aviv. But nobody answered her. Nicole and Yaron confirmed they could hear it too.

Then the volume increased exponentially, like someone turning a control knob up to ten. To Nir, the sound was like a massive swarm of bees, and it was emanating from the warehouse.

Filipescu began shouting while staring at his screen. Dima translated. "He says he has signals. Big ones—1,380 MHz. Communication protocol identifies them as Blowfish A2."

"Of course!" Lahav sounded like he was about to burst. "Makes perfect sense! KSS used the Blowfish A2 in a mortar attack against the Siniya refinery in December."

"*Douăzeci și cinci! Douăzeci și cinci!*" Filipescu had turned his screen toward Nicole.

"*Russkiy*," shouted Dima.

"*Dvadtsat' pyat'*!"

Dima looked right at Nir, his eyes big. "Twenty-five military-class UAVs are receiving signal from that warehouse."

As if to confirm Filipescu's information, large doors slid open on the side of the warehouse. One by one, Blowfish drones drifted out and shot straight up into the sky. Nir's eyes followed them a hundred meters, two hundred, five hundred, a thousand, until they were no longer discernable to the naked eye. What was visible as they rose out of sight sent ice through his veins. A package wrapped in brown tape dangled under the empty belly of each drone. Wires wound out from the packages and up to the drones, making them look exactly like what they were—bombs capable of blowing huge, gaping holes into the crowning architectural jewel of the Middle East.

CHAPTER 63

W e're going in," Nir said, throwing open his door and tumbling out.

"Wait! There's something important you don't know."

"Make it fast, Lahav! We've got to get in there." Nir wasn't even trying to hide his impatience. He dropped back inside and pulled his door closed.

"The Blowfish is much more sophisticated than the drones in Abu Dhabi."

"Meaning . . ."

"If you destroy the master controller, these drones won't just disengage and crash to earth or return home like the others. The RC signal is leading them on a pre-programmed route, which is embedded into their hard drive once they take off. The only way to stop them now is to reprogram that hard drive. So when you get in there, whatever you do, do not harm the controllers."

Nir punched the ceiling of the Suburban. "You have got to be kidding me."

That changed everything. Not only could a stray

454

bullet from one of their guns doom the thousands of people in and around the Burj Khalifa on a Saturday, but the KSS men themselves could destroy the control center, making the attack a *fait accompli*.

"How do we play this, boss?" asked Avi.

"Give me a second."

Going in with guns blazing was out of the question. It would have to be a surprise attack.

"One more thing," Liora said. "Lahav, what's the speed of those things?"

"Carrying a load, you're looking at around 80 kmh."

"Nir, that means you have about 20 minutes until they reach their target."

Rather than causing him further stress, that information gave Nir some relief. His window was short, but at least he had a little time for a stealth assault.

10:55 / 10:55 A.M. GST

It was beautiful. The hum of 25 two-meter rotors spinning at maximum speed could not only be heard but could be seen and felt—a visceral experience that could never be adequately explained, only experienced. Then those beautiful Blowfish had lifted off like a miniature, lethal, aquatic-esque air force. The whir had peaked, then faded as the drones left the warehouse and rose high into the sky until there was no sound left. The silence in the warehouse became absolute.

A slow clap echoed against the metal walls.

" *'Ahsant*," said al-Qasimi. "Well done, my friend."

Despite how much he despised the man, Abbas found himself strangely pleased with the affirmation. Then he immediately chastised himself. He would not be anyone's dog, kicked around all day, then jumping up and wagging his tail when his master rubbed his ears. So rather than responding, he turned toward the computer that showed the progress of the swarm, along with two video feeds from tiny cameras he'd installed on the lead drones.

In just a short time, the fires of hell would rain down on the people of that prideful tribute to secular man's achievement. Lives would be ruined, and bodies would be destroyed. Weak-spined Sunni Islam would fear the wrath of the followers of the true faith.

Abbas signaled for Hassan and Ali to close the sliding doors of the warehouse.

"How long?" asked the IRGC man.

Abbas looked at the computer. "Twenty minutes."

Pulling out a chair from under the table, al-Qasimi sat. He called to his partner, who was still standing by the door. "Jamshid, come join me. Let's watch the fruit of our labors."

Doron and Avi took the left side of the door, Nicole the right. Both men had a Micro Galil assault rifle strapped to their chest. Nicole, however, held her SIG Sauer P226 9mm, her service weapon of choice. It was pointed at the ground with her finger on the trigger guard. She wouldn't fire unless it was necessary.

Nir had not wanted her in the first wave of the assault. She'd initially protested, thinking he was being overprotective of her again. Then he explained that she was needed elsewhere. Although she was an excellent shot with her SIG, that was not her expertise. He needed her fingers on a keyboard, not on a gun.

Once the breach occurred, Nicole's mission was to get to the controller set up, hack into the system, and reprogram the Blowfish swarm's destination. Nobody else on the team could pull that off. The odds were long that even she would be able to do it, but the job of the rest of the team was to ensure she had the chance—and didn't get shot in the process.

She watched as Doron signaled to the second squad, letting them know he was about to gain entrance to the warehouse. Yaron signaled an acknowledgment from where he stood with Dima and Filipescu. The Romanian had insisted on joining the fight, pulling a .45

caliber pearl-handled silver Colt 1911 out of his messenger bag. When he'd racked it and smiled, Nicole thought he looked every bit the part of the Eastern European gunrunner.

Quietly, Doron asked, "Assault 3, you in place?"

A click sounded over the com—Nir affirming that he was ready to go.

After they'd approached the warehouse, Nir had low-run around to the back of the building, and Nicole knew he'd make sure he stayed below the window line. She'd also seen him take his 9mm Jericho, but rather than adding a Galil, he'd opted for an M16. Under the rifle was mounted an M203 single shot 40mm grenade launcher. One grenade was loaded already, and he'd stuffed four more in his vest. He was ready.

Avi inserted a lock pick into the door handle and began flicking a small bar to trigger the tumblers. *In and out, in and out,* Nicole thought as she took deep breaths. Although she'd now spent more than a decade serving in the Mossad, this was the first time she'd ever participated in a field assault.

Lord, please protect us. Take down these enemies who want to do evil. Give me the strength to do what needs to be done for the saving of many lives.

Avi cursed, pulling the pick out and starting again. Time was getting short; nearly ten minutes had passed while they'd waited for the ramsad's permission to raid the building. Nir's first inclination had been to go in without informing Efraim, but Nicole had reminded him that such a strategy was potentially career and freedom ending. She was grateful he'd acquiesced. He was a good man, but he sometimes let his passion for doing the right thing lead him into doing the wrong thing.

Flick, flick, flick, and Avi's face spread into a smile. With a subtle twist of his wrist, the handle turned and the door cracked open. With two clicks on the com, Doron signaled the other teams that they had breached. As they'd done in Abu Dhabi, they would let flash-bang grenades give them the advantage. At the front door, Avi and Doron each readied an M84, pulling its circular primary pin and its triangular secondary pin but holding tight the safety lever against the perforated steel body. Yaron and Dima did the same. Nicole's adrenaline spiked, and she felt a fluttering in her stomach.

Lifting his hand, Doron used his fingers to count down.

Five . . . four . . . three . . . two . . . one.

CHAPTER 64

Surrounded by drone cases acting as a shield, Abbas leveled his AK-74. Ten minutes earlier, after the drones had departed, al-Qasimi had called his partner to watch the attack on the computer. But Jamshid had not left his place by door. He was pressed against a wall, his attention riveted to something outside.

Snapping his fingers, he waved for al-Qasimi to come to him. Abbas followed along. At the door, they both leaned in next to Jamshid, who started saying something to al-Qasimi in Farsi.

"In Arabic," said al-Qasimi. "Our friend and his men are involved in this too."

Jamshid glared at Abbas. "I have been watching that black Suburban down the road. Immediately after the drones left, the passenger door opened and a man wearing a tactical vest stepped out. Then, just as quickly, he stepped back in."

Al-Qasimi swore. "How could they have found us?"

"All we need is 20 minutes," said Abbas. "We need to delay them only that long."

"That's if we want to die here. I for one do not. Can we take the equipment and flee?"

Abbas shook his head. "We can't risk disconnection of the RC controllers. I don't know what would happen if they separated."

"And if we destroyed the equipment?"

"Again, I don't know. Maybe they'd continue their flight. Maybe they'd crash to the ground like the ones in Abu Dhabi. I don't know this equipment well enough."

Al-Qasimi swore once more. "You are supposed to be the expert, you worthless fool!" He turned to his man. "Have you seen any others, Jamshid?"

"Just the one SUV, but I expect more to come. I suspect they're planning an assault."

"Of course they're planning an assault!" The Iranian soldier walked away, stood for a moment, then came back. "Okay, let's be ready for them. As you said, we just need 20 minutes." He looked at his watch. "Correction. Seventeen minutes."

Now Hassan and Ali were ready by the front door. Al-Qasimi and Jamshid were behind cover by the sliding doors. Abbas was in his small shelter near the controllers. It was his job to ensure that nothing happened to shut down the deadly flight of the drones.

Ali signaled, telling them all there was activity at the front door. Taking a deep breath, Abbas readied himself for the attack.

Nicole slipped her SIG into its holster in order to free her hands as Avi eased the front door open. Opening her mouth, closing her eyes, and covering her ears, Nicole prepared for the repercussion from the flash-bangs. Instead, she heard gunfire erupting from inside. Nicole opened her eyes in time to see Avi fall to the ground. Doron must have tossed his grenade into the building because he was reaching for his gun, but Avi's flash-bang was rolling toward her. Instinctively, she dove away, squeezing her eyes tight and pressing her hands against her ears.

Boom!

The high-decibel noise slammed into her head, disorienting her even with her ears covered. Closing her eyes had helped little, but the extreme light caused her vision to be covered with a large blue spot. Disoriented, she lay on her back groaning. When the ringing in her ears began to die down, it was replaced with the sound of gunfire and voices talking about a man down and points of entry. Slowly, her senses began to return, and her mind started processing her surroundings.

The blue spot dissipated. Turning, she saw Avi, still on the ground. Beyond him, Doron was firing his rifle through the door. Nicole unsteadily scrambled over to Avi, who was bleeding from a wound to his upper arm and one to his hip. Taking hold of him by his armpits, she tugged as hard as she could. He slid roughly under her effort, and she dragged him to safety, away from the doorframe.

She had to hold her watch still for a moment before she could make out the numbers. They were down to eight minutes.

"Doron!" He looked over, and she tapped her watch. He nodded and turned back toward the warehouse.

11:04 / 11:04 A.M. GST

Nir had used a strap to shimmy up a pipe to a high window. He had then belted himself in, his boots against the outer wall and back leaning into the loop. Removing a rope coiled around his shoulder, he tied one end to the drainpipe and fed the other end through a carabiner attached to his belt. As quietly as he could, he rubbed a spot through the opaque layer left on the window by decades of dust and salt air. But when the gunfire started, he smashed the window with his elbow.

He heard the first flash-bang go off. Then the second, although that one seemed unusually distant. Two more echoed throughout the warehouse from the direction of the sliding doors.

"Man down! Man down!" It was Doron's voice, which meant either Avi or Nicole was in trouble. Nir started to pull back to run around the building. He had to know if Nicole was okay. But he stopped. The whole team was counting on him. It was imperative that he stay in position. Looking back inside, he scanned the warehouse.

The gunfire dissipated as the hostiles tried to deal with their disorientation. Across the large room, he saw Dima and Yaron entering through the sliding doors, guns at the ready. Shots were fired, and the two Caesarea agents dropped to the cement floor. Yaron rolled to the right behind some boxes, and Dima bolted back for the doors.

Nir spotted muzzle flashes. Two men in Emirati clothing were firing from behind a large forklift, well protected from a frontal assault. Nir, however, was not in front. Putting one of the men in the sights of his M16, he pulled the trigger. The bullet entered the man's skull from behind his left ear, and he dropped to the floor. The second man, his white *kandura* splattered with the red of his partner's blood, ran for a secondary position.

Interesting, Nir thought as he scanned the warehouse floor. *It looks like they've put some thought into this.* He could see at least five places that had been built up, which would potentially provide good cover. Maybe he could use that information to his advantage.

Gunfire had started again from the front door.

So gunfire to the left. Gunfire to the right.

And the spot in the middle is the control center. Lovely.

"Assault 2," Nir called to Dima and Yaron as he aimed his rifle toward the main entrance. "One hostile down. A second has reset behind the lumber to your right."

"Assault 2. *Root.*"

Two men in camouflage uniforms spread out a barrage of bullets from some offices. Doron was returning fire. Nir lined one man up and pulled the trigger. The militia soldier pulled back, and the round slammed into an inner wall with a puff of sheetrock. Nir fired again, but the man had dropped to the floor.

Something suddenly smashed into Nir's rifle. Pain radiated through his hands, and the M16 clattered to the cement floor. A second shot shattered what was left of the windowpane, and tiny glass shards peppered his face. In rapid succession, he button-released the strap, rolled his body headfirst through the window, and slid toward the floor. Grabbing the rope, he did his best to slow gravity, but his damaged hands couldn't get a solid grip. He landed hard on his back.

11:05 / 11:05 A.M. GST

Once the first bullet took out Jamshid, it was obvious they were flanked. Abbas had spun around looking for the source of the shot but could see nothing. Only when gunfire was directed toward the offices did he tilt his gaze upward and see a man shooting through a shattered high window.

The upper windows had been a concern for Abbas, but al-Qasimi had convinced him that, because they were so high and there was no stair access, they shouldn't worry. Besides, the sound of glass breaking would be enough of an alarm to let them know an assault was coming from behind. What they hadn't accounted for was the noise of the covering gunfire.

Lining up his rifle, he depressed the trigger. It was a direct hit, but on the man's rifle, which fell to the floor. *Are you kidding me?* Angry at his bad luck, he fired again, only hitting glass. Suddenly, the man came flying through the window in a front flip, then dropped hard to the floor, landing on his back. Abbas put him on his bead, but before he could pull the trigger, two rounds whizzed past his ear followed by the sound of the shots.

Abbas dropped to the floor. When he popped back up, the man was gone.

CHAPTER 65

SITREP," Nir said as he stumbled to a stack of tractor tires. He'd seen this location from his high vantage point and figured it was likely the fallback of the man who'd just killed his M16.

He heard Yaron's voice. "Assault 2, we have one hostile, but he's got good cover and sounds like he's not short on ammo."

Doron's was next. "Assault 1, we're pinned down by at least two. I can't get Nicole through. Avi is alive, but he's not in good condition."

There was no way to get Nicole to the control center without exposing her to gunfire. But without getting her there, hundreds or thousands would die. The decision was painful but easy.

"Nicole, go to the sliding doors now. On my signal, run for the control center. It's in the middle of the floor. Everybody, lay cover fire but not toward the stacks of cases. I need to take care of a hostile there, and I don't want you taking me out by accident."

God, if You're here, watch over Nicole. She's one of Yours.

"Nicole, are you in place?"

"Ready."

"Okay, on my mark. Go!"

Nicole sprinted across the floor. The noise was deafening. At any moment she expected to feel the flesh-tearing slam of a bullet.

God, help me! God, help me! God, help me! She prayed as she ran. She saw movement to her right. It was Nir plowing into a stack of black plastic cases.

She turned back toward the control center. It was coming up fast.

The sound of the gunfire changed. The hostiles were firing back. The cover was breaking down.

She kept running.

Finally, she reached the table, dropping into a chair and spinning toward the laptop. Her heart sank. A gaping hole was in the middle of the screen, and what hadn't been torn away was completely black.

Think, think, think! She felt the underside of the laptop. It was still warm, and she could sense a subtle whirring. *The computer isn't dead. It's just not functional.*

A bullet whizzed by her ear, and she dropped to the floor under the table.

"Lahav, are you on?"

"I'm here."

"The computer screen is shattered. If I can connect in through my laptop, will I be able to control the drones?"

"I would think so. You see, they both—"

"Dima, tell Nicolae to bring me my laptop! Fast! We're down to four minutes."

11:07 / 11:07 A.M. GST

Abbas knew cover fire when he heard it. When everyone shoots on automatic all at once, it's because they're trying to distract from something else. *What are they doing?* Then he saw it— or her. A woman, of all things, sprinting across the floor toward the control center. *That's not a journey you'll complete.* He took aim, but then the cases behind him exploded forward.

Someone careened into him from behind, and Abbas flew into the front wall of his shelter. He landed on a hard plastic corner, and his assailant landed on his back. Air expelled from his lungs. A fist hit him on the side of his head once, then twice. But he'd trained for this scenario. He lurched his hips upward and twisted, throwing his passenger off balance. Spinning underneath his attacker, Abbas connected his fist with the man's chin. It was a well-placed blow, dazing his opponent. With one more hip bounce, he launched the man from on top of him.

He recognized his enemy from the window. They both got to their feet. The man pulled a pistol from an underarm holster—a Jericho 941.

An Israeli? In the UAE? What is this?

But that thought was just a flash in his mind. Abbas kicked out and swept the Israeli's feet out from under him. The man landed hard on his back, his head hitting the cement. The gun clattered away. Abbas pounced, but his challenger rolled away. He landed hard on the floor. A fraction of a second later, the man was on his back. An arm wrapped around his neck and squeezed.

It didn't take long for the corners of his vision to gray. He flopped and twisted, but the man's hold was too strong. With the last of his strength, he reached into a cargo pocket, his fingers grasping for its contents. Finally, he found what he was looking for. He knew he didn't have much longer. Pulling his hand from his pocket, he used his thumb to push up on the flip button of the Gerber FAST knife, releasing its serrated-edge. Swinging his arm down, he plunged the weapon into his attacker's leg.

The man screamed and released his grip. Gasping, Abbas rolled off of him, pulling the knife out as he went. The Israeli tried to get up but dropped back to the floor. Abbas pounced. He landed on top of him, then pushed himself up to straddle him. Lifting the blade, he said in Arabic, "You shouldn't have interfered, Jew."

The first bullet struck the man in the temple. The second went through his left cheek. And then he fell to the floor.

Nicole slowly lowered her SIG Sauer. She wanted to rush over and check on Nir, but her body seemed rooted to her chair.

It had to be done. It was him or Nir.

She'd fired a gun many times and prided herself on her accuracy. But this? This was not that. This was not a paper target. This was not a training course. A human being was dead, and she'd killed him.

Someone ran up next to her and began speaking. Nicole ignored the voice, staring at the spreading pool of blood around the dead man's head. *Lord, forgive me. If there had been another way . . .*

Hands grabbed her arms and shook her. She recognized Filipescu. He was yelling at her in Russian and pointing at her laptop. Like waking from a bad dream, Nicole snapped from her fog. She pointed to Nir, and Filipescu nodded and went to check on him.

"Lahav, are you with me?"

"Always and forever," he said.

Normally that would have creeped her out, but now she laughed. That was the stupid battleground humor she needed to focus.

"Lahav, I'm hardwiring in. Give me a minute."

"How about 30 seconds? We seem to be running short of minutes."

Yaron's voice came through the com. "One in

custody. Right side cleared. Dima's coming to give you some help, Doron."

Nicole typed on her keyboard, busting the complicated firewall.

"Three minutes," Lahav said.

Images suddenly appeared on Nicole's laptop. "I'm in."

"What do you see?"

"Code of some sort on the bottom half of the screen. Two view boxes up top that look like they're giving real-time video from the drones. I can see the city passing by and the Burj in the distance. We may not have the time we thought."

"Can you type in the code screen?"

Nicole tried. "No, it's got me locked out."

"You need to make yourself administrator. Hurry! Then mirror your screen to me."

Nicole went into a control prompt and overrode the administrator protocol.

She heard a series of shots from the offices.

"Two down," Doron said. "Offices cleared."

"Clear the rest of the warehouse, Dima." The strain in Nir's voice belied the pain he had to be in. "Doron, tend to Avi."

"*Root*," they both said.

"I'm in," Nicole said.

Filipescu appeared at her side. With bloody fingers, he pointed to his RF sensor, then held up one finger.

"Lahav, we have one minute. Talk to me." The

Burj towered into the sky on the video screens.

"Okay, one second. This is . . . What the . . . Hold on. Okay, got it."

Nicole could see details in the building's windows. Filipescu held up four red-smeared fingers on one hand and five on the other. "Talk to me, Lahav."

"I can't explain it. You've got to give me control. Make me administrator. Now!"

Nicole typed as fast as she ever had. "Go, Lahav! Go!"

Letters and numbers appeared at the bottom of her screen, line after line at lightning speed. In the view boxes she could see people on the ground looking up, no doubt wondering at the strange buzzing machines racing toward their destination.

Filipescu showed her a two and a zero.

"Twenty seconds, Lahav!"

Still the lines raced across the screen. Nicole could no longer see the top of the building. It was out of screenshot.

"Oh, Lord, save those people," she whispered.

Suddenly, the view turned toward the ocean. The drones raced ahead, over the freeway, past the Burj Al Arab displaying its great sail, and out to sea. The last thing she saw was water approaching at high speed. Then the feed went dead.

CHAPTER 66

TEN DAYS LATER
AROMA ESPRESSO BAR, TEL AVIV, ISRAEL—
FEBRUARY 25, 2020—14:00 / 2:00 P.M. IST

It was a beautiful, cool day in Tel Aviv—light clouds, 18°C, an easy breeze coming in off the Mediterranean. Nir breathed in a deep lungful of air as he limped along the sidewalk. It was good to be alive, and the only thing that could possibly make it better was waiting for him at Aroma two blocks up the street. He could have parked much closer, but the day was just too perfect to go directly from car into building.

He'd just come from visiting Avi Carmeli in the hospital. The Emiratis had given him good care for the first few days following the conclusion of Operation Joktan. When he was stable enough, a Mossad Gulfstream had brought him home. Each day since his friend's return, Nir had stopped by his room at Tel Aviv Sourasky Medical Center, commonly known as Ichilov. Avi would recover, but the damage to his arm meant his days in Kidon were over.

A cloud passed in front of the sun, and the air cooled enough to send a chill through him. His leg ached, but he pushed forward. The irony of his being stabbed like he was yet surviving had not escaped him. Twelve years earlier he'd pulled the same desperate move on the Xhosa gunman who was about to take his life. Nir was lucky to limp away from his wound, but the South African militant had not fared as well.

It had been a long week and a half. Moments after the drone swarm plunged into the Gulf, Dubai police burst into the warehouse. The Kidon team had immediately surrendered their weapons and were taken into custody. Avi was rushed to the hospital, but Nir's leg wound was simply field dressed before he was taken to police headquarters. There, he was finally introduced to Lieutenant General Dhahi Khalfan Tamim, who still wasn't Nir's biggest fan despite what had just happened. The feeling rapidly became mutual. Thirty minutes into Nir's interrogation by the chief, most of which hearkened back to the assassination of Mahmoud al-Mabhouh, the head of SIA, Abdullah Al Rashidi, had shown up.

For Nir's team going off on their own, Al Rashidi brought with him threats of trials and imprisonment for all the members. Nir's only response to the tirades of both men was "Call the ramsad." After a full hour of interrogative futility, Al Rashidi had done just that. Two hours later, Nir and his team were on a private flight to

Tel Aviv. Nir had wanted to stay with Avi, but Al Rashidi demanded that the rest of them get out of his country immediately.

The café was up ahead, and he could see Nicole sitting at what had become their customary table. His step quickened and his pain lessened as he approached the door. Her face brightened when she saw him.

"Hey, old man." She nodded toward the cane in his right hand, then stood and kissed him on the cheek.

"Don't knock it. It's got a two-shot .380 built into the handle." He'd managed to say it without smiling.

"Really." He heard the skeptical note in her voice.

Nir made as if he were going to pull off the cane's handle, then chuckled. "No, not really. But it would be really cool if it did."

Nicole laughed and squeezed his arm. "Sit down. My treat today."

He watched her walk away as he lowered himself into a chair. Much of the flight home had been with her sitting next to him, her head on his shoulder. The first time in combat shakes everybody, especially if they're forced to shoot someone—and even more so if it's at close range. They said little in the low light of the plane. Every now and then, he could hear her softly crying.

Nicole came back with two ceramic mugs. "You know my first question."

"Avi's doing okay. It was hard telling him he still has a place with Caesarea but not with Kidon. It wasn't a shock to him, but I could see the hurt. Physically, though, he's improving. He has another surgery in two days to further repair his arm."

"Poor guy. Not only does he lose his position but his team—essentially, his second family. That's got to be hard. I'm going to run by Ichilov to see him when we're done. I promised him an iced espresso."

"That'll be good."

Nir had replied with a tone surprisingly somber. He hadn't thought about how deep the ramifications were for Avi. It was imperative to ensure he knew he would always be a member of the family even if he couldn't be part of the team.

Nicole smiled. "Now answer my second question."

"Nicolae."

"You know me too well."

"It's looking like he'll be deported to Romania. Tamim was determined to prosecute him for his tech smuggling despite the ramsad's protests. But the ramsad called the prime minister, and it looks like he's intervened. The Romanian prime minister is actually excited to have him home and is looking to give him a position in their intelligence service."

Nicole laughed. "I can't picture him in a government job."

"Absolutely not. But I guess if even Lahav can get scared straight, there's hope."

Nir shifted in his chair. If he remained in one position too long, his thigh began to burn. The doctor who performed the surgery said it would be like that for a few months but he should get back full function.

Rumors were that the discussions between the ramsad and the prime minister had other, more far-reaching ramifications. Apparently, the two men had hit it off well. They'd each committed to connecting the Mossad and the SIA more closely in the interest of peace and a growing relationship between their countries. That goodwill had spread to the Israeli prime minister, and now there were talks about the two governmental leaders meeting in person. Their eyes were continuing to look forward to the peace plan expected to come from Washington later in the year.

"So enough talking about other people. How are *you* doing, Nicole?"

She sat quietly for a moment, and he sipped his latte as he waited.

"It's strange. I don't think much anymore about that man—Abbas. He was going to kill you, and I stopped him. I don't feel any guilt—"

"Nor should you."

"Nor should I. He put himself in that position. I

478

didn't. But to be honest, I do still have nightmares about that moment, and I'm guessing I will for a while."

Nir nodded, a tightness in his throat. He hated to see Nicole having to deal with the aftermath of the operation and her part in it. "I'm sorry to say it will be with you for a long time. I have night visitors from time to time. Lately, it's been Abu Mustafa. Not just him jumping out of the helicopter, but what I . . . you know . . . what I did to him before he jumped." Emotion welled up inside. He did his best to stifle it with a long draw from his latte, then set down his mug.

Nicole swapped hers for his. "Again, I don't think much about killing Abbas. I think a lot more about what would have happened if I hadn't killed him. Or what if you hadn't stopped him from killing me. Honestly, it's two very different emotions."

That statement surprised Nir. "What do you mean?"

Nicole spun Nir's empty mug a few times before answering. "Okay, so if I had died in that warehouse, it would have been a tragedy in the sense that there are people who love me and they would have been very sad."

He shifted again. He still couldn't bring himself to think about that outcome.

"But, Nir, for me, it wouldn't have been a tragedy at all. I would be with God because I've accepted Jesus as my Savior. I know that for a fact. That's why even when I was running across that warehouse floor, I was never scared of being killed. I was scared of the pain of getting shot, but of dying? Not at all."

"No, I get it. I call it battle mode. You can't think of dying; you just have to focus on getting the job accomplished."

Nicole was shaking her head. "It's not that. I actually did think of dying while I was sprinting across that floor with bullets whizzing around the warehouse. What I'm saying is that when I thought about it, I wasn't scared—not at all. What did scare me was the thought of you dying."

The conversation was starting to make him uncomfortable, but Nir figured he'd ride it out a little longer. "Why is that? I mean, what's the difference?"

Nicole took his hand. "Nir, if you died, it would be a double tragedy. We who love you would be heartbroken"—Nir noticed the plural pronoun—"but what would make it worse is that you wouldn't be with God."

Now he was really uncomfortable—and a little offended. He was about to say something when Nicole continued.

"Listen, I know that sounds harsh, but aren't we at a place where we don't have to soften our words or dance around things?"

Ouch. I guess we are, but here I am hurt by her just saying what she believes.

He nodded.

"Tell me, aren't you afraid of dying?"

Again, Nir nodded. "Not that I think about it much."

"But when you do, there's fear. That's natural. That's how I was too. But that fear is totally gone now, because I know Jesus has given me eternal life. That means when this body dies, my soul will keep living with Him."

"That's what you believe."

Nicole smiled. "That's what I *know*. Do I seem gullible or delusional or ignorant to you? Am I the kind of person who would fall into a mind-control cult and believe all sorts of crazy things?"

Nir laughed. "No. Although I almost got you with that gun in the handle of my cane thing."

"You wish. Something happened to me, Nir. You knew me before, and you know me now. What changed me is not delusion. What changed me is Christ. And He can change you too."

"Do I really need that much changing?" He smiled.

"We all do." She squeezed his hand again. "And it's just a prayer away."

Stretching his leg out to buy a little time, he considered what she said. It made a lot of sense. Nir hated funerals and avoided them whenever possible. Every Memorial Day, a day when most

481

countries celebrated with family picnics and sales at furniture stores, the entire country of Israel shut down and truly mourned those who had lost their lives defending the nation. He usually spent it at home alone, drinking just a little too much so he wouldn't have to think about the day his friends and family would cry if he perished fighting for his people. It would be amazing to have all that fear about death gone with one prayer.

He drained the last of Nicole's latte. Maybe one day he would try Christianity, but today was not the day. Nicole just kept failing to grasp one fact. Jesus was for the Gentiles, and Moses was for the Jews.

"Listen, Nir. I'm not trying to force you into anything. It's a personal decision. Just think on it."

"I promise I will," he said, jumping on the out she was giving him. "Now, let's change the subject to something light and breezy, like what happened in Iran."

Nicole slapped his hand. "Rude. I know we need to talk the Iran operation through sometime, but not now. Let me finish dealing with the effects of this operation before we jump back to an old one."

"Fair enough. Maybe instead we can talk about dinner tomorrow night. Manta Ray, down by the beach? Start with a little yellowtail sashimi, then move on to the filleted sea bass?"

"That's a conversation I can get into." They talked a while longer, about his need to get back to Yael Diamonds before the business fell apart and her photo shoot next week in Bermuda. An international relationship would not be without serious hurdles, but if that's where they were headed, Nir was willing to give it his all.

When it was time to go, they stood. Nicole said, "Don't forget your cane, old man."

"Careful. It's loaded."

They laughed as she tucked her arm in his and walked to the counter to order an iced espresso for Avi.

AUTHORS' NOTE

Why fiction? After establishing a strong presence in the nonfiction market, why turn now to storytelling? There were a number of reasons, but, first and foremost, a fast-paced, exciting story is just plain fun. And in this crazy world of cultural change and viruses and political mischief, don't we all need a little more good, clean fun in our lives? Our hope with this first Nir Tavor Mossad thriller is to entertain you to the extent that you'll be forced to lose a little sleep at night because you won't want to put the book down.

However, there is more to the book than just an exciting story. In Amir's nonfiction offerings, biblical and geopolitical truth is supplemented by anecdotes and humor in order to make the book a more enjoyable read. In fiction, the opposite is true. The entertainment of the story is supplemented by truth in order to give the book a higher purpose.

To that end, we kept three key goals in mind as we wrote this book. First, we want to reveal more clearly the geopolitical situation of the Middle East, especially in light of the expanding peace brought about by the Abraham Accords. Fighting against the pacifying trend is Iran and the ever-expanding instability that its terrorist regime brings to the region. A second goal is to portray some of the struggles Israel faces when it comes to survival. The necessity of the Mossad's creation and the fact that it has become the premier global intelligence agency is a direct result of the precarious nature of Israel's existence. Finally, we want to show the spiritual and cultural struggle of an agnostic Jew as he is confronted with the reality of Jesus Christ.

The scenes within the overall story are typically fictional events told within real historical, cultural, and geopolitical context. The one exception is the targeted killing of Mahmoud al-Mabhouh in Dubai, UAE. That event is told as it actually happened with only a few minor modifications so that we could insert our characters into the action. The militia group Kata'ib Sayyid al-Shuhada (KSS) is real, as is its usage of UAV warfare and its connection to the Iranian Islamic Revolutionary Guard Corps (IRGC).

The plot of this book is both practical and probable. Maybe UAV attacks won't take place in the locations laid out in our story, but they will happen. Drone terrorism is the wave of the future, and it will likely not be long before the Western world learns that firsthand.

Still, there is no reason to be afraid. Jesus Christ loves you and has given His life for you, and it is His "perfect love [that] drives out fear"

(1 John 4:18). By giving your life to Him, He will give you peace for today and the promise of eternal life for tomorrow. Turn to Him; He is waiting for you.

Awaiting His return,
Amir Tsarfati
Steve Yohn

Center Point Large Print
600 Brooks Road / PO Box 1
Thorndike, ME 04986-0001 USA

(207) 568-3717

US & Canada:
1 800 929-9108
www.centerpointlargeprint.com